PENGUIN BO

You Spin Me Round

ally O'Reilly lives in Brighton with her husband and two children. A former *Cosmopolitan* magazine new journalist of the year, she is also a runner-up for both the *Cosmopolitan* short story prize and the Ian St ames Award. Her first novel, *The Best Possible Taste*, is published by nguin.

By the same author

The Best Possible Taste

You Spin Me Round

SALLY O'REILLY

PENGUIN BOOKS

PENGUIN BOOKS

Published by the Penguin Group
Penguin Books Ltd, 80 Strand, London WC2R ORL, England
Penguin Group (USA) Inc., 375 Hudson Street, New York, New York 10014, USA
Penguin Group (Canada), 90 Eglinton Avenue East, Suite 700, Toronto, Ontario, Canada M4P 2Y3
(a division of Pearson Penguin Canada Inc.)
Penguin Ireland, 25 St Stephen's Green, Dublin 2, Ireland
(a division of Penguin Books Ltd)
Penguin Group (Australia), 250 Camberwell Road,
Camberwell, Victoria 3124, Australia (a division of Pearson Australia Group Pty Ltd)
Penguin Books India Pvt Ltd, 11 Community Centre,
Panchsheel Park, New Delhi – 110 017, India
Penguin Group (NZ), 67 Apollo Drive, Mairangi Bay, Auckland 1310, New Zealand
(a division of Pearson New Zealand Ltd)
Penguin Books (South Africa) (Pty) Ltd, 24 Sturdee Avenue,
Rosebank, Johannesburg 2196, South Africa

Penguin Books Ltd, Registered Offices: 80 Strand, London WC2R ORL, England

www.penguin.com

Published in Penguin Books 2007

1

This is a work of fiction. Although some real places and events are used in the story, others are entirely the product of the author's imagination, and the characters described are not real and any resemblance that any of the characters may have to real people is entirely coincidental

Set in 12.5/14.75pt Monotype Garamond
by Palimpsest Book Production Limited, Grangemouth, Stirlingshire
Printed in England by Clays Ltd, St Ives plc

ISBN: 978-0-141-01655-9

For Noel

There they all were, all the lovely sisters, giggling and shivering and bawdy and prim, and I turned and turned again, gloating at the numbers before and behind my motley, frost-defying sex.

Because sex is all we really had in common.

Jill Tweedie

1. London, 1985

'Friendship is optional, and a matter of free will. Family is mandatory, and forced upon one.'

Netta was complaining at one end of the phone line, and Jane, her older sister, was saying this at the other. Jane had a congratulatory First in Greats from Oxford University. Netta had recently arrived at Goldsmiths College to study Communications. Jane's university life had glittered with interesting, intoxicating friends. Most of them had parents who regularly appeared on BBC2, or ran small countries, which was nearly as good. Netta was less fortunate. She was in the third week of her student life, and though she had met lots of people, not one of them was in the least intoxicating. She winced at Jane's deployment of the word 'one'. They were from an unremarkable background just outside Crewe, but her sister's high intelligence had sent her ricocheting into a different social class. Having babies had only served to make her spikier and posher. Since coming down from Oxford some years earlier, she had produced three children in quick succession with her perfect husband Richard, an elegantly superior academic.

'If only it was that simple . . .' Netta inserted one finger into the curls of the phone flex. She had narrow, well-shaped hands, which she supposed was an advantage of some kind.

'What do you mean? You've always had plenty of friends.'

'It's different here. University friends are meant to be different. I want to find a soulmate . . .'

'So bloody intense!'

'I can't help it. But I just seem to get sucked in by all the wrong people. Everyone comes into my room. All the weirdos, anyway.'

'You're too nice to everyone.'

'No I'm not.'

'Yes you are,' said Jane. 'You plunge in without thinking, and then get saddled with duds.'

Netta watched as two Geographers walked past, complete with rucksacks. 'Coming to the lager festival?' asked one, winking at her. 'Only fifty pence a pint.'

'Wet T-shirt contest later on,' said his slightly shyer friend. They giggled at this, overwhelmed by their own sexism, and scurried away.

'Duds are pretty thick on the ground. Anyway, it's weird, being shoved into student life like this. I think I'm too old – twenty, after all. Halls of residence are a bit like those huge vats of Quality Street.'

'Whatever do you mean?'

'A sort of unlucky dip.'

'Unlucky what?'

'Dip. You know, with lots of really crap flavours, like the ones with purple wrappers that taste of sick.'

'Talk sense, Netta, for God's sake. This is the kind of conversation I have with the children.'

'Some of them own fluffy slippers,' said Netta, in a low voice.

'Speak up, can't you? The children are having a percussive moment.' In the background, Netta could hear saucepans being bashed together. 'I don't want to discourage it, they're showing a marvellous sense of innate rhythm.'

'Fluffy slippers,' said Netta, in a louder voice. 'Or tartan ones. The sort ancient incontinent men wear in old people's homes. They change into them when they get back from lectures.'

'How perfectly vile.' Jane finally sounded impressed. Clearly this had been unheard of at Balliol. 'Doesn't sound very cutting-edge. I thought Goldsmiths students would all be wearing hi-tech boiler suits and so on.'

'No, well, this place is full of . . .' Netta watched a Lycra-clad dancer shimmy past, perfectly petite in her stripy leg-warmers. She knew Jane would say 'morons', and wanted to think of a less elitist way of putting it. 'Do you think people turn into stereotypes on purpose? Maybe it takes the pressure off.'

'The reassurance of the gang,' said Jane. 'Remember how I had to offload that awful separatist Persephone and her terrible women-only crones? They were all into Andrea Dworkin and the power of men in pornography. One might have expected better things from people who have risen to the top of the system academically. She's reading for the Bar now, you know.'

Netta thought uncharitably that all of Jane's Oxford friends had specialized in non-stop languor, never happy unless they had a medieval column to lean against. She grimaced. 'One couple have the same haircuts and the same navy jumpers, and they got together at the Freshers' Ball.

Now they're engaged or something. They're eighteen, for God's sake.'

Jane maintained a tactful silence, safe in the knowledge that the really fascinating people would be spending their undergraduate years among the dreaming spires as she had done.

'I suppose there must be someone out there,' said Netta at last. 'Someone on my wavelength.'

'Once you find your college friends, you'll never lose them. They're your peers,' said Jane. If she was trying not to sound smug, she was failing badly. 'Remember my Ophelia in the OUDS production? The performance was in the cloisters at New College.'

'How could I forget?' Netta could still see Jane, tripping about with those bloody wild flowers. 'Her' Ophelia had been a hectoring head girl, eminently sane. Jane's dramatic career had peaked several years earlier when she had excelled as Lady Bracknell in the school play. Her voice carried well, but she lacked range.

'Still know everyone in the cast. Scattered all over the world. Marvellous, isn't it?'

'Inspirational.'

'Good, good. Glad to help.' Jane's super-intelligence did not alert her to irony. 'Well, I have to go now. I'm about to sing an aria to Little Richard.'

'Bleeding hell, Jane, he's only a baby! Don't they have Trumpton any more?'

'Never too early to sensitize a child to the romance of *Rigoletto*.'

'I hate opera. All those Diana Dors bosoms.' Now she was wondering why she had phoned Jane in the first place;

then she remembered. There wasn't anyone else. Her schoolfriends were all blissfully happy with their new chums, laughing beautiful hysterical laughter at Sussex or Exeter or UEA. She didn't like to bore them with her bad side. So there was only Jane. And somehow, before talking to her sister, Netta always convinced herself that there would be warmth and understanding between them. Sometimes she almost thought the temperature was rising – but then Jane would initiate a chill.

A barely audible sigh drifted into her ear. 'Just . . . be yourself, Nettie, you know that's what Mum would have said.' Jane suddenly sounded tired.

'If she was alive, I'd be boring her instead of you.' There were tears at the back of Netta's voice now. Shit. She would not collapse into self-pity. She would not be pathetic about it. But she could see her mother now, standing smiling at the school gates, a wide orange hairband failing to control her wild black hair. Margaret would never let Netta know when she was coming to meet her from school, and this was an unusual treat, as she was generally too busy and disorganized to make the time. Forward planning wasn't her style: she was a glorious amateur when it came to motherhood. So when Netta did see her waiting, she felt a surge of intense joy. Margaret had a special little wave for these moments, an ironically cute twiddling of her fingers, as if she was laughing at the whole idea of her being there, like a proper mum.

Jane's reply dragged her back into the present. 'Yes, well. Maturity thrust upon one,' she remarked. 'Twenty-six years old, three children of one's own and in loco parentis to you.'

'With Dad old soako parentis.'

'Quite.' Jane did not like Netta's jokes, or references to their father's love of the demon drink. An Oxford man himself, David Royce had subsequently underachieved, and ended up teaching History in a secondary modern. After the death of their mother, he had left his job and bought a village pub with the money she had left him. This had not been a wise move. While the regulars caroused in the snug, he would down purposeful amounts of G and T, and then go upstairs and sulk in his dark, empty flat. Jane was impatient now. 'Carpe diem, Nettie, lively up yourself. You know, in the Bob Dylan phrase.'

'Bob Marley.'

'I said Bob Marley.'

'No you didn't.'

'Yes I bloody well did. I know who Bob Marley is. Or was. He was a Rastafarian musician from Jamaica who died of cancer at the age of thirty-six. Bob Dylan's an American Jewish singer/songwriter, who's turned all Born Again. Happy now?' Popular culture was Jane's only weak area, and she sometimes swotted up on it, goaded on by the fact that Netta had an exhaustive knowledge of trivia and showbiz gossip.

'Okay, who or what is Dead or Alive?'

'Shut up.'

'You don't know.'

'Shut up. It's not a proper question.'

'It is a proper question. You're showing your ignorance. I'll give you a clue. You Spin Me Round.'

'Look, just fuck off, will you?'

'It's pop music, Jane. It was number one in March.'

6

'Anyway. Irrelevant. What I'm saying is – you must get out and about. Rather than pratting about like the most hideous wallflower at the youth club dance.' Netta could tell that Jane was trying to be kind.

After hanging up, she stood for a minute, staring around her at the scruffy hallway, reluctant to go back to her room. The pay phone was at the bottom of a flight of lino-covered stairs, next to the heavy fire doors which led out into the concrete quad. She might as well have gone to college in the Soviet Gulag in search of a cosy, old world ambience.

She realized she was not alone. Belinda was sitting on the bottom step of the stairs, with a tea towel tucked into her top like a giant napkin, eating sausage and chips. Belinda sprang from a long line of Somerset butchers, and did not know how to cook, so she ate sausage and chips every day. She had a puffy, veal-like complexion and fluffy blonde hair.

'You made me jump,' said Netta.

'Sorry,' said Belinda, with a full mouth. 'It's lonely in my room.'

'Don't worry, it's fine,' said Netta.

'Want a chip?'

Netta accepted one.

'I miss my mum, that's the main trouble,' said Belinda.

'So do I.'

Belinda munched in silence for a while. 'Yeah, but it's easier for you, isn't it? You must be used to it by now, if she died when you were twelve.'

'Must I?' said Netta. Was she used to it? She felt a cold

ache at the thought of time carrying her away, trying to reduce her mother to a tiny dot on a distant horizon. Her memories of Margaret were intense: magic lantern pictures, brighter and more beautiful than real life. But she didn't edit out her mother's oddness and incompetence; it was all there, in brilliant flashes, exploding across her mind. The terrible sandwiches she used to make: egg shell in the egg mix; holes in the bread caused by the manic application of fridge-hard butter; eye-watering quantities of thoughtlessly slathered Marmite. Netta's mouth prickled now, as if she had just taken a bite. Suddenly, she was on Prestatyn beach, aged nine, watching a line of doleful donkeys mooching along in a sandstorm. She and Margaret were sitting side by side, sheltering behind a canvas windbreak.

'What are the sandwiches like, darling?'

'Horrible.' The lump of meat in her mouth seemed to be indestructible. It had no taste left. She thought it might be there for ever.

'Really horribly horrible?'

'Even worse than usual. What did you put in it, Mummy?'

Margaret rolled her eyes. 'Sorry. *Sorry*. It's brisket. It's disgusting. Daddy told me I had to save money. And it's extremely good for you.' She smiled at Netta, smoke pouring out of her nostrils as if she was a friendly dragon. Then she produced a big white pocket handkerchief. 'Spit it out in here, and we'll gorge on chocs.' The chocolates were tiny, doll-sized bars, each wrapped in sparkling blue paper. Netta could still taste the cool milk chocolate, feel the sand stinging her cheeks, and hear the waves crashing on to the beach. But the sense of love and security she had felt, behind the windbreak with her mother, had gone for ever. The memory of how it had all ended, her mother a skeleton, clawing at her with some final message she hadn't the strength to communicate, wasn't in the magic lantern gallery. It didn't need to be: it was with her all the time.

She watched Belinda eating her chips. Upstairs, in the room next to her own, she could hear the sound of Prudence, the Punk from Preston, banging biscuit tins together, out of time with Poly Styrene and X-Ray Specs. She was having a 'men-only' party, hoping that one of her guests would agree to have sex with her, and had asked Netta to stay out of sight. This was flattering in a way, but not exactly a sign that they had formed a bosom friendship. Although she wasn't beautiful, Netta's fair, girlish looks seemed to get men over-excited. Her chief attraction was her wavy mass of golden hair. Whole building sites had been known to go wild when her hair made an appearance. She sighed – but then caught sight of a scribbled notice which was pinned next to the phone:

TO LET
LARGE ROOM AVAILABLE IN SPLENDID
VICTORIAN HOME. ICY DRAUGHTS,
GARDEN VIEWS, CHARMING LOCATION AND
ONE SMALL BUT PERFECTLY FORMED
FLATMATE (FEMALE). TEN MINS FROM
BLACKHEATH STATION.
CALL PILAR ON 692 733 FOR DETAILS.

Netta was filled with sudden determination. 'Feel free to go and sit in my room, Belinda,' she said kindly. 'You can use my heated rollers if you want.'

'Can I? Brilliant,' said Belinda. 'And there I was, thinking the evening would be all downhill after the chips.'

When Netta dialled the number, someone picked up the phone right away.

'Yes?' A woman's voice.

'Is that Pilar?'

'Speaking.' The voice was clipped Ealing, but somehow unconvincing.

'I'm calling about the room.'

'Sorry. It's gone. Or rather, it hasn't gone exactly, but there's a whole world of nutters and weirdos out there, and no doubt you are one of them. I'd rather pay twice the rent than spend any more time attempting to find the one person in South London with unfetid breath and a healthy indifference to watching endless videotapes of *Brideshead Revisited*.'

'I hate *Brideshead*. I live in a nuclear bunker,' said Netta, desperation rising in her voice.

'Not a peace person, are you? I've got one of those already. My old flatmate has taken herself off to Greenham Common.'

'It's not literally a nuclear bunker, it just looks like one. I'm in a hall of residence. And I can't stand peace people.'

'Why not? Are you a Tory?'

'No. It's the dodgy headgear that puts me off.'

'Gawd, yes. Embroidery and earpieces.'

'Pompoms and strings under the chin.'

'Multicoloured wool, using all those odd bits at the bottom of the basket to save the planet.' Pilar sounded friendlier now.

'Inca animal life, mainly llamas.'

'Flower-child hair-weaving disease.'

'Bloody awful snoods.'

'Look, why don't you come over? Just for a chat. I'm not promising anything, though. I don't want to be incarcerated with some social outcast, standing in my personal space, ranting on about astrology. What star sign are you, by the way? I'm a Gemini, fatally divided.'

'Scorpio.'

'Dark, mysterious and into the occult?'

'Blonde, blabbermouth and frightened of the dark.'

'Perfect. Where's your hall of rez?'

'Camberwell. Miles away.'

'Bugger that. Get a tube to Charing Cross, then you'll need to jump on a train.'

The house, Dartmouth Villa, was set back from the road, hidden behind a huddle of overgrown trees and a high stone wall. Netta pushed open the wrought-iron gate and, not seeing a path, began to cross the damp, muddy lawn, snail shells cracking under her feet. She looked up at the looming house. It was almost institutional in size, a red-brick villa with a grand sweep of stone steps up to the front door and rows of windows glaring down at her. Some of these were boarded up, and the house itself was half-obscured by the rampant shrubbery and the ivy which twined around the drainpipes, reaching up as far as the eaves. She climbed the stone steps to the front door, which was opened almost immediately by a red-haired woman with small, neat features.

'Hello,' she said. 'Blimey, look at all your lovely hair! I knew you'd be pretty. Come in.' There was something strangely vivid about her, like a Hollywood film star seen through the wrong end of a telescope. She had a husky voice, partly Estuary, partly clipped Celia Johnson. Netta assumed that the aim was to sound more upmarket than she actually was. What made her so appealing Netta couldn't quite think – maybe it was the retro spectacles with pointed sides, which made her look clever in an off-centre way, or the fact that she had a black Soubranie clenched between her lips.

'Do you live here on your own?' asked Netta, stepping into the hall.

'Just in the top half. The downstairs belongs to a famous feminist who lives in Spain. She owns the whole house, in fact, and rents it out. Her daughter lives there now, and her son drops in from time to time. They are seriously out to lunch, the pair of them.'

'What sort of out to lunch?' Netta asked.

'Emily is a French student and she thinks she's Françoise Sagan. Totally pretentious, all Gitanes and "l'amour", and she's kind of dormant unless there's a man in the room. Tom's an extremist. He shoots statues, did you ever hear anything so wanky? I don't see much of them. Mostly, they're in North London, hanging out in super-cool squats. You know, that North London shit.'

Netta certainly did know that North London shit. Jane lived in a flat-fronted house in an Islington square, complete with a palatial drawing room with pompous invitations propped up on the marble fireplace. But if anything, this house was built on an even more epic scale. She stepped into an immense hall, its ceiling almost invisible in the gloom. A baronial staircase curved up in front of them, but it was uncarpeted, and the hall itself was a mess of old bicycles and half-used pots of paint.

'Bloody hell,' said Netta, looking around at all the closed doors, and upwards at a vast, cobweb-infested chandelier. The magnificence impressed her more than the mess. She began to laugh nervously and thought – don't say too much. Don't screw it all up. 'So you're often here all by yourself?'

'Yeah,' said Pilar, leading the way up the stairs. 'Kind of spooky, isn't it?'

'D'you have to will yourself not to think about the house in *Psycho*?' They had reached the landing now, and Netta half-expected to see stuffed birds glowering down at them. But all she could see was a row of old wardrobes, topped by cardboard boxes.

'Not really. I've never been scared of the dark. Is that going to be a problem for you? Easily spooked?'

'God, no. I just sleep with my head under the duvet.'

'You'll love it here,' said Pilar. 'I know you will.' Her reluctance to share the flat seemed to be completely forgotten. 'This is your room, if you like it,' she said. 'Afraid me and Mel – my absent Greenham chum – have already bagged the best ones.'

'So she still lives here some of the time?' said Netta, looking inside. The room seemed to be as big as the entire floor she lived in at Bromley Hall. The fact that there was hardly any furniture may have added to the sense of scale – a great tract of bare floorboards led to a long window at one end, and all the room contained was a chest of drawers and a double mattress on the floor.

'Oh yeah, she's all over the place. Ideology, you know. Addles the brain.'

'How much is it?'

'Thirty-five a week. Plus bills. Bit steep, really. I'm down for a hard-to-let flat, but they have to get the tramps out first.'

'It's just amazing.'

'If you want it, it's yours.'

'I'll take it.'

'Won't your hall of residence make you pay for the whole term?'

'I'll sort that out later.' Netta had a small fund of money that Margaret had left her. It was for Emergencies Only. Jane had spent hers on a stash of elaborate gowns to be inflicted on innocent undergraduates at May Balls. Netta had been waiting for an equivalent need – and this seemed to be it.

'Good,' said Pilar. To Netta's surprise, she threw her arms around her and gave her a hug. 'I'm really glad!' She pulled Netta through another door off the landing. 'This is the kitchen.' A cold room yawned before them, with black-and-white tiles on the floor and old-fashioned cupboards. She picked up a chipped brown teapot and put it down again. 'Gin, I think,' she said, and opened a bottle. They drank all of it, out of cracked teacups, and laughed till it got dark.

*

Jane helped Netta move her things into the new flat the following Saturday, but didn't appear to be very impressed with her decision.

'Where will you work?' she said, dumping a cardboard box full of old copies of *The Face* on to the mattress. She was flushed and breathless, and putting on weight, Netta noticed. But it almost suited her – she had an indelible, inked-in prettiness that nothing seemed to spoil.

'What d'you mean, where will I work?'

Jane's glance flashed around the high room. 'There's no desk. Not even so much as a bookshelf.'

'You don't have to read if you're doing Communications,' said Netta. She knew this was rubbish. 'You just have to watch loads of TV. It's all about popular culture, magazines, the mass media. All the stuff you're too poncy to enjoy. I don't have to sit here reading books. That's not very rock and roll. I need to be . . . out on the street . . .' But she ran out of steam at this point.

'Honestly, Nettie, what do you take me for? Of course you need a desk! I'll see what we've got in our attic. I'm sure I'll be able to persuade some hire-van to come south of the river . . .' Jane opened the empty wardrobe and looked inside it, frowning.

'Thanks a lot. No need to make South London sound like East Germany.'

'I'm only trying to help. Don't you want to show Dad what you're capable of? Horribly musty smell in here.'

Netta banged the wardrobe door shut. 'I don't give a damn what Dad thinks I'm capable of. He's a stupid, rotten old drunk. He has no idea about anything. He thinks I'm a complete thick-head in any case, and frankly I wouldn't care if —'

'Really, Netta, stop ranting! No one could call him stupid, I draw the line there. It's a tragic waste, the ruin of a brilliant mind.'

Netta did not point out that she was the person who actually phoned their father, and had a relationship with him, however imperfect. Until she left for college, she'd been working in the pub, helping behind the bar, and making him his nightly supper of grilled chops and beans. His lack of respect for her was a bond between them: he had no respect for himself, either. She hated to think of him being alone, no matter how much he annoyed her. Jane preferred to admire him from afar, nurturing the myth of Wasted Genius and avoiding his alcoholic breath. But Netta realized she had better keep quiet if she wanted more help with the boxes. Pilar was nowhere to be seen, and was unlikely to be the removal-person type, in any case.

'Okay, okay, I'm sorry. He's a Great Man In His Way.' This was one of their father's favourite catch-phrases. He believed in Great Men, especially if they were flawed and sexist, like Kingsley Amis. It was harder for him to identify with the Dalai Lama.

When Jane's car was empty and the room was stacked with boxes, they both stood looking at it for a moment. The euphoria which Netta had felt as they drove out of the dreary concrete quad overlooked by Bromley Hall had not entirely evaporated. None the less, it was hardly a perfect scenario. The room looked bleak and unwelcoming and the piles of boxes just made it seem abandoned, like some forgotten store room.

'It'll be fine. I shall sort it out before I go to bed,' said Netta, stepping over a pile of LPs. Chrissie Hynde stared up from the top one, all androgynous attitude, a flash of red among her monochrome men.

'The house is impressive enough,' said Jane grudgingly. 'Just don't know how you can stand living like some maladjusted hippy. I had a study-bedroom with a dressing room attached in my first year. Up that stone spiral staircase – d'you remember?'

'Yup.' Netta was beginning to sort listlessly through her piles of belongings.

'With Persephone opposite, of course. Talk about bad luck! Though she was still sleeping with men in those days. Before the separatism set in, I mean.'

'Yup. Good old Persephone.'

'She had waist-length hair the first time I saw her. I thought she was like Rapunzel, high up in her tower.'

Now Netta was looking at some heated rollers. Was there a place for heated rollers in her new life? 'D'you want these? Spruce yourself up before a dinner party?'

'You must be joking. Chuck them out. She cut it all off with nail scissors. I nearly died when I saw her.'

'Tragic.' Netta stood up. 'Well, at least you met your true friends in the end. Like you said. The people you still know.'

Jane smiled tightly. 'People like Richard,' she said. 'Success stories.' She looked at her watch, and a look of panic crossed her face. 'He'll want me back by now,' she said. 'This is the most solo childcare he'll have done since Little Richard was born. And he's got a student coming round this afternoon.' She pulled her car keys out of her bag, as if to placate his absent spirit.

'I thought you might like a cup of tea.'

'No time. Anyway, that kitchen looks like a public health hazard. If I come round again I'll be bringing my own bleach and rubber gloves.'

'Suit yourself.'

Jane walked out of the room with the tiniest hint of a waddle. Netta stood for a few moments, feeling angry and graceless, then rushed to the top of the staircase. 'I mean – thanks, Jane! And everything . . .' But perhaps Jane didn't hear. There was just the sound of her old Beetle revving up outside, and then driving away. A wave of loneliness made Netta clench her hands, then she braced herself to call her father and tell him about her escape from Bromley Hall.

2

Netta was musing over stationery in the college shop. It was two months since she had moved into the house, and Jane's desk had finally arrived. Some new notebooks were vital to create the appropriate ambience of a study-bedroom.

'Funny thing about girls,' said a voice by her elbow. 'You love all that crappy paper stuff. Cutesy notepads, coloured felt pens, novelty thank-you notes. And you're all suckers for cuddly toys.'

Netta turned to see a pale, scrawny man standing behind her. He had mousy hair, a washed-out face and – big mistake – a bandanna tied around his spiky quiff.

'Sorry, do I know you?' she asked.

He scrutinized her, eyes narrowed, as if he was trying to work this out. 'Think so. Almost sure you do.' He took a biro from a box on the display counter and scribbled with it, experimentally, on the pad of paper. She noticed that he had scrawled the words 'Sex God'.

'Actually, I'm lying,' he said. 'I never saw you in my life before.'

'No. That's what I thought.'

'But you definitely remind me of someone.'

Netta, who was used to reminding men of someone, was not impressed with this. 'Now, why doesn't that surprise me?' she asked. 'Do you do much work on your chat-up lines, or do you just say the first thing that comes into your head?'

'How d'you mean?' asked Quiff, eyes wide open in disbelief. 'That wasn't a *line*. That was me reacting with total honesty to external stimulae. Christ, do you think I make a habit of harassing girls in the college shop?'

'It's not "girls",' said Netta.

'What's not girls?'

'The word. The word is not "girls". It's "women".'

'Oh yeah. Right on, sister. You don't look like the sort that needs to plait your own leg hair to me. Leave that to the sapphic tendency, darling. Attractive young person like yourself.'

'Are you in some kind of 1970s time-warp? You'll be saying "chicks" next.'

'I would never use the word "chick". What do you take me for? Jessica Lange, that's the one. You look exactly like Jessica Lange. Only with more hair. Which is good.'

'I'm afraid I'm going to have to ask you to fuck off,' said Netta. 'This conversation is a complete waste of time.'

'Brilliant,' he said, scribbling again. This time he produced the phrase 'Girls on Top'. 'I like a lady with a bit of spunk. And I can reliably inform you that today is your lucky day.'

'Lucky in what way?'

'I am able to offer you a personal invitation to see the best band in the area. Façade, the thinking person's Dépêche Mode, the muso's Visage, a Simple Minds for the punk faithful, New Romanticism for the Unromantic . . .'

'Would this be your band, by any chance?'

'It certainly would,' said Quiff. 'Let me introduce myself. Bryan Sullivan's the name, enigmatic front man is the game.'

'I'm afraid I'm busy.'

'I haven't told you when the gig's on yet.'

'I'm busy all the time.'

'Right, washing your hair, reading the fucking *Women's Room* – don't worry, I know the score.' He sighed, and tossed the biro back on to the counter. 'Look, you could be passing up something a bit special here.'

'I could?'

'Perhaps I should fill you in about my track record. Serious stuff, you know. First in English and Drama, editor of *Metropolitan Student*, and I've written my own play: *Cosmo Boy*. Get it? About a glossy magazine in a parallel universe where men are the oppressed sex. I'm not just some brainless college stud.'

'I didn't have you down as any kind of stud.' She turned away, and practised her signature with two different types of pen.

'You're a tough one, Netta Royce,' he said, looking over her shoulder. 'Nice name, though.'

She turned to him, finally losing her temper. 'For God's sake! I don't know you! And I don't want to know you. Isn't it obvious? All I want to do is buy some effing stationery in, okay, possibly a stereotypically girly sort of way. But I need it, we all need it, paper for writing on, pens to write with. And I absolutely *loathe* fluffy toys. All right?'

'All right – point taken.'

But she was furious now. 'I'd just like to make one

thing clear. I've only ever owned one item that was in any way frilly or girly. Muffles. He was a pink, generic fluffy thing. Kittenish, doggy-like, teddy-oriented. I dunno. Maybe he was a fucking Womble. My old boyfriend gave him to me, thinking, like you, that being female means you must automatically adore anything furry with a bow round its neck. He never bothered to find out if this was true in my particular case.'

'So what happened?'

'I gave both of them the boot. Muffles went to Oxfam. Boyfriend went to North Staffs Poly. We didn't stay in touch.'

'If he was pink, Muffles must have been a girl. I mean, woman.'

'Very funny.'

'Sorry.' Netta was surprised to see that he looked embarrassed. He smiled at her. 'Look – forget I said all that.'

'I don't care what you said. I'm just trying to buy some notebooks.'

'There's no point me trying not to be a disgusting sexist pig at my advanced time of life. I'm twenty-three, you know.' He pulled two tickets out of his pocket. 'Anyway. Fucking bollocks. You hate my guts. You might even have hairy legs. But it would be great if you could come to my gig . . . it's in the college bar, tonight . . . just – you know. Be there, or be square. You might surprise yourself and like it. Bring a friend.'

Netta looked at the tickets, which said: 'Façade: dance to the beat of a different drummer.' They were badly photocopied, and featured a smudged portrait of Bryan in serious bandanna mode. 'Thanks,' she said, suddenly embarrassed in her turn.

He shrugged, and followed her to the till. She bought some lurid notebooks, suitable for the image of a Communications student, and he bought a KitKat.

'We're huge – Façade – really mega,' he said, when they got outside. 'A and R men coming along tonight, as it goes. Serious stuff.' But then, looking furtive, he pulled a whole wad of tickets out of his pocket and gave her those as well. 'Bring all your friends,' he said. 'Bring anyone.' And he hurried away, bumping into a group of Drama students as he went.

That evening, Netta grinned to herself as she opened the front door of the house. She rushed up the stairs two at a time. 'Hey, Pilar, guess what . . .' she began. But stopped, seeing a large rucksack lying on its side at the top of the stairs. 'Pilar . . . ?'

'In here, darling!' came a cry from the bathroom. She saw that the door was half-open, and light and steam were drifting on to the cold, dark landing. Pushing the door open wider, she went in.

Pilar was lying in a bubble bath. Her body was completely hidden by the foaming suds, and only her head was visible. But she was not alone. Another head was poking out at the opposite end of the bath – a blonde, shaggily cropped head, regarding her benignly through the gently rising vapour.

'Hello, darlin',' said the head, all affability. (Why was everyone calling her darling today?) 'You must be Netta.' She had a loud Yorkshire accent: her voice boomed slightly.

'That's right,' said Netta. 'And . . . are you Melanie

Moon?' She recognized the woman's cherubic face from photographs stuck to the kitchen door, and her name from the post piled up on the hallstand.

'Certainly am,' said the head. 'You can call me Mel. We're all friends here.' Even naked and half-submerged in soapy water, she had an air of effortless command.

'Want to slip your things off and squeeze in between us?' asked Pilar. A white arm came out of the water and picked up a glass of wine. 'We can make space, can't we, Mel?' Her voice was warm and giggly.

'Not really,' said Mel comfortably. 'Where would my feet go? If they weren't . . .' And here there was a lot of splashing and laughing, and Mel finally heaved herself out of the water. She was heavy-breasted and big-hipped. 'I've had enough of luxuriating,' she said, wrapping herself in a big red towel. 'Get in and take the weight off your embarrassment.'

Netta hesitated. Somehow, she felt that she would be at a disadvantage whatever she decided to do. Clothed, she would seem prudish. Naked, she would feel, well . . . naked. But naked seemed the way to go. 'I met a total tosser called Bryan Sullivan today,' she said as she pulled her jeans off, hoping to sound matter-of-fact.

'Oh, we know all about him,' said Pilar, holding out her empty glass to Mel. 'He's famous. He used to be The Worst Man at College. Now he's got some wanky sabbatical and he's just The Worst Hanger On. Fill her up, will you?' Netta tried not to notice the intimacy of her tone, or mind the 'we'. After all, she herself was the interloper. Mel had more reason to feel threatened than she did. But feeling threatened did not seem to be Mel's style. Netta lowered herself into the warm, fragrant water as Mel disappeared in search of wine. She found she was sitting between Pilar's outstretched legs.

'He's written a play called *Cosmo Boy*, apparently. Sort of gender-reversal thing.'

'Fancies himself to death,' said Pilar. 'Thinks he's a bloody genius.'

'Being a genius is a disease that mainly affects blokes. Like heart disease and gout.'

'Ooh, hark at you,' said Pilar. 'Get down off your soapbox! Isn't it cosy, being girls together?'

'Certainly is,' said Netta.

'Are you okay?' Pilar's smile was warm and flirtatious.

'Fantastic!'

Mel had returned and was offering Pilar her drink. 'And one for the new woman in our midst,' said Mel, handing another brimming glass to Netta.

'Very nice of you,' said Netta, taking a sip and setting it down.

'Who were you talking about?' asked Mel.

'You know, that wanker Bryan Sullivan,' said Pilar. 'One of those horrible Union hacks.'

'The *Metropolitan Student* man?'

'Yeah. Biggest git on campus.'

'Oh, I know him all right,' said Mel. 'I shagged him in my first year. One of those little accidents we all have along the way. Once we'd fucked a couple of times, he literally talked all night.'

'He's got a gig tonight,' said Netta. Her naked voice seemed to be firmer and brisker than her clothed one. 'At the college bar. He gave me a load of free tickets.'

'Well, we've got to go somewhere, so why not?' said Pilar. She was sponging her shoulders. She had very beautiful collarbones.

'Suppose,' said Mel, towelling herself dry. 'It'll feel a bit weird, appearing in the bar when I'm never in a seminar.'

'Christ, join the rest of the human race,' said Pilar. 'You don't have to be at Greenham Common to not turn up for anything. Most people just stay in bed in Streatham.'

'They're called Façade. Dancing to the beat of a different drummer,' said Netta. 'Sounds on the pseudy side.'

'Are you kidding? Fucking Norah, we *have* to go!' said Mel. 'It's bound to be good for a laugh.'

She began to dance around the bathroom, wearing nothing but a layer of talcum powder, which made her look like a portly ghost. 'Get into the groove,' she began in Madonna-falsetto, then, in a bigger voice, to the tune of 'Frère Jacques': 'We are women, We are women,/We are strong, We are strong,/We say No, We say No,/To the Bomb, To the Bomb.' As she sang the word 'bomb' for the second time, she dropped a wet loofah into the water between Pilar and Netta. Foam shot into the air.

'This is the last voice you will ever hear!' squealed Pilar, leaping out of the water and chasing Mel out of the bathroom. Netta could hear them yelling, 'When Two Tribes Go to War – One Is All that You Can Score!' until they put the stereo on at full volume.

By the time she was bathed and ready, they were both in full battledress. Mel was wearing a man's dinner suit with a glittery T-shirt underneath, and Pilar wore a party frock which sparkled with scarlet sequins. They were standing side by side in front of the gilt-framed living-room mirror, outlining their eyes with kohl.

'You look great,' said Pilar, smiling over her shoulder at Netta's black dress.

Mel smiled at her in the mirror, more vaguely. 'Bit ironic, but it's like being in the Army, being a Greenham woman,' she said, as if they were in mid-conversation.

'Really?' said Netta. Pilar seemed not to be listening, and was putting on a lot of navy-blue mascara.

'What's it like at Greenham, then?'

'Cold.'

'That's it – cold?'

'Cold and hard work and quite boring, a lot of the time. Most of your energy goes into surviving – keeping the fire going, cooking food, clearing up. The bits where you get to shout at the police are few and far between, unfortunately.'

'Sounds like complete crap.'

'Well, it's not.' Mel was tweaking hair gel into the front portion of her hair, so that it spiked upwards. 'Being with other women is what makes it all worthwhile. The bonds you make – I've met some of the . . .' But then Mel glanced at Pilar and broke off. 'There's basically a lot of singing, a lot of laughing, a lot of . . . warmth.'

'So it's cold, but kind of warm at the same time?'

'Exactly. The warmth is from humanity. Or womanity, whatever you want to call it.'

'Bit intense.'

'Exactly. You want to go a bit crazy, when you're home on leave.'

'I can imagine.'

'So I'm looking forward to a really good night out.'

'Aren't we all?' said Netta.

'Which in my case means getting the beers in, and having a bloody good shag.'

'Me too,' said Pilar. 'Simple souls, aren't we, really? Just one step up from the amoeba.'

Mel nodded. She was now rolling something pink and shiny on to her cheeks. 'I'm a male chauvinist pig, trapped in a woman's body.'

'Desperately Seeking Spam,' said Pilar.

Netta, who had been rooting about in her bag for a lipstick, looked up in surprise. 'Spam? Spam's revolting. I mean – I wouldn't say no to a kebab, later on . . .'

Mel turned away from the mirror to look at Pilar. 'Oh, Pee,' she said, in tones of mock horror. 'Haven't you told her about Spam? Frigging hell! She knows *nothing*!'

'What d'you mean?' asked Netta, looking from one woman to the other. 'Spam's luncheon meat. Isn't it?'

Pilar turned towards her to reveal her heightened, artificial face. 'Spam, Ms Royce, is Meaningless Male Flesh,' she said, twirling across the room so that her skirt flew around her.

'As if there was any other kind,' said Mel. She took a cigarette packet out of her pocket and handed it round.

Netta had only ever slept with two men, one of whom had later presented her with Muffles, the fluffy toy from hell. She decided to keep this quiet. 'I think I must be a bit of a romantic,' she said.

'Bloody Norah,' said Mel. 'Have you met any men lately? What is there to get romantic *about*?'

'Well, love, I suppose. Finding the person you can love.'

'How sodding boring. We want Fun. F.U.N.' Mel looked deadly serious.

'Not always easy to achieve, a total and utter one-night stand, but it's a beautiful thing when it happens,' said Pilar.

'Crikey,' said Netta. She thought of Jane, mired in monogamy. 'Well, I'll try anything once,' she said.

Mel beamed, and lit their cigarettes. 'Hold them up!' she commanded. 'Pilar, come on, hold yours up!'

They all held their lighted cigarettes towards the ceiling like the Three Musketeers. 'Right – we're in this together!' said Melanie. 'Here's to the Spam Hunt!'

'Serial shaggers for sexual equality!' said Pilar.

'They do it to us, and now we do it to them,' said Mel. 'Fuck 'em and forget 'em, that's what I say! All for one – and one for all!'

'One for all!' they chorused, laughing and taking a simultaneous drag.

3

The college bar was crowded. They had to evict some old people from their chosen table: adult education types sipping halves of shandy before pottering home.

'Right. There are a number of issues here,' said Mel, taking an inaugural gulp of her snake-bite. 'First, bear in mind that we are *fucking* attractive. We look good, and we can speak as well, which is more than you can say for some of these dance morons. Second, we don't want more than one shag – we just want to borrow a half-way decent bloke for one night only. And third – we're not going to wait to be asked. That's the beauty of it – assertiveness. We're not going to sit around oozing feminine charm. We're going to find some appropriate blokes and hit them over the head with it.'

'Hit them over the head with what?' Pilar was gazing round the bar abstractedly, drinking her rum and black.

'Feminine charm, Grandma, wake up,' said Mel. 'I'm just explaining the strategy to our new recruit.'

'Pretty clear on the lie of the land now, thanks,' said Netta. 'But I still think we'd be better off somewhere with fewer members of our platoon trying to pick off the enemy troops. They're really out in force tonight.' She nodded across at a posse of dancers from the Laban Centre, who were lying in wait on the way to the Gents.

'Just see it as healthy competition,' said Mel.

'Get pissed first, and it'll all fall into place,' said Pilar.

Mel looked stern. 'Come on, it's not your bloody execution! What's up with you?'

'Nothing.'

'Could have fooled me. You're doing this guilt thing again, aren't you?'

'No I'm fucking not!'

'What guilt thing?' asked Netta. 'Guilty about what?'

'Oh, you know.' Mel was smiling at Netta. 'Pilar already has a steady boyfriend. One day he'll come down here and sweep you off your feet, won't he, Pee? Or haven't you told her about Roops, either?'

'No, I have not told her about Roops. I haven't told her my whole bloody life story,' said Pilar. She took another glug from her plastic glass. 'Rupert is my fiancé,' she said unexpectedly.

'A good match,' said Mel, nodding. 'Apparently, these things still exist in Bishop's Stortford.'

'He's not from Bishop's Stortford, he's from Cambridge.'

'Marrying up?' asked Netta, thinking of Jane and Richard.

'A girl called Debbie from Bishop's Stortford must marry a man called Rupert if he comes from Cambridge,' said Mel. 'You can tell she's an English student – she thinks she's in a Jane Austen book.'

'Debbie?'

'My real name,' said Pilar, looking decidedly irritable. 'I'm not ashamed of being called Debbie, thank you very much. I just prefer the name Pilar, and I'm used to it now.'

'Come on, there's a bit more to it than that,' said Mel. 'You were called Debbie for the whole of the first term.

Then you threw a massive wobbly and everybody had to call you Pilar. Deep down, in my heart of hearts, I still think of you as Debbie.'

'So what is it?' asked Netta. 'Debbie or Pilar?'

'Okay – here's the full story,' said Pilar. 'I called myself Pilar after the woman who ran the hotel my dad used to take us to on the Costa Brava. She was really glam. And – okay – Debbie is a crap name. Number two – Rupert is at Durham University, his dad's a GP, and yes, he is a bloody good match, no matter how snotty trademark down-to-earth people from Hebden Bridge want to be about it.'

'So do you feel guilty about Spam Hunts?' asked Netta.

'In my opinion, there is still such a thing as wanting to have a good time while your boyfriend isn't looking,' said Pilar. 'What he does in Durham is his business, and what I do down here is my business.'

'Correct. Which means it's time to stop being such a typical, guilty, Catholic girl,' said Mel. 'You don't have to be honest with men. It's not in the job description.'

'Yeah, okay, okay. I feel great.'

'Him by the bar, look, he's quite nice.' Mel was looking at a tall, narrow-faced boy who was buying a lot of crisps. He wore a striped T-shirt and baggy trousers, and had a little black hat attached to the back of his head.

'Looks like an Art bastard to me,' said Pilar, who still seemed to be having trouble getting into the spirit of the thing. 'That type only like girls with pipe-cleaner legs and green hair. They're tribal.'

'We'll soon see about that,' said Mel, marching towards him.

'She really likes you,' said Pilar after a second.

'Yes.' Netta watched as Mel engaged the fashionable man in animated conversation. 'She's great!'

Pilar leaned forward confidentially. 'Melanie has always been the centre of attention,' she said. 'Only child of doting parents.'

'I see.'

'They worry about her. It's their life's work. They send her food parcels, in case she can't get the right type of tea down here. She's never dared to tell them she's living at Greenham. They're scared of breathing, scared of the bloody air. The type that should never have children.'

'Sounds pretty grim.'

'It *is* grim. Whereas I'm overshadowed by two wonderful brothers. They can do everything. Rugby. Quadratic equations. Currency dealing.'

'I've always been second best to my sister.'

'There you go – Mel's never had to share the limelight with anyone. And it shows.'

'But you still like her.'

'Like her? She's the best person I know. She's the sister I never had.'

Netta sipped her drink, trying to assimilate the concept of a sister being something desirable.

Mel returned, bearing a tray of brimming drinks and beaming. 'Phew-eee, adrenalin rush or what?' she said, plonking it down. She had bought chasers for all three of them.

'How did it go?' asked Pilar. 'Have you tapped off?'

'Afraid not. He's a really sweet bloke, though. Doing Sociology, not Art, for your information.'

'So why is he wearing all that trendy gear?'

'Because he's gay. So gay, in fact, that it's actually his name. "Call me Gay Jeremy," he said. So that's it.'

'Not much room for bisexuality there, then,' said Netta.

'I would never be a bisexual,' said Mel. 'You're either one thing or the other.'

'What if you sleep with both sexes?' Pilar suddenly looked interested.

'Gay or straight – it's your choice. But you can't do both. Once you've decided, swing the other way and you're just – having a lapse. In whatever direction it happens to be.'

'I don't see why it has to be so rigid,' said Netta.

'Did you learn that at Greenham?' asked Pilar.

'Being at Greenham's not about being brainwashed, you know.'

'Really? You keep very quiet about what goes on there.'

'Women could change the world,' said Mel. She was still looking round the bar. 'If they stopped wasting their energy on men.'

'Oh, bloody hell!' Pilar was laughing so much that she choked on her drink. 'Now I've heard everything! Melanie – no one has wasted more energy on men than you have!'

'Well, that's going to change.'

'I thought we were on a Spam Hunt.' Netta had caught sight of Bryan, with a large group of Student Union hacks.

'Good point,' said Mel. 'Right,' she said, wiping the back of her mouth with her hand. 'The next one's going to be a heterosexual, and he's going to say yes.'

The next one certainly was a heterosexual, but Netta couldn't help feeling surprised by Mel's choice. He was a short, squat, ginger-haired Welsh rugby player whose nick-name was Mutant. It was a name which suited him so well – his slightly unfortunate arrangement of features having been pummelled into an even worse position in the course of his rugby career – that his Christian name had been forgotten. 'Say hello to Mutant,' said Mel, as she squeezed through the crowd in search of some wall to snog against.

'Hello, Mutant,' said Netta, by this time on her fifth drink. She was wedged against the bar with Pilar. The surge of student drinkers held her trapped, so that all she could do was extract more money out of her bag from time to time, and buy more booze. Dancing was out of the question, and she had hardly seen any men worth even thinking about.

'Hello, good-looking,' said Mutant. 'I still can't decide which of the three of you has the best tits. Been trying to work that one out all night.'

'Interesting project,' said Netta. 'Well, all the best. I don't expect I'll be seeing much of you in future.'

'You never know,' said Mutant. 'You might be the lucky one next time.'

Netta said nothing, but waved her hand at him in a pantomime 'goodbye'.

'What's the next thing down from spam?' she asked Pilar. 'Luncheon meat? Brisket? Puréed testicles? Because . . .'

'Absolobly no fuckin' idea . . .' Pilar had lined up three vodkas in front of her, and drank them all down, one by one. 'All for one, all bloody gone,' she said lucidly. Then: 'I'm thinking of divorcing Roops, you know . . .'

'Divorcing? Don't you need to get married first?'

'Shpeakametaphoric . . .' Pilar stopped and took hold of Netta's shoulder. 'Meta-Phoric-Ally. Don't love him, y'see. Don't *love* him.'

'I thought it was about economics.'

'Sex no good,' said Pilar. 'Sex no good at all. Best time I ever had was with—'

'Aha! If it isn't Ms Jessica Lange.' Bryan's head appeared through the crush of bodies. He had a mad look on his face. 'Saw you across a crowded room with your gorgeous nymphettish chum, and I thought – it cannot be! Ms Netta Royce has come along and graced us with her—'

'We're only here because we had nothing else to do.'

Bryan ogled Pilar in her red sequins. 'Believe me, I am sincerely and humbly grateful to have you here on any terms,' he said. 'Feel free to insult me at your leisure.'

'On a Spam Hunt,' said Pilar, speaking with exaggerated clarity. 'Seekers After Spam.'

'She means we're looking for non-eligible men for shagging purposes,' said Netta. 'When does your band start playing?'

'Oh, in about half an hour,' said Bryan. 'Going to be a totally brilliant gig, I'm telling you. Did I say some A and R people are coming?'

'Yes, you did. And I don't even know what A and R people are.'

'Recording company types,' said Bryan. 'It's a big deal, make or break.'

'Well, good luck,' said Netta. 'Hope it all goes well.'

'If the worst comes to the worst, I can always make do with shagging you meaninglessly later on.'

'We do have some standards in place. I wouldn't get too excited if I were you.'

'You old flatterer,' said Bryan. 'Just can't keep your hands off me, can you?' But he was obviously more interested in the drunken Pilar. 'Fancy coming up to my room for an early audition?' he asked, touching her naked shoulder.

'Most probably,' said Pilar. 'Might well get round to it at — whoops!' She had somehow caught her hemline in her stiletto heel and collapsed on the ground in a heap of sparkling red.

'God's sake, get up, Pilar,' said Netta, attempting to pull her to her feet. But Pilar was heavier than she looked, and it was only when Bryan hauled her up from the other side that she made it back into what passed for a standing position. Now, however, she could only remain upright if she was wedged against the bar. Bryan kept hold of her in a territorial manner which irritated Netta.

'Need more vodka,' said Pilar. 'Must say, heaps better now. Hair of the dog really works.'

'Is that really a good . . . ?' began Netta, but Pilar sent her such a furious look that she thought better of it. She was only a first year, after all, and only a trainee friend, not a fully-fledged one yet. Pilar's true friend was now just a pair of grasping hands, wandering over Mutant's back as if she was Charles Aznavour smooching with himself on stage. Netta took the bottle of beer which Bryan passed to her, and looked from one face to the other: his, flushed and purposeful; Pilar's, composed, but with crazy, glittering eyes. There could be no reasoning with her tonight. And why should anyone interfere, anyway? Pilar was sliding down the side of the bar again, and Bryan was hauling her upwards. Only this time, when she achieved a standing position, he kept his hand inside her dress, and without Netta seeing quite what happened, their mouths were suddenly slobbering together in a kiss so animal-like and all-consuming that she began to back away. She did not want a ringside seat if they were going to fornicate in the middle of the bar. Something about this clinch made her uneasy. Did Pilar really want this to happen? Was this really hedonism? Girls being powerful? Or something more traditional? Something humiliating, that Pilar would regret?

Suddenly, she felt angry with Bryan. It was all too sordid, too calculated. 'The point is, you need to be on stage,' she said, stepping forward and tapping him on the back. 'In . . . about ten minutes, probably.'

He broke off, face smeared in lipstick, and gave her a startled look. 'What?'

She pointed to her watch. 'Make-or-break time? Or are you chucking it all in for lust?'

Pilar smiled at him muzzily, obviously wondering who he might be. She had the drunk's gift of lurching into total inebriation without warning.

'Let's go and dance to Bryan's amazing band,' said Netta, taking Pilar's arm and half-dragging her away.

'Good – good decision,' said Bryan. He adjusted his bandanna and followed them up the stairs towards the main hall.

Netta stood in the half-empty room, propping up Pilar and staring at the empty stage. 'Ladies and gentlemen – I give you – Façade!' shrieked a girl from the Student

Union, hard and sporty in stretch denim. There was some ragged clapping, and a few ironic whistles. Nothing happened for a short time, and then Bryan appeared, looking paler than ever, followed by his band: two very thin blokes and one very fat woman. The fat woman took up position behind her keyboard. Then a small, plump woman tripped on to the stage, and appeared not to know where to stand. It was Belinda. After a while, she wandered to the centre and stood staring up at Bryan, as if struck dumb with horror. One skinny bloke twanged his guitar morosely. The drummer, whose arms looked even thinner than his drumsticks, began bashing around and beating his cymbals. Bryan was making a strange keening sound. Netta realized that this must be their first song. It went on for a very long time. Belinda remained silent. When it finally ended, Netta looked at her watch again, and was surprised to see that only three minutes had passed. There was silence from the audience – not even booing. Bryan stepped up to the microphone and said, 'Eat your heart out, Icicle Works!'

There was laughter now from the few knots of people who were standing around. 'Icicle Works?' yelled one voice. 'They could wipe the fucking floor with you, mate! Icicle Jerks, more like.'

'Flock of Turkeys,' said another voice. 'They could have you!'

'This is a song I wrote after I found out my girlfriend had emigrated without telling me,' said Bryan. But there was a lot of feedback, so he had to say it again. That was when the booing did start. 'Australia wouldn't be far enough,' shouted a female voice. Bryan ploughed on, apparently basing himself about equally on David Sylvian and Leonard Cohen, but with all the cheeriness removed.

'I can't stand this,' Netta hissed into Pilar's ear.

'Can't stand up,' said Pilar, which was true.

'No way you could fancy him now!' said Netta, though in fact she felt quite sorry for Bryan. She hated human suffering in any form.

'Fancy who?'

'Bryan! You were snogging with Bryan!'

But another song had started, and the crowd was entering a state of advanced hate. Bryan broke off, and said: 'You're such a great audience we're going to reward you with a personal favourite of mine, our special version of "I Should Be So Lucky" by the lovely Kylie Minogue ...' A wall of sound greeted this: an impressive amount of noise, given the small number of people assembled in front of the stage. Now Belinda appeared to be singing – or was it some other sound? Her mouth was open, but not very wide. Netta could just about hear Bryan intoning: 'I should be so lucky in love ...' when the whole cacophony was drowned out by an explosion of competing sound. At the other end of the room, someone had switched the disco lights on and started to play Spandau Ballet at maximum volume. There were cheers, and a few people wandered away and started to dance. The stage went dark.

'Let's get out of here,' said Pilar, suddenly speaking with intense clarity again. 'Slight chance I might be sick later.'

'Right,' said Netta. 'We'll head for the loo.'

'I'm staying right here, bossy boots,' said Pilar.

'Suit yourself,' said Netta. She was beginning to tire of her babysitter role. 'I'm going anyway.' And she stomped off, deafened by the baying audience and the throbbing disco.

She sat in the Ladies for some time, elbows on her knees, staring at the floor. Friends, she thought. The only sort that would really be any good would be the ones who weren't actually people. Perhaps she should build one, like Frankenstein, and bring it out for social events. She looked at a sentence scrawled on the toilet door: 'A woman needs a man like a fish needs a bicycle.' This made no sense at all. Gender wasn't the problem, or at least, no more of a problem than everything else. She realized that she was drunk too, just not as drunk as Pilar. Oh dear. Pilar. She'd left her alone, in that dress, barely able to remember her own name. She pulled the chain and hurried out of the cubicle.

There was no sign of Pilar upstairs, so Netta rushed down to the bar, where she saw her wrapped around the unmistakable figure of Bryan. His lust must have survived the trauma of his humiliation. A scrum of rugger buggers was standing around them, so at first she couldn't make out what was going on. But when she wriggled through the crowd, she saw Bryan and Pilar snogging furiously, and being timed by their audience. Cheers went up as she reached the ringside. 'It's gone ten minutes!' yelled one bloke, a Northern baldie who had lost his hair before his spots cleared up. 'Let's time them bonking later on!' yelled another specimen – Netta couldn't even bring herself to look at him, but formed an impression of facial hair.

'Here's her mate!' said Baldie. 'Who do you fancy, love?'

'You know, it's a funny thing,' said Netta, 'it's just so hard to choose between you.'

'A lot of women say that,' said Facial Hair. 'Animal magnetism, that's what it is.'

'That must be it,' said Netta. 'Need to have a teeny word with Romeo over there. Would you mind attracting his attention for me?'

'He's otherwise engaged!' chortled a few voices, but Northern Baldie tapped him on the shoulder. 'You're in demand tonight,' he said. 'There's another one here now.'

'Hello, Bryan,' said Netta. 'Can you put Pilar down for a minute?'

Bryan looked annoyed. 'I'll be right with you . . .' he said. His tone was sarcastic. Pilar, her lips liberated from his, stood blinking uncertainly until someone handed her a drink. Bryan squeezed through the crowd. 'What's up?'

Netta took his arm and led him to a quiet corner. 'I need to speak to you privately.'

He stared at her. 'What about?'

'As if you couldn't guess!'

'No, you've totally misread me there! I really can't guess at all. Enlighten me. What the fuck is going on?' He took a cigarette out of his packet and lit it without offering her one.

'Pilar is pissed.'

'Is that so? Do you mean to tell me they're selling alcoholic beverages here? I thought it was against the law for under-eighteens – oh shit, sorry, we're all *over* eighteen, so there doesn't appear to be a problem. Of course she's pissed! We're *all* pissed.' He exhaled smoke in a furious rush.

'Are we?'

'Well, if you aren't, you've only got yourself to blame. Maybe your poker-up-the-backside attitude isn't helping. You need to loosen up a bit.'

'I just think you're being really selfish. I think your behaviour stinks, in fact.'

For a moment, Bryan just stared at her. 'Who the fucking hell do you think you are?' he asked at last, speaking very low. 'Who the fucking hell gave you the right to stand here and lecture me, practically a complete stranger, about the fucking rights and wrongs of who I shag? Who the hell *are* you?'

'I'm Pilar's friend,' said Netta. But she knew this sounded pompous.

Bryan took such a long drag of his cigarette that she expected it to turn to a long plume of ash before her eyes. 'You were upstairs, weren't you? You saw what I just went through?'

She hesitated. 'It didn't seem to . . . go down very well, did it?' she said.

He laughed now, with a dangerous look in his eye. 'Don't miss a trick, do you? Nothing escapes your finely honed perceptions. No, it did not seem to *go down* very well. It went down like the proverbial lead balloon. It went down like the atom bomb on Hiroshima. It went down like Oliver Reed's trousers in *Women in Love*: it went down like –'

'For God's sake!' said Netta. 'Why are you torturing yourself?'

'Why am I torturing myself?' He rolled his eyes and groaned. 'Why the fuck are *you* torturing *me*? All I want is a bit of compensation, a bit of carnal knowledge. Or in other words, I'd like to get my leg over with the lovely Pilar. Is that too much to ask?'

'Yes, it is. She's bloody drunk and incapable!'

'Christ, I'm not much like some moustache-twirling Victorian cad, am I? It's 1985, we're all equals. Don't forget you told me all about this brilliant Spam Hunt idea. I'm just a forgettable shag. My take on that is – glad to be of service. Some blokes might say you girls were being a tiny bit sexist. But not me. I'm totally pro-female. You can't fault me on that.'

'Is that why you hang out with the rugby club?'

'Hang out with them? I don't even know them. They're animals. It's not my fault they came over and started all that Snogging Olympics crap.'

She shook her head. 'I don't give a shit what happened to your band. If you fancy Pilar, wait till another time. This isn't fair, and isn't right.'

'You are unbelievable.' He crushed out his cigarette, pulled his bandanna off his head and wrapped it round his wrist. 'Do you have any idea how often I get propositioned by a woman?'

'Quite a lot, I should think.'

He raised his eyebrows.

'Not because you're attractive, obviously. But you're not exactly shy and retiring, are you?'

'Oh yeah, I mean, I get the looks, the come-ons, from time to time. But then it turns out – silly old Bryan! I got the wrong end of the stick. They fancied my *mate*, or they want to be my fucking *friend*. They didn't want to shag me at all. You've always got to be on the lookout for those telltale signs that girls are backing down. A serious offer is a gift from God.'

'Hasn't it ever crossed your mind that if you treated women with a bit more respect, you might not get the bum's rush quite so often?'

He pulled his bandanna off his wrist and stuck it back on his head, at a slight angle. 'Listen. Your friend is the business. Funny, good-looking, sharp. You know? I *like* her. I am not the Yorkshire Ripper. I am not Mr fucking Goodbar. I'd take her to the bloody pictures if she'd come with me. Even the pissing West End. I'd take her to see *Another Country*, top-notch entertainment. G and T at half-time, the whole works. But all things being equal, including the sexes, I will settle for a shag. That's the kind of guy I am: flexible.'

'So why don't you ask her out? When she's sober? When she can tell what you look like?'

He looked nonplussed. 'A real man would tell you to piss off,' he said.

'Well, what kind of man *are* you?' She noticed that the rugger buggers had disappeared. Pilar had slumped down the wall once more, and was lying unconscious on the ground, open-mouthed and snoring. Someone had thoughtfully pushed a plastic half-pint glass down the front of her dress.

Bryan followed Netta's gaze. 'Okay, you win,' he said. 'Career as a rock star, finito, chances of bedding nubile Titian-haired nymphet, zero. Story of my fucking life.' He shrugged, sighed and walked away.

4

Netta's first thought the following morning was that someone was having a baby in the next room. The noise was harrowing and very loud. 'EEUUUGGGGG!!! Huff! Huff! Huff! EEEUUGGGHHHHHH! Ahhhhhhhh!' She raised her head from the pillow. Strangely familiar, she thought now. Oh, yes. She replaced her head on the pillow, and then on second thoughts put it on top of her head. It was the sound of someone having sex. More specifically, it was the sound of Mel having sex with Mutant. After a lot of yelling, Mel started on the road to orgasm – or fake orgasm, who could tell? 'Yesss, that's good. Oooh . . . yesss! Mmmmmmmmmmm! Euggh! EUGGH! EEEUGGGHHHHHHHHH! EEEUUG-GHHHH! EUGGGHH . . .'

But these blissful noises were suddenly interrupted by loud banging. 'Nice cup of tea for you both here! Are you decent?' called Pilar. She sounded remarkably together for someone who had been on the verge of hospitalization the night before.

Silence for a moment, then an almost experimental: 'Mmmmmm . . . Ooohhhh! Euggghhh!' followed by more banging.

'And a couple of rounds of toast and marmalade! Or Mutant, are you more of a Special K boy? I can pop in with some cereal if you like. Just give me a shout.'

A longer silence. Then Mel's voice, sounding strained: 'Piss off, Pilar. It's not funny.'

'Who's trying to be funny? I'm just being your perfect flatmate. Room service for all occasions.' Netta heard the sound of the door opening, and a muffled shriek. 'Gawd, the smell of sperm in here,' came Pilar's voice. 'Mmmmm, let's get this window open. Heavens, how did you manage that . . . oh, I see. Those are *your* legs, Melanie. Morning, Mutant. Lovely day. Bit of fresh air. There you are. Much better. D'you know, I think I'd recognize your bottom anywhere, after that mooning thing you were doing at Skol night. Really distinctive buttocks – sort of mottled, aren't they? Has anyone ever told you that? And the funny thing is, Melanie's surname is "Moon". Did you know? I wasn't sure if you were on surname terms yet, or what . . .'

About ten minutes later, Netta heard the sound of footsteps running down the staircase, and the front door banged shut. Then there was silence. Netta waited for the outburst from Mel, but none came. She got up, felt the rasping chill of the unheated room, and wrapped herself in her duvet before wandering into the living room. In spite of the cold, Pilar was wearing a tiny baby-doll nightie and fluffy slippers. She was reading a copy of *Spare Rib* and eating a boiled egg with a fastidious expression on her face. It was hard to keep track of her moods.

'Aren't you hungover?' Netta asked. 'I mean – I don't think I could face an egg, and I was about a millionth as drunk as you were.'

'Thanks,' said Pilar, eyeing her coolly. 'I'm quite used to getting the beers in, you know. I don't need a sheepdog to round me up.'

'You were in a pretty bad state, if you don't mind me saying so. Although I know it's none of my business.'

'Well, exactly, it isn't, actually,' said Pilar in her poshest voice. She returned her eyes to the article she was reading. Netta sat on the chair opposite, feeling deflated. Then she saw that Pilar's shoulders were shaking. Was she shivering? Or crying? Or . . . laughing? To her relief, she saw that Pilar's eyes were shining with amusement, and suddenly she burst into uncontrollable giggles. 'God – imagine! I nearly screwed that awful Bryan! D'you think he'd have been able to stop talking about himself for long enough to do anything?'

'I think he'd have had a damn good try,' said Netta. 'He seemed pretty keen.'

'God.' Pilar took another spoonful of egg. 'What was his play called, again?'

'His play?'

'I thought you said he's written a play.'

'Yes – *Cosmo Boy*. Role-reversal thing.'

'He loves himself so much, that Cosmo Boy. You wouldn't want to boost his self-esteem any further, would you? He'd practically go into orbit. Such a wanker.' She smiled gleefully at Netta, as if finding such a specimen to nearly sleep with was a feat of ingenuity in itself.

'He was a bit upset about his band,' said Netta. 'And he was kind of gentlemanly, in the end.' She hated to see people treated unfairly, even men. 'I doubt if I'd have been able to have a sensible conversation with Mutant, for instance. I'm not sure if he can do reasoning just to order like that, in any case.'

'It's certainly not his strong point.' Mel was standing

48

in the doorway. She was fully dressed, in baggy dungarees, check shirt, monkey boots and black donkey jacket.
Outsize 'wimmin' signs hung from her ears, and her hair
was hidden under a trilby.

'What's all this?' asked Pilar, turning to look at her. 'I
thought you'd be wearing nothing but a sheet and a selection of love bites.'

'Off to the launderette.'

'Don't tell me you actually fancied that man?'

'It's not a question of fancying, it's a question of urges.
Unfortunately.' Mel did not appear to bear Pilar any
grudge for the interrupted orgasm. 'I thought you said
there was toast and marmalade.'

'I ate it.'

'Well, come on, make some more, then. Getting me
out of bed under false pretences. Christ. You scared the
pants off poor old Mutant.'

'Or on to him, more like,' said Netta, as Pilar flounced
into the kitchen.

'He'll get over it,' said Mel equably, taking the seat that
Pilar had vacated and picking up the copy of *Spare Rib*.
'He's not fully evolved, which will help his recovery along.
Very minimal wiring.' She flipped through the magazine.
'You should read this stuff,' she said. 'Plenty of answers
in here.'

'I'm not looking for answers.'

'Why not?'

'I haven't even thought of the questions.'

'Oh, right. Just want to keep it all vague and woolly,
do you?'

'Well, do you know any?'

49

'Any what?'

'Answers.'

Mel sighed. 'Well, for a start, what we think is controlled by how we've been educated, and we've been educated by the patriarchy.'

'And what is the "patriarchy", anyway?' asked Netta. 'A load of men with white beards?'

Mel leaned forward. 'Last night, with that stupid bloke, I knew all the moves. No problem. But all of a sudden I felt like a man in drag – I mean, it was like I had learned all these lessons about how to be a girl, but it wasn't really me. The real me is trapped inside.'

'For goodness' sake,' said Pilar, coming in with a jar of marmalade and a spoon. 'Being a girl is fun, it's the biggest romance of your life. Girls are lovely. What d'you want to do, wear those horrible dungarees all the time?'

'Einstein wore the same suit every day,' said Netta.

'Einstein was a bloke,' said Pilar.

'I'm going to the launderette,' said Mel, chucking the copy of *Spare Rib* on to the table and wolfing her toast down in two enormous bites. 'Then I'm going to do some serious research. We need facts, hard facts, if we're going to change.'

'I love the "we",' said Pilar. 'I'm planning to stay exactly the same. A cross between Goldie Hawn and Joan Ruddock. Adorable, sexual, socially aware but not scary. You've got to be smart, Melanie. Ideology isn't smart, it's just about tidying everything up. We all need a bit of mess.'

They looked around the room. The dusty bookshelves contained few books, but were overflowing with bills, postcards and old newspapers, while each end was hung with coats and jackets. An ironing board had been standing in the same corner for weeks, piled with seedy hairbrushes, pots of lip gloss, empty biros and unused Tampax. But perhaps the most depressing sight was the row of desiccated spider plants on the mantelpiece, the wizened brown relics of previous good intentions.

Just then, the front doorbell rang. 'Shit,' said Mel. 'Mutant's back. What the hell does he want now?'

'Probably going to propose,' said Netta. 'I would if I were him. I've never heard anything like it.'

'You must have led a very sheltered life.'

'Isn't anyone going to see who it really is?' asked Pilar. She looked down at her skimpy nightie. 'I can't go down like this. I look like a child prostitute.'

Mel disappeared, sighing heavily. 'I'm not marrying him, whatever happens,' she said. When she returned, she was accompanied not by a ginger-haired Welsh half-back, but by a tall woman with prominent breasts and waist-length brown hair, some of which had been mildly backcombed. She had saucer-like eyes, bleary with black eye-liner, and was carrying a basket.

'Hi . . .' she said, drooping into a chair. 'Sorry . . . I've lost my keys. I'll disparu downstairs in a bit, soak away my sins. Thought I'd share my ennui with you for a while first . . .'

'Emily!' said Pilar. 'God – haven't seen you for weeks. What's been going on?'

'I fell in love,' said Emily, drooping even more. 'L'amour, l'amour, quelle bore.' She exhumed some cottonwool and face cream from her basket, and began to wipe off her eye make-up.

'Not again!' said Mel, pouring tea. 'Fertile hunting ground, north of the river. What was this one like?'

Emily regarded her lopsidedly, with one blacked-in eye and one little nude one, which appeared to belong to an albino mouse. 'I neither know nor care,' she said. 'He could be dead, as far as I'm concerned. He's certainly spiritually moribund.'

'So what did you see in him?' asked Pilar. There was an unfamiliar edge to her voice.

'He had beautiful feet,' said Emily. She blew her nose on a crumpled handkerchief. 'I've always had a weakness for feet.' She began to remove the make-up from her other eye with rough, sudden movements, as if she had been forced to wear it for an uncongenial theatrical part.

'I'd still be a virgin if I had high standards in that department,' said Mel. 'If the worst comes to the worst, they can always keep their socks on.'

'There's only one solution if nice toes are your thing,' said Pilar, getting up and stretching.

'What's that?' asked Emily, both eyes blinking lashlessly now.

'Fuck girls, of course.' Pilar shimmied out of the room, smiling prettily.

'She's very rude,' said Emily to Netta, not looking in the least offended.

'Very,' said Netta. 'I'm Netta, by the way. The new person.'

'Oh.' Emily appeared to have no interest in this. Indeed, she appeared to have no interest in anything, now that the subject of her failed affair had been dropped.

Mel looked irritated and returned to *Spare Rib*, tapping

the open pages with a pencil. 'It's all here, if anyone can be bothered with it,' she said.

'All what?' asked Netta.

'The sex war. Women's rights. The whole lot.'

'Oh, yawn,' said Emily. 'I really, really don't need any of that.'

'That, Emily Birtwistle, is where you are very much mistaken,' said Mel. 'You of all people, with your famous feminist mum! Don't you ever feel ashamed, poncing about like Little Red Riding Hood, with that stupid basket?'

'Very funny, coming from you,' said Emily. 'The person with the worst boyfriends of anyone I ever met.' She took a half-eaten sandwich out of her controversial basket and began to eat it. 'Anyway,' she said, revealing a certain amount of lettuce. 'She's on TV this morning. You should turn it on.'

Netta was impressed. 'On TV? Why?'

'She's gone to Greenham.'

Mel looked up, startled. 'What for?'

'I dunno. Probably because you all get in the press so much. No one bought her last book.'

As Mel switched the television on, the doorbell rang for a second time. 'I'll get it,' called Pilar, now fully dressed. 'Bound to be Mutant with a lovely diamond solitaire.'

But this time it was Bryan. He looked ill and uncomfortable. Pilar was smiling in a superior manner. 'Bryan's come for a cup of tea. He's trying to be a human being,' she said.

'Jesus,' said Mel. 'Now I've heard everything.'

'How did you find out where we live?' asked Netta.

Bryan grimaced and took Pilar's diary out of his pocket. 'Pilar . . . lost this,' he said.

'How careless!' said Netta. 'And what a stroke of luck for you, finding it just lying around.'

'Don't kick a man when he's down,' said Bryan. 'I'm staring a lifetime of obscurity in the face.' He looked at Emily. For some reason, she had put on a pair of sunglasses and was tossing her hair about.

'Shame about the gig,' said Netta, sinking deeper into her encircling duvet.

'It was the worst thing that's ever happened to me,' said Bryan. He offered his cigarette packet round at high speed, obviously hoping no one would take one, then sat down on the floor. 'I told the band it was all over. In future, the audience really will be listening to the beat of a different drummer. One who can play the drums, for a start.'

'You seemed to be short of a good tune,' said Netta. On the TV screen, a winsome female reporter was standing in front of Newbury courthouse, in front of a group of women turning cartwheels. 'These ladies have left their homes and families to make this protest,' said the reporter, as they began dancing round in slow motion, sticking their tongues out and waving at the cameras. 'They deserve our respect, at the very least . . .' Then the scene changed. Cool blue sky, barbed-wire fences, and lots of policemen in tall helmets standing around looking grim and embarrassed. And on the ground, a group of women lying down, like so many toddlers having a group tantrum.

'There she is!' said Emily. 'What a complete and utter mess! Hideouser and hideouser . . .'

She was pointing at a middle-aged woman lying sprawled on the ground. Her frizzy grey hair stuck out around her, and she was dressed in purple and green. A microphone was thrust into her face, and the winsome reporter's voice said: 'Flora Birtwistle, a lot of people associate you with 1960s Women's Lib – can you tell me what brings you here today? Are you going to be a spokesman for Greenham Common?' Flora propped herself on her elbows. Netta saw that she had an aristocrat's haughty bearing.

'I am most certainly not the spokesperson for the Women,' she said. 'Each woman can only speak for herself. All I am saying is that you cannot ignore thirty thousand of us. Women have come here to . . .'

Another head popped up in front of her, and a scrawny woman with cropped hair started reading from a piece of paper. Her voice was barely audible, but she seemed to be as determined as Flora was to dominate the scene. She read: 'We Choose Non-Violence Because We Believe It Is Impossible To Achieve A Non-Violent Society Through Violent Means . . .'

'Can I have your name?' interrupted the reporter.

'I Am A Woman!' said the woman. 'There Are No Leaders At This Camp.' Flora's frizzy hair was visible behind her, and she seemed to be trying to get back into shot, but the woman pressed on: 'Non-Violence Is A Philosophy Which Springs From A Belief That All Life Is Worth Love and Respect, And That While . . .'

'I think the viewers of this programme would like to know who is expressing these opinions.' The reporter now sounded like a starchy head girl.

Flora's face appeared again, and she took the paper from the other woman, whose scowling face disappeared from view. 'My name is Flora Birtwistle. I am a feminist, writer, mother and spokeswoman for no one but myself,' she declaimed. 'But the women have agreed this wording: "While fighting evil, one does not have to destroy the person perpetrating it, but rather 'compel' them to one's point of view–"' A policeman's bulky legs were suddenly visible behind her. She glanced backwards, as if assessing how much time she had left, then shouted at the camera: 'NON-VIOLENCE AND NON-COOPERATION MAKE IT IMPOSSIBLE FOR EVIL TO CONTINUE. ALL YOU NEED IS YOURSELF – AND A GROUP OF OTHERS WITH YOU –' As she spoke, she was lifted bodily by the policeman and dragged from view, and the screen was chaos, the camera lurching, then blanked out by the large hand of the law.

Emily chortled with delight. 'Arrested! They've arrested her! Oh, I pity those poor bastards, I really do! I hope they know what they've let themselves in for...' Her earlier lassitude had disappeared, and while she spoke she kept glancing across at Bryan, as if gauging his response. She was still wearing shades. 'I could never do that!' she announced. 'So unfeminine! And that awful woman with her – hideous in the extreme...' Her hair flew around her, her eyes peered over the tops of her glasses. Netta suddenly saw that she was back on stage, now that there was a man in the room.

Bryan's reaction was presumably the one Emily was hoping for. From the moment the broadcast started, he was transfixed, and he laughed joyously while they were reading out their written statement. 'Oh, nice one!' he kept saying, and 'It's brilliant, it's like they're spoofing themselves. No need to take the piss out of this lot, let them do it for themselves . . . cut out the middle man!'

Mel took no notice of this. She turned the TV off, frowning intensely. 'Got to go . . .' she said.

'What's the hurry, all of a sudden?' asked Pilar, returning with a trayload of tea things. 'Why don't you have some tea before you go to the launderette?'

'I'm not going to the launderette, I'm going back to Greenham.'

'But why now this minute?'

'It was on the news. Flora's turned up and been arrested,' said Mel. 'I didn't even know she was there! What's she up to, Emily? I thought she was baking her own bread in Andalucia.'

Emily shrugged. 'I dunno. She got bored with Spain, I suppose. She's just desperate to be relevant again. You know Flora – she's an attention-seeking missile.' She flicked her hair around again, and aimed a coquettish glance at Bryan.

'Arrested already! She didn't waste much time,' said Pilar. 'What did she do?'

'They'll probably say she was causing an obstruction. That's the usual non-charge. What worries me is that she's trying to take over the whole show,' said Mel. She spoke abstractedly, as if this wasn't what she was really thinking about.

'Is that so bad?' asked Netta. 'Maybe she'll get Greenham in the news more often.' She was thinking of her impossible essay, 'Images of Women at Greenham'.

So far all she had managed to do was assemble some unintelligible ravings from the *Daily Mail* and various *Guardian* articles which compared the Greenham women to the suffragettes.

'It's just the other woman – the other woman who was there . . . she's Jude,' said Mel, rooting about in her bag. 'Yes, got enough money . . .'

'Jude?' Pilar raised her eyebrows enquiringly.

'Jude Blackman.'

'Who's Jude Blackman?'

'She's . . . well, she's just fantastic.'

'Fantastic in what way?' Pilar was pouring tea very calmly. 'You haven't mentioned her before.'

Mel was pulling on a hairy old sweater. 'Just a really, really strong person.'

'Great. But who is she?'

'She's . . . well, she's my best friend.'

Netta didn't see Pilar's reaction to this. The phone was ringing in the hall, and she dashed to answer it. 'Hello?'

'Isn't it about time you came round for dinner?' Jane was obviously in no mood for social niceties. 'Or are you only bothering to contact me when you need to move house – or acquire new furniture? How *is* the desk, by the way?'

'Fine. I mean – thanks, and everything . . .'

'Think nothing of it. There's more to family ties than crude exploitation. One would like to think.'

5

'God, you're thin.' This was not a compliment. As if to demonstrate the point, Jane continued: 'You look like something from bloody Ethiopia. Make sure you eat your supper this evening.'

They were sitting together in Jane's basement kitchen in Islington. It was a beautiful kitchen, if kitchens can be beautiful, with a red-tiled floor, stripped pine shelves lining the walls and a huge table dominating its centre. Christmas decorations in various degrees of readiness littered every surface: Jane made all her own, though she had never been particularly dextrous. The children, meanwhile, were making their own mess. Six-year-old Toby and his little sister Charlotte were watering the cat, apparently unimproved by their exposure to opera. And Little Richard was slowly dribbling puréed spinach on to his snow-white bib, to form a stain of deep and indelible green.

Netta bit her lip and looked down at herself. Since moving into the flat, she had adopted Pilar's habit of only eating from the college snack bar. In the evenings they snacked on salt and vinegar crisps and dry-roasted peanuts – pub fare. No wonder Netta felt so at home: it reminded her of working behind the bar with her father. It was true, her arms were getting rather stick-like. She liked the feeling of being pared down to her essential nothingness. Jane, on the other hand, was sitting in a great heap of sleeveless

Sloane jerkin and newly acquired extra flesh. She had once been so perfect, with her dark skin and almond eyes, that Netta had ached with jealousy. Now she was turning into a dumpy matron, although she was still only twenty-six.

'No one can be bothered to cook in the flat,' Netta said. She did not want to talk about Mel and Greenham or the peculiarities of Pilar. Jane wasn't interested in hearing about Netta's world, in any case, only in talking about her own. Sometimes, it was hard to believe that they were related to each other at all. Netta had always admired Jane, but with a baffled feeling of inadequacy. When she was tiny, the love she felt had been unquestioning, devoted. When she was older, she began to resent Jane's automatic assumption of superiority. As a girl, Jane had been in possession of absolute certainty. Either something was perfectly obvious – how pi worked, for example – or else in need of further explanation, in which case she soon found out what the further explanation was. Whereas Netta came at things sideways. She wasn't sure what made sense. Why write on the lines of exercise books? Neatly, with a joining flick at the bottom of each letter? When it made just as much sense to write in the space above, floating free? When she wrote her name, carefully, with the required flick, she wondered what 'Jeanette Royce' actually meant. Education seemed to be about copying everyone else. The best impersonations reaped the greatest rewards. The eleven-plus was an example of this. Jane triumphed over the neatly cryptic questions, winning a special prize for getting the highest marks in Cheshire. Netta remembered the pink faces and jubilation, Margaret pouring out the celebratory sherry, David hugging Jane, and Jane saying, 'All I did was fill in some silly boxes.' But everyone knew that she now had concrete evidence of cleverness. Six years later, it was Netta's turn to face the silly boxes. The questions tortured her, devious and inscrutable. 'If the code for UNKNOWN is VPNRTCU, what does OCWYWGS mean?' She had twisted round in her chair, suffering over past papers, and once kicked Jane when she came over, bright and exact in her grammar school gym slip, offering advice. Her failure had been even less surprising than Jane's success. On the day the dread letter came, consiging her for ever to the life of an intellectual also-ran, Jane surprised her by giving her a copy of *Pride and Prejudice*. It was Jane's favourite book, but she had found Netta an abridged, easier version. The rage Netta felt against Jane hadn't lasted long, though. And passing or failing some stupid exam didn't really matter, after all. A year after Netta started at the local secondary school, Margaret found a lump in her breast. Six months later, she was dead.

Netta tried to shake these thoughts out of her head. She fixed Jane with a positive smile. 'How are you all?'

'Well, I never see Richard. I hardly know who he is. Toby won't eat anything green. Charlotte's best friend at nursery's just been diagnosed as "gifted" by some doom-brain psychologist. And the baby is possibly autistic. But you don't want to know about all that.'

'Yes I do.'

'No you don't. If you did, you would visit us more. How often can you be bothered to get over here? Twice a year? Including your token Christmas visit!'

Netta looked in a bemused way at the presents she had bought from Selfridges on the way over. She had no idea if the suit of armour or glittery fairy outfit or giant teddy were already features of the nursery upstairs. What she did know was that wrapping them up in the Ladies at Piccadilly Circus had been no mean feat, and they had cost her almost twenty pounds. But forward planning never had been her strong point. Jane and Richard had had to make do with a bottle of champagne from Oddbins. It was characteristic of Jane that she expected to receive Christmas and birthday gifts well in advance. Her obsession with forward planning was the polar opposite of Netta's scatty impulsiveness.

'Oh, come on, Jane. It's more often that that. Don't be ridiculous,' said Netta. 'Anyway, aren't you busy with your friends most of the time?'

'Friends! Ha! None of them have children, have they? Most of them are still partying all night. You'd think children were some alien bloody life form.'

'But . . . but you always say you met your soulmates at Oxford.'

'They might be my soulmates, but they don't live the way that I live. I suppose I bore them.'

'Bore them? Surely you don't mean that?'

'I do mean it. I've grown dull, dull, dull, servicing the needs of all these other humans, with never a second for myself.'

'You should go out sometimes. Get out of the house.'

'It's all very well for you. Maybe one day you'll be a mad housewife – and find out what it's like!'

Netta tried to take this in. Jane was usually so smug. She wondered what was going on. She had never seen her in this light before: as unfree as any suburban hausfrau.

Perhaps her exquisitely bourgeois surroundings made no difference at all.

'Can't go anywhere. One can't trust babysitters with babies. And Richard never wants to go out in any case. Children take up time and energy, you know. You have to give of your best.'

'I'm sure you do.'

'Read *Catch 22* when I was seven, remember that. And of course Richard was an infant prodigy, so it's in the genes.'

Netta looked at her watch – this was bang on cue. She had been there for fifteen minutes, and had already been reminded of Jane's intellectual gifts, with a bonus mention of Richard's high IQ thrown in.

'I'm sure you're doing the right thing, what do I know . . .' Back into those old familiar roles, thought Netta. We torture each other, just by existing. Jane had indeed been an absurdly intellectual schoolgirl. Her success at the eleven-plus was just the beginning. She had streaked ahead of her classmates and was ensconced at Oxford before her seventeenth birthday. Unfortunately (Netta thought) her extreme beauty made everyone fall in love with her as soon as she first cycled down the High. She had been like Zuleika Dobson, minus the mass suicides, and by the fourth term she had ensnared star historian Richard Tyler, who was several years older than she was and working on his PhD. He had the advantage of being even cleverer than Jane, so much so that he rarely spoke to normal people, and he had his own mysterious beauty, though of the bespectacled sort. They had been married now for six whole years, following their perfect spring wedding.

Netta had not been asked to be a bridesmaid. Richard's two sisters had fulfilled this function instead. She remembered them now, looking sheepish in their own spectacles, which had clashed with the wreaths of lilies they were obliged to wear.

'Eight years since Mum's death,' said Jane suddenly. 'Remember how the stream at the bottom of the garden was frozen over? The day she died?'

'Was it?' Netta hated talking about Margaret's death: the element of competition made her cringe. Grief had not brought them closer. It had sealed them into themselves. Jane had literally howled throughout the funeral. Both David and Netta had been cowed into silence by this astonishing sight. Now, Jane seemed to lay claim to bereavement, and occupy it with the full force of her personality. Sometimes, Netta wanted to say – you know, such a coincidence! Did you know, *my* mother died at just the same time that *yours* did? And the childish part of her wanted to wail – she belonged to me! You always had Dad. And you've still got Dad. Which meant that she was just as bad as Jane, competing for prime position at the edge of the void. But it was true that David worshipped Jane.

Jane rolled her eyes. 'Doesn't it mean *anything* to you?'

'Look, you're the official custodian of our family memory, so why don't you just get on with it?'

This comment seemed to please Jane. 'Sometimes I think I'm turning into her,' she said. 'One spends so much time wiping squashed banana off Helen Oxenbury books. All closes in.'

'Are you . . . not happy?' asked Netta, looking at Little

Richard's green bib. She couldn't remember seeing Margaret wipe squashed banana off anything. She thought of all the hours she and Jane had spent sitting in the car with their fizzy drinks and crisps, while David and Margaret made merry inside some country pub.

'Well . . .' Jane's face was blank. Netta was so used to her setting the agenda, telling her what to think about every aspect of life – even when Netta made it clear she didn't want to hear – that this uncertainty was strange. 'I can't say anything,' was all Jane came out with at last. Then she seemed to stir herself. 'More tea? Coffee? Or something alcoholic – is the sun over the yardarm yet?'

'I thought you never drank till they were in bed.'

'It's Christmas, isn't it? Or the run-up, which is worse.' Jane, not usually a keen drinker, poured out two rather large glasses of white wine. She took a sip and looked visibly cheered. 'Richard's upstairs, but will he be taking any part in Poison Hour? I think not. Therefore – nothing for him.'

'Glad to hear it. All the more for us. What's Poison Hour?'

Jane was now spooning some peach-coloured gunge into Little Richard's mouth. 'This is Poison Hour. Tea time, bath time, whinge time, bed time. If you weren't such a very busy auntie, you'd be here more often and you'd know that.'

Netta decided to ignore this. 'Is Richard working on something in particular?'

'He's always working on something in particular. Of course. Never urgent, though, just his life's work. Whereas we are his hobby . . . Toby, sit down.' In the background, Mozart's Horn Concerto continued on its melodious way, ignored by everyone, but obviously doing wonders for the children's synapses. Netta noticed that, as well as taking frequent gulps of wine, Jane was also reading from a large book propped on a recipe stand on the Welsh dresser.

'What's that – the meal you're making later on?'

'Shakespeare's sonnets,' said Jane. 'Richard's doing something with tuna – I shan't be going near a recipe tonight.'

'So you feed the children, drink wine and read Shakespearean sonnets all at the same time? You're like Superwoman, only with culture attached?'

'Superwoman has a job, if I'm not mistaken. And I did have one of the finest minds in my year. Need to feed my brain, otherwise just – atrophy. Or go mad.'

'Which one are you reading?'

Jane returned to the dresser and proclaimed: 'Being your slave, what should I do but tend/Upon the hours and times of your desire?/I have no precious time at all to spend,/Nor services to do, till you require./Nor dare I chide the world-without-end hour/Whilst I, my sovereign, watch the clock for you,/Nor think the absence of bitterness sour/When you have bid your servant once adieu . . .' She had a lovely reading voice, soft and deep, and most unlike the one she used for every day. Without pausing for breath, she dashed across the kitchen, smeared gloop off Little Richard's face, unleashed him from his high chair and announced, 'Bath time! Toby, up the stairs! Charlotte, follow me.' And they were gone.

Savouring the sudden quiet, Netta looked around her. The shelves of the old pine dresser displayed an organized muddle of Clarice Cliff china, pots of crayons, odd gloves and bright plastic beakers. On the wall hung a bright pinboard, covered with the children's artworks and snap-shots of each of them at various stages of development. Next to the noticeboard was a family portrait, taken just after Little Richard was born. He was in his father's arms, regarding the world with the stern, self-centred expression typical of small babies. Jane, her smile almost psychoti-cally serene, sat next to Richard, with Charlotte on her knee. Toby sat in front of his parents, gazing mournfully into the camera like a lost Edwardian boy. Netta turned her attention to the washing spinning reassuringly round and round. Her chaotic flat seemed very chilly and austere compared to this sophisticated homeliness.

'Hello, young stranger!' Richard was apparently able to tear himself away from his studies once the children had vanished upstairs. Netta could never remember what Important Research he carried out at King's College, and had no idea what lay behind his expression of calm superi-ority. All she knew was that he seemed to gaze out at an irrelevant world. To say he didn't have small talk was an understatement – he didn't have medium-sized talk either, or even quite big talk which did not relate to the finer points of the struggle for universal suffrage, his specialist field. While Jane seemed housewifely before her time, Richard was apparently suspended for ever in a state of undergraduate bliss.

He kissed her. His skin was stubbly and scratched her cheek. In his glasses, she saw a glimpse of her own reflection. She looked away quickly, not sure why this was so unsettling. Richard always had this effect on her – he made her feel not only intellectually outclassed, but emotionally disoriented as well. She had always chosen to interpret this feeling as dislike. The very first time Jane had brought him home, Netta tripped over a loose rug at the top of the staircase and went flying down, screaming with fear and embarrassment. Richard, standing at the bottom, had caught her as she fell. She still remembered the shock: haughty face in agonized close-up, little zits around his nose, thick lashes behind heavy lenses. Then the way they both pulled away, laughing with embarrassment. She was really just a child then – thirteen, still unable to believe that Margaret had gone for good.

'How are you?' she asked, in her silly, flibbertigibbet voice. 'Happy pre-Christmas! Jane told me you're busy, as usual. Working too hard, and everything.'

'Did she?' Richard had his back to her, and was pouring a drink. 'I thought the general idea was that I spend too much time upstairs, avoiding parenthood.'

'Well – don't you? I bet you think children are women's work, or something. Not really the New Man type, are you?'

Richard laughed, unhappily, she thought. 'Maybe I should go up?' he said, looking behind him and peering up the stairs. 'When I do, I seem to be even more annoying than the children. One hasn't quite mastered the expertise, or perhaps I'm just congenitally incompatible with Pampers. I suppose Jane has been telling you how absurdly little use I am . . .'

'No, she . . .'

But then Jane's voice came wafting down the stairs. 'RICH-ARD! Are you down there? I can't believe this! How about a bit of help? God almighty . . .' Then followed a great, non-specific wail which could have been

68

some or all of the children. Or perhaps Jane herself. Richard put his glass down and bounded out of the room. Netta watched him go, and sighed. She looked at the sonnet again, and carried on reading where Jane had left off: 'Nor dare I question with my jealous thought/Where you may be, or your affairs suppose,/ But like a sad slave, stay and think of nought,/Save, where you are, how happy you make those.'

'Thing is, I was an Exhibitioner, Richard. Exhibitioner. All got to go somewhere. Responsibility pass it on to the next . . . fine young minds . . .'

'What I don't get is, why do women have to turn into 1950s housewives, just because . . .'

'Darling, no one doubts the fineness of your mind, it's just the amount of wine you seem to . . .'

The three of them were slumped around the kitchen table. They had a side each, which was probably appropriate. Netta could see three empty bottles among the debris of tuna and salad and zabaglione, and Richard was opening another. A small part of her mind was still clear and sober, and worrying that Jane had never drunk quite like this before. However, a bigger part of her mind was itself too sodden with drink to formulate coherent thoughts. Instead, it was tuning into something rather exciting in the atmosphere, something she couldn't quite identify. She watched as Richard filled her glass.

'After this, I really must go,' she said. 'I mean, thank you so much for this lovely dinner and everything, but I really have had quite enough, and I've got lectures tomorrow so . . .'

'Don't go yet,' said Richard, smiling away. 'You've hardly got here.' He was beaming at her. He had beautifully regular teeth, so that his smiles were a form of showing off. 'This is a very interesting conversation. I knew there was an intellectual inside you, trying to get out!' She preferred Richard when he was being supercilious: at least she knew where she stood. Now, she had the distinct feeling that she was being patronized. She wondered why Richard had married her sister. Once it had seemed so obvious. Jane was clever, she was beautiful, she had a tense, combative energy which made things happen. Everyone wanted her. But now? Maybe once he had landed her, he had set out to neutralize her. Or maybe the neutralizing was accidental. Whatever the intention, he was certainly succeeding.

'Yeah, okay. So I'm not studying Wittgenstein. But it's fascinating, you know . . . looking at how the media works.'

'Must be people we know who'd be useful to Netta. Contacts in The Media. Don't you think so?' Jane's expression had changed to one of almost comical concentration. 'Who do we know, Richard? Fenton Brasier, didn't he go to Reuters and do something extraordinary? Always people one knows – who do we know, Richard?'

'I don't know anyone useful, in that way,' said Richard, irritation in his voice. 'We can't just call up people like Fenton. I haven't set eyes on him for years.'

'Oh, you're so . . .' Jane's eyes veered around the kitchen, with its hanging strips of garlic and bowls of shining fruit. Netta sensed her claustrophobia. A strange fear crept around her, but she couldn't have said what she was frightened of. She thought of the names-to-conjure-with at Oxford: Thurston Davidge, Kitty Cava, Imogen Spencer-Dingwall and Fenton himself, of course. She thought of Jane punting along the Cherwell, Netta's hand trailing in the water, while Jane laid waste to the world in her clipped, aggressive phrases, her perfect, neat profile attacking the sky. In those days, Netta had had no doubt that Jane could do anything she wanted. Men were just a fawning backdrop, anxious to please, joking about Bede while toasting teacakes in front of her electric fire. Now it was all gone, all closed into these four walls, this star-prize boffin of a husband who seemed to regard his wife with aloof bafflement. How had they managed to leap forward into middle age so prematurely? And yet Jane had always seemed to want it this way. She had been impossibly grown up at six, and now there was a logic to her being a thwarted, dumpy twenty-six.

'Why can't we – do anything?' asked Jane. 'Why must everything be so narrowed down? It's like these little bits of research you do, Richard, finding a tiny niche in Chartism that no one else has spotted yet, or cared about . . . Why has everything got so small? I always wanted a big life.'

'You always wanted children,' said Richard. 'You've got everything you wanted.' He had found a cigarette and was lighting it with a long kitchen match. 'Why is the world "small", Jane? You have a wonderful life – children, friends, reading, conversation. We've got enough money. My career is going well . . . I've got that trip to New York coming up, remember. Incredibly important symposium, I'm really far too junior to be there. And if you did want to work – so be it. We'll sort out a nanny and . . . off you go.'

71

'Iss just . . .' Jane was staring at him as if she wasn't sure who he was. 'All very well for you, buggering off to America, very important person, no problem there. But I feel so . . . hemmed in. Children like . . . it's like . . . walking through treacle. Can't do anything. Can't unmake the 'sponsibility.' Tears began to roll down her face. 'Can't unmake this particular 'sponsibility, anyway.' Richard went towards her, but she pushed him away. 'Bed,' she said. 'Sleep. I have to. Knitting up something of care. 'Night, Netta.' She gave Netta but not Richard a blurry kiss, and was gone.

Afterwards . . . afterwards went on for a very long time. In the days, months and years that followed, Netta would think of various possible versions of the rest of the evening, all of which featured her behaving with some degree of virtue or good sense. In one version, she left as soon as Jane went off to bed. In another, she washed up first. In a third, Richard sobbed in her arms, but wiped his eyes and resolved to be a better husband after some wise words from his perceptive young sister-in-law. In a fourth, he kissed her hand at the front door, and, when she got into the taxi, she saw him shake his head slowly, as if dreaming of might-have-beens.

But somehow, it went like this.

'Shit.' He stubbed his cigarette out. She noticed that his hand was trembling. Suddenly noticed everything about it, in a burst of drunken hyper-clarity: the square nails, the hairs on his fingers, his grown-up wedding ring.

'What?'

'Shit.'

'What is it, Richard?' She had never known him so monosyllabic.

72

'That dreadful diatribe of Jane's . . . I suppose it struck a chord with me.'

'But why?'

'Oh . . . you know. In vino veritas.'

'Which bit was veritas?'

'The bit where she said she felt hemmed in.' He looked across at her suddenly, and their eyes jolted together. Not that, thought Netta. Surely not.

'I must go,' she said. But it was like being in a dream: her limbs were immobile. For what seemed like hours, he said nothing, and neither did she. They stared at each other. Then Richard said very softly, 'It was last summer – when I first realized . . .'

'First realized what?'

'How beautiful you are.'

The room lurched. Netta took an unwise slug of wine. 'God – really – Richard. You're just pissed. You married the beautiful one.'

'It's not just your face. It's you. You know it's you.'

'I don't know anything of the sort, Richard. You're just addled with drink.' She stood up to leave, but found the floor was undulating strangely.

'No I'm not. Sit down, you're not going yet. Have you got any cigarettes?'

'Yes, loads.' They both lit up, drew in the smoke, and vice was somehow curling round them in the air, the possibility of sealing off the past and the future, and doing things which were only permissible in a passing second. Then there was a blurred bit, which Netta never could remember clearly, then a period when she appeared to be looking up at the kitchen table, followed by what Pilar would call a 'skirmish'. A skirmish was anything sexual, short-lived and unresolved.

Clarity loomed again. She was struggling upright, hair at odd Kate Bush-like angles, she noted in the black of the kitchen window. Richard's glasses were no longer on his face: they were watching them from the kitchen table. She had hardly ever seen him without his glasses. His eyes were urgent, shining.

'I need you.'

'You don't need me,' she said. 'A woman needs a man like a fish needs a bicycle, so, by implication, a man needs a woman like a bicycle needs a . . .' She smoothed her clothes down, looked round for her bag. 'Anyway, you're a bicycle who's already got a . . . bicycle pump.' Everything seemed so complicated – she found her wallet, but where was everything else? For a moment, she didn't even realize this was Jane's kitchen, but felt they were on top of a high tower, overlooking the sea. He was the forbidden prince. She was under a spell. There was no escape.

He seized her arm. 'She won't have me. She doesn't want me. Do you know when we last had sex?'

'No! *Don't*. Don't . . . please don't tell me anything . . .'

'I have to tell you. I must tell you. This is my only chance – don't you see?'

Then they were sitting at the table again. Richard had produced a bottle of whisky. He was telling her a long, long story about how gorgeous and scintillating she was, what a free spirit, what an admirable, witty, inspiring, modern girl. Richard, who usually looked at her oddly when she said anything, as if he had never heard anything so stupid. Richard, who had married her older, cleverer, prettier sister. Richard, who had everything, wanted her. He poured more whisky, whispering of his terrible dilemma. Netta's gorgeousness and scintillatingness and beauty seemed to fill the room – bourgeois notions of morality shrivelled under her admirable, witty, inspiring, modern gaze. Their hands were clasped together across the table. Their limbs were clamped together under the table. Jane seemed a very, very long way away. And when she woke up, she would have him for ever, whereas Netta had just this one night. She thought again of the time she tumbled down the stairs when she was thirteen. Right into his arms. Had it been dislike she had felt all these years, or an attraction that was too destabilizing to identify? Wanting Jane's husband would have been the worst humiliation of all. But now was not the time to find out. This was her booze-mind, and she knew her booze-mind only too well. It wanted two things: attention and sex.

Then . . . 'Oh my God! I love you! My darling! My darling . . .'

'I love you, I . . . aaahhhh!'

There were still some clothes on, but not the important ones. Clenching hold of his buttocks as he shrieked into her, muffling his shouts in her hair. A shuddering climax, during which she stuffed a National Trust tea towel into her mouth, a Clarice Cliff teacup crashed to the floor and neither of them noticed. Lying there, looking up at the garlic, past Richard's silent, sweating shoulder. Turning her head, she saw the first glimmerings of dawn through the window. High above them, a cry: the sound of Little Richard calling for his first feed.

6

When she got home, Netta locked herself in the bathroom, pressed her back to the door and closed her eyes. What had she done? Scenes from the night before – or early that morning – kept playing through her head. Could it be true? How was it possible that she had done this? She, who had advised Bryan to leave Pilar alone when she was drunk? Who did not do Spam Hunts, who was waiting for someone special? Jesus God! Her eyes flashed open, and she willed herself to stop seeing Richard's face. What had she done? She was in physical pain, her limbs ached, her head ached, her chest was tight with fear. An irreversible step had been taken, so that now everything she had once taken for granted must be realigned. Whether it was love or lust or jealousy or masochism, or a little bit of all of these, she couldn't say. All she knew was that she had done something which could not be undone. She had committed a big, grown-up sin. And now, she must think about what might happen next. How would she speak to Jane? To the children? To Richard, most horrifying of all? ('Oh, darling, darling!' And her own operatic groans. It had been good. No, she would rephrase that. It had been bad. It had been bad on a scale she did not yet understand.) How could she ever go there again, and sit in that kitchen, listening to Jane going on about her narrow, unrewarding life! How could she ever go anywhere?

She caught sight of her reflection in the mirror and went closer, hardly conscious of what she was doing. Her face looked the same, apart from the fact that she had dark circles under her eyes. There was no mark of adultery on her. Adultery. Such a heavy, old-fashioned word. To be an adulterer at twenty seemed absurd. She had assumed that the term itself was out of date: you couldn't commit this biblical sin, because in the modern world marriage was outdated. Now she knew better. She mustn't let herself think about the perfect spring wedding, or Richard's bespectacled sisters in their unfetching wreaths. The memory threatened to seep into her mind, but she blocked it out. Instead, she shook her hair out around her face, her pretty, vapid face. Stupid, stupid girl. If a person committed a mortal sin, what could they do afterwards? Retire to a nunnery? Do penance? Go to confession? She could see the shortcomings of atheism now. No prayers, no ashes, no rosary beads or Hail Marys. Doing wrong was permanent, yet meaningless. She couldn't even call it 'sin'. The action just existed.

She hated that girlish reflection now, and she hated her floating yellow hair. Her face seemed to be marooned in a blonde explosion which had no limits, an infinity of man-catching gold. But of course, it was a cop-out, blaming her hair. Hair does not make moral decisions. The worst thing of all was that she wasn't simply sorry – she was excited. She was still trying not to see Richard's eager face bearing down on her, smiling, smiling, then suddenly serious when he . . . when he . . . She shook her head. She nearly looked at herself now, nearly squared with that spoilt child's face. No one must ever know. She would keep silent, let time heal over the wound, like scar tissue. So that eventually, all that would be left would be a barely visible mark on everyday life, something that Jane would never notice. How could that work, though? Because she, Netta, would always know. Scar tissue might form on the outside, but what would happen on the inside? Suddenly, she caught sight of a pair of nail scissors, and remembered Persephone, who had transformed herself at Oxford by hacking off her hair. Picking them up, she began to snip away, beginning at the front. Her reflection immediately looked so peculiar that she proceeded with a desperate intensity, so that in a few moments great hunks of hair were resting on her shoulders, falling on the floor around her and covering her feet. She cut around her ears, as close as she could go, she slashed at the hair she couldn't see on the back of her head. Finally, she realized that she had forgotten to cut a long, curling, blonde strand which hung directly in front of her face. She chopped this off and stared hotly at the result. In the mirror, she saw a nine-year-old boy with sticky-out ears and a sulky mouth.

A sudden bang on the door. 'Have you died in there or what?' called Pilar. 'Some of us are doing real degrees, you know. It's Emily Dickinson today.'

'Coming,' said Netta. She looked at her silent reflection, then flicked back the lock and stepped into the hall.

'Bloody hell!' said Pilar, who was wearing pink pyjamas and tiny bunches. 'What happened to your hair?'

'I cut it,' said Netta. 'Change of image.'

'God.' Pilar peered dubiously round Netta's head. 'I hope you don't mind me saying this, but the back looks even worse than the front. It's *terrible*, Netta. Why didn't you go to the hairdresser's? I've got a lovely little man at the Greenwich Clipper who'd have done something really . . .' She stopped. 'Net, you look really strange – kind of insane. And you reek of booze, as well.' She put her hand to her throat as if she, Pilar, had never consumed more than two demure glasses of Babycham of an evening.

'Yeah, well, I was out on the razz.'

'I thought you were at Jane's house.'

'I was.' Netta hesitated, but only for a second, then said: 'I had sex with Richard.'

'You had what?'

'Sex with Richard. Speccy Richard. Perfect, priggy boffin Richard. My brother-in-law. Under the kitchen table. At Jane's.'

The more words she spoke, the more terrible it sounded. Unshockable Pilar clutched at the doorframe, a stunned look on her face. 'That's absolutely bloody outrageous,' she said. 'Or . . . is this a joke?'

'I'm totally serious.'

'Serious? Christ almighty! Where the hell was Jane?'

'Upstairs. In bed. Drunk. He said he loved me.'

'Oh, so that makes it all right, does it?'

'No, I was just . . . filling you in.'

'Well, consider me filled. That's your sister's husband you're talking about, not some bozo from your course. These people are married. Committed. Parents.' She stared hard at Netta, as if trying to look behind her face. 'I just cannot believe you did this.'

'God, don't you think I feel bad enough already? Don't you think I know what I've done? I feel like a bloody murderer – I don't need you to stand in judgement . . .'

Tears began to spill down her cheeks, but they were hotter and harder to shed than she would have liked. The morning light had not quite killed her drunken amorality: she suspected that they were ninety per cent Frascati.

'I'm not standing in judgement. I'm expressing an opinion. I'm just . . . totally gobsmacked. This is family.'

'I know it's family. For fuck's sake, Pilar! I didn't think you'd be so—'

'So . . . what? And if him being married wasn't enough to put you off, couldn't you even control yourself given that the person he happens to be married to is your own bloody sister? Family is where you're from. The people who love you. The bottom line. Where can you go to if you betray them? My dad did that, and he never got over it.'

'What do you mean?'

'He thought he could ignore his commitments, leave my mum, and me, and my brothers, and go off with his floozy, scot-free.'

'And . . . couldn't he?' asked Netta in a small voice.

'Oh, no. He didn't know what had hit him, once he'd really made the break. Walked out when I was thirteen. "I think you're old enough to understand that a man has urges," he said to me. I should have killed him. If I'd had a gun in my hand, I would have blown his head off.'

'What happened then?' Netta's voice was so quiet now it was hardly a whisper.

'He never got over my mum. Never. The one thing he didn't bargain for was that other men would want her. And the more time went by, the better she looked. She had a new boyfriend every year, used to ditch them at

Christmas, actually, just after they gave her the prezzie. Always insisted they bought her something gold. Till she met Bill, that is. The man of her dreams.'

'Did Bill give her the best present?'

'Correct. He's absolutely bloody loaded. The richest man in South Woodford. And meanwhile, Dad and Fat Sandra were slugging it out in his horrible Dallas-type mansion. Literally miserable as sin. What goes around, comes around.' Pilar's face was hard and sharp as she spoke. 'Fuck with anything, Netta, but don't fuck with family.'

'I didn't exactly plan it,' said Netta, which sounded completely pathetic to her own ears.

'Yeah, well, forgetting your flat keys and handing your essays in late may qualify you as endearing little Miss Scatty Knickers. Getting them down for Brother-in-Law qualifies you for something else.'

'Look, I've had enough of this! You've no bloody idea! Just leave me alone . . .' Netta grabbed the phone off the hallstand and carried it into her bedroom, slamming the door behind her. Outside, there was silence for a moment, then the sound of Pilar filling the bath. Netta wanted her to come in and give her a hug, tell her it was all right, no such thing as absolute morality these days. But she knew there was indeed such a thing as absolute morality, and that she had offended against this hidden, human code. Where did that leave her, though? What should she do now? She looked at her watch – not even nine yet – then at the phone. She longed to call him. Longed to be assured it had really happened, longed to make amends, longed to . . . what? She was trapped – just as trapped as Jane was, now. She saw her sister weeping at Margaret's funeral, saw her filling her glass with wine the night before, desperate, angry. Jane was already unhappy – and now Netta had betrayed her in the crudest way possible. Just as she was about to return the phone to its usual place, it rang, and she picked it up instantly.

'Hello?'

'It's Richard.' He sounded as if he had been running.

'Richard! Are you all right? Where are you?'

'Jogging. I'm out jogging. In Greenwich Park – or rather, I was. I'm in a call box now, obviously.'

'Oh – well, I'm glad you called. I think I'm in shock!' There was a slight laugh in her voice, but her legs were shaking so much that she sat down on the bed.

'Right.' His voice was tight and desperate. 'Well, I'm calling you to say that as far as I am concerned, nothing happened. Nothing. Happened. Okay? I won't be telling Jane anything about it, and I suggest that you don't either. Not now, and not ever. Do you understand me?'

'Look, there's no need to be all rude and bolshie about it! Of course I'm not going to say anything to Jane. Do you think I'm mad? It was all just a stupid drunken mistake! Apart from the fact that it was practically incest . . .'

'Quite. We were temporarily insane . . . in any case I hardly remember . . . the evening. A lot on at work – I've been overdoing it.'

'God, yes. I totally understand.' She struggled to think properly, to locate normal life. 'Besides, we don't even like each other, do we? You've always thought I was a complete moron. And I've always thought . . .'

There was an odd pause. 'You've always thought – what?'

'Oh, I dunno.' Sober up, sober up! she commanded herself, feeling her gabble factor about to sweep her towards further disaster. 'I've always thought that you were a bit snooty, I suppose. I mean – you know. Not my type.'

'Well, I . . .' Richard sounded taken aback. 'I would never have described you as a moron, Jeanette. Really, what a thing to say! I've always found you rather – entertaining.'

She shook her head. 'Oh, Richard! How could we have done that?'

'With surprising ease, apparently.'

'It doesn't seem easy now.'

'Quite,' said Richard again. 'I couldn't agree more. It was a momentary and utterly meaningless aberration. And I love my wife. My beautiful, clever, adorable wife. The mother of my three children.'

'And she loves you.'

'Yes.'

'And she's my sister.'

'Quite.'

'And that's all there is to be said.'

'Yes.'

When Richard had hung up, she looked at the receiver for a moment, wondering how she was going to manage to lie to Jane for the rest of her life. Just as she heaved herself to her feet, the phone rang again. With trembling fingers, she picked up the receiver for a second time. 'Yes? Richard?'

'Richard who? This is Bryan.'

'Oh.'

'Trying to get hold of that Emily girl.'

'She's on a different number.'

'Well, I've only got one fifty-pence piece, so can you get her for me?'

Emily came bounding up the stairs, and giggled into the receiver till his money ran out. 'Oh, Bryan!' she kept trilling. And then, 'Not that sort of model! The sort with clothes on . . .' Then she ran down again, with hardly a glance at Netta.

Netta slumped down on the bed just as the phone began ringing for a third time. Almost weeping with irritation, she said, 'For God's sake! She's gone back down . . .'

'Jeanette, it's Richard.'

'Hello, Richard.'

'You . . . er . . . left something.'

'Left something?'

'In the kitchen.'

Her mind rushed through a list of possible incriminating objects. 'What was it?'

'Some kind of hair accessory.'

She remembered – a glittery velvet band she used to scrape her hair back when it needed washing. 'It doesn't matter,' she said. 'Chuck it away.'

'Really? It looks rather . . . pretty.'

'Richard, it's just a hairband.'

'Oh, quite.' He paused. 'That's it, then.' And once more the phone went dead.

She sat very still for a long time. Then, after she heard the door bang, and Pilar's footsteps had skittered down the stairs, Netta ventured cautiously into the living room. She lit a cigarette, hands shaking as if she had the DTs. She felt that she could barely walk – but then, sitting down briefly on the sofa, she realized that she couldn't sit down either. The walls seemed to be bearing down on her, the stale dullness of everyday life was too much to take. It was a weird emotion. She could hardly say she liked Richard. If he had a single redeeming feature, she couldn't think what it was. He was arrogant, vain and self-obsessed. And he had cheated on his wife. (Just as she had cheated on her sister.) Did she want him? Was this philandering hypocrite the man for her? No. But she seemed to have tuned into some essential aspect of his personality that she had never been aware of before. His words ate at her; the knowledge that so few hours separated her from his passionate, whispered declarations made her feel dizzy. She thought again of the moment when she had caught sight of her reflection in his glasses. Why did he unsettle her in this strange way? What was real, and what was not? How many things could be true at the same time? Had he no morals? (Had she?) If there was a simple explanation, a coherent conclusion to be drawn, she could not think what it might be. She couldn't bear this. She must leave the house. She must go. Stubbing out her cigarette, she forced her arms into the sleeves of an old leather coat of Pilar's, snatched up her bag and ran out of the house.

She walked fast, sweating and muttering to herself. Before she knew it, she found she was in Deptford. The High Street, never a cheery prospect, was looking particularly depressing today. All the big stores had long since abandoned this dingy, forgotten thoroughfare, and the shops that remained were either weirdly niche, like the rad-femme bookshop, or grimly functional, like the grotty all-hours supermarket which sold cheap tea towels and instant coffee to the cash-strapped. Fragments of litter blew listlessly across the road – eerily empty of traffic, as usual – and an old tramp was pushing a broken pushchair full of Carlsberg Special along the pavement. Interesting, she noted, in spite of her mental state. This was her father's favourite drink. He might have been on the streets himself by now, if he wasn't so middle class. As it was, there were always friends and relations visiting with chicken soup and historical biographies. He hated this, of course, and would have preferred to be left alone. He was the sort of publican who loathed the human race. She'd always assumed that Jane was his inheritor, and that all his negative characteristics had been handed down to her. But now, she wondered. Her accidental shag with Richard was both self-destructive and cruel. The kind of thing her father himself might have done in his drunken, womanizing heyday. Jane would never do anything so underhand. She stabbed people in the front, if there was any stabbing to be done. Netta suddenly saw herself in the shower, Jane's hand on the knife. Psycho Killer. She must stop these thoughts. She must control herself. Yet what else was there to think about? Dimly, she felt that if she kept moving, she would leave some of this behind, as if her memories were in a physical place. But as she rushed along the road, the pain seemed to increase. Her mind was hot and busy. What could she do? Where could she go? She saw a phone box, and suddenly felt that she must speak to Richard. Urgently, soon, now. Why was he so angry? She needed to talk to him so that she could resolve this turmoil. Yes. Must clarify the situation. Put across her point of view. She didn't know his number at the university, but he might still be at home. The urine-scented phone box was well stocked with dodgy calling cards: 'Blonde, hot and sexy', 'Young girl, anything goes', 'Naughty Nanette Newman, Nice Big Boobs'. (Was that one serious?) But the phone itself was working: there was a dial tone. She hesitated for a moment, then phoned Jane's number, pushing the dial round as fast as she could so that she didn't have time to change her mind. A police car screamed by just as she heard a voice at the other end. Richard? Or Jane? No way of knowing. She shoved the money in, hands shaking.

'Hello? Richard?'

'It's Jane. He's left for work. Is that you, Netta?'

'Er – yes. I was just phoning . . . to say thanks for last night.'

'A little surplus to requirements, I would have thought. In the circumstances.'

Netta closed her eyes, and felt the nausea lurching in her stomach.

'He . . . told you then. He said he wasn't going to.'

'Well, it's happened before, and I've no doubt it will happen again. No one is perfect.'

This seemed uncharacteristically forgiving. 'What do you mean?' asked Netta, opening her eyes again to stare at another card: 'Raunchy Chick'. 'What did Richard tell you?'

'Oh, you know, the usual. Can't hold my drink. Can't do anything, apparently. The way I spend my days amounts to nothing, while the way he spends his amounts to A Life's Work.'

'You were fine. A bit tipsy, that's all. I was plastered. Anyway . . .'

'Anyway, what?'

Anyway, I'm Judas Iscariot. Anyway, I screwed your husband. 'Anyway, Richard was pretty far gone himself . . .' Casually mentioning his name like this seemed almost as duplicitous as casually borrowing his body.

'Yes. He's in a vile mood this morning. Jogged round the park and then came back snarling and sniping at everyone. Yet somehow, this is normal behaviour, part of adult enjoyment, whereas I'm punished for peaking too soon and going to bed in a slightly lachrymose spirit. Don't ever get married, Netta, it just isn't worth the hassle.'

'I'm not planning to,' said Netta. 'I don't think I'm marriage material.'

'Then you are very lucky. I suppose you're phoning up for a lift? The whole thing went completely out of my mind last night. It's the way things are now – I can only retain information if I write it down.'

'A lift?' Netta felt that she was about to remember something unpleasant.

'To Dad's. For Christmas. For goodness' sake, Netta! You haven't even got any kids. I had a photographic memory before I procreated.'

Netta wondered how she had managed to put this out of her mind. Presumably because a family Christmas was just too horrible to contemplate.

'What . . . were you planning to do?'

'It's the festive season, Netta. The options are pretty limited. No doubt I'll be called upon to organize the usual exhausting parade – tree purchase on Christmas Eve, carol service in the village church, turkey with all the trimmings. Plus present-orgy for the children – the same thing we do every year. By the way, Charlotte has three fairy outfits already.'

'So . . . you've opened the presents I bought for the children?' Netta felt irritated in spite of all her wrong-doing. 'That's not very festive, is it?' She had a sudden memory flash of Christmas with Margaret – fire roaring, torn wrapping paper strewn across the floor, and her mother doing the Charleston with a paper hat on while the turkey burned. Her Christmas lunches were legendary – everything was either charred or stone cold. But no meal since had ever quite lived up to them, the mad banter, the glugging red wine, her mother's laughter as she ignited the plum pudding. There was always far too much brandy on it, and one year the blue flame singed the paper streamers she had looped across the ceiling.

'One likes to check. Reduces the likelihood of Yuletide tears and tantrums.'

Netta was about to say – don't you trust me? But she thought better of it. 'Maybe we should do something different, for once.'

'Whatever for? It's nice for Dad. And you know what Richard is.' Jane laughed sourly. 'Addicted to ceremony.' ('Oh, my darling! Oh, my darling! I love you!' Skin on skin, sweating with lust.)

'Bollocks.'

'What do you mean, "bollocks"?'

'I can't come.'

'Don't be so ridiculous! Of course you can come. Don't be selfish. You know Dad's been really low lately.'

89

'He's always really low.'

'He might be a natural melancholic, but he's been worse than usual recently.'

'I know. I'm the one who has to see the miserable old git, remember. I'm the one who bloody *lived* with him till a few months ago. And now this . . . purgatory. Fuck. *Fuck*.'

'What on earth is wrong with you?'

'I can't come.'

'Netta, you are being utterly pathetic. It's Christmas. You have to be there. It will look weird if you aren't.'

Netta took note of this. Of course, nothing must look weird. Everything must be abnormally normal, now and for ever. The subterfuge started here. 'Okay. But I don't want a lift. Thanks.' She thought of a typical Tyler car journey – Richard pointing out features of historical interest (even on the M6), while Toby and Charlotte squabbled over their colouring books and Little Richard was mildly sick. Jane would busy herself with her operatic arias, oblivious to everything. And Auntie Netta would sit among them, oozing unrequited illicitness in her lacy basque, fishnet stockings and suspenders. 'Naughty Netta. Nice Big Boobs'.

'Why not? You're always broke.'

'I'm behind with my essays – I'll do some work on the train.' This, at least, was true. The lateness of her essays seemed to be the only aspect of her life that she could be honest about.

7

'Where the hell have you been all day?' Pilar was toasting pitta bread under the grill, and sipping from a tall glass. The kitchen cast a feeble warmth and light across the dark landing. Netta, shivering, wrapped a woollen scarf around her neck and buttoned up the leather coat.

'Out.'

'Out where? That's my coat, by the way.'

'I just walked. I know it's your coat – sorry. I thought you wouldn't mind.'

'Don't mention it. What's a coat, when you're used to nicking husbands?'

'Fuck off.'

They watched the pitta for a while.

'Just . . . walked?' Pilar turned to look at her enquiringly. 'Where to?'

'I dunno. I wanted to keep moving. Escape from being me.' She crossed and recrossed her arms. 'God, Pilar! I'm all over the place!' She waited for Pilar to speak, but the silence lengthened between them.

'I suppose you think I deserve to feel like shit.'

'Well – don't you?'

'Yeah, thanks very much. That doesn't actually move me on very far. I did this . . . thing. Now what? What can I do to make things better? Or is that impossible – am I cast into the outer darkness for ever?'

Pilar turned back to the grill. 'Don't be so effing melo-dramatic. Okay, maybe I was a tad OTT. It's . . . all that stuff with Dad, and his evil, conniving ways. Of course, it's your business, not mine. Up to you how you carry on.'

'It is your business, though! I want it to be your busi-ness! You're my best friend!'

There was another silence. Netta remembered that this was what Mel had said about Jude. They were like little girls in the school playground. But then Pilar smiled at her, managing to look ironic and forgiving at the same time. 'Have a bloody drink, darling,' she said. 'We're all human. You did something crap, and now you feel crap, and you deserve to feel crap. There's no need for me to make you feel any worse.' She poured some lager into a glass and handed it to Netta.

'Thanks.' Netta sipped, and shivered again. 'Can we turn the oven up? I'm fucking freezing.'

Pilar opened the oven door, turned up the gas to number five, and they sat in the expensive warmth, sticking their hands out towards the visible flame inside the cooker.

'Bleak's the word for it,' said Pilar. 'No money, Arctic weather, bloody Christmas rubbish around the corner . . . and bloody fucking awful essay crisis to cap it all.'

'God, same here. Bloody fucking awful essay crisis is doing my head in.'

'Still that Greenham twaddle?'

'Still the Greenham twaddle. What's yours?'

'Totally boring "Imperfect Enjoyment".'

'Never heard of it.'

'It's a poem by the Earl of Rochester. Some old roué who suffered from premature ejaculation,' said Pilar, with an expression of distaste. 'The only interesting thing about him was he swung both ways. But of course we don't touch on that. We like to focus on the whoring side in our tutorials – it's as close as Rod Bamber comes to getting his end away. Once you've discussed Restoration rumpy-pumpy with your forty-eight-year-old bald tutor, there's not much more life can offer, really.'

'I can imagine,' said Netta. 'Still, at least it must give you an insight into what it feels like to be a man.'

'Surprisingly crap, apparently.'

'I suppose that perspective might be useful one day. When you're married to Rupert, for instance.'

'Yeah, great, I'll be miles more understanding when he suffers from brewer's droop,' said Pilar. 'Sometimes I think I know enough about men. I'm sick of The Male View. Blake, Swift, Dickens, D. H. Lawrence, James bloody Joyce . . . the whole lot of them. All blokes – and all stark, staring mad.'

'They should call it Bloke Lit,' said Netta, nodding. 'Newspapers aren't any better. Wall-to-wall chaps. Perhaps Mel's right.'

Pilar shrugged. 'She's always right. That's the trouble with Mel. She's always right, and she always gets her own way.'

They were silent. Netta wondered if Pilar needed Mel, and wasn't sure if she could fill a Mel-shaped space. Since Mel had returned to Greenham, Pilar had been absent and distracted; she ate less and drank more. Sighing, Netta caught sight of her own essay, which was lying on the kitchen table. She picked it up. A testy letter from her anorexic tutor, Effie Spink, had appeared in her pigeon-hole, wanting to know if pastoral issues were holding up its production. Now, she was trying to think of a pastoral issue she could use as a convincing excuse. She looked at the title again. It was: 'The media distorts the truth about minority groups and "ordinary" people in the news by using stereotypical images – or by creating such images when they do not already exist.' Discuss, with reference to a current news story, such as the miners' strike or Greenham Common. Underneath were her notes. 'Hags? Witches? Prejudice against the dirty lesbians.' Then, in a different biro, she'd scrawled, 'Witch hunt. Salem. Arthur Miller, *Crucible*. Ducking stools? What images of witches in the past??? *Macbeth*.' And that was it. Three months of analysing the media, and this was the best she could do. To hell with it. To hell with the whole damn thing. Her desire to not-think was overwhelming. She would act, not analyse.

'I know what,' she said.

'What?'

'Let's have an end-of-term party. A proper do. Cocktails. You know – sophistication. Something to look forward to.'

Pilar brightened. 'Yes! Great idea. Something with style. We can announce people as they sweep up the staircase.'

'If we roped Emily in, of course, we'd have the whole house. It would be brilliant.' Netta pushed her chair back and took a notepad and pen out of a drawer. 'Let's make a list. Invite all the mean, moody, sexy men we can think of.'

'And a smattering of duds,' said Pilar, opening another bottle of lager. 'Otherwise, it's going to end up being one of those disgusting wimmin-only dos.'

Filled with bureaucratic zeal, they planned it all: cleaning and decorating the house, buying food, alcohol, decorations and new frocks, hiring glasses, compiling disco tapes . . . everything. Finally, they produced a list which had one hundred and sixteen items on it, which would cost two hundred and seventy-three pounds.

Even Pilar, grand in matters of over-expenditure, baulked at this. 'We can't do everything. Let's slim it down.'

'The booze stays.'

Pilar swigged her beer. 'Obviously the booze stays. It's a party, for God's sake. In fact, we may need more Irish whiskey for the Manhattans.'

'The frocks stay.'

'Clearly the frocks stay. But we should check out the attic. Emily found a fantastic lace dress up there once. Twenties flapper thing. There's loads of stuff up there.'

'But doesn't it all belong to her family?'

'The Birtwistles are posh hippies. They aren't into vulgar ownership. They leave all that to nouveau riche people like me. And they sure as hell don't give a shit about people wearing their mouldy old dresses.' She screwed up her eyes, scanning the list. 'We should scrap the food as well.'

'Bit uncivilized, a party without food.'

'Fuck it. We want divine decadence, not dips. Splurge on booze and forget the food. That's what I call style.'

Over the next few days, they put the plan into action. Emily readily agreed to extend the party into the downstairs half of the house, but was too busy having sex with

Bryan to do much to help. Pilar was unbothered by this. Her energy seemed endless. First, she insisted they move all the bikes and accumulated junk out of the hall and into a large garden shed at the bottom of the orchard. Then she discovered a stepladder under the stairs, and a cache of mops, buckets and dusters. Setting to, the two of them cleaned the house from top to bottom, hoovering, sweeping, polishing and rubbing at ancient stains until they vanished. Netta was surprised how happy she felt as she scrubbed away, even though it took two whole days, and was delighted to find that that beneath the layer of dust and grime which covered the hall carpet there was a beautiful pattern of curling leaves. Perhaps being a housewife wouldn't be so bad after all. When they finally finished, they were both flushed and sweating. Linking arms, they processed regally down the neatly swept staircase.

'Dame Jeanette Royce and Her Serene Majesty Pilar Christie!' cried Pilar. They looked up at the chandelier, now winking at them prettily in the late-afternoon light.

'Just a "Dame" to your "Serene Majesty", am I?'

'That's the title they gave to dear departed Grace Kelly, so it must be pretty downmarket,' said Pilar. 'Fur coat and no knickers.'

They looked down at the hall and into the cavernous ballroom which opened off it. 'Fantastic,' said Netta. 'I'm sure Princess Grace would have felt very much at home here.' She glanced at the stack of black and silver invitations on the hall table, the result of their shared design skills and further expense at the photocopying shop round the corner. 'All we need to do now is post these and buy up Oddbins, and we're through.'

Pilar gave one of her Technicolor smiles. 'It's going to be a completely fucking brilliant evening,' she said. 'I can feel it in my bones.'

Gay Jeremy was the first to arrive. He and Pilar had palled up since the Spam Hunt evening. He was wearing a white tie and a white tuxedo and – from a distance – looked achingly perfect with his slicked-down hair and sharp cheekbones. But as usual he was worried about his teeth. 'Don't look at me!' he commanded as he came through the door. 'I'm hideous! I know I look hideous!'

'Rubbish . . . you look fabulous–' protested Netta.

'Crap,' said Jeremy. 'You two are beautiful. Goddesses. I look like a sick hamster, compared to you.' He eyed them both with agitated desperation and wriggled in his jacket. 'Hired this thing. Naff or what? Should have inherited it!'

Pilar twirled towards him. Their scavenging in the loft had been a success: she had found a sea-green ballgown, which trailed shimmering panels of chiffon from its wide, rustling skirts. Netta had also done well, and unearthed a close-fitting dress which seemed to be made entirely from silver beads.

'Jem, darling, look me in the face,' said Pilar. He turned his face towards her – they were almost the same height – and she kissed him on each cheek, leaving two symmetrical scarlet imprints. 'You look The Business. You will be the coolest person here. No question. So don't whinge – all right? You are totally and utterly adorable, and if you stopped whingeing you would be the perfect man. Okay?'

'I can feel my cummerbund digging into my spare tyre,' said Jeremy. 'It's very lowering.'

But Pilar pressed a finger to his lips. 'Shut The Fuck Up,' she said. Jeremy started to laugh and watched himself in the mirror. Netta watched him too. She wanted the party to begin in earnest, so that she could dive into some mindless social scene. Now that the preparations were over, her crime had returned to stalk her again. She had suggested to Pilar that it would not be a good idea to invite Richard and Jane, and Pilar, pressing her lips together, had deleted them tidily from the list with her black felt pen. But it wasn't quite as easy as that to delete them from her mind. She was grateful for the tight, weird dress, which seemed to hold her in, acting as an artificial skin. She felt that everything beneath the enclosing layer of beads was a jelly of self-disgust. Her lips were painted dark purple, giving her an appropriately vampiric, undead appearance. She wondered how long she would feel like this, and whether it would be for ever.

But now the doorbell was ringing again, and guests began to flood in: a ferment of Geographers, people from Birmingham, Art bastards, rugger buggers, Drama twits and Welsh virgins, talking and laughing and shimmering in their cocktail best. Bryan arrived with Emily and Belinda the Butcher's Daughter. Netta felt a twist of apprehension as the guests herded up the stairs, where Pilar was waiting for them, wielding the cocktail shaker like a maraca. Four shakers were lined up on the kitchen table, alongside a mass of intoxicating ingredients, while recipes for Dry Martini, Pina Colada, Black Russian and Tequila Sunrise were stuck on the fridge.

There was no way that Pilar would be staying sober that night.

Emily loitered at the bottom of the stairs and looked around her. She was wearing a long, droopy dress – which partially exposed her unfeasibly full bosoms – and long, droopy earrings. She'd applied so much kohl that the whites of her eyes seemed to be peering out of subterranean holes. But she had adopted an animated, party-girl expression: it was a mixed gathering and she was in the full glare of the footlights. 'You've certainly been hard at work,' she said. 'I don't think the house has been as clean as this in Mum's lifetime.'

'It was fun, in a way.'

'And I see you've dug out one of Gran's old frocks. Très chic.'

Netta flushed. 'Pilar was positive you wouldn't mind.'

'It's, fine, fine. Family history – I could never wear one of Gran's little numbers. She was a suffragette, you know. Smashed her way into a Bond Street jeweller's with a rock-filled muff. She didn't take anything, of course. Far too grand. I think she died in that one, actually.' Emily nodded at Netta's dress.

'What – you mean – she died for the cause? Like the woman who threw herself under a racehorse?'

'Emily Wilding Davis. I was actually named after her. Embarrassing!' Emily giggled. 'No, this was years later. Gran had a stroke at the Rotary Club fancy dress. She was eighty-eight.'

Netta looked down at the ramparts of beads, feeling queasy. 'It *is* quite a weight,' she said. 'Sort of holds you in.'

'Anyway, Mum will be very impressed with all this.' Emily gestured at the freshly polished chandelier and the tracts of clean carpet in the hall.

'Impressed?'

'When she turns up.'

'You mean. . . she's coming?'

'Yes – she phoned earlier.'

Netta felt a new wave of unease. She had invited Mel without asking Pilar. This was not subterfuge, exactly, it just never seemed like quite the right time to mention it. She had seen this as a way of initiating détente between them. She shouldn't have interfered. Perhaps Flora was coming with Mel. If so, she couldn't imagine that any good would come of it.

'Does she want to keep an eye on us? Make sure we don't trash the place?'

'Oh, Flora's not bothered about anything like that! No. But there's something up, I think.'

Bryan approached with a full glass and handed it to Emily. He shot Netta a cautious glance. 'See?' he said. 'I'm a boyfriend now. Fully house-trained.'

'He's quite wonderful,' said Emily, wrapping herself around him. She had unusually long arms.

'Very impressive,' said Netta. She noticed something was different. 'Where's your bandanna?'

'Dumped it,' said Bryan. 'Ex-proto pop star now.'

'Really? Are you a proto something else, instead?'

'Yeah – proto tabloid hack.' He pulled a mini tape recorder out of his pocket. 'Searching for hot stories. Let me know if you hear of anything.'

'Flora's coming later,' said Emily.

'I know that . . . I was thinking of something more earth-shattering. Like the beginning of World War Three, or the death of Ray Bans.' His gaze was drifting down her droopy top. 'But . . . nice one. Along the right lines.'

Netta lost them in the crush as a wave of guests swept her up the stairs. The assault was led by the Welsh virgins.

'I'm feeling reckless tonight,' said one, whose name was Myfanwy, or Miffy for short. 'That's the thing about college. Used to be Saturday night out in Cardiff, that was your one big chance. Get out, get drunk, find some nice boy from the valleys and have a massive snog before you both threw up. Now, everything is so much more spread out. You can do all that stuff every night of the week.' She batted her spidery lashes. 'It's like Christmas every day, for someone sheltered like me.'

'Had oral sex the other night,' said her friend. 'Cunnilingus, you know. First time. I still don't know what he was called – it was magic! And the beauty of it is, I'm still intact, technically.'

Netta tried to think of something to say but found that her mouth was dry, and the sight of even more people pushing their way up the stairs towards the kitchen and the cocktails filled her with a sudden panic. She felt as if she was on the edge of a precipice, with no words, nothing in her mind that could protect her from tipping over. She badly wanted to get drunk – but then she would lose control, and veer from no words to spewing out the wrong ones, words that would incriminate her and twist what was already bad into something worse. So she slid quietly along the landing, opened the door of her room and slunk out of sight. For a while she stood completely still in the dark, grateful for the cold silence. Beyond the door, the noise rose and rose – from chatting and laughter to frenzied hilarity. The cocktails were obviously going down well. She could hear Pilar getting more and more regal as she progressed towards complete inebriation. Then she heard Bryan's voice, and Emily's kittenish party giggle.

'On the lookout for hot stories,' he said.

Pilar's snorting laughter followed this. 'Hot stories? Christ! This place is full of them. The stuff I could tell you . . .'

Netta stiffened, and pressed her ear to the door.

'Bad behaviour is what makes the world go round, don't you think?' Pilar was saying. 'Where would we be without the sexual miscreants, the Earl of Rochester, good old Bowie, and even my own dear flatmate . . .' Netta did not hear Bryan's reply to this, as she had flung the bedroom door open. 'Gawd's sake!' said Pilar. 'There you are, you bloody old trollop . . . thought you'd buggered off somewhere for a spot of incest.'

'Shut up, Pilar.'

'Though I suppose it was only in-law cest, really, wasn't it?'

'Pilar, I said shut up.'

'What's all this?' asked Bryan. 'Incest? Sounds good.'

'Pilar's drunk.'

'Don't get your knickers in a twist, dear,' said Pilar. 'There's no one here who knows anything about it.'

'Anything about what?' asked Jane.

8

Jane was wearing widowy black lace. She did not smile at Netta. 'I can't believe your flatmate, who barely knows me, had the decency to invite me to this party, while you, presumably, thought I would cramp your style. Or perhaps you just see me as irrelevant stodge, the mumsy big sister with incarceration instead of a life. Mmm?'

Netta wished she had not only stayed in her bedroom when she had the chance, but hidden under the bed. She felt her body swaying gently. Only the dead suffragette's dress was holding her together. 'Is Richard here?' she managed to ask.

Jane pursed her lips. 'No. Richard is babysitting, for once. I thought it was my turn to get out and have a little fun.' She looked around her uncertainly at the heaving crowd and the row of cocktail shakers on the table. 'Though why I thought that might be possible here, I have no idea.'

'Brilliant. I mean – that you got here. Great . . . I mean . . .' Netta tried to arrange her stuttering mind. She wanted to keep the truth at a safe distance, without telling any more lies. 'I meant to invite you. We just ran out of invitations, and I forgot . . .' This was the worst of all worlds, both unconvincing and untrue. Then, floundering further: 'But I knew that Pilar would remember . . .'

'Really.' Jane shook her head. 'Sometimes I wonder if you like me at all. Now you're just making me feel like the Bad Fairy.' She turned and disappeared into the crowd. Netta wondered, with a twist of protectiveness, who Jane would find to talk to.

'Shame to leave her out,' said Pilar, rattling another shaker.

'What's the big idea? I specifically asked you not to invite her – and you might have told me . . .' The irony of these words brought her up short. It seemed that neither she nor Pilar was scoring very highly in the total honesty department. Netta poured her first drink, with clammy hands. 'I mean . . . supposing she'd brought Richard along as well? This is serious, you know, Pilar.'

'Of course it's fucking serious, doom-brain,' said Pilar, speaking at a higher than average volume. 'That's the whole point. You can't go and stick your head in the sand and pretend you're not related to her, just because you screwed up.'

'Screwed up? So I'm not the only one.' Belinda the Butcher's Daughter was wearing electric blue, which gave her face an Arctic pallor. Her small eyes were fixed on Bryan and Emily smooching by the bathroom door. 'I'm a butcher by blood, but I'm a big softy at heart.' Her round eyes were full of yearning.

'God, you don't want to worry about him!' said Netta. 'That man is Britain's leading wanker. Really.'

'A total dick-head,' said Pilar. 'He tried it on with me, you know. Netta had to rescue me in case I lost my virginity.'

'Bryan is an inspiration, a wonderful, amazing person,' said Belinda, on the brink of tears. 'You don't know what he's really like. I thought we understood each other, and now he's taken up with that . . . that . . .'

'I think you'll find it's "those",' said Pilar. 'Those tits.'

'He's just not like that!' said Belinda. A single tear rolled down her cheek. 'I could have half the men at college, but all I want is him.'

'Gor blimey, love, you've got your whole life ahead of you,' said Pilar. She filled a glass from the cocktail shaker in her hand. 'Have a bloody drink.'

'Thanks,' said Belinda. She took a sip. 'Wow! What's this?'

'Black Tequila,' said Pilar ominously.

'Does that exist?' asked Belinda.

'It does now.'

Netta noticed that Pilar's intensity-rating had been turned higher. 'Can you remember what you put in it?' she asked.

'Don't patronize me, Ms Royce. 'Course I can. Loadsabooze. Tastes fan-bloody-tastic.'

'Like cough sweets,' said Belinda. But she looked more chirpy, and disappeared down the stairs.

'Pilar, you're on the slippery slope,' said Netta. 'And – whatever you do – will you please, please keep your mouth shut about my recent misdemeanours? Especially now Jane's here, your surprise guest.'

'Blood's thicker than water,' said Pilar. She was pouring something out of another shaker now. 'Though not necessarily thicker than a Bloody Mary.'

'For God's sake!' Netta spun away, knowing that it was useless to reason with Pilar once she was in serious drinking mode. She felt a chill. Downstairs the front door had crashed open, wintry air was blasting into the hall, and she could hear singing. Could it be carol singers? But as she dashed along the landing, Netta realized that this wasn't a carol, but another kind of song: 'We are women, we are women,/We are strong, We are strong,/We say NO, We say NO,/To the Bomb, To the Bomb.' It was the Frère Jacques-inspired ditty that Mel had entertained them with in the bath. Then a loud cry went up: 'Nukie, nukie, nukie! Out! Out! Out!' and there were loud cheers from the rugby club. 'The lezzies are here!' they crowed. And two figures were climbing the staircase towards her: one, tall, blonde and bulky, was Mel. The other, a scarecrow-like figure with grey frizzy hair, Netta recognized from the TV screen. Flora Birtwistle, her landlady. Each of them was carrying a plastic bucket.

'Mel! You made it!' said Netta.

Mel hugged her. She smelled like Bonfire Night. 'Who invited those bastards in the hall?' she said.

'We invited everyone.'

'Well, you're bloody mad. They're a bunch of woman-haters.'

'What, even Mutant?'

Mel shot her a sharp look. 'This is Flora,' she said. 'My partner in peace.'

Flora was smiling with assured magnificence. She didn't actually bow, but created an atmosphere of bowing. 'You may have heard of me.'

'Oh yes,' said Netta. 'You wrote a book called *Housebound Harridans* in the 1970s. I found a copy in the Salvation Army shop the other day.'

This did not appear to be the right answer. 'I think you will find my body of work extends well beyond the 1970s,' said Flora. She handed Netta a bucket. 'We have brought you sustenance for the evening.'

'Bucket of curry,' said Mel. 'Two buckets, in fact. Fresh from the campfires of Greenham Common. All we need to do is stick it in a saucepan and warm it up. Got any rice?'

Pilar staggered out of the kitchen. 'Mel,' she said, then stopped. 'Flora.' Mel went forward to hug her, but Pilar was giving out a strong force-field of disapproval. 'Who . . . invited you?' she asked.

'I thought *you* did. We got a lovely black and silver invite. Why? What's up? Aren't you pleased to see me?'

'I assumed you'd lost interest in what goes on here. With so much going on at Greenham.'

'But . . . we're still flatmates! Still friends . . .'

Pilar did not seem to hear this. 'What was that you were saying about buckets?'

'It's curry,' said Mel. 'Great party food. It'll soak up the alcohol a treat.'

'No way,' said Pilar. 'We are not having buckets of curry at this party.'

'Why ever not?'

'This is . . . party with standards. Create ambience of old-fashioned politesse. Traditional style and–'

'Don't be so daft.'

'No curry. No way. We've spent ages getting this thing ready, and now you're trying to ruin the whole thing!'

'I like a nice curry, myself,' said a Welsh virgin. 'If we had one here, it would save us having to go out for a chicken vindaloo at three o'clock in the morning.'

'Curry it is, then,' said Mel. She took her coat off, to reveal a T-shirt and jeans underneath, neither of which was very clean, and carried her bucket into the kitchen. Flora, meanwhile, was unfurling various banners and hanging them over the banisters. Netta went half-way down the stairs and read: 'SAY NO TO CRUISE' and 'DART-MOUTH VILLA – A NUCLEAR-FREE ZONE'.

Pilar had backed against a wall to steady herself, and looked as if she had been pinned there. 'Cocktails,' she said faintly. 'Gorgeous fabulousness . . . now it's turning into a squat party.' She took a swig of Black Tequila.

'How can you worry about trivial matters like that?' asked Flora. She was now busily pushing people away so that she could arrange a selection of books on the chest of drawers which dominated the wide landing. Netta saw that they were all written by her, and concerned the conventional subjugation of women via the washing and sorting of socks. Leaflets about the arms race were dotted among them. 'We're not here by accident, you know. We're here to recruit.'

'Recruit?' Pilar's voice was even fainter. She was fading away, like Tinkerbell.

'For Greenham,' said Mel, now wearing a pinny and coming out to collect the second bucket. 'If you had something to believe in, Pilar, maybe you wouldn't need to get pissed all the time.'

Netta had had enough. Whether Flora was taking over Greenham she had no idea, but she was certainly taking over the party. She slipped down the stairs, past Emily snogging Bryan, past Mutant swigging beer, past Jane asking Belinda what the schools were like in Taunton, and pushed her way into the outside air. Her naked shoulders were seized by icicle fingers as soon as she closed the front door, but she sat down on the front step with a great sigh of relief.

'Fucking women,' she said out loud.

'Fu-fucking . . . what?' She looked up. There was no outside light, so she had only the glare of the windows to see by: it was a cloudy, starless night. A figure stretched up towards the dark sky. It was a man, dressed in leather. He seemed, from her lowly position on the ground, impossibly tall.

'Fu-fucking women . . . did you say?'

Staring up at him, she had an impression of the Presidents of America, carved into Mount Rushmore. A noble, bony face, high above.

'Yes, I did,' she said. 'Just a moment of weakness. Don't worry. I know men are even worse.'

'Un-un . . .' The word seemed to get stuck in his throat, as if he was choking on a consonant. Then, he shook his head, and a great flood of words came out. 'Undoubtedly. I couldn't agree more. We are the unfair sex.'

'At least you know your faults.' She could see him better now, the heavy dark fringe of hair falling into his eyes.

'Two thousand years of conditioning have fucked us up big time,' he said. 'And I . . . and I'm a prime example.'

'In what way?' asked Netta.

The mysterious man said nothing.

'I mean . . . not wanting to be rude, but are you fucked up in any particular way? Or just generally fucked up big time? Generically?'

She saw the man was nodding thoughtfully. 'Semi-evolved,' he said after a while.

'Semi-what?'

'Evolved.'

'You mean – like the missing link?'

'Sort of.' He paused. Pauses seemed to be his big thing. 'Never . . . talk about my . . . f-feelings.'

'Nothing unusual in that. It just means you're a bloke.'

'And I have a mor . . . a mor . . . a morbid desire for penetrative sex.'

Netta rather liked the sound of this. 'I wouldn't give yourself too much of a hard time about that,' she said. 'I think you'll still find a few women old-fashioned enough to join in with a bit of unreconstructed fornication. Though speaking personally, of course, I do appreciate that the crude usage of the penis is overrated.' Listen to yourself, said her mind. You should bloody know, when it comes to crude usage. You're the expert in the field.

He looked down at her. She looked up at him. Her breath came in short gasps: it was shockingly cold. But she had decided that she would like to know this man better, even if he liked – as seemed probable – Joy Division.

'Come inside,' he said. 'You'll freeze to death out here.' His stutter seemed to have disappeared. He pulled her up, his leather jacket creaking like a ship's rigging. The veins stood up in the backs of his elegant, sinewy hands. Suddenly, partying seemed more attractive.

'I don't suppose you like dancing to Wham! by any chance?' she asked.

'No,' he said. 'I never dance.'

As they stepped inside, the music stopped abruptly and the lights went on.

'What . . . ?' Netta looked around, blinking. Flora and Mel were standing by the stereo. 'What's happening?'

Her new friend groaned out loud. 'Oh shit, I knew she'd pull something like this.'

'It's Flora Birtwistle, the feminist!' she said to him reprovingly.

'It's . . . it's my bloody mother,' he said.

'So you're Tom, the statue-shooting man?'

He said nothing: his eyes were fixed on Flora.

'Hello, everyone,' boomed Flora. The guests stared at her dumbly. 'Now . . . listen to me, please.' Her voice carried effortlessly – she had the kind of accent that would have quelled rioting sepoys during the Raj. 'I will only keep you for a few minutes,' she said. 'Your time is precious, and so is mine. More precious than we realize, perhaps.'

'Get on with it, then!' called Bryan.

'All right, if people are listening, I'll be brief. This is a recruiting pitch. Our country has never been under greater threat of annihilation than it is now. Hundreds of Russian warheads are pointing at our cities.' ('Crap,' whispered Tom. 'She can't even get her facts right.') 'You might say – like a lot of people do – well, there isn't anything I can do about it. But that's where you're wrong. There *is* something else you can do. You can join us at Greenham Common. Provided, of course, that you are female. This is a nationwide call to women.' Booing followed this.

Tom stepped forward and looked up at his mother. For a second, he didn't speak. Then, he said: 'It . . . it . . . it . . .'

'It – what, mate?' asked Bryan. 'It's a bloody liberty?'

'It's an outrage!' said Tom at last. 'It's a bloody outrage, to ex . . . to exclude men like this. When you know . . . when you know I've been campaigning against the Bomb for years. But because I'm a man, it doesn't count. Even though I'm your son!'

Flora seemed barely to register that he was there. 'Of

course, the support of our menfolk is vital,' she said grandly. 'In the form of . . . financial donations . . . and so on . . .'

'It's a women-only protest because it's men who start wars in the first place!' said Mel. 'It's a women-only protest because all men are innately violent! Okay?'

'Men are just as capable of being non-violent as women,' shouted Tom.

'The pigs pick on men,' said Flora. 'Which means it's easier for a women-only protest to be peaceful. Go away and find your own causes to fight, Tom. You would be much more useful somewhere else.'

'No one could force me to leave Greenham,' said Tom. 'I have squatter's rights.'

'We can't have men at the base,' said Mel. 'Women need space to get away from power-tripping.'

Netta was approaching the stereo. If she put the music on loudly enough, perhaps she would be able to drown out the battle of the sexes. However, the scene wasn't quite over yet.

'What about Thatcher?' shouted Bryan.

'She's a man!' said Mel.

Bryan tried again. 'What about Israeli girl soldiers?'

'Sexist bastard!' Mel was yelling now.

'What about Mahatma Gandhi?' called Mutant. '*He* was a bloody pacifist, wasn't he?'

'Shut up, Mutant!' cried the other rugger buggers.

'Please feel free to purchase copies of my book, *The Sock Dropper's Misogyny* – only two ninety-nine,' said Flora.

'Or a bowl of genuine Greenham Curry for just fifty pence!' said Pilar, appearing behind her. 'Made of uni-lateral turnips and anti-nuclear carrots. Raising funds for those gallant girls at the base!' She looked the worse for wear, and was wearing an orange pompom hat and an old anorak, which did not go with her sea-green dress. In one hand she carried a bucket, in the other an outsize ladle.

'Oh, for God's sake!' said Mel. 'Stop taking the piss!'

'That's a good one. Thass a very good one. Plan this sodding . . . ambass'dor-you-are-spoiling-us party for months . . . bloody years, actually, then you come here . . . sab'tage the whole . . .' But Netta had managed to switch the stereo on again, and now people were beginning to dance to the Buzzcocks.

She saw Jane moving towards the front door beyond the gyrating bodies and wild arm-waving.

'I'm off,' said Jane, buttoning up her coat. 'Not much like the parties we had at Oxford. Not much wit between the lot of them.'

'No. Wit isn't very big at Goldsmiths.'

'Your flatmate seems to have joined the Catholic Church,' said Jane, as she pulled on her gloves. 'At least, I think that was what she was on about. She certainly seems to think that you would benefit from a trip to confession.'

'She's just pissed, as usual,' said Netta.

'Complete basket case, as far as I can make out. I wouldn't trust her as far as I could spit.' Jane's voice was suddenly vehement. 'What does she know about love and marriage, a tart like that?'

'She's not a . . .' began Netta. But she had caught sight of Pilar sobbing, ladle in hand, being comforted by Miffy, the virgin from the valleys. When she turned back, Jane had disappeared.

9

The next morning was bruisingly bright. Four women sat slumped in the Creekside Café, none of them quite cutting the dash they had the night before. Pilar's face seemed to have shrunk, and she held her cigarette in wizened little fingers. Mel was flushed and smelled strongly of Pina Colada. Emily, hidden behind shades, sighed dramatically from time to time. Netta had no idea how she looked herself, as she was currently avoiding eye contact with her reflection. But her insides felt as if they had been removed, microwaved, then shoved back into her body in no particular order. Cruel rays of sunshine illuminated the congealed brown droplets which clung to the sides of the HP sauce bottle on their table, and highlighted each fallen sugar crystal which lay glistening on the dirty checked tablecloth. No one had managed to start eating yet: their breakfast had arrived with unwelcome promptness, and stared up at them, harrowing in its eggy, bacony, greasy reality.

'How could you?' said Pilar, who was the only person who had stuck to toast.

'It's great hangover food,' said Mel, slicing up her fried egg so that the golden yolk burst forth from its membrane and ebbed across her plate.

'I don't mean the fucking food,' said Pilar. She drew tightly on her cigarette and sent smoke out of each nostril.

Mel paused with a forkful of egg close to her mouth. 'How could I what, then?'

'Trash our fucking party.'

'"Our" – I like that! "Our" – does that mean you and Netta? Like you're Darby and Joan? She only moved in five minutes ago.'

Netta, feeling as if her head might follow the example of the exploding egg yolk, stared out at the flighty winter sky.

'All the work that went into it! All the fun we had – and then you ruined it, with your stupid anti-nuclear antics. No one gives a shit, Melanie! Why don't you just grow up?'

'Don't squabble,' said Emily from behind her shades. 'Life's depressing enough, isn't it? Sort of fawn.' Bryan had not stayed the night, but had insisted on leaving at three a.m., when the fags gave out, claiming that he needed to be available to pursue possible news leads on Sunday morning. Now Emily sat in a dishevelled heap next to Pilar, exuding sexual gloom.

'I'm not squabbling,' said Pilar. 'I'm simply stating the facts. Barging in like that. With those fucking leaflets! Gawd – we all know Flora is a pain in the backside . . .' ('Hear, hear!' said Emily.) '. . . but why did you have to join in?'

'You'll thank me when we're all incinerated,' said Mel. 'When your skin's dropping off, and your hair's falling out, and your eyeballs are sliding down your cheeks.'

'Thanks a lot,' said Netta, who had just taken a mouthful of her own fried egg. 'Nice image.'

'It's just bad manners,' said Pilar. 'If Greenham's so bloody important to you – more important than your friends – I don't know why you don't just stay there.'

Mel munched food for a while. Netta wondered if she was unabashed by Pilar's remarks, or just protected from them by her hangover. 'Funny you should say that,' she said.

'Funny I should say what?'

'That I might as well stay at Greenham.'

'Why?'

'I'm going to spend Christmas there.'

'What . . . you mean – Christmas Day?'

'Yup. Me and Jude and whoever else wants to join us. It's not exclusive, or anything.'

'But we promised each other we'd spend it in London! In the flat! Avoiding the horror of Christmas crap . . . *The Two Ronnies* . . . snoring round the mince pies . . . farting dads . . . for God's sake, Mel! You know Mum's gone off on a cruise! I'll top myself if I have to sit there while my fucking father and Fat Sandra bicker over the bleeding Bendicks! You promised!'

Mel looked embarrassed. 'Yes, well, I've made a pledge with Jude now. She's quite damaged. She needs someone like me.'

Pilar's small features had almost reached vanishing point. Her mouth was tense with fury, her eyes narrowed. 'Pledge? Can't you do anything without making a big deal out of it? What kind of pledge?'

Emily unfolded a paper napkin and draped it over her face. 'Wake me up when it's all over,' she said, leaning backwards. 'This is insupportable.'

'We want to be together,' said Mel, peeling open a pat of butter and spreading it across her toast.

'Together.' This was not a question: Netta could see

that Pilar was steeling herself for something. There was a moment's silence.

'We're just good friends, like I said . . .' Mel was now focusing her attention on a sachet of marmalade which was proving difficult to open.

'And . . . ?' Pilar stubbed out her cigarette. 'And?'

'Well, we're in an ongoing process of deconstructing our desire.'

Pilar stared at Mel, open-mouthed.

'Deconstructing . . . what?' asked Netta, who had planned to keep quiet. 'Like . . . Meccano, or something?'

Mel didn't look at her. Instead, she kept her eyes fixed on Pilar. Her voice was light and carefully modulated. Netta realized that she had rehearsed this speech. 'What I mean is . . . in lay person's terms . . . we have both been brought up – conditioned – to fancy the opposite sex. But we both agree that we only want to have sex with men – as much as we do want to, which isn't much – because society has disallowed our lust for other women.' She hesitated, and her gaze finally flickered to Netta, and then to Emily, still hidden under the paper napkin. 'If you can call woman-to-woman attraction lust, which I'm not sure about. It may be an offensive noun.'

There was another silence. Netta watched the paper napkin slowly rise and fall to the rhythm of Emily's breath.

'Bollocks,' said Pilar. 'Only a straight woman could shag Mutant – and he's not even the worst one you've had.'

'Why does it matter, anyway?' asked Netta.

'It matters because we've all been programmed,' said Mel.

'Bollockser and bollockser. No one's programmed *me*,'

said Pilar. 'I could just as soon shag a woman as a man. It's all the same thing – sex, pure sex.'

'Now, that *is* bollocks,' said Mel. 'Coming from the practically-engaged Queen of Bishop's Stortford.'

Emily finally emerged from the veil of her napkin. 'I must say, that does rather strain credulity,' she said. 'You're a girls' girl.'

'I sure am,' said Pilar. Turning to Emily, she kissed her on the mouth, the little sliver of her tongue probing its way between Emily's lips. A silent second passed. Emily gave a shudder, then her right hand fluttered on to the back of Pilar's white neck. After a few moments, Mel cleared her throat. 'I think you've made your point, Pilar. We don't want to get chucked out of here before we've had time to eat our fried bread.' The two women pulled apart, blushing and laughing.

'Well,' said Emily. '*Well.*' She pulled one hand through her untidy hair. 'I shall certainly have something to tell Bryan when I see him.'

'Exactly,' said Mel. 'Just a spot of titillation for the rugby club. As if women shagging is just some safe little turn-on for the boys. *That*'s not going to change the world. There's a bit more to sexuality than that.'

'Like what, exactly?' Pilar was looking rather pleased with herself.

'Snogging like that! You can't be a lesbian – you're not even a proper feminist! It's just window-dressing . . .'

'Or window-shopping!' giggled Pilar.

Emily began to wrap her long scarf around her neck. She picked up her basket and rooted around inside it for a while, though it was not clear what she was looking for.

Then she stood up. Her face was still pink. 'Do you think women are up to the necessary mind games?' she asked. 'I mean, to keep you in the state of misery in which obsession can flourish?'

'Women can be crap,' said Netta, with some feeling. 'I reckon we can give men a run for their money in that area . . .'

'The whole point of men is that they behave badly,' said Emily. With that, she turned and wafted slowly out of the café.

'She hasn't paid,' observed Mel.

'She didn't eat anything,' said Pilar. 'She tasted *nice.*'

'Stop showing off,' said Mel. 'I don't know what you're trying to prove.'

'She was a good kisser,' said Pilar.

Mel rolled her eyes.

'God's sake, Pilar,' said Netta. 'Whatever are you up to?'

'Okay,' said Pilar. 'I'll let you in on it: Operation Girl Dating.'

'I'm not sitting here and listening to this.' Mel pushed back her chair and stood up. 'You can't "date" girls, just like that! It's political!'

'Nonsense,' said Pilar. 'You just want it to be political. You take it too seriously, darling. Like that awful Radclyffe Hall book you lent me – *The Well of Loneliness.* If ever a central character could have done with a sense of humour, it's that Stephen. Why did she call herself an "invert", when "girl" would have done just as well? And did she need a name for what she was anyway?'

'Because the whole of society was stopping her from

being honest, that's why,' said Mel. 'Why do you have to be so fucking obtuse?'

Netta looked at each of them in turn, puzzled. 'What's Operation Girl Dating?'

'Spam Hunt Nouveau – the meaningless shagging of girls,' said Pilar.

'Now I've heard everything.' Mel hoisted her rucksack on to her back. 'I'm off. I used to think Greenham was a bit weird, and the rest of the world was practically normal. Now it seems like it's the other way round. Maybe Greenham is where I belong.'

'Maybe,' said Pilar, beaming at Mel. 'See you around. And give my regards to Jude . . . hope she works it out with that deconstruction stuff.' Mel smiled thinly, then marched out into the street.

'I can't think why we hadn't thought of Operation Girl Dating before, can you?' asked Pilar, watching her go.

'Perhaps because . . . we're heterosexual? At least – I *think* we are.'

'So what? Come on, don't be a spoilsport. Let's beat Melanie at her own game – and have a bit of fun while we're at it. We'll start this Tuesday – the night they let women into Heaven!'

Netta never quite agreed to Operation Girl Dating – the very idea made her feel sick and giddy, like the time the School Wanker had decided he was obsessed with her, and took to following her along the corridor, moaning, 'I love you, baby,' before posting passionate little notes into the collar of her blouse. But it had been easy to sort out her attitude to the School Wanker in her mind. She hated him. He made her feel sweaty with revulsion. He smelled funny. And his hair grew low down on his neck. Her mental attitude to shagging girls was harder to define. Of course, kissing a woman might be perfectly wonderful. In many ways, logically, it should be preferable to kissing a bloke, who may not care much for dental hygiene, and might recently have consumed a kebab. But logic did not come into it. Wanting to kiss a man came from somewhere quite other: the loin area popularized by D. H. Lawrence. This inchoate yearning zone did not deal with issues of Colgate and stray onion shards. However, she was reminded of how the School Wanker had made her feel when she thought about Heaven, and the women who might want to go there. She was frightened. She was frightened and angry. She was frightened and angry and she wanted to run away. She thought of it now, and her legs started to tremble, visibly, under the kitchen table. But it was too late to do anything about it. She looked at her watch. Any minute now, they were due to leave the flat and head for the notorious temptations of the club.

She stared at herself in her compact mirror – white-faced and pinched-looking, not a pretty sight. Good. But maybe that didn't come into it – lesbians were commendably unlooksist. To blend in, she had hidden her body inside a uniform of black jeans and a black T-shirt. She turned her attention to Jeremy, who was twirling hysterically round the flat. He was worried about the newly fitted brace on his teeth. It had been her idea to invite Jem along: she thought there would be safety in numbers, and also he might know about the theory and practice of poppers and other aspects of gay disco. However, he was

in a vulnerable mood, having recently visited an ortho-
dontist. 'Maybe I shouldn't come out to play?' he said,
smiling unhappily at her and showing his metal-filled
mouth. 'I just *am* Jaws.'

'It's a great S and M look,' said Netta, looking dubiously at the cab company card she had found in the
bottom of the fruit bowl. Mel counselled the exclusive
use of Ladycabs, a women-only cab service, for reasons
of safety and remaining unraped. But Netta did not know
the number, and did not share these extreme views about
the risks of mixed-sex taxis. She gave a hard sigh,
surprising herself, and picked up the phone to call their
usual cab firm. 'Just stay calm, Jem. You'll be the sexiest
person there.'

'Of course, I'll be in a vicious circle now – no one
fancying me, no love action, all because of never going
anywhere.' Jem was pirouetting round the room, looking
down anxiously at his long narrow torso.

'Can't you sit down till I've finished putting my slap
on?' asked Pilar, who was applying yet another layer of
lip gloss. She looked ravishing in a tiny leopard-skin top
and baggy army trousers.

Jem couldn't. 'My dad's a policeman.'

'What's that got to do with anything?'

'It makes me nervous.'

'God, we're all fucking nervous,' said Netta. She
slammed the receiver down for the third time: the number
was continuously engaged.

'Anyway, I'm burning calories,' said Jem. 'Vital to be
super-slim, now I've invested in metal teeth. Did you
know that diet cream cheese only has half the calories of

non-diet cream cheese? Still horrendously fattening. I wept when I found out. Basically, you're better off with Edam.'

Pilar pulled on a leather bomber jacket. 'Have you got *any* male chromosomes, Jem?' she asked. 'Only, I'm beginning to wonder if you're a biological impossibility.' She looked at Netta. 'Gawd, is that your outfit?'

'Yup.'

'Sorry to say this, Net darling, but it's crap. You've got loads of stuff that's miles better than that. What about the glittery boob tube?'

'Oh, come on, Pee! I bought that for a joke!'

'Black PVC trousers?'

'They give me thrush.'

'Fucking hell, girl! You've got to have a bit more dedication than this. You look like a frigging poly lecturer.' She whisked out of the room, and returned seconds later with a tiny amount of material and a pair of shiny black boots. 'Put these on.'

'No way.'

'Put these on, or the date's off. We're meant to be having the maximum amount of fun!'

In her bedroom, Netta struggled into a pair of black tights, zipped herself into Pilar's tiny black skirt and pulled on the boots. They were thigh-high and had long stiletto heels. Her image in the mirror was scary in the extreme.

Pilar wolf-whistled when she tottered back into the living room. 'Go get 'em, heart-breaker!' she said.

'I don't want to go get 'em,' said Netta. 'I want to stand very quietly in the corner, drinking a lot of Grolsch.'

'Bullshit,' said Pilar. 'Christ, Net, where's the sodding

cab? Here, let me do it.' Moments later, a taxi was beeping outside in the street.

By the time they drew up outside Heaven, both of them had caught Jem's hysteria. He had described the forth-coming scene with such vivid anxiety that they were infected with uneasy excitement. Even the cab driver, delicately boned with a soft African voice, said he might be along for a boogie later on. 'In Kinshasa, we have none of these things,' he said, accepting their large tip with a gentle nod. 'In Kinshasa we have only the most basic whorehouses.'

Jem gave Netta what looked like a bottle of eye drops as they approached the entrance. 'Amylnitrate!' he said. 'Take a few drops when you're dancing. You'll feel fantastic for about eight seconds!'

'Cripes,' said Netta. 'What happens then?'

'You're on your own,' said Jem. 'Anything is possible.'

As they paid the catatonic doorman in his spiky leather dog collar and military cap, Netta felt an unfamiliar sensa-tion. Fear? No. She realized it was the feeling of sound. Throb, throb, throb. Like something pulsing from the centre of the earth. It was the noise of Heaven, metro-nomic, addictive. She followed Jem on to a vast circular dance floor, blinded by darkness and the lightning flash of green lasers. Here, the music was a surging, soaring cacophony of screaming strings and alien vocals, pounded into rhythmic patterns. Looking around, she began to see more clearly. There was a huge glitter ball spinning high above her head, and dancers everywhere, glimpsed through the laser beams and dried ice. Some, like the doorman, were dressed as stage-Nazis, others wore hardly anything, jeans slung so low that you could see the beginnings of their pubic hair, their naked chests shining with sweat. But most were dressed unflashily in check shirts and jeans. It was their behaviour which would have alarmed her father, in deep snog on the various raised platforms that surrounded the dance floor, or dancing together with narcissistic abandon, together and apart, always self-conscious and alert to the possibility of inspiring the next bout of passing lust.

'I can see what that amylnitrate business is about, now!' she shouted to Jem.

'What?' Jem was looking over his shoulder. He was undergoing a curious transformation. He seemed to have got over the trauma of his teeth, and was flexing his body in its tight black T-shirt. In fact, now he had reached the club, his confidence and glamour had increased. When the lights caught his metal teeth he looked like a rent boy from the Weimar Republic whose steel dentition made his services more sought after.

'Living in the moment, darlings! Go for it!' he cried.

'What?'

Pilar handed her a bottle of beer. 'Where are all the women, then?' she shouted.

'No idea!' Netta looked around. Oddly, it occurred to her now, this was more like being in a man's world than anywhere she had ever been: romantic love must be a female invention after all, designed to keep the rampant male in line. The idea that sex and love were related in any way seemed to have been left outside in Villiers Street. Here, there was no prospect of torturing yourself with guilty sex, or deceit and heartbreak. Men spun past each other, or lurched together, locking arms and bodies, then spun apart. Accidental, ruthless, intense. This was what sex was all about. Then she caught sight of some women. A group of serious feminist types, with short hair and sensible glasses which glinted in the disco lights. They weren't dancing; they seemed to be approaching the evening in a state of extreme seriousness. Perhaps coming here was part of their academic study.

Pilar swigged fiercely from her bottle. 'It's okay,' she said. 'I've seen her!'

'Seen who?' Netta shouted into her ear. Pilar had tiny ears, perfectly white and dainty, so that the diamanté chandeliers which dangled from each lobe looked out of scale.

'Girl of my dreams!' Pilar was holding her arm and yelling now. 'Looked straight at me!'

'What?'

'Like that film. Remember? *Coup de Foudre.*'

'Cool as what?'

'Isabelle Huppert!'

Then Pilar disappeared.

Later – but she wasn't sure how much later – a figure appeared out of the darkness. It was a girl, thin, with bobbed blonde hair and a cool smile. 'I am Christiana,' she said.

'Oh.' Netta's mind was full of whirling music, drink, confusion. Where was this woman from? The accent was almost familiar. Did she know her? Christiana came closer. Heaven receded.

'I like you,' said the girl. Oh, that was it. Scandinavian,

like the chef in the Muppets. The girl faded slightly, the club came into clearer focus.

'You don't even know me,' said Netta. It was the first time she had had to point this out to a woman.

'I don't mind,' said the girl. No bloke had thought of that one as yet. They always felt they had to reassure you with their deep feelings and emotional longevity. 'I don't mind' was kind of appealing. But at the same time . . . closer still now. She had long, pale eyelashes, fronds of spiked hair sticking up around her forehead, palest green now in the reflected light. She smelled of garlic.

'I'm Netta,' said Netta, not sure if this committed her to anything.

'Come,' said Christiana, and took her hand in a taut, bony grasp. Netta tried to gauge her level of sexual arousal. It was low, she thought.

'Look, I . . .' she began. Christiana turned towards her, pulled her close, and kissed her on the mouth. The kiss was both softer and harder than she had expected. More insistent. Until she had witnessed Pilar's performance in the café, she had assumed that lesbian smooching would be a bit half-hearted. Now she knew better. Christiana's tongue was in her mouth, touching her own tongue, and yes, that feeling was familiar, a falling away, a loosening inside . . . oh dear. Yes. The sapphic thing might be quite possible after all, it might be quite . . . She felt thin fingers insinuate themselves under her shirt, close softly around her back. Her own hands twisting by her sides. Control. Control was what she needed. Control was melting away . . . Heaven had stopped receding now. Heaven was inside her head.

Netta was never sure what happened next, exactly, but she appeared to be pushing her way through the heaving, gyrating, sinuous bodies, among the wet torsos, the finely muscled backs. 'Jem? Pilar? – where are you?' She felt the panic rising inside her, saw again the puzzlingly erotic kiss among the fried eggs. A hand fell on her shoulder, and she screamed out loud – though no one could hear her over the pulsing disco beat. She turned to see a strangely familiar figure. Tall, and dark, and dressed entirely in black leather. She looked up at the gaunt Elizabethan face.

'Tom?'

'I knew it was you!' Tom's face gleamed. 'The girl from the party.' When he spoke, the music and mania seemed to fade away, and she found she could hear him perfectly clearly. 'Have your sh-shoulders warmed up yet?'

'Netta,' she said. 'My name's Netta. Yeah, they're fine now.'

'Good.' He smiled down at her.

She smiled back. 'Strange evening.'

'You mean then – or now?'

'Then. I'm still waiting to see how "now" pans out.'

'Was it strange?'

'The Greenham soap-box business, the arguing – the Black Tequila?'

'Hard to say. Most of my evenings are strange.'

'Why?'

'Don't know. Weird things seem to follow me round.'

'What are you doing here? I didn't know you were gay.' She bit her lip: stupid girl.

'What *do* you know about me? We only met for five minutes.'

'You're Flora's son, and you're a peace campaigner, and sometimes you live at Greenham Common.'

'Impressive. What's my star sign?'

'Emily told me. I'm not . . . nosy, or curious or anything . . .'

'I'm not gay.' He laughed. 'I'm not anything.'

'So what are you doing here? Did you come with some friends?' She looked behind him, half-expecting to see a bunch of like-minded Goths. But it was impossible to imagine him hanging out with any kind of gang. She looked up at him again. 'Just remembered something else about you. You never dance.'

'Correct.'

'So . . . straight, non-dancing peace man at mindless gay disco Mecca?'

'I'm here on a mission.'

'Of course,' she said. 'Silly me. What kind of mission?'

He handed her a flyer. It said: 'Men for Peace: Why Women Are Making War a Gender Issue, Act Now to Fight for the Right to Non-Violence.'

'Have you had many takers?'

'A few. But I got the impression they were hoping to have sex with me.'

'Maybe you should have taken them up on it. The good-looking ones.'

'I told you, I'm not gay. I wouldn't know where to start. I don't really do sex at all.'

'Why ever not?'

'Too confusing. Takes up too much time.'

She laughed, pleased to discover that he had a sense of humour.

He bent close to her. 'It's all shit, you know.'

'What's all shit?'

'The idea that all men are intrinsically violent.' Two stage-Nazis pushed past, dripping chains.

'Of course it's shit. Everyone knows it's shit. Everyone normal, I mean. You've got this whole Greenham thing out of proportion . . .'

'I'm not sure we know each other well enough for you to p-patronize me.'

'Patronize you? All I meant was . . .'

'One day, women will get bored with being in the right.'

'I was just . . .'

He had stopped smiling now. 'Perhaps you could hand some of these out for me. If you run across any non-violent men. And if you can . . . you know. If you can be b-bothered with a lost cause.'

'No problem,' she said. 'Where are you off to – going to start your own peace camp?' But when she looked up, he had vanished in a puff of dried ice.

'Here,' she said, handing a leaflet to what she thought was a tall, Teutonic male. When she looked closer, she realized it was Christiana. And with a jolt of alarm she saw that Christiana was beautiful, with stark cheekbones and clear green eyes. Not a cuddly look, but reminiscent of the Rutger Hauer replicant in *Blade Runner*.

'Don't be scared,' said Christiana. 'It's your first time, I can tell. We'll go somewhere quiet. Come.' She held her hand out again, and Netta found that her own hand was lifting to meet it, so that their fingertips just touched across the space between them.

'No!' Did she say it, or think it? This time she really

was running away. She pushed her way through the crowd without looking at anyone, or noticing anything: she had to go. Half-way to the door, she saw Jeremy, surrounded by an admiring crowd, talking and laughing, his teeth flashing. His eyes met hers, but she knew he couldn't see her, they were worlds apart now. There was the exit: she charged towards it, and then out into the dark, eerie quiet of the arches. Without stopping to assess any possible dangers, lurking rapists or other hazards, she ran even faster, wobbling in her high heels. She reached the street, ran to the far end and turned left into the Strand. Ran hard till she got as far as Trafalgar Square. She charged past the National Gallery, hurried across the road and hurled herself on to a night bus just as it began to pull away. On the top deck, she collapsed into a seat and tried to catch her breath. 'Jesus,' she said aloud, and stared out of the window as the bus circumnavigated the familiar square, chugging past the fat stone columns of St Martin-in-the-Fields. Then she closed her eyes and rested her hot forehead against the window. Her mind was full of dried ice, and the image of a tall, leather-clad man, appearing from nowhere and disappearing just as mysteriously.

10

The next morning she woke suddenly. Her mouth was furred and dry. She was fully dressed, and her spiked heels had torn the duvet cover. Groaning, she pulled out her earrings, which had left painful red welts in her ear lobes. Why was she still dressed? She hadn't even been that drunk. It was as if, as soon as she had got home, she had shut down automatically, unable to do anything but sleep. She groaned again, and rolled out of bed and on to the floor. The winter sun was pouring through her bedroom window: she hadn't even closed the curtains. A strange guilt nagged at her, and she tried to run the events of the evening through her mind, but all she could see was those Nordic, Rutger Hauer cheekbones. No one was going to give her any points for Operation Girl Dating. Like Emily, she was obviously addicted to misogynistic males, the endless vortex of waiting and every kind of gender-divided rubbish that kept women down. The guilt must be the Richard-and-Jane guilt, the guilt she would have to get used to.

Her stomach rumbled noisily. When had she last eaten? She couldn't remember. All she knew was that it had been a very bad idea to go out the night before. Apart from the fact that it had been – interesting – to bump into weird Tom. He seemed unlikely, she thought now, so different from men like Bryan or the awful rugby club.

So lean, and long and – intense. Believing in things didn't normally bode well for sex appeal, but he managed to get away with it. And he seemed detached, disconnected, above mundane concerns. But there was no time to think about this now. Mundane concerns were making their own demands. Today – for once – she had a lecture to attend. A famous feminist was coming to address the Communications students. Netta had never heard of her, but she had some funny Russian-sounding name. The word was that this woman was widely hated in America, due to pushing a new brand of feminism, and had been slow-hand-clapped in campuses from Alabama to Alaska. At one university – Netta thought it was UCLA but couldn't be sure – she had been pelted with rotten eggs. But she was not an easy person to intimidate, and had brought her own putrid eggs as a precaution. She had bombarded the audience with these, to dramatic effect, and had been briefly arrested, but released to appear on the Johnny Carson show, where she traded insults with Joan Rivers. Somehow, this appealed to Netta. She tottered out on to the landing, running her fingers through her cropped hair. What was that woman's name again? Dada Tchaikovsky? Lulu Bronovsky? Her mind was a mess of cluttered and misremembered information. The flat was in a similar state. Clothes were littered everywhere. Pilar's trademark shocking-pink bra was draped across the chest of drawers, so the cups stuck out like fake breasts. Her black and pink lace knickers had been carefully arranged over a half-open drawer, so that the overall effect was of some surreal bikini, hanging in mid-air. Then, she heard the front doorbell ring, and a sudden intuition made her gather Pilar's clothes up and stuff them out of sight before rushing to the top of the stairs. Emily – still in her dressing gown – was opening the door to a tall, floppy-haired man wearing a tweed jacket and baggy trousers.

'*Mon chéri!*' she said, flicking her hair into his face. 'How lovely to see you!' She kissed him ebulliently on both cheeks.

'Emily, perfectly lovely,' he said in an abstracted, Sloane voice. 'Just popped in to see Pilar.' He peered up the stairs and caught sight of Netta.

'Hello there,' he said. 'Are you the new girl?' He was staring her up and down, taking in the hooker's boots and the expanse of thigh.

'Sort of,' said Netta, concentrating on standing upright in her ridiculous heels.

'I'm Roops,' said the man, with an ironic smile. 'You know, Pilar's intended.'

'Gosh,' said Netta, copying Pilar's Celia Johnson voice, 'What a tremendous surprise!' She hobbled down the stairs, smiling till her face hurt. 'Sorry about the . . .' She looked down at her outfit. 'Late night.'

'Is she in? It's all a bit unannounced, I know. Just dashed down to see my cousin at Bedford College – she's had a bit of a funny turn. Highly strung, you see.' He stepped backwards as she approached, as if fearing she might tear his clothes off.

'Well, I'm not entirely sure . . .' said Netta, trying to make her mind work more quickly. If Pilar's underwear was on the landing, then logically Pilar must be on the premises. But had she come back alone, or brought a Girl

Date with her? She decided not to risk it. 'Actually, no . . . she's . . . she just nipped out.'

'Perhaps I'll just have a quick cup of tea, if that's not too much of an imposition?' said Roops, trying to side-step Netta so that he could get to the stairs. 'Wait for her till she gets back . . .' At that moment a piercing cry, unmistakably Pilar's, came from the bathroom. This was followed by snorts of laughter, also unmistakably Pilar's. Rupert, who had been scratching his ear in a nervily posh-ness oblige sort of way, looked up in consternation. Netta rushed up to her bedroom, scrawled: 'Roops alert!' on a piece of paper, thrust it under the bathroom door, then dashed down the stairs again.

'Hi, hi . . . tea would be fine, except we've run out of milk – Emily, you don't have any milk, by any chance?'

Emily was doing a lot of hair-tossing. 'I don't drink milk,' she said. 'I've got some crème de menthe, though. Looks like you've been up all night, so – you could just carry on where you left off. Would you like some crème de menthe, Roops? It's very good for the creativity, so I'm told. Colette used to drink it in bed, when she was pencilling away at her œuvre.'

'Did you hear that peculiar noise?' asked Rupert. 'Seemed to be coming from your bathroom. Sounded awfully like Pilar.'

'Yes,' said Netta, mind now empty of all relationship-saving devices. 'As a matter of fact, I think she must be in after all. I just got up, and kind of assumed she must be out. Sorry about that. I mean, do come up. I'm sure she'll be out of the bath in a minute.' Upstairs, she heard a door open, and the sound of running feet.

Rupert gave her an angry look. 'You're actually standing in my way,' he said. 'Why did she make that extraordinary sound? Is there something going on? Has she got a man up there?'

'No, definitely not, absolutely not,' said Netta, relieved that she could at least be honest about something. 'Perhaps we could borrow some crème de menthe, Emily? Just in case – and – maybe you'd like to come up too? We could have a little party?'

Rupert was staring at her as if she was mad. Emily writhed again. 'I can't leave the phone,' she said. 'Bryan could ring any minute.' But she disappeared and returned a moment later with a half-empty bottle.

By the time they reached the living room, Pilar was sitting at the table, reading *Daniel Deronda*, wearing a pleated navy skirt, a flouncy Lady Di blouse and a velvet hairband. When she saw Rupert, she leaped from her seat and threw her arms around him. 'Darling!' she said. 'Whatever are you doing here?'

Feeling faint with tension, Netta looked at her watch. The lecture started in just under an hour – she had no time to lose if she was going to get to the refectory in time for the coffee and ham roll she desperately needed. No time to change. But where was her bag? She ran to her bedroom.

'Good morning,' said a voice, cool as an ice-strewn fjord. 'Coincidence, don't you think? We must be fated to meet again.' Christiana was sitting naked in her bed, paging through a copy of *Blitz*. Her neat white breasts were almost dwarfed by huge nipples. 'By the way, I'm your lover, not Pilar's. In case there is any doubt,' said Christiana.

Netta wondered how she could be so stern with her nipples pointing over the bedclothes like mini hand-grenades. 'Hi,' she said, picking up her bag with hands that were only shaking very slightly. 'In that case, I'd better thank you for a lovely evening. And . . . what an interesting time we had in the bath! Doing whatever it was. Afraid I have to go now, though. Lecture. Perhaps we can catch up later on.'

Christiana was smiling at her in a manner Netta didn't much like. 'It was good to meet you,' she said. 'And Pilar, your beautiful friend.'

'She's engaged, by the way,' said Netta.

'Yes,' said Christiana. She threw the duvet to one side, and started to dress: her clothes had been tossed on to the floor by the bed. Pilar certainly was a speedy operator. 'I could see it was something like this. Waiting to be owned by a man. A slave ring, to say who is going to take you over. Not such a good thing.'

'Slave ring? That's a bit heavy, isn't it?'

'How could you ever understand? A person who is too frightened to follow her own desire?'

'It's not like that,' said Netta, aware of the note of defensiveness in her voice. 'I get into enough trouble dealing with one sex. Life would be even more complicated if I was sleeping with the wrong women, as well as the wrong men! It's not a black and white issue.'

Christiana was dressed now, and stalked to the front door. Netta followed, and neither of them looked back at the courting couple, who were giggling together on the same chair. 'It doesn't look black and white to me, either,' said Christiana, when they reached the bottom of the stairs. 'It looks only black. You're all lying, and you know it.'

The New Cross train was late arriving at Blackheath station, and when it finally appeared Netta flung open one of the doors, thoughts of giant nipples and rotten eggs filling her mind. Her progress was impeded by her boots, which obliged her to take tiny geisha steps. As she entered the carriage, she almost fell over a tiny woman sitting in a seat by the door, her short legs sticking out at an angle. She was writing something in a notebook. Netta noticed that her heels were nearly as high as her own, and her tiny body was swathed in an expensive fur-trimmed coat.

'Sorry,' she said, righting herself. 'I didn't see you there.'

'No, well, this is a lousy stupid carriage,' said the woman, hardly looking up. 'Nine million-year-old train stock you have here, covered in vomit and shit and I don't know what. Don't put that in their tight-ass Dickensian guide books, do they? Nice boots.'

'Thanks,' said Netta, sitting down opposite her. The woman wrote for a while, and Netta sneaked another look at her, struck by her harsh New York accent. She was an odd-looking person, with enormous, red-framed glasses and a small, over-made-up face. But her most distinguishing feature was her wiggishly symmetrical bob, which glinted in the winter light.

'I have a question to ask you,' said the woman after a while.

'What sort of question is it?' said Netta. 'I'm afraid I don't know much.'

'It concerns popular culture.'

'That's good. As long as it's nothing to do with feminism.'

The woman gave her a pale, beady look. 'Would you not consider yourself to be a feminist?'

'Not in the current climate, no,' said Netta.

'Why not?'

'It's a bit like being a Born Again Christian. You have to sort of . . . join. You can't just think something. It needs to be part of a proper systematic way of looking at the world.'

'What kind of systematic way of looking at the world?'

'I don't even know. I'm on the outside.'

'Have you never thought of trying to find out? By reading a book, perhaps?'

'Yes – of course! But I keep falling asleep. During the small print.'

The woman laughed. 'The small print. Very nice. Yes.' But her smile was thin. 'My question has to do with *Charlie's Angels*. You ever see that show?'

'Oh yes. Everyone did.'

'Question is – who replaced Farrah Fawcett-Majors when she left to fail to make it big in Hollywood movies? I'm thinking Shelley Hack, but my mind is playing me tricks lately. Somehow, that doesn't feel right to me.'

'It was Cheryl Ladd,' said Netta immediately. 'I actually preferred her to Farrah Fawcett. Never did go for that scary Jaws smile.'

'So why I am thinking Shelley Hack?'

'She was in the last series they ever did. She was meant to be some kind of upmarket Harvard person. But no one liked her.'

'Alas, poor Shelley,' said the woman, writing this down. 'The masses can't cope with brains and beauty in the same package.' She waved her hand at Netta. 'Thanks for that. Go to the top of the class.'

The woman didn't speak again till they were drawing into New Cross station. She closed her notebook and thrust it into her bag. 'Well, our meeting has been most instructive. You getting off here too?'

Netta nodded. 'I'm going to see some crazy Russian feminist who throws rotten eggs.'

A wry vermilion smile. 'So that's all you know about her?'

'Pretty much.'

'Hell, who *gives* a shit? You Brits are a fucking inward-looking bunch of mediocrities, is what I find,' said the woman, marching away so rapidly that she had disappeared by the time Netta had paid in cash for the ticket she had failed to buy at Blackheath.

Netta munched her roll, sitting at a rather grubby table that had recently been vacated by a bunch of Art bastards, including Damian, the drunk one. She looked at her essay, which she was finally handing in. She had finished it, sort of, but it had turned into a peculiar rant, which she did not think would pass muster as a piece of academic study. But it was now so late that she supposed she ought to give it in. Staring at the words, she wondered if they made any sense.

'Working hard, are we?' said a complacent voice. She looked up. Belinda the Butcher's Daughter was lowering a bacon sandwich on to the table in front of her.

'This course is a bloody nightmare!'

'Don't say that.' Belinda took a big bite of sandwich. 'Why not?'

'I've just transferred from Art and PE.'

Netta nibbled at her own sandwich, to stop herself from shrieking with horror. Belinda was the sort of person she had consigned to a particular type of stupidity – a PE level of stupidity – and now here she was on the same course. While Communications wasn't overloaded with boffins, exactly, there was a certain hard-and-sharpness among the students, a streetwise cynicism they hoped might serve them well in future newsrooms. There was no one like Belinda.

'Did they just . . . let you switch? No . . . IQ test, or anything?'

'They were fine about it,' said Belinda. 'Anyway, that's no problem for me. I've been in Mensa, you know . . .' She chewed for a while. 'They told me a lot of people have dropped out.'

'Really?' Netta hoped the course tutors didn't think that she was one of them. Her attendance had become more sporadic since moving into the flat. She looked at her essay, her head aching.

'It was Bryan who got me on to this,' said Belinda. 'After the band broke up. Which was tragic, of course. But he told me I had a talent for it.'

'Talent for what?'

'Communication. He said I should go far.'

'I'm sure you will,' said Netta. 'In some direction or other.'

'Anyway, I expect you're looking forward to this big

lecture this morning.' Belinda spilled the contents of her bag on to the refectory table. She had purchased themed stationery in honour of her reinvention as a Communications person. Everything matched – her notebooks, loose-leaf files, even ballpoint pens. Everything was pink, and covered with shiny scarlet hearts. 'It's the sort of area that we women can make the most of,' she said. 'Getting information, you know. Noticing what's going on. My dad always says to me – feminine intuition, that's what makes the world go round. You don't need that in an abattoir.'

'No – what do you need? Electronic prods to stick up a pig's arse?' Bryan had arrived and was making himself comfortable in the empty seat next to Belinda.

'I was just singing your praises,' said Belinda. 'Mr Communication himself.'

'English and Drama, darling, that's my special field,' he said. 'Journalism is just a craft skill.'

'So versatile!'

'I heard them killing pigs in a farm once,' said Netta, bored and irritated by Belinda's devotion. 'It was the worst thing ever. The screaming sounded human. They knew they were about to die.'

'It's the natural way,' said Belinda.

'Don't expect old DeeDee Chapinsky is a veggie,' said Bryan. 'Just not that sort of girl.'

'DeeDee who?'

'The lady who's come to talk to us today,' said Belinda. 'Miss DeeDee Chapinsky is the New Feminism. She's very, very big.' Belinda wrote her name in curly-wurly piggy lettering at the top of the first page of her heart-infested notebook. Netta felt more uncomfortable still.

She got out her own notebook and wrote spikily: 'DeeDee Chapinsky – The New Feminism – Key Points'.

'Funny her being Russian,' she said.

'Russian? Christ, Netta, she's a Yank,' said Bryan. 'Even I know that. Might even do a little profile of the great woman for *Metropolitan Student*. Are you sure your finger is one hundred per cent on the button?'

Netta frowned. 'Is she from New York, by any chance?' She felt so flummoxed as they hurried off to hear Miss Chapinsky that she left her essay lying on the table.

The lecture hall was full. Netta had only been to a few lectures so far, and they had been sparsely attended. This was probably because of their titles: 'Seminality in the Age of Pravda', 'Self-censorship versus Censoriousness in the Global Village' and 'Why Subjugation Matrices Stalk the Newsroom'. Only the most ardent and ambitious students, screwed up over their notes in knee-length sweaters, had turned up for these. Today, this hardcore group had been joined by all sorts of people. Most of them were women. There were even a few dancers and Welsh virgins, sitting at the back.

Netta followed Bryan and Belinda along a row of seats half-way up the hall, where there were still a few spaces, and sat down. The platform below her seemed to be free of eminent feminists, Russian or otherwise. She could only see Effie Spink, her demented tutor, sitting alone at the long desk, picking threads out of her bright orange cardie and rocking to and fro very gently. Netta marvelled again at her uncompromising thinness: she was a woman who appeared to be constructed entirely from anxiety and bone.

Gradually, the hall filled up and the buzz of voices grew. Effie Spink got up, looking at her watch, and the voices quietened.

'This is a very important event,' she said in her reedy, classless voice. 'This is the first time that we've had the pleasure of hearing from one of America's new wave of feminists. Of course, you will all know her by reputation – co-founder of *Herself* magazine, star columnist of *The New Yorkess*, and the author of a truly seminal volume of short stories: *Lipsmacking Lolitas*. These are just a few of her quite astonishing achievements. Please join me in welcoming . . . DeeDee Chapinsky.' This was followed by some polite clapping. It took Netta a moment to realize that Effie wasn't alone on the platform after all. The tiny woman she had met on the train had been sitting there all the time, her head so low down that she had been entirely hidden from view by the desk. Now, as she crossed over to the lectern, Netta saw that her bulbous, truncated body seemed likely to be overbalanced by her large breasts, which were housed in a hideous leopard-skin jacket. And her high heels forced her stocky, muscular legs into a Barbie-doll parody of sexiness.

When she reached the lectern, it towered over her, and she peered up suspiciously, then shrugged and marched round to stand in front of it, arms folded, legs slightly apart. She had no notes, but stared at the students with a casual air of aggression. 'Darn nuisance,' she said. 'The whole world is designed for people who are too long in the limb, people who can stand behind a fucking lectern and rejoice in mindless complacency about the simple fact that they are over five feet tall. These people know nothing, I'm telling you. Being this height has given me all the insight I need. I've stared up too many nondescript nostrils to let anyone look down their nose at me. I'm a winner – it's a life choice.' She paused, and stared belligerently around the room. 'Of course, this is not the prevailing wisdom, which would be that not only am I subjugated because of my inch-impairment, I'm also the victim of the curse of femininity! What the hell's a girl to do?' The students stared at her, immobilized, biros suspended in mid-air. Netta stared too. 'I'll tell you what,' said DeeDee. 'A girl should get real! She should embrace her female status. Not assume – whoopee! Here I go! A cute little victim! How can I get society to accommodate me? What special favours shall I demand, in my cute little assertive voice, piping up for positive discrimination, a helping hand up the ladder of oh-so-unequal opportunity? Go for it, girls. You British have a role model to be proud of – your own Margaret Thatcher, who achieved everything in a man's world, on a man's terms . . .' The audience was silent, apparently numb with shock, until the door at the bottom of the lecture theatre suddenly burst open and two women trooped in. One was tiny and pale, with cropped black hair. She was carrying a banner which read: 'DOWN WITH DEEDEE'. The other one was Melanie.

DeeDee Chapinsky unfolded her arms. 'Right,' she said. 'Let's get one thing straight. If women are losing out in life, they need to fix it. No question. The point is – and I am a big academic, let me tell you, not just a lowly hack, points are my forte – the point is, how should women fix it? Are the methods they are so far utilizing sufficiently effective? Which brings us neatly to the reason you are all sitting here in front of me, with your bright little passive faces, waiting for me to tell you what to think. The media – the newspapers, television, radio – this is where women can start to forge a new identity. But is the influence of women in the media being used for the good? I don't think so. Half-baked half-wits aren't going to change things for the better. I want to save feminism from the feminists. Once upon a time, we had a feminism to be proud of: Amelia Earhart, Martha Gelhorn, Edith Cavell. These were not women who whined about rights! These were women who took life by the throat and wrestled it to the ground! Did they blame other people for their problems? Did they mention the patriarchy? I think not!'

She turned and marched to the desk, and flicked the switch of an overhead projector. A picture of a voluptuous woman in a black bra and suspenders flashed on the screen behind her.

'What's wrong with that image?' she asked.

'Offensive to women!' shouted Mel.

DeeDee Chapinsky took no notice of this. Another image flashed up, this time of a Greenham woman in a woolly hat. 'This image offends me,' she said. 'Why? Because it is an ugly image. It makes women look stupid and humourless and dowdy. Why do we have this problem with female beauty? Why can't we celebrate it, like the Japanese or the French? What are we afraid of? Why are we so prudish and puritanical?' The cropped woman – who Netta assumed must be Jude – started to make a peculiar ululating sound. Melanie, like a barbershop harmonist, chimed in with a series of unearthly wails.

DeeDee Chapinsky was not put out in the least. 'These are not questions I want you to answer. They are rhetorical, in that, so to speak, they are part of my rhetoric.'

'Dodgy! Dodgy!' shouted Mel. 'Female beauty is a capitalist commodity! Shame on you!'

'Outlining the orifice subjugates us to men!' cried Jude.

DeeDee raised one eyebrow. 'Ambiguity lies at the heart of all gender issues,' she said. 'Sexual desire is a contradiction in itself. Our spirit does not observe the rigid categorization of oppressor and victim. So – I say – who needs to come out as gay? If you come out as gay, you have to suppress your attraction to the opposite sex. I like my apartment to be tidy – I like to see clear surfaces, empty floors, I like peace and harmony and the soothing colour beige. Spill a glass of red wine on my cream carpet and I swear I will have you dead. But do I want this same pared-down lack of contradiction in my sex life? No, sir, I do not. Feminists should sleep with each other, for sure. Life is short. But they shouldn't close the door on men, either. If you want someone, then welcome them into your bed. It all adds to the gaiety of nations.'

'The personal is political!' shouted Jude.

'Sleep with men and you're sleeping with the enemy!' came Mel's voice.

DeeDee crossed the stage and glared down at them. 'Yup, it's the Stalinist sisterhood,' she said. 'But you know what I say to you? Welcome to the goddam party. Ladies, please feel free to disagree with me. Maybe I am bullshitting you. Maybe the world is harsh and cruel if you are born with a vagina. But hey! Women are tough. We can take it.'

Neither Mel nor Jude seemed to welcome the idea of an intellectual free-for-all. The ululating and wailing grew louder and louder as DeeDee Chapinsky covered more or less everything: love, sex, rape, men, women, housework, beauty, money, success and farting during intercourse. She ended with a great flourish: 'What I say to you is this. Life is like *Charlie's Angels*. Some of us are Farrah Fawcett. We got the looks. We get the breaks. No problem. Some of us are Cheryl Ladd – we do a good job, we get success, but it's never going to be the big time. But none of that is a charter for whining, kvetching loser-talk. Victims? Kiss my ass. If girls are powerful – then go for it.'

She beamed around the room malevolently. There was a second's silence. Mel and Jude seemed to be struck dumb. Bryan, grinning, dashed down the steps two at a time, clutching his Instamatic camera. Netta leaped to her feet and started to clap. DeeDee, looking up, recognized her and began to laugh. 'And here she is! Please, everyone, look behind you at the modern face of the women's movement! Observe the shameless use of exposed thigh, the celebratory killer boots, the ironically shaved head that still says – I am all woman! Ladies and gentleman – long live the New Feminism!' The applause gradually gathered momentum: enthusiastic, but masking an air of English bafflement. Netta, blushing, sat down and tried to pull her skirt over her knickers. But she had already caught Melanie's furious gaze.

11

'Friend of yours, is she?' asked Bryan, who was regarding Mel with amusement, his camera still slung around his neck. 'You want to be more careful who you hang out with, darling.'

'Bugger off. What do you know about female friendship?'

This seemed to amuse Bryan a good deal. 'Great, brilliant, got to get these photos developed,' he said, dashing away.

The hall emptied quickly – DeeDee Chapinsky disappeared instantly, as if the end of her speech had entirely exhausted her interest in the place. But Mel and her scary-looking friend loitered at the front, whispering to each other and rolling cigarettes. Netta stood up, wobbled to the end of her row of seats, and made her way cautiously down the steps. Mel licked her Rizla paper and smoothed it down with her square, ringed fingers, watching her approach.

'What an outfit,' she said finally. 'Who did you come as? Hot Gossip?'

'I wore this to Heaven last night,' said Netta, flushing. 'It was Operation Girl Dating. It's just a matter of context.'

'Really?' Mel was unsmiling. 'Operation Girl Bloody Dating indeed! There's more to life than partying. From where I'm standing, it all looks totally – desperate.'

'Desperate?'

'Fiddling while Rome burns. It's like nobody wants to face up to what's going on.'

'You mean – the arms race?'

'Gordon Bennett – the race is over! The war could start any day. Men like Reagan don't give a shit about ordinary people. Women have to do something – and so what do you do? Put on those bloody stupid boots, and prance about like Penelope Pitstop. It's beyond belief. Isn't it, Jude?'

Netta noticed Mel's friend looking at her crotch, and tried to pull her skirt down. 'I just told you – the outfit was for a laugh,' she said. 'It was Pilar's idea in any case. Then I overslept – and so here I am.'

'If you're comfortable with being a sex object, then it's your decision,' said Jude. Her voice was disconcertingly quiet – like a child's whisper. The effect was not so much conspiratorial as secretive, as if what she had to say was not for the ears of the unworthy.

Netta's flush of embarrassment had changed to one of annoyance. 'Yeah, well, thanks a lot,' she said. 'Nice to meet you at last, Jude. I've heard all about you.'

'I've told Pilar and Netta what good friends we are,' said Mel, sounding a little nervous, Netta thought.

'It was very touching,' said Netta. 'Not just good friends, either. *Best* friends.'

'Mel is my soulmate,' said Jude. Or that's what Netta thought she said. She resisted the temptation to move closer, feeling that that would mean she was being manipulated. Perhaps it was time to go. 'Well – see you, Mel,' she said.

'See you.' But there was a pained look on Mel's face. As Netta turned away, she said suddenly: 'Say hello to Pilar for me!'

'You could always say it yourself. Come round before you go back. Or phone her. She misses you, you know.'

Mel shrugged. 'She doesn't understand what's going on.'

'You haven't given her a chance.'

'She's not interested.'

'How do you know that?'

'She just . . . doesn't see things the way I do.'

'Well, try talking to her about it.'

'I *have* tried. One day soon, there won't be any kind of world to live in. And that'll be because women abdicated all responsibility, and decided to let men run the whole show.'

'That's *bullshit*, it's *bollocks*, it's just the most simplistic load of *crap* I ever . . .'

Jude turned to look at Netta, and said, in her coded whisper, 'Why don't you come with us?'

'With you where?'

'To Greenham.'

'But I've got . . .' Netta wasn't sure if she wanted to say 'really high boots on' or 'an essay to write'. The essay was about Greenham, of course. She stared from one face to the other. 'I've . . . why would I go to Greenham?'

'Change your life,' said Jude. 'It's Embrace the Base day today.'

'Embrace the what?'

'Base. Thousands of women linking arms around the fence. Nine miles long, it is. So there'll be nine miles of women.'

'Like – a demonstration? People getting arrested?'

'A peaceful celebration,' said Jude. 'Woman-power.'

'Totally non-violent. You're more likely to get beaten up on Deptford Broadway than you are to get hurt at Greenham today. Unless you feel like lying down in front of a tank, that is –' added Mel.

'No, I really don't.' Netta thought for a moment, suddenly struck by the drama of the idea. The fear of nuclear war was something she normally pushed to the back of her mind. She should face up to it. She should face up to a lot of things. And if she went, she might be in a better position to help Pilar see things from Mel's point of view. She hated the aura of gloom that descended on Pilar when the partying stopped, the feeling that no one could compensate for Mel's defection. 'Well, I suppose . . .'

'See how the other half lives,' said Mel, lighting up airily, though smoking was strictly forbidden in the lecture hall. 'The half that gives a shit.'

How this led to her climbing into the back of a scruffy green Dormobile (called Vera after Vera Brittain) Netta couldn't quite remember afterwards. Perhaps she was still drunk from the night before. But the fact was that as soon as she had agreed to go with them – as an inappropriately dressed day-tripper – the mood changed. They were in the same gang. Jude did not exactly say anything, but exuded friendlier vibes, and handed round chocolate and even Kendal mint cake, which struck Netta as a very professional touch. Conversation wasn't necessary, anyway. They sang all the way to Greenham. Netta didn't know the words, but they were fairly basic and easy to learn, and usually sung to familiar, nursery rhyme tunes or Beatles melodies. Her favourite was this one, to the tune of 'Get By with a Little Help from My Friends':

'What would you do if I closed down your base?
Would you fire silver bullets at me?
Lend me an ear and I'll sing you a song
And you'll walk out and link arms with me.
Oh, I'll ban Cruise with a little help from my friends
I'll do more with a little help from my friends
I'll stop war with a little help from my friends.'

She wondered what Jane would have made of their choral efforts. *Rigoletto* it was not. This accumulation of sound made Netta slightly hysterical and pink in the face: she wound the window down and roared at passers-by. 'I am like a MOUNTAIN ...' she yelled at a stodgy-looking traffic warden, and 'I go on ... and on ... and ON ...' as they raced past a bus stop in the outer suburbs beyond Wimbledon.

By the time they got closer to Greenham it was early afternoon. Hills rolled away on all sides, dotted here and there with huddled farm buildings and morose cows. Then they turned into a narrow side road and drove through tranquil woods. Netta was surprised at this vision of Olde Englande – she had imagined a bleak and cheerless land-scape. She looked upwards and saw a filigree of twigs and branches reaching up to the sky. The anorexic white limbs of the silver birches reminded her of naked human bodies.

'We'll park here,' said Mel, pulling off the road abruptly.

They got out into the slicing air. Fortunately, Netta had found an old anorak in the back of the van, and a long knitted scarf, like the one that Tom Baker used to wear in *Doctor Who*. But she had no gloves, and had to stick with her precarious boots. There was no sign of an army base. It looked like a nice spot for a picnic, if the weather had been warmer.

'Where are they, then?' she asked Mel, who had disappeared inside an enormous tweed coat.

'Where are what? The women?'

'The nuclear missiles.'

Mel looked serious. 'Wait and see.' She nodded to Jude and they started walking along a muddy path through the trees. Netta followed, suddenly feeling apprehensive. Her heels pronged deep into the mud, and she had to force them to the surface with each step, so her progress was slow.

After a while, Mel stopped and pointed. 'That's it,' she said. 'That's the old Common. People used to graze sheep there.'

Netta saw that beyond the trees wire mesh separated them from a flat area of grass, with a cluster of buildings and humped shapes at the centre, enclosed by yet another, inner fence.

'Are those the missiles in the middle?'

'Silos,' whispered Jude. 'The missiles are inside. Each of those warheads is a hundred times more powerful than the bomb they dropped on Hiroshima.'

'Jesus.' Netta stared at the high barbed-wire fence, the stout concrete pillars, the wire mesh stretched between them, and the spiked coils of barbed wire which wriggled along the top. There were even watchtowers – like the perimeter of a concentration camp. It looked evil. In the supermarket, or the pub, it was impossible to believe that there could be such a thing as a nuclear attack. Normality was too powerful. But this was a different world. She could see some khaki soldiers in the distance, holding weapons. She wanted to call their bluff. This can't be real. You're only pretending to be soldiers; we're only pretending to be scared. At the same time, the fear coiled around her like barbed wire itself. This was it, then. These weapons pointed at cities in the Soviet Union; and Soviet weapons pointed at them. It was like a poker game, with hidden faces.

Jude stood up. 'Come on,' she said, 'let's go.'

They walked until they reached a high double gate in the fence, closed across a tarmac road that led to the silos in the centre, which were sealed off by a second inner fence. Netta looked around her in surprise. She hadn't expected to see so many women – or that they would look like this. There seemed to be hundreds of them. Some seemed barely old enough to be allowed out on their own, with their fresh faces and pigtails. Others looked like grandmothers, faces hidden behind their twinkling old-lady spectacles, smiles denture-perfect as they linked arms. And it wasn't just that they varied in age – women of every sort were here: cheery, scrubbed matrons who looked like vicars' wives, frilly secretarial types in flattering pastels, wild hippies with leaves in their hair. Fierce lesbians – with shaven heads like Netta's – were in the minority. Soldiers and police stood around inside, looking studiedly nonchalant, as if they hadn't happened to notice that there were so many women staring in at them, shouting, singing, eating and generally creating noise and chaos. Netta realized that the mental image she had formed was of a motley crew of misfits and man-haters, huddling around their cauldrons. But now she was here, it looked more like a tribal feastday. Everywhere she looked, she saw bright hair, flushed cheeks, vivid colours, flowers, silly earrings and bizarre hats: deer stalkers, pixie bonnets, hand-knitted berets, Inca caps with ear-pieces, and ribbon-decked trilbies. And she needn't have worried about looking stupid in her porn-queen heels, either. One woman was wearing a ballgown and tiara, with a tartan rug over her shoulders for warmth. What would the *Daily Chronicle* have to say about that? If she had been a perfect student, she would have made some notes. As it was, she just gawped at the scene, forgetting herself completely for the first time since the Richard Shag.

'It's amazing!' she said to Mel.

'See?' said Mel. 'What did I tell you? And there were you, thinking that we were dragging you along to a bloody funeral. Come and look at the fence.' They scrambled up a muddy slope. The fence was barely visible, partly because so many women were standing in front of it, and partly because it had been turned into a giant, living tapestry. An array of strange artefacts and bizarre symbols of their lives had been woven into the wire mesh. Diaries, recipes, photographs of children, balloons, rag dolls, even an aubergine, which had been lashed to the fence with pink ribbon. 'We could eat that later,' said Mel, showing her old-hand credentials. Then, with a virtuous expression, she sellotaped a copy of the UN Universal Declaration of Human Rights to the wire.

Netta read the words, which she recognized from the kitchen fridge at Dartmouth Villa:

> Women are half the world's people
> who do two-thirds of the world's work.
> They earn one-tenth of the world's income
> and own one-hundredth of the world's property.

'Very political,' she said, not sure whether to be annoyed or impressed by rad-femme awareness and forward planning.

'What are you going to add?' asked Mel, tearing sello-tape with her teeth.

'No bloody idea. I haven't got anything significant with me . . .' She searched through her bag and found an empty packet of Silk Cut. That would do. On it she scrawled:

> I'll die my own way, and in my own time, thanks all the same.
> Love Netta

'How touching.' But Mel linked arms with her. Netta was a proper Greenham person now: she had made the grade. 'No idea where Jude has buggered off to,' said Mel. 'Let us proceed around the perimeter.'

Nearly all the women there were doing the same thing. They walked very, very slowly, partly because of Netta's heels, and partly because the path was solid with womankind. Netta kept her eyes on the mysterious area beyond the wire. Police cars crawled by, soldiers marched in twos and threes, flags fluttered in the cold breeze. It was normal life in an abnormal world. 'Like *Alice Through the Looking Glass*,' she said to Mel. But Mel, who was not widely read, did not know what she meant. On their side of the fence, all was hubbub and laughter and chat. Women were everywhere, part of a continuous human wall surrounding the base. All walked hand in hand or with their arms wrapped round each other, singing and talking and calling out to the soldiers, 'Come on, why don't you join us?' 'Which side are you on, the side of life, or the side of death?' Some soldiers looked embarrassed, some professional and detached. One smiled at Netta in what she couldn't help feeling was a flighty manner. He was on the side of life, presumably. After a while, by some invisible signal, all the women stopped walking and turned towards the fence. Mel produced two shining objects from her pocket and handed one to Netta: it was a handbag mirror.

'Turn it towards the base!' said Mel. 'So they can see their own madness!' Netta realized her looking-glass idea had been more accurate than she had supposed. All the women flashed their mirrors at the wire fence, the woven offerings, the soldiers and the empty space beyond. And a great, weird sound went up from all around them, a sound like women keening from the beginning of the world. Netta thought she was laughing with delight as she yelled her own protest, but she suddenly realized that tears were pouring down her cheeks. Real tears, this time, not Frascati ones. She felt as if she was facing down death.

12

After she had been keening for a few moments, Netta became aware that somebody was tapping her on the shoulder. She was so carried away with her banshee howling and her aural journey back into the primeval mists of time that it took her a second to register what this sensation was. Tap. Tap. There it was again. Not quite hard enough to be painful, but almost. Tap. Tap. *Tap*. She turned, unwillingly. It took her a moment to focus, after staring at the bright lights of the base, which had dazzled her in the gathering afternoon gloom. Eventually, she realized she was looking at the perfectly made-up face of a middle-aged woman wearing a dashing fur hat. The perfectly made-up woman was holding hands with a young girl, who looked about ten. The girl was chubby and pink-cheeked, and her cerise ski jacket and sugar-pink trousers seemed to have been chosen to tone with her face.

'Erm, sorry – am I standing in the way or something?' enquired Netta, puzzled. 'Is there – can I help you . . . ?'

'I doubt it very much,' said the woman. 'I doubt if anyone here can help themselves, never mind any other member of the human race.'

Mel had turned round too now, and was staring at the woman, looking even more baffled than Netta felt. 'We can get out of the way if you want to see the soldiers,' she said. 'It's quite a sight. Is this your first time at Greenham?'

'I wouldn't say that, exactly,' said the woman. 'My name is Audrey Orton-Avery. You might have heard of me. I make regular appearances in the press. I live just across the road, over there, at Chiverton Chase. And this is my daughter, Abigail.'

'Hello, Abigail,' said Netta.

'Hello,' said Abigail shyly. 'I'm in favour of mutually assured destruction.'

Mel laughed, slightly hysterically, Netta thought. 'Yeah, MAD – I'm looking forward to it myself,' she said. 'I've laid in a few bottles of gin so I can go out well and truly sozzled.'

'You're not in favour of it *happening*, Abigail darling, you are just confident that it's an effective and safe deterrent,' said Audrey Orton-Avery.

'That's right,' said Abigail. She was not a pretty child. Her features were set close together, leaving a lot of space around the edges of her face.

'Well, if you're that relaxed about it, you're very lucky,' said Mel. 'There's no need for you to stand out here in the freezing cold, is there? With us unilateral loonies. You can go back inside your nice big house and have a cup of tea.'

'Don't patronize me, please,' said Audrey Orton-Avery. 'We multi-lateralists enjoy freedom of speech just as you do – in fact, we appreciate the right that you seem to want to hand over to Soviet control. Do you know *nothing* about the atrocities of the Soviet Union? Or is that a silly question? I know some of the ladies here can barely read and write.' She pushed between the two of them and began tearing peace symbols down from the fence, starting with a photograph of Winnie Mandela.

'I regard your behaviour as an act of violence,' said Mel.

'Poppycock,' said Audrey Orton-Avery. 'What utter rot. Violence is what happens when the KGB comes knocking on your door. Peace is what we had here, in the Home Counties, before you came along and polluted the landscape.'

The women all around began to mutter among themselves. 'Shame,' said someone. Then came an emphatic voice that Netta recognized. 'My dear lady,' it said. 'My dear lady, no one would question the need for free speech! I am myself a veteran of every key free-speech rally in living memory.' The crowd parted and an imposing figure appeared. It was Flora, in full Boudicca mode, complete with scarlet cloak.

'I am not here to be "dear ladied" by anyone,' said Audrey. 'I am here to show my daughter that this is not how proper women behave. You are a blot on the landscape, and a danger to society.' Now a ring of women had formed around them. There were more cries of 'Shame on you!' and 'Women are powerful!' Netta glanced nervously around her. The lights of the base cast sickly shadows over Flora, Audrey and her child. The faces of Mel and Jude – who had silently appeared at Netta's side – were in shadow. The harsh arc lights made the evening sky seem darker. Her feet were hurting – she wondered what her toes would look like when they finally emerged, probably twisted tightly together like the bound feet of some poor oppressed Japanese woman. Perhaps she would be maimed for life, for the cause of beauty if not for Greenham. But her brain was hurting even more. The crowd of women was beginning to shout louder: 'How can you *say* that? How can you *believe* that, when you're a mother yourself?' And Audrey, implacable, stared them down. Netta thought of the aristocrats being carted off to the guillotine in their tumbrils.

Whether Flora was a tricoteuse or a latter-day Marie Antoinette it was hard to say. Her voice now carried effortlessly over those of the rest of the crowd: 'I can't help feeling that this would make an excellent television debate.'

'Oh, for fuck's sake,' came Mel's voice, equally strident. 'Lay off the bloody media for five minutes, Flora! This is about Greenham. We haven't got any leaders, and we don't want women sticking their face in front of a microphone every day . . .'

Now Audrey's operatic tones: 'I'll thank you to watch your language. There is a child present.' She cleared her throat. 'I see this place is riven with disputes. Of course the point I am making is . . .' But her point was drowned out by more howls and cries. From the other side of the wire, Netta heard a man's voice calling, 'Ladies, ladies, calm down . . .' and turned to see two chuckling soldiers. She began to shout herself: 'Can't we all just . . .' And then she saw Abigail's pink face, wet with tears.

'Abigail?' she asked, tottering across the hostile circle and touching the child's shoulder. 'Are you all right?'

Audrey pulled her daughter closer to her side. 'Of course she's all right, she's—'

But Netta, suddenly hot with fury, said, 'I asked Abigail, not you.'

The little girl looked up at her. She seemed to have got younger since the shouting started. 'I believe in . . .' she began. But then she bit her lip, and her tears flowed faster.

'Believe in . . . what?' asked Netta. Everyone had gone quiet now. She staggered down to her knees, which was a blissful relief. 'Boy George?' Abigail looked blank. Netta tried to cast her mind back to childhood. '*Jackie*? *June* and *Schoolfriend*?'

'It does look rather messy,' said Abigail at last, very quietly.

'What does?'

'All this . . . the camp and everything.'

'You mean . . . the peace camp? The women?'

'Yes.'

'What about the base, Abigail?' Mel's voice was kind, though she was incapable of abandoning the party line. 'Don't you think the fence looks a bit messy as well? And all those ugly buildings . . . ?'

'Leave her alone,' said Netta.

But now Abigail wiped her face. 'I tell you what,' she said. 'You can come and look at it out of my window.'

'What, all of us?'

'Yes.' She hesitated. 'If Mummy says so.'

Jude's whisper sounded deafening in the silence. 'I think that is a brilliant idea. What do you think, Audrey?'

'It's Mrs Orton-Avery to you.' There was a pause. 'In the interests of free speech . . . follow me.' The crowd of women began to murmur again, with surprise and – Netta thought – relief at the prospect of getting out of the cold for a while. Mrs Orton-Avery raised her hand. 'But please don't expect tea,' she said firmly. 'I regard you as the enemy within. If it wasn't for true democrats like Margaret Thatcher, you would all be shot.'

'Boots off, coats off and hand-washing in the sink, please.' Chiverton Chase was mock-neo olde-worlde, featuring Tudorish half-timbering and red brick turrets. It had probably been built in the 1930s, Netta guessed. Now it presided over lawns as big as parade grounds, battalions of rose bushes, cohorts of fat Labradors. Audrey had ushered the women into a utility room that was big enough to accommodate a crack SAS squad. Abigail watched them, dry-eyed, with fascination.

'Ever seen anyone this muddy?' Mel asked her, as she prised off her soil-caked wellies.

'No,' said Abigail. 'Only the dogs, once, when they fell in the water.'

Netta was disturbed to find that her feet retained their pointed shape even after she had removed her killer boots. She hobbled to the sink and cleaned herself up. The room was square, with walls of exposed brick, and two washing machines. The air stank of bleach. Cleanliness was clearly important at the Chase – Netta noted the Domestos bottles standing to attention on a high shelf. But Audrey wasn't taking any chances. She had produced a can of perfumed body spray and was squirting it around in the air.

'Do you people *ever* wash?' she asked. 'The last time I had to endure a stench like this, I was helping out in a Sally Army shelter.'

'The Quakers let us clean up and refresh ourselves at their place in Newbury,' said Flora. 'But we don't need to go more than every two weeks or so. Dirt warms the spirit, my dear lady. We deplete ourselves with depilatories, you know.'

Audrey made a small exploding sound. 'One thing I *will* say for Joan Ruddock is that she does at least look like a lady who knows one end of a mascara brush from the other,' she said. 'Not to mention how to apply deodorant.'

'Good old Joan,' said Mel. 'Living proof that you can be a real girl and still want to ban the Bomb.'

'Follow me,' said Audrey. And they followed her: Abigail, Jude, Mel, Netta and six other women, of varying ages and sizes and with differently horrible socks. Flora brought up the rear, looking around her at the polished wood floors and oak panelling with a superior expression. They climbed the wide staircase, which was carpeted in cream. Netta noticed with automatic alarm that small crusts of mud were dropping from their clothes, so that the pristine stairs were littered with tiny brown stars. The landing, unfortunately, was also carpeted in cream. A beautiful teenage boy stood at a bedroom door.

'What's going on, Mum?' he asked. 'Have they been billeted on us?'

'Peace ladies, Sebastian darling,' said Audrey. 'We've invited them in to promote democracy. Abigail's idea.'

'Abigail had an idea? I suppose there's a first time for everything.'

Audrey tutted. 'Very rude, dear,' she said indulgently. Without thinking, Netta took Abigail's hand, and Abigail held on tightly. Audrey opened a bedroom door at the far end of the landing. The room was pink – carpet, ceiling, walls, bedspread, everything. 'Now you'll see what we have to put up with,' she said. 'Come in, come in, get on with it. We'll have to get the Hoover out after you've all gone, whatever happens.'

On the left side of the room there was a long mullioned window with a window seat, dotted with plump pink satin cushions. It was quite dark now, and the sky showed through the panes only as an expanse of dense blackness. 'You can't really see our view properly,' said Audrey. 'But over there – beyond the RAF base – there are the most wonderful woodlands, where I used to play as a girl. Sydmonton Common – a magical spot. Bluebells as far as the eye could see.'

'Of course, when you were a child, there was already an airbase here,' said Flora, peering out into the dark. 'They built it during the Second World War.'

Mel knelt on the window seat. 'Yes, Mrs Orton-Avery. The base that you can see right in front of you. With all the lights and the fences and watchtowers.'

'I find it a reassuring sight,' replied Audrey. 'It shows us that we can do something. Britain is still strong. It represents *order*.' They all looked out at the black sky and the starkly lit area of ground. In truth, there wasn't that much to see, apart from some soldiers and a very slowly moving police car. The atmosphere was one of sci-fi calm. Audrey tapped on the glass and pointed. 'Whereas – look, look – even in the darkness – there – among the trees. Disgusting. In the twentieth century! *Disgusting!*'

'What?' asked Mel.

'A friend in peace is answering the call of nature,' said Flora. 'Down there, do you see?'

Netta tried to search the view for the offending person, but could only see the shuddering trees. 'Not so much ground cover in the winter, I suppose,' she said. 'And you must get a very cold bum.'

Abigail giggled, but withdrew her hand from Netta's.

'There's no need for that, Abigail,' said her mother. 'We all know what we think about lavatory function in this house. People who laugh at that sort of thing are on the same level as people who say "toilet". But that's not all – look – look . . .' To Netta's surprise, she picked up a pair of binoculars from the window seat. 'The things my daughter has had to endure! Women . . . *kissing*. Like teenagers. And look at the . . . look at the mess . . .' She handed the binoculars to Netta.

'Go on then,' said Mel. 'Take a peep.'

Netta peeped. At first, all she could see was the stubbly frozen ground and the trunks of bare trees. But after a while, the glasses found something. Two women, washing up in a small bowl. One was talking a lot, dipping a mug in and out of the water. The other was listening, head down, a tea towel in her motionless hands. After a while, she looked up and said something which made them both laugh. Netta was frustrated that she would never know what they were talking about. She raked the binoculars around further. Not so good this time. A young woman with long plaits, assiduously picking her nose. Rooting round with great precision, and examining what she found on the end of one index finger. 'It's just voyeurism, isn't it?' she said, lowering the glasses before she had to watch

167

the young woman eat a bogey. 'Can't you just leave them to it?'

'The point is, these woods used to be empty,' said Audrey. 'Now we have debauchery, destabilizing influences – a health hazard, for goodness' sake. Can't you see that? Can't you tell the difference? You wouldn't want hundreds of boat people on your doorstep, would you? Hordes of . . . Palestinians? Without lavatory provision, or proper standards? And we don't want . . . you lot.'

'No, I think we all do see that, quite so,' said Flora. 'I shall be much more careful to do my crapping well out of your line of vision from now on, so I do thank you for the opportunity to protect my own privacy.'

'Yes, thank you kindly, Mrs Orton-Avery,' said Mel, exchanging a swift glance with Jude. 'And that reminds me of something. Just a quick favour.'

'What sort of favour might that be?'

'Can we use your toilet before we go?'

13

'Jeanette, take off your bloody hat.' It was Christmas Day, and the Royce/Tyler family was sitting shivering in the garden of the Golden Goose. The ordeal of lunch was over, and David had insisted that they all troop outside. He disliked drinking indoors: indeed, he considered such behaviour to be bordering on the homosexual. Outdoor drinking was mandatory, even in winter. Netta wondered if her day at Greenham had toughened her up. She didn't mind sitting outside all that much. It seemed less claustrophobic than being indoors, with her sins and family members pressing close. Richard in particular was behaving strangely, staring at her one moment and snapping at her the next. She was counting the hours till she could escape. She looked at David, standing at the end of the table, swaying slightly. His face, which had once been beakily handsome, was now collapsing into itself. Alcohol, of course, and a diet of grilled chops and baked beans. He was in a mood of precarious bonhomie, and he had a double brandy in his hand. His fourth, Netta estimated.

'I'm freezing, Dad,' she said.

'It's the warmest Christmas for twenty years, what utter piffle,' he said, squinting up at the feeble sunlight.

'Well, sit down and enjoy it,' said Jane, huddling into her coat. She jiggled the pram in which Little Richard was snoozing between piggy grunts, and took a sip of wine. Richard, Netta noticed, was hardly drinking anything at all, and kept stalking about, examining things, as if he was a master detective, and engaging Toby in platonic dialogues about this and that: the shape of beer glasses, soil formation, the life cycle of the bumblebee and so on. Perhaps, having erred on the perfect husband front, he had decided to concentrate on being a perfect father instead. If only she could be a perfect something! She longed to find a way of absolving herself or making it up to Jane. (Without Jane knowing, of course.) She looked around at the pub garden, at the pretty wrought-iron tables and the lawn sloping down to the river. Beyond the slow-flowing water, she could see the familiar shapes of trees, punctuating the landscaped fields in a mysteriously reassuring way. She did not know if they were oak, ash or elm: but she recognized them from her earliest childhood. Her head ached, partly because she was straining to think of safe things to say, and partly because that childhood was lost for ever now.

'Sit down? I'm not an old woman,' said David. He waved his arm dismissively at his two daughters. 'Or a young one. Pubs aren't for sitting in, Jane, they're convivial places. Hail fellow well met, drinks across the bar.'

'Unless you're serving,' said Netta. 'Then you're about as convivial as Scrooge. Do the regulars still call you Old Grumpy?'

'Have it your own way, Dad, I'm not going to argue on Christmas Day.' Jane took a comfortable, longer drink. 'Stand up if you want to. I must say, it's very pleasant out here,' she said. 'Scenic . . . and refreshing.' The Golden

Goose was handily situated in the middle of the rather self-consciously cute hamlet. It had once been the hub of the village, and was still popular, but David Royce had put off a number of former customers with his long, rambling yarns and sudden, snarling self-justifications. Some had started frequenting the White Hart in the next village, though it was an ugly roadhouse.

Now Richard appeared, with a child round his neck, and Netta studied her drink. 'What's the matter, Charlotte?' asked Jane. 'Can't you leave Daddy in peace?'

'Go and play by the river bank,' said David inscrutably. His general view of grandchildren was that they were what he termed 'surplus to requirements'. He gave the small back view a piercing look. 'She's not all there,' he said. 'You were reading Voltaire at that age.'

'Rubbish, Dad, you're mythologizing history,' said Jane. 'It's true, though. She reminds me more of Netta than she does of myself. It's Toby who takes after me. Obsessed with knowledge: quite amazing.' Netta noticed that the improving encyclopaedias from Father Christmas were piled up on the table, awaiting Toby's attention. For him, there was no escape.

Charlotte turned to stare at David, a cunningly vapid expression on her face. 'I'm boring,' she said. Netta smiled in spite of herself. Then she saw Richard's eyes were fixed on her. She gulped some wine.

'Shall I take Charlotte?' she asked into the void between them. 'Then we can both be boring together.' Richard turned away, as if he hadn't heard. Charlotte, however, twisted in his arms.

'Want Netta! Want Netta!' she said. 'Daddy hates me!'

She wriggled her way out of Richard's arms and came and sat on Netta's knee, kicking her painfully in the stomach as she did so. Then she pushed one hand inside Netta's T-shirt and grabbed hold of her bra strap, this being her comfort position when sitting on Jane's lap. She smelled of sugar and shampoo. Netta's face was hot and she tried to look away, but still saw Richard giving her another strange look. Did he think she was to blame for their transgression? She wished so much that she could run away.

'Absurd child!' he said to Jane, taking the seat next to hers, and they both laughed. He leaned towards her, saying something in an undertone. Netta had good hearing, and she caught: 'Hard to know which of them is the more immature.' Jane's face was shining: she looked like a flirtatious sixth-former. What would Jane do if she found out? Who would she blame? It was a marriage Netta had blundered into, something no one on the outside could understand. She breathed deeply; the cold winter air suddenly seemed so sparse that she felt she was being asphyxiated.

'I had two friends at nursery,' said Charlotte, breathing her sickly breath into Netta's face. 'Amelia and Other Charlotte. But they hate me now.'

'I'm sure no one hates you, Lottie,' said Netta.

'Well, I hate *them*. They sit in the painting corner and I do dressing up.'

'There must be *somebody* you like at nursery.'

'Not really. Sarah wets her knickers, Rosie bosses you about, and Miranda's got a funny smell.'

'Children are always absurd,' pronounced David. 'Some

of them turn into respectable human beings as they get older, some don't. To me, babies were always your mother's domain.'

'Things are different now,' said Jane.

'I don't see how,' said David. 'After all, Richard's the one with the career.'

There was an unpleasant silence.

'Jane does everything well,' said Netta, then wished she hadn't, remembering that this was one of the comments she had made before she and Richard had started tearing each other's clothes off.

'I wouldn't expect you to understand,' said Jane. 'I've got options now I would never have had twenty years ago.'

'Really?' said David. 'And what might those be? You've made precisely the same mistake I did: thinking Oxford is the passport to the world. It's not. It's a calling card. You need to work if you want to get further.'

'You must admit an Oxbridge degree does make a difference,' said Netta, driven by guilt to protect Jane from their father's tactless stream-of-consciousness. David liked to entertain himself with pointless disagreements. 'Goldsmiths is just a melting pot for mediocrities.'

'Don't be so bloody silly,' said Jane. 'Running yourself down for no reason.'

David sighed. 'Really, Netta, why do you say these things? I'm sure Smithfield is marvellous in its way. All you have to do is find your niche in life, though God alone knows what that will turn out to be. Maybe some women's magazine will have you, maybe you can turn out some little articles about going to the hairdresser's or how to catch a man.' He picked up his glass. 'At least you have your life ahead of you: I've got nothing. Nothing but the demon drink.'

'You've got us,' said Netta, thinking: I'm going to cry if things carry on like this. She concentrated hard on keeping her eyeballs dry, sucking the unshed tears into her head.

'You have your own lives to lead. You don't need me. I'm irrelevant now . . .' David put his glass down and stared across the farmland beyond the river. 'I'm not cut out for living on my own. Can't stand solitude, and can't stand visitors. Your mother would have been so much better at it.'

'She'd have known how to cook more than a mixed grill every night, that's for sure,' said Netta. 'Come on, Dad, buck up.'

'Very true,' said David. He wiped his eyes. 'Bugger this brandy.' Then he held up his glass. 'To Margaret – a wonderful woman, and a perfect wife.'

They all raised their glasses. Calling her a perfect wife really *was* mythologizing history, Netta thought. Margaret had been gloriously terrible at being a wife: her clothes clashed and oozed cleavage, she hated housework, gave calamitous dinner parties and argued violently with both David and their friends. People came in and out of her life with giddying speed, attracted by her noisy exuberance, but frightened off by her unpredictable moods. Netta saw her mother as a wonderful Bad Fairy: she remembered her in a whirl of dark hair and blurred make-up and insulting remarks. But when she became an invalid, she had mellowed slightly, and Netta used to read Maigret stories to her while she lay in bed. Netta could see the sickroom now – rumpled bedclothes, piles of glossy magazines, plastic sick bucket close to hand. Margaret did not like to be nursed; she wanted to be entertained. 'Dying is so bloody boring, Nettie,' she had said one day. 'Promise me you'll just fall under a bus.'

'Promise,' said Netta.

'Where are we in the story?' She nodded towards their current Maigret book, *Maigret Sets a Trap*. It was the thirteenth they had read together. When they started, Netta had been an indifferent reader, as she was an indifferent everything when it came to academe. By the time Margaret died – just before the end of *Maigret and the Madwoman* – Netta read fluently, with accents and dramatic pauses, her voice rising and falling in the quiet room with theatricality and flair. Sometimes, she had caught her mother smiling at her, and not, she suspected, really following the story at all. And it was only years later that she realized what Margaret had done. She had given Netta her own world, the world of words.

'Maigret's pretending he caught the murderer, so he can catch him in real life.'

'Oh yes, that's right. Man after my own heart. Honesty is overrated. Words of wisdom from your dying mum.'

'Stop talking about dying. It's not funny.' Netta had taken up the book, and began to read: 'Maigret made a mistake. Would another man, in his situation, have avoided it? That was a question he was often to ask afterwards, and of course he never found a satisfactory answer to it . . .' She read on and on, and the narrow streets of Montmartre rose up around them, the smell of Gitanes wafted out into the night air, Maigret turned up the collar of his raincoat and pursued his man, doubting himself, but never doubted by Netta or her mother.

'Netta, are you with us or not? I just asked you if you want a refill.' David knocked back the remainder of his drink, then burped quietly. 'Any more for any more?'

'Richard, can you sort that out?' asked Jane. When he had gone, she turned to look at Netta more closely. 'Why *are* you wearing that ridiculous hat?' she asked. 'It makes you look like Compo.'

'And you have such charming hair, dear,' said David, who was clearly now the worse for drink. 'Jane has it in the brains department, and God knows, she's quite something special in the looks arena as well. So . . . you might ask, where do you fit in? Studying newspapers . . . no one could blame you for feeling you've drawn the short straw . . .' He hesitated, as if unsure how to move on to a bracing conclusion. 'Not all of us are born to excel. Not all of us have the capacity. But you do have a wonderful look of your mother – and beautiful hair. That must be some compensation.' Extreme insults could only follow after compliments as fulsome as this.

'Thanks, Dad,' said Netta. 'Thing is, I went to the hair-dresser's, asked for something radical, and they went a bit too far. I'm going to keep it covered up till it grows out a bit – it just looks foul.' It was typical of her father not to notice that she had been wearing the Compo hat since she arrived on Christmas Eve.

'Take it off, for goodness' sake,' said Jane. 'Your haircut's not that terrible. It looked okay at your dreadful party.'

'I just feel better with it on,' said Netta.

'Although it is slightly reminiscent of those women in Belfast who've been tarred and feathered for sleeping with soldiers . . .' said Jane.

'Well, thanks for being honest,' said Netta.

'Who the hell's going to be honest with you, if you can't trust your own family, that's what I'd like to know!' said David. 'Here we are, all together – what's left of us – and we all stand together, all for one and one for all.'

Netta shifted Charlotte on to one knee, reached into her bag for her cigarettes and lit up. She thought of Mel and Pilar holding their fags in the air. The Three Musketeers. It might be possible to be 'one for all' with friends; it certainly wasn't possible with family. 'I don't want your honesty,' she said after a moment.

'What do you want, then, from your family?' asked Jane. 'Deceit? Betrayal? Lies?' She gave a short laugh, a question mark in itself. 'By the way, if you must smoke, do you mind going down to the bottom of the garden? I don't want the children dying of lung cancer before they've done their O-levels.'

Netta obediently handed Charlotte to Jane, picked up her drink and went down to the fence that bordered the river. Toby, obviously not concerned with lung health, followed her. 'What's your least favourite way to die, Auntie Net?' he asked, cocking his head like a cute little puppy.

'Blimey!' said Netta. 'I've never thought about it.'

'Not cancer, then? Like Grannie?'

'Well, cancer was pretty damn horrible, I can tell you. But there are so many really agonizing things to choose from,' said Netta, realizing too late that this was probably not the sort of thing that grown-ups usually said to him.

'Well, okay, here are some choices.' Toby ticked these off neatly on his grubby fingers. 'First, decapitation, which means having your head cut off,' he said, with a nod acknowledging that she might have problems with his terminology. 'Could be quick – but would they get it right? Sometimes, even executioners took – maybe, seventeen goes. Second, burned alive. So imagine the way my hand felt when I touched the frying pan on Pancake Day, multiplied by – a million? Could be even worse than that. Number three, disembowelment, which means . . .'

'Toby, we know what disembowelment means.' To her alarm, she saw that Richard had followed them. He sighed heavily and shrugged. 'It's not as if he watches video nasties. He absorbs it, via osmosis.'

There was a short pause. Netta felt the pressure of Richard's gaze. 'My worst way of being killed would be radiation sickness,' she said brightly. Her eyes were fixed on the soothing shape of an ancient tree. She imagined it flattened to the ground like wind-blown grass. If the world vaporized, her sordid crime would disappear. She imagined all of them vanishing in a white glare.

'You can't have radiation sickness on a battlefield,' said Toby. 'Idiot!'

'Really, Toby, apologize at once! You mustn't talk like that to your aunt,' said Richard.

'I can tell you how horrible radiation sickness is, if you're into that sort of thing,' Netta offered. 'Give you a list of some really disgusting symptoms. That's what real violence leads to in the real world.'

'What about being impaled, which means stuck to the ground with a massive spear?' Toby's face was determined:

it was Merrie Olde English retro-violence or nothing.

Richard groaned. 'Toby, go away! I'm talking to Netta.'

'The Tudors used to crush people to death with rocks and heavy doors!' protested Toby. 'They did! They did, Daddy! I thought you were a historian . . .' But he was wandering away towards the garden fence.

Netta stared into the distance, smoking hard. What was there to say? Richard was silent for a moment. Then he sighed. 'It's all the most tremendous mess, of course.'

'What is?'

'Us.'

She dragged harder. 'There is no "us", Richard. We just did a very, very bad and stupid thing. Now we have to pretend it never happened.'

'Yes, well.' He turned to face her, then glanced quickly over his shoulder. But Jane and David were laughing over their drinks, and well out of earshot. 'It's not quite as simple as that, is it?'

'Isn't it? I thought we had agreed not to mention it again? Surely that's the best thing for everybody!'

'Silence is not an option. I need to talk to someone,' he said, leaning closer. 'To sort this situation out – this situation with Jane.'

'See a marriage guidance counsellor, then.'

He laughed ironically. 'I assume that's a joke. There's no one I can talk to. No one I can admit these things to.'

She waited, dreading what was coming.

'Only you.'

Just then there was a scream, and a splash from somewhere on the other side of the fence. 'What . . . ?' Richard whirled around. 'Toby?' But the child had disappeared.

They ran to the end of the garden. There was a hole in the wire there, just big enough for a small body to squeeze through. 'Toby?' called Richard again. 'Toby, where the hell are you?' There was silence from the other side, apart from the slow gurgle of the river. The dusk was drawing in, and all that Netta could see was the purple grass, tussocky and uneven where it came to the river bank, and the spiked reeds beyond.

'What's going on?' called Jane from the terrace. 'What's happening?'

'Nothing – just – just finding Toby . . .' Richard called back.

Netta, with a swift look at his white, scared face, wriggled through the child-sized hole in the fence.

'Netta – what are you . . . ?'

'He could be in the water for all we know,' said Netta, heaving herself to her feet on the other side. Richard tried and failed to climb the high wooden fence, which was overgrown with fierce brambles and had been reinforced with barbed wire. Then he kicked at the hole, which was far too small for him. Netta turned and faced the river – then heard what sounded like a cry, and another splash. She pushed her way forward, forcing back the branches and wiry bushes which lay just beyond the pub garden, and stumbling over hummocks of grass till she reached flatter but boggier ground. Each footstep left a yawning, sucking hole behind.

'Toby?' she called. 'Toby?'

And then she reached the riverside, and saw him in the water. His face was hidden; his anorak hood was up, so that she couldn't see his head properly. He looked like a floating corpse. She caught her breath, almost screamed, but instead she threw herself into the icy water. At first, it was so agonizingly cold that she almost lost consciousness, and she could hardly move her arms and legs. The freezing weight of her clothes threatened to pull her down beneath the aching surface of the water, but there was no time to kick them off. She thrashed about, panting for breath, until she reached him. When she felt the shape of his floating body, she clasped him in her arms. He was horribly still. She twisted him round so that she could see his face. His eyes were closed and his cheeks were bloodless. She held the information in her mind, refusing to panic. Now she needed to get back to the bank, but found that the current was stronger than she had expected and was pulling her slowly towards the centre of the river. Sobbing for breath, she struggled against the mute power of the water. Voices from the garden carried over to her with surreal clarity. 'Where is he?' 'Where is she?' A hysterical scream from Jane and yelled instructions from her father about how to get down to the river bank without climbing over the fence. Then Netta turned and fought against the current, pulling back the ice-cold water with one arm and hugging the dead weight of Toby to her with the other. Somehow, she came closer to the edge, and managed to crawl on to the muddy bank just as she saw feet pelting down the path towards her. Richard threw his son on to his back, blew into his mouth, then turned and took a breath, then blew again. The rhythm was perfectly controlled, and completely desperate. For a moment, nothing happened. Netta stood, dripping, hands clamped to her mouth. She didn't feel the cold now. She didn't feel anything. She could only watch. Then – suddenly, miraculously – Toby choked, wriggled and produced a spume of watery grey vomit.

'Daddy!' he said, muffled by Richard's body, as his father held him in a sobbing bear hug. 'Daddy! I'm heavier than I thought. I thought – being reasonably small – the water would make me float, if I jumped in with my hood up. The experiment was a total failure.'

The rescue was not enough to satisfy Jane. She couldn't understand how Toby had managed to get into the water in the first place. She sat in the rocking chair by the fire, tilting to and fro and holding Toby tensely to her. His bright eyes were watchful and calm. 'How could you?' she kept saying to Richard. 'How could you? How could you possibly not notice that he'd got through the fence? You know how dangerous it is down there.'

Neither Richard nor Netta looked at each other. Netta was drinking port, perched on the window seat at the far side of the room. This was a long way from the fire, and there was a cold draught, but while she wanted to hear what Jane had to say, she thought it wise to keep her distance. Richard was pacing up and down, while David was upstairs, reading to Charlotte, which was an unusual challenge for him. Above the sitting room, Netta could hear the juddering of Charlotte's bed, and her delighted squeals as she jumped up and down.

'It was just a moment – a second!' cried Richard for the hundredth time. 'It's not as if he's a toddler, Jane. For God's sake! One expects him to be able to go out of one's sight for that long without practically drowning – it's insane.'

'Don't try and justify this,' said Jane in a low, furious tone. 'I'm prepared to put up with a very great deal, Richard, but not that. Apologize, and then shut up.'

'I *have* apologized! What the hell do you want from me?' cried Richard. This was theoretically true, but he was bad at saying sorry as if he meant it. It did not suit him to be in the wrong.

'Dear God,' said Jane, suddenly covered in tears. 'When I think what nearly happened! When I think what I nearly lost!' Trembling, she laid her head on top of Toby's. His eyes were still open, watching the flickering flames.

Netta felt that she had heard enough, and began to edge out of the room. Richard, seeing this, said, 'If I have to apologize, then at least you might thank your sister for saving his life!'

Jane did not look up. 'Thank you,' she said in a muffled voice. 'You saved my life as well as his.'

Netta paused, about to carry her glass up the stairs to her attic bedroom. 'It was . . . it was the least I could do.'

After two days of extreme tension, Richard drove Netta to the nearest station. She had tried to avoid this, but failed. When they reached Stafford, he turned the engine off and sat for a while, looking at the reclining windscreen wipers.

'You saved Toby's life,' he said. 'No one else could have got through the fence. He'd be dead if it wasn't for you.'

'I just did the obvious thing,' said Netta, turning to unlock the car door. 'Anyone would have done the same. If the hole had been bigger, you'd have rescued him yourself. It was just lucky I was there.' She waited till the door was open before saying: 'And you know, Jane was right. We should have noticed what Toby was up to. The reason we didn't was because we were having that – awkward conversation. If I hadn't pulled him out in time, just think what that would have meant. We've done something terrible as it is.'

He touched her arm, but she struggled out of the car, then turned to face him. 'I have to go,' she said. 'My train's due any minute.' She hesitated. 'Neither of us is going to win any prizes for virtuous behaviour.'

Richard peered up at her through the open passenger door. 'This is crazy,' he said. 'Nothing makes any sense.'

Netta sank her head lower down inside her muffled scarf. 'One thing that does make sense is that you didn't lose your son. He's fine. Everything is fine. So now – don't fuck him up by flirting with flirtation. It's all done with – finished.' She slammed the door hard, and saw Richard bang the steering wheel before turning on the engine and backing out into the road with furious haste. She watched him drive away, then went on to the station platform and looked up and down the long bleak vistas of track that led north and south. The sky was grey and heavy with snow. As the first few flakes began to fall, instantly turning to ice as they touched the ground, she thought of Mel and Jude and the Greenham women, hunched together in these conditions for months. (With just the occasional break to recruit more women, or harangue the unacceptable face of feminism.) The scale of what they were trying to achieve made normal human misdemeanours – such as adultery – seem insignificant. She thought of the day they had linked arms and walked

184

around the base. And an idea began to take shape in her mind. The shock of nearly losing Toby was much more powerful than the relief that she had pulled him out of the water. But even so, she had been in the right place at the right time. If she hadn't been there, he would almost certainly have died. What she did – good or bad – could make a difference. Now she would go back to Greenham Common and prove her worth, not to the rest of the world, but to herself.

14

As the train drew into the station and she climbed on board, she began to think about the problem of putting this plan into action. How, exactly, would she get there? She knew Greenham was somewhere near Newbury, and that was it. And once there, what would she do? She was not sure how to find Mel, or even if Mel would welcome her with open arms, given that she was so taken up with Jude. She had a mental image of herself standing there forlornly with her backpack, alone in an Army search-light. Besides, dashing off to join the peace women would not go down well with Pilar. She had been a little cool since the Richard-crime, though she had insisted this was all in Netta's imagination. And she had been scathing about her day trip with Mel and Jude, insisting that she didn't want to hear anything about Jude at all. Then Netta had another idea, though a rather challenging one. She wouldn't go to Greenham on her own. Somehow, she would persuade Pilar to go with her.

How she was going to do this she wasn't absolutely sure. But perhaps the thought of seeing Mel again might be some inducement. In spite of her studiedly offhand atti-tude, Netta knew that she was missing her old flatmate. Her hit-rate with women was high – she was currently seeing Miffy, the wild Welsh girl, and seemed unusually smitten. But this didn't take up all her time – or her emotion.

Netta had found a half-written note on the living-room table, scrawled while Pilar was downing a bottle of wine, judging from the empty bottle of Bulgarian red left on top of the crumpled pages. Pilar had started by enquiring calmly about life at the base, but ended up in a ranting lament, accusing Melanie of everything from faking her sexual orientation to stealing cheese. By the time Netta had finished reading, she realized that she'd committed another crime: invading Pilar's privacy. By bringing the two of them together, Netta felt that she could help them repair their friendship. She couldn't see quite how she would do this, but she could try. Having met Jude, she didn't think she was much of a substitute for Pilar.

As she reached Dartmouth Villa, she heard footsteps hurrying along behind her. 'Bloody freezing, isn't it?' said a familiar voice. 'Not exactly what I would call le temps du choix.' She turned and saw Emily, hand-in-hand with Bryan. She was all smiles now the vortex of waiting was over. In spite of the intense cold, she was coatless, wearing a clingy black sweater which accentuated her large bosoms.

'You look very serious,' said Bryan, who looked very serious himself.

'I've decided to go to Greenham,' said Netta, then wished she hadn't.

This seemed to cheer Bryan up. 'What for?' he asked. 'What would a fun-loving, woman-person-about-town like you be doing, hanging out with a bunch of hideous lesbian girls?'

Netta glared at him. 'Saving the planet? Pulling humanity back from the brink of mass destruction?'

'At least you haven't got any delusions of grandeur,' said Bryan.

'It beats posing around pretending to be a pop star.'

'That was social satire,' said Bryan, pushing open the rusty wrought-iron gate. 'My audience was just too thick to see it.'

Emily was tossing her hair and pouting a lot in Man Awareness Mode. Netta thought how nice it must be to have such straightforward needs. The fact that she would collapse in a heap of self-loathing if Bryan left her was a price worth paying. 'Of course, you're bound to run into Mum,' Emily said. 'She practically runs the whole show, these days. Tell her I'm pursuing the modelling option – that should get her going.'

'Mental case,' said Bryan. Netta assumed he meant Flora, rather than Emily.

'Self-obsessed,' said Emily, moueing like a guppie and skewering her hair into a half-hearted bun, so that most of it came tumbling back down again. '*Très toddleresque.*' She laughed, though this remark did not strike Netta as being particularly amusing. The aim was apparently to show her animal high spirits. 'Which gate are you off to?'

Netta frowned, not knowing anything about gates. 'I'm putting myself in the hands of Fate,' she said.

Emily shook her head. 'You'll need to do a bit more planning ahead than that!' she said. 'Each gate has a camp round it – there's Orange, Yellow, Blue, Cinnamon, Rainbow – where my mother hangs out – God knows what else. And they're all different – you know, some separatist, some madly hippy-dippy. All sounds like nonsense to me, but Tom's the expert on all this. He hides in the trees, did you know? Undercover peace Goth.'

'Sounds very noble and romantic,' said Netta.

'He's only doing it to annoy Mum. I told him that last weekend. He went all the way to Camden to have a shower. He's seen Melanie at the camp as well, of course. He watches them from his hide.'

Now they were entering the dark hall. 'Didn't think you were arse-brained enough to be a Greenham girlie,' Bryan said to Netta. 'You seemed like you had more sense.'

'Banning the Bomb makes pretty good sense to me.'

'I still don't get it,' said Bryan. 'Why go to Greenham Common? Just send ten quid to CND if you're that bothered.'

'Flora was on *Nationwide* again last night – very irritating for the other women, I should think,' said Emily. She led them into the downstairs sitting room, switched on the gas fire and crouched down next to it, blocking out most of the heat.

'If attention's what you want, Greenham's certainly the place to be,' said Netta. 'They're in the papers again today.' She took a copy of the *Daily Chronicle* out of her bag: the headline 'Harridans from Hell' had caught her eye, together with an unflattering photo of some peace women arguing with the police.

Bryan grabbed the paper and read the article with a strange expression on his face. 'Been trying to pitch ideas to this lot, and they're so fucking snotty about it,' he said. 'Attitude's like – go away, little boy. Go and edit your student rag.'

'Isn't that a full-time job?' asked Netta. 'With a salary? Bit greedy, trying to do other things as well.' She took

.

her coat off and plumped down on Emily's balding velvet sofa. The downstairs of the house was both grander and colder than the upstairs, and the air was harsh, even with the gas fire blaring gallantly away. She took out her cigarettes and lit one for warmth.

'Bryan's desperate for fame, aren't you?' said Emily. 'Name in lights. Notorious!' She beamed at him. 'We're two of a kind.'

'Let's just say I need a new direction, now that Façade has bitten the dust,' said Bryan. 'Fancy myself in the tabloids, digging for dirt. Kill an Argie and win a Metro, sort of thing.'

'You could do worse than coming up with a new angle on Greenham,' said Netta.

Bryan looked thoughtful.

'What's this about Greenham?' A sharp voice, Pilar's voice. But as she came towards them, laden with crackling carrier bags, Netta saw that her face was anything but sharp. She looked white and puffy and had obviously been drinking, though it was only five o'clock. 'Post-Christmas prezzies,' she said, by way of explanation. 'Daddy's money. He gave me two hundred pounds. All wrapped up in gold paper and with a red velvet bow on top. Couldn't be bothered to think of something particular for me, but at least I can make the most of the sales. He's such a shit.' She took one of Netta's cigarettes. 'You all up to something?'

'Nope,' said Netta, standing up. 'Let's go upstairs, Pilar.'

'She wants to run off to Greenham with you,' said Bryan.

'*Folie à deux*,' said Emily.

'Very funny. Trains are up the spout, anyway,' said Pilar.

'All cancelled from Lewisham. Tiny bit of snow.' They looked out of the window, and the flakes were indeed starting to pile up on the window sill. Pilar pulled a bottle of wine out of her capacious handbag. As she opened it – with the corkscrew she carried everywhere – Netta noticed that there was a lipsticky love-bite on her neck.

Emily went to get some glasses and Bryan paged through the *Chronicle*, chuckling ironically to himself.

'Pilar,' Netta whispered urgently. 'Pilar! Will you come with me?'

'Where to?'

'Greenham!'

'Whatever for?'

'To see Mel!'

'No need to go capering across the countryside to see that sanctimonious cow. It was bad enough you going – she's bound to assume it's some sort of victory. I'll see her when she gets back.'

'But that might not be for months.'

Pilar scowled and shooshed smoke out of the corner of her mouth. 'Look, be realistic. Do I look like peace person material?'

'Anyone can be a peace person. I saw a woman there in a ballgown and tiara.'

'Okay, fine. Let's look at it another way. I don't *want* to be a fucking peace person. They're nuts, it's a waste of time, and there is frigging snow on the ground. Plus, I've still got tons more shopping to do. I want to get a little negligee for Miffy.'

'But Pilar, I have to do this,' hissed Netta, trying to make her voice even quieter, as Bryan was now looking over at them with interest. She tried appealing to Pilar's lapsed-Catholic side. 'Don't you understand? It's a way of making reparation – you know. Route to God-free absolution.' Pilar looked at the end of her cigarette thoughtfully. 'And you must be a bit curious about Jude.'

'Bound to be pug-ugly dungaree-witch,' said Pilar. 'Why would I need to see that?'

'Oh, come on!' said Netta. 'I need your help! I screwed up. So, so badly! Now, I want to try to put things right.'

Pilar seemed to consider this. 'No trains,' she said finally. 'No way of getting there till it melts.' She flicked ash on to the fireplace, disregarding the need for an ashtray. 'Anyway, I've got a date with the lovely Miffy.'

Then Netta had a flash of inspiration. 'Taxi,' she said. She knew that Pilar couldn't resist conspicuous cab-consumption.

'What?' But Pilar's eyes had lit up already. 'All the way to Greenham?'

'It's a different world. It's worth going there, just once. Honestly.'

'You can't afford it.'

'Yes I can. If we go halves.' She tried and failed to remember how far below her overdraft limit she was. 'And your dad sent you all that money. This can be your Christmas present to Mel.'

'Hmm. I suppose Miffy can wait for her frilly lingerie.'

Pilar spent over an hour assembling the right outfit, and eventually decided on a floor-length fur coat – a gift from her father, and clearly not a fake. She put it on with an evil, Cruella de Ville glint in her eye. Instead of a rucksack, she plumped for a spotted vanity case. 'Make-up,' she said, wrapping a cerise angora scarf around her neck. 'For those ongoing repair jobs.' Netta, in her layers of sweater, scarf and cagoule, thought it tactical to keep quiet. As long as Pilar went with her, she could wear a gold lamé bikini for all she cared.

By the time they hailed a taxi, it was after midnight. The journey itself was slowed down by a blizzard, and once they got off the motorway, the roads were covered in ice and snow. By the time the taxi dropped them off – the driver having spoken not one word during the entire journey – it was daybreak.

'Is this Greenham?' asked Netta, her teeth beginning to chatter already. 'Are you sure this is the right place?'

'It's Berkshire,' said the cabbie. He pointed to a white sign which said as much. 'And we've been through bleedin' Newbury. So – job done.'

'Charmed, I'm sure,' said Pilar. 'I take it you weren't expecting a tip.'

'Just glad to see the back of you,' said the cabbie. 'The way I look at it is, the Communists have got their own people there.' He seemed to have decided it was safe to share his views with them now. 'No one can deny that Margaret Thatcher is the best leader we've had since Winston Churchill.'

'It's certainly hard to imagine Neil Kinnock at Number 10,' said Pilar, taking an imperious drag. 'There's something so servile about him.'

'Come on,' said Netta, taking her by the elbow and propelling her along the road. 'For God's sake! Try and enter into the spirit of the thing. Think rad-femme.'

'Where are we going?' asked Pilar, as the taxi sped away. 'What are we doing?'

'Hitching the rest of the way,' said Netta. 'Can't be far from here.' But she didn't feel as confident as she sounded. In spite of Pilar's fur coat, she suspected that to the burghers of Newbury and the surrounding farming community, they would look like Greenham hags par excellence.

The reaction was worse than she had feared. Some drivers just tooted their horns and yelled things she could barely hear as they sped past – she could make out '... KIN LESB ...' as they went, or '... eed is a good fu ...' But the worst people were those who stopped. This happened twice. The first time, a smart new Mini Metro drew up some distance ahead. Netta struggled to a slow jog, the rucksack banging her back as she went. Pilar tootled along behind her. Finally, they drew near to the car. The driver was a young man, alone, with music playing on his cassette tape. It was 'In the Name of Love' by the Thompson Twins.

'Hi,' she said, when he leaned over and wound down the passenger window. 'Can you take us as far as Greenham Common?'

'Have you ever had it up the arse?' asked the man. He had dark skin and floppy black hair: just the type that Netta found attractive.

'I'm sorry?' she said, genuinely distracted by his good looks. 'What was that?'

'I said: Have You Ever Had It Up the Arse?' The man was speaking slowly and distinctly this time.

'Erm, no, I can't say I have,' said Netta.

'Well, if you get in, I'll give it to you now,' he said. 'And I'll use this.' He held up something which Netta took to be a monkey wrench. Pilar treated him to her most regal V-sign.

The second car stopped twenty minutes later. 'If this one wants to bugger us, we're saying yes,' said Pilar. By this time Netta was beginning to think she might just collapse at the edge of the road. Perhaps they were walking in the wrong direction – surely they should have reached the camp by now? She felt light-headed as she staggered towards the red saloon car. She could see that there were children in the back.

'Hello,' she said, as the woman driver leaned across and wound the window down. 'I wonder if you could take us as far as Greenha –' But she was stopped in mid-word by a great splash of tepid liquid. As the car drove off, the sound of children laughing delightedly filled her ears. She wiped the liquid away with an old tissue – the smell was familiar: Ribena. Not urine, then, that was some relief. But it clung sweetly to her skin: a dirty, sickly layer.

'Vermin,' said Pilar. 'Housewives are vermin.'

But Netta had seen something. 'That's the base,' she said. 'Look – over there.' They could see trees, a high barbed-wire fence, and a scattering of sleeping women. She pulled a map out of her pocket which she had torn off the kitchen door. 'That'll be Cinnamon Gate,' she said. 'Rainbow must be further round, hidden in the trees.'

Pilar gazed at the gentle woodland around her. 'Pretty!' she said. 'Apart from . . . that – barbed-wire fence thing.'

'Not what you expect, is it?'

'Like . . . the Shire,' said Pilar. 'Hobbiton.'

'The Shire meets Mordor,' said Netta.

They followed a narrow footpath that led through the frost-sharpened grass and the white trees till they reached a small clearing in the woods: a flat area of trodden-down grass littered with old boxes, washing-up bowls, cooking pots and plastic chairs. In the centre was a campfire, burning low and surrounded by flat stones. On one side of it was a pile of firewood. On the other were four hunched sleeping bags, muffled in plastic sheeting, the occupants burrowed inside. Netta and Pilar peered around them.

'This it?' asked Pilar, now fully awake and shivering. 'Everyone?'

'Maybe they've dropped a neutron bomb already,' said Netta. She frowned. It was a very different scene from that of her first visit, the hording raggle-taggle women and bizarre outfits. She wondered if the snow was to blame.

'Hilarious.' Pilar bent down and picked up a leaflet which was lying on the ground with her clumsy, mittened fingers.

POSITIVELY CUNTS

Women – Reclaim Your Genitalia!

Across the world, gay men and disabled people are calling for the right to be called by what they REALLY ARE. QUEER NATION says men are queer, not 'gay'. CRIPPLES ANONYMOUS says that if you are wheelchair-bound, you have the right to the word CRIPPLE not some euphemism which ducks the issue that your legs DON'T WORK and that you are treated like a second-class citizen by people who identify as able-bodied. Now women need CUNT POSITIVISM, which states that if you are the proud owner of a vagina, the Anglo-Saxon word for it is CUNT. The patriarchy wants to make your sex safe by turning it into a cosy or overtly medical word. This coyness is actually caused by a deep hatred of, quite literally, OUR SEX. Without CUNTS there would be no human race. So it's no surprise that in a patriarchal society, CUNTS are seen as the ULTIMATE OBSCENITY. Women who agree with this are facilitating their own oppression.

Women who call a CUNT a CUNT are CELE-BRATING THEIR TRANSCENDENT SEXUALITY.

A man's penis dangles pointlessly outside his body. He pisses with it and fucks with it. Our CUNTS are designed only for sex and having children – no wonder the patri-archy can't cope with them.

WOMEN ARE ANGRY – AND ALL WOMEN WHO WANT TO BE FREE OF THE OPPRESSION OF THE USELESS PENIS MUST CELEBRATE OUR HIDDEN, POWERFUL SEX.
POSITIVELY CUNTS – JOIN US OR COLLUDE WITH THE OPPRESSION OF YOUR OWN CLITORIS.

For more information, come to Rainbow Gate and ask for Jude Blackman.

'Gawd,' said Pilar. 'Imagine what Radclyffe Hall would have made of that.'

'She'd have passed out on the spot, I expect.'

Melanie's head had appeared at the top of one of the sleeping bags.

'Surprise!' called Pilar. 'Hello, darling!'

'What . . . ?' Mel stared at them for several seconds with narrow, red-rimmed eyes. 'It's more than a surprise, it's . . .' She struggled out of her sleeping bag with difficulty, her progress impeded by her multilayered outfit. When she finally emerged, she still looked like a sleeping bag. 'You can't just . . .'

'Can't just what?' Pilar's smile glitterered with girlish menace.

'Show up like this . . .'

'Why not?' said Netta. 'If it was okay for me to come along before, why are you being so funny about it now?' She was suddenly aware they were staring at each other across a tundra of frozen grass. 'I mean – hello, Mel. Happy post-Christmas. Nice to see you.'

'Hello,' said Mel. 'Sorry. I just – didn't expect to see Pilar.'

'Aren't you going to give me a kiss?' said Pilar, rushing over to Mel and wrapping her arms around her.

'You stink of booze,' said Mel, pecking Pilar on the cheek. She looked at both of them dubiously. 'Just a day trip again, is it?'

'Nope, we're here to stay, apparently.' Pilar took a bottle of whisky out of her bag. 'And we're bearing gifts!'

Mel took the whisky without smiling. 'You're wearing a dead animal,' she said, looking at Pilar's coat.

'It's lovely and warm,' said Pilar. 'Try it on.'

'I'm a vegetarian.'

'No you aren't.'

'Yes I am.'

'What, the kind that eats bacon sarnies and veal?'

But the conversation was interrupted by another voice, low to the point of inaudibility. 'Morwumm' was what Netta heard at first. She turned to see Jude crawling out of her sleeping bag. She approached them slowly. The bones of her face were visible through her frost-white skin. Her hair was shaved close to her head. Her body was swaddled in black. She looked like Death itself. 'Hi, Net,' she said in Netta's ear. 'Welcome to Rainbow Gate.'

'This is Pilar,' said Mel. 'Neither of them will be staying. I don't think they're really that committed.'

'Bleedin' cheek!' said Pilar. She was lighting a cigarette. 'I'm totally unilateral! Aren't I, Netta?'

Netta sighed. 'Not exactly,' she said. 'We're here more in a spirit of solidarity.'

'Passion,' whispered Jude.

'What?' Netta leaned close again, feeling as if she was being sucked into some strange force-field.

'You need passion to be part of this,' said Jude. 'Cunt-positive rage.'

'Sorry . . . ?'

'Must say, thought there would be more girls here,' said Pilar. 'Bit sparse, isn't it?' She looked across at the two remaining sleeping bags, as if hoping that one of them might contain a snoring Isabelle Huppert.

Mel shook her head. 'I just don't get why *you're* here, Pilar. You were sarky as anything at the party. This is a cause I believe in, you know. I'm not here for a laugh.'

'Well, I've come because I want to do something good,' said Netta, then bit her lip because it sounded so stupid.

'And I've come because Netta made me,' said Pilar. 'Plus, I'm a passionate unilateral person, like I said.' She was looking around the clearing, her thin face impassive above her fluffy pink scarf. 'Although I do feel I've been misled. Netta seemed to think that when we got here it would all be one big happy family. Not just the four of you.'

A third figure was now shambling to life – Flora, her hair frizzed into Brillo-pad bangs by the outdoor life. She grabbed both of them in a strangely impersonal bear hug. 'Women of the world, unite!' she shouted commandingly, looking around at the silent trees. 'Dear, dear people!' Netta thought she might be about to make a speech, but instead she started combing the knots out of her hair. 'You must join us, of course, in the activities of the day,' she said. 'Our planned invasion will be glorious! Glorious! It will be our privilege to see the vile weapons at close quarters.'

Jude said something inaudible, and they all leaned towards her. 'Democratic,' she said. 'It has to be a democratic decision.'

'We'll take a vote,' said Mel.

'A vote on what?' asked Netta.

'It's simply a cloak for dictatorship,' declaimed Flora. 'This place is like a banana republic.'

'An Action,' said Mel.

'What's an Action?' asked Netta.

'Invading the base,' said Mel.

Now, the last figure had come to life. A very, very old woman – at least sixty, Netta thought – was crawling over to the campfire on her hands and knees. She added some branches to the glowing embers and fanned it to a healthy blaze. Next, she put on a pair of immense, bug-eyed spectacles. Then, finally, she spoke, in strong Cockney tones. 'Did you ever hear that old saying . . . ?'

'Racist,' muttered Jude. 'We've already agreed that saying is racist.'

'Too many chiefs, and not enough Indians?'

No one else spoke, so Netta said, 'Er – yes, I have.'

'Well, I'm Betty. And I'm the Indian. First I'll make us all a nice brew, and then these ladies can tell each other what to do.'

Netta went with Betty to the standpipe, where they filled a billycan with water. 'Why aren't there more of you?' she asked, as Betty hummed a tune which was probably something by Vera Lynn. 'Where is everyone?'

'We *are* a bit thin on the ground, aren't we?' said Betty. 'The weather doesn't help – you do get these fair-weather types. Personally, I like a bit of privation. Part of the war generation, you see. Pit yourself against it. And it reminds me of the Russians – just people just like us, with their balls freezing off. Only we don't have any balls, physically, of course. You can't really say freeze your vagina off, with it being tucked away inside, can you? Wait till Jude gets on to that subject – it's her party piece.'

Netta frowned, trying to follow this. 'But – are there more women at the other gates? There were hundreds of people here last time I came – and they can't all have been here just for the day.'

Betty turned the water off and laughed. 'Oh yes. Plenty more. Special circumstances at our gate. They all buggered off to Cinnamon Gate, two days ago. Fourteen women – I counted.'

'Why?'

'Can't you guess? They were going barmy. Jude's a nice girl, but she thinks she's running the Politburo. Flora's an interesting lady, but half the time, she comes on like the bleedin' Queen of England. Might as well have Maggie and Mr Andropov living here, for all the agreement we get. It's murder trying to get anything done.'

'And Mel is always on Jude's side, is she?'

'Oh yes. Starry-eyed about her, she is. It's all too much. No wonder the others decided they'd had enough.'

They were walking along the perimeter fence now. Netta looked through the diamond shapes of the wire mesh at the silos, which had a strangely festive appearance in the snow.

'Weird enough, isn't it?' said Betty. 'Enough to drive anyone round the twist.'

Netta nodded. 'Evil,' she said. 'Totally evil.' All her life, she had wanted to be relevant, at the centre of things. And now here she was, and she wished she could be somewhere else. But nowhere was safe from this.

As they approached the clearing, Netta said, 'So why did you stay? When the other women went off?'

'I'm a creature of habit,' said Betty. 'And they need me here, you know. The Indian. And the funny thing about it is, they always end up doing what I want – it's always a sort of log jam until I say what I think we should do. By the time we get to that stage, they're grateful to do anything. Without me, they'd just sit there arguing till the end of time.'

After Betty had made the tea, they all sat round in a circle, each person hunched on a small square of carpet to avoid sitting in the snow. Mel was holding an empty hot-water bottle. 'Okay, everyone. Are we agreed there is no chair?'

'Agreed,' whispered Jude.

'Right. This hot-water bottle is the conch. You only speak when you're holding it. If you want to speak, hold up your hand.'

Flora held up her hand and took the hot-water bottle. 'I want to know if we're going to cut the fence.'

Jude held up her hand and the bottle went to her. 'I say no,' she muttered. 'Cutting the fence is an act of violence. We should climb over it.'

Flora's turn again with the bottle. 'They've reinforced it. There's more barbed wire at the top. It's irresponsible to expose ourselves to unnecessary injury.'

Now it was Mel: 'I totally disagree with that.'

This went on for ten minutes, until Betty raised her hand for the last time. 'I vote we cut the fence,' she said.

So it was agreed. This was followed by a much longer discussion about what to wear. On the table was a Womble theme, Easter bunnies, Christmas angels and Bananarama. Mel and Jude favoured the Wombles. Flora liked the surreal visual impact of premature Easter bunnies, but her keenness on visual impact was seen as proof of her obsession with appearing on television. Pilar fancied herself as a Christmas angel. Netta was keen on Bananarama. Betty pointed out that unless all the themes were embraced, there wouldn't be enough costumes to go round.

It was only when Netta was half-way through the hole in the fence, her bottom wrapped in Pilar's pink angora scarf (an improvised ra-ra skirt intended to conjure up the mental image of Siobhan Fahey, the best-looking Bananarama girl), that she realized that she didn't know what to do once she got inside.

'Go for it, go on!' said Womble Mel, as she held the wire surrounding the hole open as wide as possible. This was the friendliest she had been so far.

'Go for what?'

'Head for the silos, over there!'

'And then what?'

'Climb on top!'

'What happens if they catch me? The police – or the Army?'

'Don't you know? Didn't you read Jude's handout?'

'What – the cunts one?'

'Bloody Norah – it's too late now! Just run for it – I'll catch you up. And go limp if they arrest you. Oh, and – don't tell them your real name.'

Netta looked up. Ahead of her, Christmas Fairy Pilar was skipping along, still in her furs, sporting a wreath of tinsel. She gave another wriggle, felt one of the naked points of wire tear into her flesh, fell headlong on to the grass on the other side, rolled over and began to run across the white, frozen ground.

15

Netta hurtled towards the dancing figure of Pilar, not daring to look left or right, expecting to see battalions of soliders rushing towards her. Behind her, she could hear panting and gasping, which she hoped was Mel, and not some enormous squaddie.

When she reached the inner fence, the three of them caught hold of the wire with their hands for a moment, and stood there, breath rasping.

'Got to get in!' wheezed Mel, puce in the face, frosted breath clouding the air. She began to work away with her wire-cutters, struggling to get the steel beak to cut the thick metal strands. From somewhere, Netta could hear the sound of men's voices shouting. Pilar looked behind her coolly, as if she was planning to ascend to the heavens if there was trouble of any kind. But the snowy expanse of ground was empty. Netta saw that Mel had already made a small hole in the wire – almost big enough to wriggle through, if you were skinny.

'Just . . . need to make it a tiny, weeny bit . . . wider . . .' said Mel, cutting away. 'Nearly there. Just think, you'll be dancing on top of those weapons in no time.'

'Shit,' said Netta, suddenly seeing some figures rushing towards them.

'What?'

'Police. They've spotted us.'

'Fuck! I only need . . .' Then she looked up quickly, as if judging the distance of the small group of men jogging towards them, and appraising Pilar and Netta's bodies. 'Go through,' she said urgently. 'Go through now – you're both miles thinner than me . . .'

Netta squirmed through the hole. The sound of running footsteps was coming nearer, and she ran on, even faster than before, till she came to the first silo. She looked up at it – flat-topped, grey and monolithic, it reminded her of an ancient Mayan tomb.

Pilar was next to her. 'This is bleeding hilarious!' she said. 'I could really get into this gung-ho stuff. All it needs is some really foxy women. Love among the missiles.'

'How do we get up there?'

'Dunno. Let's just go for it and start climbing.'

They scrambled up the side of the silo, pulling themselves up with hands that were half frozen inside their gloves. Breathless, half-giggling and half-sobbing, they finally reached the top. They skipped to the centre, joined hands and began to dance, while what seemed like the whole of Berkshire slowly revolved behind them, spread out like a panoramic Christmas card.

'Phewee,' said Mel, scrambling up and breaking into their circle. Her clothes were ripped and her hands were bleeding, but she was grinning, she was the old Mel. 'Fantastic, isn't it? Makes you proud to be a woman.' They began to spin faster and faster, so that the sky and the landscape became a shimmering blur. Netta looked at her friends' laughing faces, and thought she had never been so happy – or so frightened. Everything seemed to be brighter, more sharply illuminated, especially her own emotions.

'Boozers against the Bomb!' cried Pilar.

'Greenham Women Are Everywhere!' yelled Mel.

'Girls from Crewe Say No to . . . Cruise . . .' said Netta, slightly losing her momentum when she saw four policemen marching towards them, looking slightly embarrassed.

'Right, ladies, we are arresting you for trespass and anything you say may be used in evidence . . .' said one of the policemen. 'Name, please?'

'Lady Olga Maitland of Women and Families for Defence,' said Mel. And with that she lay down on the ground.

'Edith Piaf,' said Pilar. '*Je ne regrette rien.*' She stretched out next to Mel, giggling.

Netta felt faint. This was it, then. She was about to be arrested. What would her father think? What would Jane make of it? 'Barbara Cartland,' she said, stretching out in her turn.

'You can't kill the spirit,' Mel shouted up at them. 'We are women and we are strong!'

'Come on, my love,' said another policeman, jarringly perky. 'Up we come! No harm done!'

'I'm not your love,' said Mel. 'Please don't use inappropriate terms of affection. I find that patronizing . . .' But her voice was fainter now. They were carrying her away.

'I demand to see my solicitor,' said Pilar. 'I'm entitled to at least one phone call.' She seemed to have a flair for civil disobedience.

'We haven't arrested you yet, miss,' said a yokelly voice. 'Won't do that coat much good, lying in the mud, now will it?'

Netta heard a high-pitched shriek as they picked Pilar up. 'Fascists!' she hissed. 'I demand my right to lie down on a silo . . .' Then she too was gone.

Now the sky changed shape over Netta's head as two policemen bent over her, their helmets dividing her line of vision with almost formal symmetry.

'Best not to talk to them more than necessary, constable,' said one. Looking up, Netta noticed his knobbly face, with cheeks that could have been stuffed with cauliflower. 'Just do what you have to.' Then she felt someone take her arms, holding her so tightly that she could feel her skin burning.

'Come on, come on, constable – get the legs. We haven't got all day,' said the first policeman.

'Right you are, sarge. Here we go,' said the second policeman nervously. Netta wondered if he was new to the job. She felt him grab hold of her legs, and then she was dangling about two feet from the ground, feeling as if she was about to be given the bumps at school. He seemed to have trouble keeping his grip, and as he reached the edge, she felt herself begin to fall.

'Watch out,' she screamed, as the sky changed its angle and she plunged downwards, her body falling towards the police constable who was already half-way down the ladder.

'What the bloody–' he squawked as she landed on top of him, her fall conveniently broken by his large frame. For a second, she lay with her eyes closed. The sergeant was groaning. 'My leg – my leg . . .' She saw her chance. She didn't have to be arrested after all. Scrambling to her feet, she fled, running hard, not knowing which direction to go. Where were the holes in the two fences? Had the police sealed them up again? Her chest was tight and she began to panic. What were they doing to Mel and Pilar? Would the next sensation she felt be a bullet, ripping her apart? Panting, she reached the inner fence, but there was no hole to be seen. Just the concrete pillars marching off and encircling the inner sanctum. She was trapped. Looking behind her, she saw that other women were dancing and cavorting on top of the silos, and more police arriving to arrest them. She started to run round the fence, hoping that the hole might still be there, further along somewhere. Behind her, voices were growing louder. The fear was now clenching her throat, like a physical force. Then someone stuck their head out of the fence ahead of her, swathed in an orange shawl.

'This way! This way!' With heaving breath, she ran even faster till she got to the opening in the fence, and threw herself through it. 'Come on – follow me!' said a muffled voice, and she followed as they charged across the snow towards the outer edge of the base, her chest contracting in pain, her feet stumbling over the rough ground. Looking back again, she saw a policeman half-way through the hole, trying to force his way through. Her legs were getting heavier, and each breath felt as if it was scraping out the inside of her lungs.

'I can't . . . can't . . .' she tried to say, but her mind couldn't even formulate what it was that she couldn't do.

'Keep going! Don't slow down!' She followed the voice blindly now, hearing her breath coming as childish sobs as she ran. Behind her, she could hear feet thumping on the ground – she would never get out, she could never get out. Then, suddenly, the hole in the second fence was in front of her, she was being pushed through it. A tumble of snowy bushes, and she found herself in a heap on the frozen ground, tangled up with the arms and legs of her rescuer. The orange shawl had unravelled, and she saw it was a tall, dark-haired man. Tom Birtwistle was looking at her with a mixture of exasperation and amusement.

'I hope you know what you're d-doing,' he said, shaking his head. 'Or rather, it's obvious you don't have a clue.'

'Don't be rude,' said Netta, struggling to her feet. 'I've got just as much right to get arrested as anyone else. You don't need an A-level in Peacenikking to run about in there.' She waved at the wire fence, relieved to feel angry with him when in other circumstances she might have been intimidated. He looked unnervingly handsome in the early-morning light, his long dark hair dishevelled by the shawl and falling into his eyes.

Tom smiled in a superior fashion, brushing himself off. His black leather appeared to have emerged untarnished from the fray, but it still creaked a lot. 'A small amount of c-common sense would help. You're practically crippled in that stupid costume, for a start. And why didn't you know about your exit point?'

'Oh, pardon me,' she said. 'Exit point? I didn't know I was signing up for the Marines! I thought I was against the military, not part of the show.' She stepped out of her pink angora skirt and bundled it up.

He laughed. 'You do need forward planning,' he said. 'But something tells me you aren't the forward-planning type.'

'Well, thanks a lot. Although, I must admit, you're not the first person to say that.'

'I'm not trying to . . . be superior or anything.'

'Really?'

'No.'

'So what are you trying to do?'

'I'm trying to help . . .'

'Why?'

'Because – oh, I don't know . . .'

'Because what?'

'Because I like you.'

She felt a surge of elation. 'Even with my weird new hair?' She ran her fingers over the blonde stubble.

'Especially with your weird new hair.'

They looked at each other. Oh dear, thought Netta. I don't want to just tumble over the edge into this, the way I fell off that silo. She needed a safety net. There must be bad things about this man. If only she knew what they were!

Suddenly, he grabbed her by the arm and pulled her into the bushes. 'Peace women,' he hissed.

'Not the Gestapo, then?' But she crouched next to him in the frosty undergrowth, listening to the sound of approaching voices.

'Men aren't exactly welcome round here, as you'll know,' he breathed into her ear.

'So why don't you bugger off then?' she whispered back, but now he squeezed her arm tightly and kept a firm grip as the voices came right up to their hiding place.

'It's an important statement, you see. We want to get the great British public to see us as an inspiration,' said a voice. Netta felt a thrill of embarrassment. It was Flora.

*

Through the dark evergreen leaves, Netta could make out that there was another woman with her. She had long, droopy hair, which gave her the appearance of a doleful spaniel, and was wearing a knitted hat which resembled a tea cosy. 'Yes, we got some good photos of you getting through the hole in the fence,' said the woman in a nasal voice. 'Action shots. They should come out well.'

'Excellent,' said Flora. 'No one else was in the way, I hope? I did worry that you might not get a good view.'

'I'm sure they'll be perfect,' said the woman.

'What I want to get across in this article is that the whole movement is in danger of being hijacked by extremists,' said Flora. 'People like me – what you might call the old guard – we represent broad feminist values. Of the best kind, it goes without saying. Now there's all kinds of nonsense going on, every kind of ragtag opinion which doesn't fit into the mainstream. The main issue – nuclear disarmament – is being overshadowed.'

The woman was silent for a second. Netta saw that she was scribbling hard. 'I understand you've only just got here?'

'Oh yes,' said Flora. 'You'll find that's very much the nature of the beast, my dear. Women come and go, rise up, and fall. All part of the same organic urge to save Mother Earth, you see.'

Tea Cosy looked up from her pad. 'But you're the one who gets the media attention.'

Flora gave a modest laugh. 'I suppose my track record speaks for itself. You got the title of my last book, didn't you? *The Sock Dropper's Misogyny*. A thought-provoking yet highly accessible analysis of the fundamentals of sexual inequality. And . . . can you put in a brief reference to Jude Blackman? I consider her to be a very dangerous person. No need to go into much detail – just make the point that she is manipulative – and irrelevant. The focus of the article is me, of course.'

Netta glanced at Tom and saw that he was biting his hand. Whether to stifle his laughter, or stop himself from screaming, she wasn't sure.

After they had gone, he covered his face with both hands. Finally, he removed them and took a deep breath. 'Stupid, stupid woman,' he said.

'Stupid? Are you kidding?' Netta shook her head. 'She seems pretty much in control to me.'

'She's *out* of control,' said Tom. 'At least, her ego is out of control. She comes here, out of the blue, and then starts exploiting it for her own ends. She's just a bloody has-been – but her pathetic career is more important to her than the nuclear threat. It makes me sick.'

They pushed their way out of the bushes and began walking along the path by the perimeter fence. Netta glanced at his face. He was staring around him vacantly, as if he wasn't sure what to do next. 'It's bad,' he said finally. 'It's all very, very bad. Any day now, they could fire off those weapons, and my mother is trying to sell a book about socks.'

Netta shrugged. 'Which is crap, I totally agree. But all parents are crap. My dad is the crappiest of the lot – he's drunk all the time and thinks I'm a moron because I'm not some ridiculous Oxbridge Exhibitioner. The only difference is that your mother is famous, which is obviously annoying in itself. What I don't get is why you have to hang around, hiding in the bushes, *watching* her be crap. Can't you go off and do something else, and leave her to it?' She was standing so close to him that she could see that the whites of his eyes were almost blue, reflecting the sky, as he gazed above her head.

'This is the epicentre of nuclear protest in the UK. Where else would I go?'

'It's for girls, Tom. It's a womany thing. They don't need you, and they don't want you. Protest in some other way. Emily told me you shoot statues – that sounds like a bit of fun.'

Tom looked wounded. 'Fun? Don't you understand anything? It was socialist anarchism, a statement about the decadent irrelevance of accepted hierarchies. An attack on obeying orders. I'm not here to make jokes. Anyway, I'm finished with all that.'

'What did you shoot them with? An actual gun?'

'Of course not! I used a wooden replica rifle with a little white flag at the end, saying "Bang bang, you're dead."'

'Right,' said Netta. 'Sounds very symbolic.' She was trying to think. He was attractive, certainly. And she also felt sorry for him, the lonely undercover peace Goth, still obsessed with his dreadful mother. But perhaps this made him a lost cause. She suspected there wasn't much chance of releasing him from his self-imposed vigil.

'Your mother does seem to be exploiting Greenham,' she said. 'Even so, I don't really see what you can do about it.'

'I don't know. I suppose if I could get my own voice heard, it would make some difference.'

'Heard by who?'

'By – the public By the press. I suppose. Then I would be fighting her on her own terms. But the papers don't want to talk to me. She's the famous one in the family.'

'Why don't you write something then? Or talk to a journalist?'

'What would be the point?'

'Maybe someone would publish it.'

'I wouldn't know where to start.'

She was aware of not thinking quite straight, of the fact that there seemed to be less oxygen in Tom's immediate vicinity. When he smiled at her – as he was doing now – the not-thinking-quite-straight was dizzyingly intense.

'Well – why don't you just tell me?'

He stared at her, then said thoughtfully: 'I just never understood why other children didn't get it.'

'Get what?'

'The first time I saw that white nuclear flash on TV – God – it just changed everything.'

'Why?'

'Because – that's what it would do. Reality, blasted into nothingness like matchwood. But everyone else just carried on watching *Blue Peter* and eating egg on toast, as if the world was safe and permanent and nothing could ever go wrong. I knew different . . .'

'But why did you know different?'

'I suppose I have to give Flora some credit. The house was always full of protest banners and candles in jars, ready for the next rally. Not to mention all kinds of radical hippy weirdos. My dad was a peacenik, too. In the end he went off to live in some commune in Denmark. Squeezed out by Flora: she couldn't stand the sight of him.'

'Poor bloke.'

'He was a complete git. Slept with everyone behind her back. Most women turned a blind eye to that kind of thing then, in the name of free love. But not Flora.'

'Was it an unhappy childhood, then?'

'How can you tell? It was quite good having a dad in Copenhagen. We used to go and visit him sometimes. And I thought all children spent their days making nuclear fall-out shelters under the kitchen table. Using pillows for sandbags, and taking in enough supplies to last till the "All Clear" siren sounded.'

'Bit strange.'

'I didn't think it was strange. Why play Cowboys and Indians when real death was so much more exciting? But other parents complained that I was scaring their kids with horrible stories about the end of the world. All I was trying to do was raise a bit of awareness . . . I suppose I was about eight by then . . .' On the subject of Flora his manner changed, and he picked up a stick and twisted it irritably in his hands. 'She was into every-thing – everything fashionable – not just feminism. A bit of anti-nuclear stuff – she marched to Aldermaston in the 1950s when she was a teenager – but it all got swamped by every other radical protest available. Anti-arms sales to South Africa, pro-black rule in Rhodesia, pro-Sandinistas and anti-armed occupation of Northern Ireland – you know the kind of thing. But since her first book came out – *Housebound Harridans*, the famous one

– she's really only been interested in one thing.' He stopped suddenly.

'What's that?'

'Getting attention. You saw for yourself.' Tom stood up and stretched his legs.

'I have to go,' said Netta.

'Me too.' But Tom caught hold of her right hand and looked at it. 'Do you play the violin?'

'No, why?'

'You've got musician's hands.'

'Bit late now,' said Netta, withdrawing her hand in case it gave too much away. 'I gave up the recorder when I was seven.'

'Right.' He looked as if he was going to ask her something, but then clapped his hands to his sides, in an exaggerated pantomime of being cold. 'Definitely have to go now,' he said. 'Have to – go and lurk in the bushes. Important job.'

'And I should find the others.' Netta felt suddenly disoriented. What was she doing? What was she thinking? And what had happened to Mel and Pilar? Even though it was accidental, she felt guilty about escaping when they had been carted away by the police.

Tom gave her a twisted smile. 'Feel b-better for that, self-indulgent splurging,' he said. 'Maybe someone will print something sensible about all this one day.' She realized he hadn't stammered once during his diatribe about Flora and his childhood. He hesitated, then turned and disappeared among the snow-laden trees. Netta watched him go, then began to tramp slowly towards Rainbow Gate.

*

'Oh, it was so funny! You should have been there, Nettie! It was hilarious!'

It was early evening. Pilar was sitting by the campfire, drinking from her whisky bottle. Mel was sipping tea, laughing quietly to herself. Jude and Flora were listening to the story of arrest, manhandling (or 'person-handling' according to Jude), incarceration and caution, told by Pilar with great panache. She seemed like an old hand already, a Greenham stalwart in spite of her dodgy furs and variable accent. (Which was more Estuary and less Ealing now that she had done her fifteen minutes of form.)

'The fucking pigs!' said Flora, with a grand sweep of her hand. 'I can't tell you the number of occasions on which I've tangled with them in my time. They tried to trample me to death in Grosvenor Square, you know. But of course, they were out of their depth. Eight thousand of us, protesting against the obscenity of Vietnam. Heady times, the sixties. We shall never see their like again.'

'The police dropped me,' said Netta, unable to say 'pigs'. 'Over the edge, by mistake. I squashed a constable, and ran away.' She felt dropped in more ways than one, as Pilar and Mel sat leaning against each other, faces bright with excitement. While she didn't want them to be at war with each other, she didn't want them to get on so well that she was excluded, either. However, she knew these feelings were unworthy of someone who had come to Greenham to stop World War Three. The trouble with big ideas (such as wanting to rid the world of nuclear missiles) was that small ones (such as wanting to be Ms Popularity Princess, 1985) were more familiar. She was on safe ground with small ideas. Twisting her hands in her lap, she wished she could understand. Why couldn't life be simple: happy times bonding with like-minded chums? Instead of all this mess. The one event which loomed out of the recent past with absolute clarity was having sex with Richard. Tom fascinated her – but their encounter hadn't made any difference to the guilt and self-hatred she carried with her. What she needed was the flip-side of that dreadful evening: the reverse experience. If she'd had some bolt-cutters, she would have been tempted to cut her way back in, lie down, and insist on being arrested with unnecessary force. Imprisonment and martyrdom would rid her of the deed. But this was unworthy too. She would be no better than Flora, using Greenham for her own ends. She glanced at the trees which bordered the clearing, wondering whether Tom was listening in again, and whether they would meet again.

'If only Dad could've seen me!' said Pilar, swigging again. 'Gawd! His little girl! He thought I was safe in Harrods, spending his dosh. And there I was, manacled in a police van.'

'My dad would have had a heart attack,' said Mel. 'He's missed a trick, with this. He should have taken out insurance cover against spawning a peace person. Safety first and last, with him. Not much he can do about it now.'

'Can't insure against them dropping the Bomb,' whispered Jude. They all bent nearer to her, but this was all she had to say on the matter.

'Father was in the Somme,' said Betty, emerging from the shadows, and chucking some firewood on to the pile. 'They dropped plenty on him there. He lost his sense of smell.'

Talk of fathers made Netta nervous. She hadn't phoned her own malfunctioning, inebriated one since leaving London. She usually called him every other day, and held the receiver a short distance from her ear, so that he could rant on about the rain, regulars and Anna Raeburn (whom he loathed with unreasonable loathing, being a secret reader of *Cosmopolitan*). Now, she was out of reach, and if he tried to contact her, he would hear Pilar's recorded message, telling him in fake Celia Johnson tones that she was probably in the library. The more Netta thought about this, the more worried she felt. In the end, there was nothing for it but to slip away and call him – the nearest phone box was some distance away.

'Dad?' Someone had picked up the receiver, without speaking. 'Dad, is that you?'

'Dad.' The voice was a croak. 'Is that who I am? Or . . . David?'

'You're both – David and Dad.'

There was another long silence. 'Hmmm. Who's this?'

'Netta.'

'Who?'

'Jeanette.'

'No it's not. You're out. I phoned you. Yesterday, I think, or last week. Or perhaps it was tomorrow? Hard to say. It's dark here, you know . . .'

She clutched the cold receiver tightly. 'Are you okay? Have you been drinking?'

'No, of course I'm bloody not, and yes, of course I bloody have,' he said. 'What do you expect? I'm a fucking depressive alcoholic.'

'I'm sorry I haven't phoned before.'

'Oh, don't worry, don't mention it. The other one called.'

'The other one?'

'Finest mind in her year. Married that pompous bugger Richard.'

'Jane.'

'Jane! That's the one. Phoned up in bloody tears, if you don't mind. What's the point of that, when she says she's calling to find out how I am? Just selfishness. She's underachieved, of course. All those bloody . . . whatsits . . . children.' Then he made a strange noise. It took her a moment to work out what it was. He was crying, she realized. She had never heard him make that sound before, even after Margaret died. The dry, bitter sobs sounded as if they were being ripped out of him.

Netta looked out at the frozen landscape that surrounded the old-fashioned phone box. A sharp wind blew through the broken panes of glass.

16

When she got back to the camp, another meeting was in progress. Flora was waving a leaflet about, which Netta realized was the Positively Cunts flier she had found when she arrived. 'Can you please define the purpose and objectives of Positively C-words, and explain without recourse to the use of absurd jargon its precise relevance to ending the nuclear menace?' The hot-water bottle was nowhere to be seen: this was an authentic argument, not a controlled exchange of views.

'Oh, fuck off, Flora,' said Mel. 'This is about women's rights. We're not all stuck in a 1960s time warp. There's more to life than Joan Baez.'

Jude began to whisper authoritatively. 'Positively Cunts is an organization which is looking at issues around women owning their own sexual organs, which are a focus for both sexual pleasure and procreation.'

'In other words, my fanny belongs to me.' said Mel. 'It's just common sense.'

Flora made a small exploding sound. 'I'd jolly well like to know who owns my sexual organs, if not me,' she said. 'I've given birth to two children. Most of this stuff is plain balderdash, Mel! You are an intelligent person . . . where does all this nonsense come from?'

'I can't get into this c-word affair,' said Betty. 'It's much too intellectual. I was born in Shadwell, you know.'

'Then follow me!' said Flora, throwing her head back in a Queen Boudicca sort of way.

Betty looked sceptical. 'I'll make us another brew,' she said, getting up and picking up the kettle.

'I can't believe you're still saying this, Flora!' Jude's whispers were more audible now. 'You know that's crap. Who owns women's bodies? Who owns our image, our powers of reproduction? THE PATRIARCHY, that's who!' Mel began to clap.

Pilar, who had nodded off with her head on Mel's shoulder, woke up and clapped as well. 'Hurrah for the patriarchy!' she said.

'Very well,' said Flora. 'Let's look at what we are against. Cruise. Nuclear war. The Arms Race. Onward and upward. We're letting gender issues take over. It doesn't matter if we use, or don't use, the c-word.'

'"Cunt", you mean,' whispered Jude.

'There's no need to say the word.'

'Isn't there?' Jude stood up. 'Cunt,' she said, speaking at normal volume. Netta caught her breath, jolted by surprise. Jude continued, still talking in conversational tones which seemed to ring out in the woodland like a sergeant major's on parade. 'What does that word say to you? It's the most extreme swear word in the English language. But it's a word that used to mean "fanny", just as simple and straightforward as that. So how come I grew up thinking that saying it was so foul? "Fuck", yes. I could say that if I wanted to be offensive. But "cunt" was beyond offensive. It was obscene – and it denigrated women. So everyone said. Only really sexist, misogynistic men would use a word like that. Then I thought – why? It's a word which represents our sex. And it's been outlawed. Is it because it's the essence of what it means to be a woman? Men say that women have penis envy. Bullshit to that. Men have cunt envy. Cunt encloses them. Cunt is not bad, cunt is everything. Cunt is our anatomical jewel.'

'You're talking about sexual politics, not the battle against the Bomb!' shouted Flora. 'We'll be a laughing stock in the press if we carry on like this . . .'

'Shh,' said Mel. 'Did you hear something?' She had turned to look behind her.

They stared at her.

'Something in the woods.'

Netta said nothing, thinking of Tom the Oedipal spy. Jude seemed to have no interest in this. She had hit her stride now. 'When men fuck our cunts against our will, we feel as if someone has shoved shit into the essence of our soul, and spend the rest of our lives trying to clean it off. Cunts are the centre of our being. When we learn to love them, we learn to love ourselves. If we reclaim the sacredness of the word "cunt" we reclaim our own sacredness as women. Is that big enough to include the struggle against the nuclear Bomb? I think it is.'

'Seconded!' said Mel.

'Thirded!' said Pilar, who had found the whisky again. 'Hurrah for cunts!'

Flora stood up too. She stretched up to her full size – which was approximately twice that of Jude – and said, 'We have to assert the logic of unilateralism. What has the c-word got to do with that?'

'The old roles don't work any more,' said Mel. 'It's not just about sharing power, it's about redefining it.'

'Rubbish!' shouted Flora.

'Cunts against Cruise!' shouted Pilar.

'Shut up, Pilar,' said Mel.

'We need a woman-centred language to create a woman-centred world,' said Jude. 'Womankind is varied and vast. But all of us have cunts. All of us have that darkness and richness inside us.'

'Stuff and nonsense! I've never heard such idiocy in my life!' shouted Flora.

Netta stood up to speak, but no one was listening. Mel was trying to get the whisky bottle off Pilar, Flora was shouting about the arms trade and *Guardian* editorials, Jude was looking quietly serene, as if the argument was over. Only Betty, returning with a full kettle, noticed when Netta turned to go.

'It's not for everyone,' she said.

'I wish I could stay,' said Netta. 'I really do. I just have to sort something out, then I'll come back.'

'They love all this,' said Betty. 'But not all of us were put on earth to theorize about Down Below. Some of us have to make the tea.'

The London train shuddered out of Newbury station. Netta stretched out her legs, realizing that she ached all over. It was tempting to imagine that by leaving Greenham, she was leaving the threat of war behind as well. But she knew this wasn't true. She opened the ludicrous Government leaflet 'Protect and Survive', which she had brought with her from the house. On the front was a picture of a mushroom cloud, in a curiously nostalgic shade of sepia, swelling magnificently above an elegant stem of silvery vapour. Below it were the following words:

If Britain is attacked by a nuclear bomb, we do not know which targets will be chosen, or how severe the assault will be. If nuclear weapons are used on a large scale, those of us living in the country areas might be exposed to as great a risk as those living in the towns. The radioactive dust, falling where the wind blows it, will bring the most widespread dangers of all . . .

'Nice bit of light reading for the journey,' said a familiar voice. 'When the day comes, I'll be heading for the fucking epicentre, I'm telling you. Get yourself in the right place at the right time and you won't know a bloody thing about it. Being vaporized when the world ends is what I call going out in style.' Bryan stood in front of her, smiling and carrying a British Rail bag which gave off a powerfully greasy aroma.

'What the hell are you doing here?' Netta asked. '*You* haven't been to Greenham, have you?'

'I don't know why you're looking so surprised,' said Bryan. 'You're the one who suggested I should check it out. Went down for a recce, and I'm reporting back to the features editor today. No point hanging around if there is a hot story to be chased up.' He settled himself down opposite to her. 'So how was it? Didn't last long, did you?'

'I've had to leave early for personal reasons – for a while,' said Netta. 'I'll soon be back.' She nodded towards his bag. 'That smells disgusting.'

Bryan fished out his sandwich and looked at it appraisingly. 'Bacon and egg,' he said. 'You just can't arse that up, can you? Even undercooked bacon has its own appeal. Unbeatable.' He took a large bite and chewed for a while, regarding her happily over his sandwich. 'Great idea, this freelancing. I can do two jobs at once. They never fucking know where you are at the Union, in any case. Perfect for me, really. Should be able to pay off my debts by Easter.'

'Lucky old you. Then perhaps you'll be able to invest in some proper food.' She didn't think she'd ever seen such a horrible sandwich in her life. The bacon slices looked like human flesh held between the pallid white slices of bread. 'Did you get any ideas, then?'

Bryan's smile faded slightly. 'Yeah, well,' he said. 'All the usual boring bull-dyke stuff, really. I need to get a sexy new angle going. I only got this work because I sold myself pretty hard. The people at the *Chronic* are under the impression that I already have quite a strong track record in nailing top stories about youth culture.'

'Whatever gave them that idea?'

Bryan winced.

'You . . . misled them, did you?'

'Well, kind of. I might have created the impression that I'm a bit more experienced than I am in reality. Though I did get something about BowWowWow in the showbiz pages of *Today* once – I sold them an exclusive when they nicked some toilet rolls from the Student Union.'

'Maybe you should stick to your real job, and try and do that properly. The *Chronicle*'s a rubbishy old newspaper, in any case.'

'Look, the moral high ground is pretty crowded, darling.

You can take your seat alongside the anti-nuclear harpies. I'm happier down here in the sewers.'

'But why?'

'I'm not complicated. I'm a strictly superficial kind of guy. I want to be famous. Not next year, not when I've paid my dues, not when I'm old and bald – right now. *Met Student* might keep me off the streets, but it's never going to make me a household name.' He leaned across and looked at the leaflets on her lap. 'What's that – "Protect and Survive"?' As she passed it to him, the Positively Cunts pamphlet fluttered to the ground. She reached out quickly to pick it up, but it was too late. Bryan had plucked it from the ground and was reading it. 'Oh shit,' he said, then, 'Hilarious! "A man's penis dangles pointlessly outside his body" . . . I love it. "Join us or collude with the oppression of your own clitoris" – Jesus. There has to be some mileage in this!'

'Do you have to be so predictable? Making a mockery of Greenham is just a cheap shot. I thought you would want to do something more interesting. Put over the inside story, not just regurgitate the usual tabloid tripe.'

The expression on Bryan's face changed. 'Now, that *is* a good idea,' he said. 'What with you being in a position to put me in the full, inside-story sort of picture.'

'How d'you mean?'

'You could do a little bit of a reporting job for me. Tell me what's going on inside these women's heads.'

'Help you write for the *Chronicle*? You must be joking. I might as well join the bloody National Front! Just go away and think of a good idea and don't involve me!'

'Why not?'

'These people are my friends. Even Pilar is there now – though I doubt if she'll last long. Just think how it would go down with the women at Greenham if they thought I'd written some insider view, behind their backs, and it had been printed in the *Daily Chronicle*.'

'Probably crush you to death with their big fat arses.' Bryan was silent for a moment, apparently enjoying this mental image. 'Only – I thought you might like the idea of getting your byline in the nationals. Person of grit and ambition like yourself.'

'No way. I want to redeem myself, not transform into Glenda Slagg.' Shouldn't have said that, she thought to herself.

'Redeem yourself? That *does* sound interesting. What have you been up to?'

'None of your business.'

Bryan sighed. 'Suppose I'll just have to hide in the bushes, and try and eavesdrop on the evil ratbags as they trip about, trashing local beauty spots in search of firewood, or looking for newborn babies to eat. I mean, let's face it, I could just make anything up and the *Chronicle* would print it. Who's to know the difference?'

Netta stared at him. 'You're not serious! Aren't there rules, professional regulations? It would be libellous. And wrong. Just wrong.' She ran out of steam, wishing that she hadn't glazed over quite so fundamentally during every single 'Law and the Media' seminar.

'Of course I'm serious. This could be my big chance. Anyway, these peace women deserve everything they get. This leaflet is factual evidence – they're off their fucking heads.'

'Bryan, you just can't make up stuff about Greenham. It would be completely irresponsible!'

'Just watch me. I can and I bloody well will. And if you wanted to get anywhere in life, instead of joining in with these half-baked, bleeding-heart bozos, you'd be the same. It's Thatcher's Britain, not Noddyland. Wake up and smell the napalm.'

'God.' She looked out of the window, trying to think. Sidings rushed by. Marooned trains, rusting and forgotten. Some hoardings. A huge ad of a man with a bunch of flowers chasing after a woman. Another showing a model's legs poking out of an egg, as if they belonged to a newborn chick. The slogan ran: 'Legs as soft and smooth as the day you were born'. Below this, someone had written in spray-paint graffiti: 'Born kicking'. She would like to do that, of course, kick her way out. But every step she took seemed to compromise her further. 'Oh, my darling! Oh, my darling!' Would she ever forget it? Could she ever put things right? Perhaps she could do something now, something to help Tom and to stop Bryan from penning some cynical little hatchet job on Greenham Common.

'Do you want to do something useful, or do you want to just spend your life being a total airhead?' said Bryan, echoing her thoughts. His good humour had evaporated completely now.

'I don't want to add to all the rubbish that's been written about them already. It's not exactly going to help the cause, writing about all that. It's going to make things worse.'

'What do you get out of being so pious? Apart from a nice warm, smug feeling about solidarity with the girls, when you don't fit in with people like them and you bloody well know you don't.'

'Apart from not alienating all my friends, nothing. I'd like to read my leaflet now, please.'

Bryan sighed and rolled the empty paper bag into a ball. 'Well, all I can say is that one day you'll regret this. When I'm the editor of *The Times* and you're washing nappies. I'm off to the smoking carriage.' He got up and turned to go.

But an idea had been taking shape in Netta's mind. She called out, 'Bryan?'

He looked back at her.

'Yeah?'

'You could try speaking to Tom. Emily's brother. He knows all about Greenham, and he thinks Flora gets too much air-play. He wants to put his side of the story.' She bit her lip. 'Tom's an idealist. Which might be beyond your comprehension. I hope you tell his story straight.'

Bryan grinned. 'Thanks for the lead. Still sure you don't want to kick-start your freelance career?'

'Positive.'

He shrugged. 'Okay. But – there was something I wanted to say to you . . .'

'Yes?'

He hesitated. 'Just wanted to say . . .'

'What?'

'Basically, if you fancy a shag, let me know.'

'You must be joking.'

'Yeah, I know what you're thinking. Who'd fancy you in that state? When your hair gets back to normal, obviously.'

17

'I want gin!' David was lying in the spare bedroom of Jane's house. It was an elegant, well-proportioned room with two long windows overlooking Fitzsimmons Square. However, it didn't appear to its best advantage at that moment, with the tramplike figure of David sprawled across the double bed.

'You can't have gin. Drink your cocoa.'

'Give me some bloody gin! I live over a bloody pub, and all I can get is cocoa. For God's sake . . .'

'Dad, you're drunk. You're killing yourself with drink. You've got to stop.'

Her father growled.

'Anyway, you're not at the pub,' said Netta. 'You're at Jane's. In London. In Islington. Remember?'

David looked down at himself as if he was trying to work out who he was. Most of the buttons had come off his grubby white shirt, and the flies on his trousers were permanently undone, presumably to give him one less chore to trouble about when he rushed into the bathroom next door. Through the gaping, zip-framed hole, Netta could see his string underpants: David was far too old to have allowed boxer shorts to enter his consciousness. Behind him, on the dressing table, was a black-and-white photo of his wedding day. Shining with boyish lust, he was holding the door open for Margaret, curvy and alluring in a tight white suit. Netta looked at the familiar picture, then at the bedclothes and pillows, creased and snarled up around his arms and legs. He had been either in bed or lolling on top of it since she had returned from Greenham four days earlier to help Jane look after him. The room stank of stale booze and old sweat.

'Little bitch,' said her father. 'I'm not your prisoner, you know.'

'Of course you're not my prisoner, Dad! For God's sake. And don't say bitch.'

'At my time of life – in close proximity to death – I can say and do what I want.'

She sighed. 'Here we go.'

'If I want to use a healthy Anglo-Saxon word like "bitch", I can. If I want booze, I can have booze. If I managed to drink myself to death, then no doubt you and your sister would be very relieved. Less trouble for you, when I'm gone. And you'll get the pub, don't forget that.'

She sighed again. 'I haven't forgotten. We don't want the pub. We'd rather have you.'

'Nonsense. No one in their right mind would rather have me.' He stared at her. 'What the bloody hell have you done to your hair? You look terrible!'

'I cut it all off. You've seen it already.'

'No I haven't.'

'Yes you have.'

'No I haven't.'

Downstairs, she could hear Jane calling. 'Drink your cocoa,' she said to him, turning to go.

*

Jane was feeding the children in the kitchen. She was wearing an old summer coat of Richard's, back to front like a surgeon's gown. There had been no further mention of the Toby near-death incident. This was the best outcome, Netta thought. Praise for saving him would be inappropriate. Analysis of how he came to be in the water in the first place could lead to more trouble. 'Thought I'd sort lunch out before leaving you to hold the fort,' Jane said. 'Nightmare, otherwise. How is he?'

'Oh, you know. Drunk and mad. Demanding gin. Although, maybe he's feeling better. He's threatening to come down.'

'Try and get him to go out for some fresh air. The brood could do with it, too. That's the curse of these cold winter days – they all go stir-crazy.'

'Okay. Bit nippy though, isn't it?'

Jane – who had managed not to sound snooty for several minutes – reverted to form. 'Netta, there is nothing wrong with a little winter cold. Take them to the Heath, that's what I do.'

'Oh, we hate the Heath!' chorused Toby and Charlotte. 'We hate Outdoors, we do!'

'What, Hampstead Heath?' said Netta. 'It's bloody miles away.'

'Bloody, bloody, bloody!' shouted Charlotte.

'Ten pence in the swear box,' said Jane. 'You're not with your foul-mouthed college chums now.'

'He's in an awful state,' said Netta, spooning some puréed apple into Little Richard's mouth. 'I do feel sorry for him. Maybe I should take some time off my course and go up there. Help out in the pub.'

'That qualifies as one of your utterly hare-brained ideas. One minute you rush to Greenham, the next minute you want to go back to Crewe. What would be the point of that?'

'He just seems so lost. And I . . .' She hesitated, feeling herself going too close to absolute honesty.

'You . . . what?'

'I don't do much good in the world.'

'Auntie Netta, are you a bad person?' asked Toby.

'Auntie Netta is Evil,' said Charlotte.

'Save the whale or something, if you're that worried,' said Jane. 'It would be easier than trying to sort Dad out.'

'So that's it then, is it? He's beyond help?'

'He certainly smells,' said Toby. 'It's like a camel's den up there.' With this thought, he and Charlotte slithered off their chairs and ran up the stairs, whooping. Little Richard gazed beneficently after them.

'He romanticizes everything, which makes it worse,' said Jane, filling the kettle. 'He used to moan about Mum all the time. And when they drank, of course, they fought all the time. Now he's reinvented their entire marriage as love's middle-aged dream.'

'He's lonely.'

'He'll carry on being lonely if he insists on living in the past. Some of us are having enough trouble with the present.' Jane looked at her watch. 'It's good of you to come so I can get to this . . . job interview.'

'Where was it again?'

Jane looked vague. 'Oh, some kind of editorial role at Demeter Books. Finding old feminist novels that are out of print and breathing new life into them.'

'Bit radical for you, isn't it?'

Jane gave a small, smug smile. 'Fenton recommended me. He used to go out with Carmella Jobson-Nash – you know, the blonde one from Lady Margaret Hall who was always stoned – she's a director there now.'

'Fenton Brasier? I didn't know you were in touch with him again.'

'Oh – I'm not. Absolutely not. I bumped into him the other day. He's practically running the World Service now. Fascinating person.'

Netta remembered a beaky young man, all angles, leching obsessively over her sister. Jane had not been fascinated by him then. The power of success, she supposed.

'He seemed amazingly dull to me.'

'I always admired the quality of his honesty,' said Jane. 'Fenton would never lie.'

Netta concentrated on scraping the last traces of puréed apple from the bottom of the jar. 'Very admirable of him.'

'It's the first requirement of any coherent moral code,' said Jane, looking away.

Now sweat was collecting in Netta's hairline. Was this a reference to Richard? To her? Or both of them? She caught sight of a National Trust tea towel, hanging neatly over the back of one of the bentwood chairs, presumably the very same towel she had stuffed into her mouth to muffle her orgasmic cries. Jane walked over to the window and looked out at the paved basement area which was full of flowering shrubs, all nameless and indeterminate to Netta, but usually a source of great satisfaction to Jane, who watered them every evening and had each one neatly tagged with its English and Latin name. Now she stared out at this small area as if it was a picturesque prison yard.

'I suppose you think my life is fairly pathetic.'

'Whatever do you mean?'

'Kids and domestic rubbish, then this fetish for reading Shakespeare. Who am I trying to fool? No one would know the difference if I spent my afternoons watching *Countdown*. Whereas all you have to do is walk out of the door to complete freedom, I was already pregnant with Toby by the time I was your age. My whole youth has been spent pushing buggies full of screaming kids to Sainsbury's.'

'Your life is perfect! Beautiful children, lovely house, really nice . . .' Netta's voice faded away. She couldn't say 'husband'.

'You know what I mean. With my education. My . . . intellectual gifts.'

'You've got brains and beauty. All the aces. Anyway, maybe today will be the beginning of your brand-new career.'

'Maybe. But sometimes . . . I think of how it'll be for you. Even after training in "communications", you'll be able to get some kind of reporter's job. While I'm chief laundry maid, intellectual capabilities irrelevant.'

'It's not actually a training course, Jane, it's an academic subject.'

'Yes, quite, absolutely. I'm sure that's an important distinction.'

Jane had the same fixed expression on her face that she had worn when she was doing her night-before notes-on-notes-on-notes revision which led to her four straight 'A' A-levels and the blissful portals of Balliol. She crossed over to the coat rack and began to pull on a black jacket. 'My interview is in two hours,' she said, rifling through a drawer and producing a pair of red leather gloves. 'And Richard will be leaving work early – he seemed rather keen to catch up with you. Nice to see him making an effort for once.' And with that she rushed out of the kitchen, into the basement area and up the steps to the street. She didn't so much as glance at her plants.

After she'd gone, Netta went up to the spare room, opened the door silently and crept in. The curtains were drawn, bordered by pallid winter sunlight. David was lying flat on his back, eyes shut, like a corpse laid out for burial. She tiptoed towards the bed and looked down at his face, which was flushed with alcohol. Gently, very gently, she touched his hand.

'Come to see if I've passed on?' he asked, his eyes flashing open.

'God, Dad, you made me jump!'

'My time hasn't come yet. It can take years to drink yourself to death. Decades.'

'Even with your tireless commitment and hard-won expertise?'

'It's no bloody joke, believe me,' said David. He sat up and swung his legs down to the floor. 'Realize now, late in life, I've got the constitution of a fucking ox. Should have been a prize fighter or something. Gone out on the lash with Ernest bloody Hemingway.'

Netta sat down next to him and put her arm around his shoulders. 'Honestly, Dad. Is drink really all there is left?'

'Till death us do part, they say. Seems like such an old cliché, till death does part you. So much air about, Jeanette, that's what I feel. So much empty space, that ought to have her in it! Where can she be? How can she just disappear?'

'We all just disappear. It's our job to disappear, eventually.'

'Bloody fucking awful arrangement, that's what it seems like to me. Can't think why we put up with it.'

They sat for a while. She took his hand. 'How about coming to the park?'

'What, with those dreadful brats?'

'Your grandchildren.'

'Of course. Genetic imprint. Supposed to make it all worthwhile. What's the oldest called again? The one that jumped in the river?'

'Toby.'

'Toby! Christ! What a terrible little know-all!'

'He's an infant prodigy.'

'Why don't they bully him at school, that's what I want to know? Got no spunk, the kids of today.' But he pulled on his sports jacket, which had been draped over a chair, the loose change jingling in his pockets. Netta realized that she still found this sound reassuring.

'I utterly detest parks,' said Toby. 'Lonely places, in my view.'

'Don't be silly,' said Netta. 'Why don't you run about and play?' Like normal children, she nearly said.

'You're like an old woman,' said David, taking a nip from his hip flask. But this term must have reminded him of the lack of Margaret, and he lurched blurrily over to the duck pond.

Netta thought her father might be right about Toby. Charlotte was arranging a group of dolls so that they could get a better view of the ducks, and he was watching her with a pinched, joyless expression on his face, as if he was learning the world for an exam. Mozart must be to blame.

'Charlotte thinks that all those ducks have different personalities,' said Toby. 'But they don't. They're just ducks. If she thought about subjects, she'd know that.'

'She's only four,' said Netta. 'And you're only six.'

'Yes, I know what ages we are.'

She stared down at him. 'Can't you just enjoy being a child?'

'I like finding things out, that's all,' said Toby. He picked up the picture book he had brought with him from the house. It was called *Animals of the World*. 'What's your favourite amphibian?' he asked.

'Crocodile,' said Netta.

'What sort?'

'Man-eating.'

'Hmm . . .' He turned the pages. 'Mine's probably a tomato frog,' he said, showing her the picture. 'They're bright red so other animals can tell they taste horrible.'

'It's a dog-eat-frog world out there,' said Netta, but Toby gave her such a condescending look that she thought it was better to keep quiet. She concentrated on trying to wipe an advancing tide of snot off Little Richard's face before it reached his protruding tongue. After a few hours with the children, she was feeling more sympathetic towards Jane than she had before. She would never have children of her own. She was not cut out for it. The greeny-yellow snot-gunge had seeped out of the disintegrating tissue and on to her fingers.

Toby was staring at the ducks again. She followed his gaze.

'Maybe it's just humans who can't tell the difference between ducks' personalities,' she said. 'Maybe they'd be obvious to another duck.'

'No way,' said Toby. 'You should read some animal books.' He was regarding his sister owlishly through his spectacles. This was an uncomfortable reminder of his father, who would be arriving at any minute. She remembered how disconcerting Richard's spectacles had looked, sitting watching from the table as he eased her T-shirt over her head. Father and son both wore the same round frames, which made them look like cartoon schoolboys. 'The thing about subjects is that you can find out all about them,' said Toby. 'But people . . .' Charlotte was toppling each doll over, into the mud, with systematic deliberation. 'People do funny things all the time.'

Netta was forced to accept the logic of this. 'Normal people have always been in short supply,' she said. 'Probably more chance of finding a normal duck.' She glanced at her watch yet again: Richard was now one minute late. Smiling and escaping would be the key – she must imitate that rare being, a Normal Person. Sexless in her baggy clothes, she hoped to melt away across the grass.

But when Richard finally appeared, she wasn't ready for him at all. He materialized by the bench without warning.

'How ridiculous,' he said, ignoring the children wrapped around his legs, crying 'Daddeeee! Daddeeee!' Pale-faced in the dusk, he was wearing a long dark coat and a woollen scarf, and looked expensive and padded against the cold.

'Ridiculous?' Netta was clutching the handle of the pushchair so hard that her hands went into spasm and she furtively tried to unfurl them, holding them in her lap. 'Why ridiculous?' Her lips were numb, so the words came out in odd, clumsy shapes. Was it the cold, or the shock of seeing him like this? She half-looked at his mouth, then remembered its soft touch on her neck, and her skin rippled with embarrassment.

'That I have to go to these lengths,' he said.

She gripped the handle harder. 'What do you mean?'

'To have a simple conversation with you.'

'You can talk to me whenever you like.'

'But not alone.'

'We aren't alone now.'

'It's a form of privacy, meeting behind a wall of children . . .' But he had caught sight of David, who was tottering towards them. He changed his tone to one of detached coldness. 'Absurd. And the baby – look at him. Covered in . . . in . . . he's ill.'

'Come on, Richard, spit it out. Covered in snot,' said David. 'Bile, shit, puke and snot – the lot of every loving parent,' he said, looking at the surging tide of tiny humans. 'At least the end is in sight for me. You've got years ahead of you.' He offered the hip flask to Richard, who surprised Netta by taking a dainty nip.

'The children are lovely, just lovely . . .' protested Netta, forgetting that moments before she had decided she never wanted any of her own. But Little Richard chose that moment to let out a keening wail.

David clamped his hands to his ears. 'Hell is other people's children,' he said.

'Honestly, Dad! Can't you stay sober till they're in bed?'

'Need a piss,' said David, wandering off again.

'Just when I thought my marital situation couldn't get any worse, we turn into a rest home for old drunks,' said Richard.

'That's a terrible thing to say.'

'True, though.' Richard moved closer to her and spoke in a tense, agitated undertone. 'We can't just disregard what happened. Things need to be clarified . . . we're operating in a grey area. It's . . . one needs to address the part Jane had to play in this.'

'Next thing you'll say is that she doesn't understand you.'

'Well, she doesn't.'

'Yes she does,' said Toby. He stared up at them, white and intense. 'Mummy understands everything.'

Netta, hardly knowing what she was doing, turned to Toby and rested her hands on his head. 'Of course she does,' she said.

Richard marched over and swept Toby up in his arms. She saw, with confusion, that his hands were trembling. She didn't want to know whether this was rage, or some other emotion.

'If you think you're doing some notional "right thing", then you are very much mistaken,' he said. 'In a situation like this, it isn't possible to be ethical.' Toby, apparently having had enough of adult discourse, wriggled out of Richard's grasp and ran away.

'What do you want to do – analyse us into doing something even worse?' She saw David coming towards them, his flies undone. He was whistling now, cheerfully and unashamedly pissed.

'I don't know what Jane is doing, leaving you in charge,' said Richard loudly as David came back into earshot. 'She knows perfectly well how immature and irresponsible you are.'

'Good Lord, Richard, what a bloody miserable thing to say!' said David. 'Nettie has her good points, you know. Mixes a perfectly respectable dry Martini, for a start.'

'Don't worry, Richard,' said Netta quietly. 'I'll try and see as little as possible of you in future.'

'Come on, kids! Time to go!' said Richard. But the children ignored him. Toby was chasing Charlotte round and round the pond, yelling, his eccentric persona and young genius temporarily forgotten.

Meanwhile, David had picked up a newspaper from a park bench and was opening it, still humming his tune. 'Something here for you, Nettie,' he said. 'Big article on Greenham – oh my word! I'm sure none of them look like that . . .'

'Like what?' Netta peered over his shoulder. At first, she couldn't take in what she saw. 'MY GREENHAM HELL' said the headline. Underneath was a long article, and a picture of Emily naked to the waist. Her breasts looked smooth and professional and she was smiling in a superior, art-school sort of way. She appeared to be chained to the perimeter fence: behind her Netta could see a group of laughing soldiers and the grey humps of the silos. But this was nothing compared to the words she saw next to the photograph: 'Reporter: Netta Royce'. Her eyesight must be going, fading in the dusk. It must be a name similar to hers, a silly coincidence. She blinked and looked again. The words were stubbornly insistent: 'Reporter: Netta Royce'. She stared harder, dull with shock.

'Well done, Nettie,' said David, beaming at her proudly. 'An article in a national newspaper! I must say, I didn't think you had it in you.'

18

On the way home, Netta read the article over and over again. At first, she couldn't believe the words were real. When she got to Charing Cross, she bought another copy of the *Daily Chronicle*, just to check that this wasn't a rogue copy, published for a joke. But the article was there again, somehow more glaring. Now she was beginning to feel angry. It was obvious that Bryan was to blame: his name was hidden away at the end: 'Additional reporting: Bryan Sullivan'. Additional reporting indeed! Why had he used her name instead of his own? What had she ever done to him? And what on earth would Mel and Pilar think? As if there might be a secret message hidden in the article, she made herself read it, very slowly, once again:

MY GREENHAM HELL
Lesbian hate police make peace camp into a war zone.

Picture the scene. Greenham Common, 1985. A dozen women sitting around a smouldering campfire. With their woolly hats, sensible anoraks and wind-reddened faces, they look more like a bunch of cheerful hikers than a witches' coven, eager to topple Margaret Thatcher and all she stands for. But, like the miners who are conducting a similar campaign against our democratically elected government, these women are dangerous not in themselves, but because of their poisonous ringleaders.

Exhibit A is Flora Birtwistle, celebrated 70s feminist and self-styled Earth Mother. (Mother of two.) Utopia for Flora would be a world in which men did half the Hoovering, half the washing up, half the cooking – and perhaps had half a penis too. But what has been forgotten in all the recent coverage of Greenham and its publicity-hungry 'spokespersons' is that Flora is using the nuclear debate for her own ends. As one of the original Women's Libbers, she concentrated on the so-called vices of husbands, not the bigger issue of male violence and global threats to peace. Indeed, her latest book, *The Sock Dropper's Misogyny*, is more of the same. And yet now, she is claiming to be a committed peace woman, appearing on TV to promote the cause of women against the Bomb. Now this high profile has led to a vitriolic clash with rival Greenham woman Jude Blackman, one of a new breed of militant separatists, and leader of lesbian fringe group 'Positively C—'.

I decided to spend time with these women to see what Greenham is really like. Spending time with them is like going back into ancient history, into a time when finding food, fire and shelter was our sole preoccupation. The peace women are a tough lot – they don't seem to notice the cold, damp, intense boredom or the fact that eating vegetable stew each night is hard on the tastebuds. How I longed for a Big Mac after 48 hours of mushy carrots and potatoes! Strangely, many of them actually seem to enjoy these daily privations. Several are also keen naturists who strip naked before climbing into their waterproof Gore-Tex sleeping bags for the night. The theory is that this keeps them warm – typical upside-down Greenham logic. 'Nature should rule our hearts and our heads,' Flora told me. 'The whole of the Western world is being driven mad by electric lighting. If we rose and slept with the sun, I don't believe we would be capable of the collective insanity of developing nuclear weapons – they are a symbol of our disconnectedness to the universe.'

So far, so loony. But what does her son Tom – an apparently normal though not particularly masculine 22-year-old – make of all this? 'Being brought up as a feminist is like being disabled,' he says. 'No women fancy you, they all want boyfriends who leave them tied up somewhere near the M6 – and of course to other men you are just a joke. It's worse than being gay.'

But if you think Flora sounds bad . . . Jude Blackman – a so-called 'political lesbian' – is the Greenham woman of nightmare. She is the kind of lesbian who really does scare the horses. Predatory as Joan Collins in *The Stud*, transposed to a damp woodland and sporting a shaven head. 'All women are lesbians,' she insists. 'The only problem is that some of them – housewives and women who wear stilettos, mainly – have been socially conditioned into thinking they fancy men. They don't, obviously, which is why so many women end up frigid, pretending they have a headache for 20 years. If they could only get away from the idea that they ought to have sex with men, they could start having a really good time.'

But is the nuclear issue important? 'Of course it is. It's all about penis-envy – have you seen the shape of those things? Pointing upwards like that? Women don't have penis-envy – men do. And they have c— -envy too.' You couldn't make it up. The saddest thing of all is, she isn't even joking.

These deluded women say this is an example of a peaceful, alternative way of life. In fact Greenham is a hotbed of rivalry, intrigue, sexual obsession and insane ideology. If you want to hear sense, listen to Michael Heseltine. But if you want a good laugh, look no further than this muddled, unhappy group of social drop-outs and failures. The confused thinking and sexual perversion is turning this one-time peaceful protest into Sodom and Gomorrah. While so-called New Man Tom Birtwistle is so mentally disturbed that he can't hold down a relationship, chief lesbian Jude Blackman stalks women like a professional Romeo, using her position to try and seduce as many women as possible. Are they putting something in the water at Greenham? Who knows. But whatever is the truth, this is a place where being a sexual misfit is the norm.

This was not quite all. Underneath the article was a series of bullet points:

Ten things you never knew about the Greenham Goddesses:
- Jude Blackman was runner-up for Miss Penge West in 1978
- 83 per cent of Greenham women are gay
- Tampons are banned because of their similarity to the penetrative penis
- Number of flushing toilets at Greenham – zero
- Weight of carrot cake sent to Greenham Common by Yoko Ono – 16 tonnes
- Make-up is banned at Greenham because lipstick 'outlines the orifice'
- Two per cent of Greenham women are also miners' wives
- 27 per cent of Coldstream Guards would rather be in Belfast than Berkshire
- Flora Birtwistle is 47
- Jude Blackman is 23

Netta lowered the paper, wondering if she was going to throw up. The odd thing was, there were phrases and sentences that looked vaguely familiar. Then she remembered the Greenham essay she had lost at the DeeDee Chapinsky lecture. That was where she had seen some of this before: she had written it herself. Bryan must have picked it up. But why had he done this? She frowned, still not able to take in the fact that her words were apparently looming out of a national newspaper, voicing opinions that she didn't have.

When she got back to the house, she saw that the light was on in Pilar's bedroom. She pushed the door open. Pilar was lying on the bed, sobbing into a paper tissue. She was still wearing her fur coat, and her pink make-up bag lay on the floor next to her.

'God, Pilar, I'm sorry . . .' Netta said. 'I didn't think you'd take it this badly.'

Pilar didn't look up, but sobbed slightly more loudly. 'Of course I'm taking it this badly! It's the end of everything!'

'No it's not! It was just Bryan, playing some stupid trick . . . nothing to do with me.'

'What's Bryan got to do with it?'

'Well, he . . .' But Netta was beginning to realize that there might be something else on Pilar's mind. 'What's the matter, Pee? This isn't about the newspaper article, is it?'

'I don't know what you're on about.' Pilar unrolled some fresh tissue from a toilet roll and wiped her nose. 'Rupert's dumped me.'

'I don't believe you!'

'D'you think I'd make it up?'

'But he's mad about you!'

'Try telling him that.' She fixed Netta with her blood-shot eye slits. 'He's broken off the engagement. Wants to "spread his wings" . . .'

'He can't mean it! He'll change his mind . . .'

'To be honest, I've always thought he was a bit AC/DC. I think he might want to shag a man.'

Netta sat down on the bed next to Pilar, but Pilar moved away. 'According to Roops, I'm too dull and conventional,' she said. 'Can you credit it? I should get an Oscar. All those Sloane hairbands, dykes shoved under the bed, vibrators hidden in the wardrobe, all those Henry James books I used to whip out to impress him – I even made him tea in that disgusting stripy teapot . . . he believed the whole lot. He thinks I really *am* the girl in the hairband! Says I need to "expand my sexual horizons".'

'That's just ridiculous!' Netta shuffled across the bed and stared into Pilar's face. 'Couldn't you have told him how . . . deceitful you've been? It's a shame to let all that shagging around go for nothing!'

'Ironic, innit? There was just no way I could convince him. I said, quite truthfully as you know, that I've slept with five women in the last three months. And of course he said I was making it all up, to try and get him to fancy me again.'

'God, that's so crazy! Surely there was some way of proving it was true?'

Pilar shrugged, wiped her wet face with her hands and led the way into the kitchen, where she poured out two glasses of wine. She handed one to Netta, then took a long drink herself. 'He is unconvincible,' she said. 'We were sitting in the pub in Greenwich, and he was coming out with all this stuff, about how I live in a small, neat world, how I'm so sheltered and pure and lovely and he's not good enough for me! I mean, what gobshite, apart from anything. He might as well have said – you're a really nice person, can we just be friends? You know. Well, anyway, I suddenly realized that Miffy was in there. She was with Mutant, actually, they must have some sort of Welsh thing going on.' The more she talked, the harder her face became.

'So what did you do?'

'Well, I waited till Mutant had gone to the bar to order himself nineteen pints of lager or whatever, and I rushed over to her and said – look, you have to tell this bloke I'm with that we've been to bed together, it's a matter of life and death, he's trying to chuck me for dullness and I'm just not having it. And she ran out the pub in tears!'

'She's in love with you.'

'What? You reckon?'

'Could be.'

Pilar shrugged. 'Maybe. Maybe Roops is in love with her. Maybe Roops is in love with sodding Mutant. We may as well be in one of those Iris Murdoch novels where everyone is called Pontius Fishwick or Alabaster Creech.'

'He'll be back. He'll never find anyone else like you.'

'If he does try to come back, he can go screw himself.'

'Oh, come on, don't go into a big "hell hath no fury" routine.'

'You don't get a second chance with me.'

'What's more important than really loving someone?'

'Bullshit. It's over. Finished. No man is indispensable.

There is a line, and if he crosses it, he's out. And boy, has he crossed it!'

'I just don't see the point.'

'The point is survival, darling. If a man starts messing me around, there's no coming back.'

'And it would be different if a woman messed you around?'

'Women are more complicated.'

'But all he wants is what you've been after all along. The chance to play away. And if he is off to sleep with a man, in a way, he's your perfect match. Your bisexual doppelgänger.'

'Oh, for God's sake.'

'You know what I mean. It can't be over.'

'It just is. That's it.'

Netta was about to say more – but she heard the front door bang below.

'It's only Emily and that prat Bryan,' said Pilar. But Netta was peering over the banisters. In the hallway below, she saw a dark figure, standing silent on the doormat.

'Who is it?' asked Pilar. She looked over Netta's shoulder. 'Melanie! Back already? I thought you were staying down there till the end of the month.'

The figure remained silent.

'I've had some fucking sick-makingly bad news,' said Pilar, sounding slightly more uncertain.

Mel didn't seem to be listening. She was climbing the stairs very slowly, leaving a muddy footprint on each one.

'I've been dumped by–' began Pilar, as Melanie reached the top.

'By her!' said Mel, pointing at Netta.

'By who?'

'By Netta,' said Mel. 'Dumped right in it! We all have. By that two-faced bloody cow!' She held up a copy of the *Daily Chronicle*. 'She's shopped us. Betrayed the peace women. Made us look like a laughing stock.'

'I didn't write it,' said Netta. 'You've got to believe me. I had nothing to do with it.'

'Oh, please,' said Mel. 'Do I really look that stupid?'

'What didn't you write?' asked Pilar. 'I don't understand what's going on.'

Mel silently handed Pilar the newspaper and she began to read it, her face completely still.

'I didn't write it,' said Netta again, aware of the bubble of hysteria in her voice. 'I know it seems completely bizarre, but that's the truth. It was Bryan.'

'Bryan? Jesus, what the buggering hell do you take us for?' said Mel. 'How *could* he have written it? It's a women-only camp. He can't have known about half the stuff that's in there.'

'He must have talked to Tom,' said Netta. 'Tom's been hiding near the base . . .' Her voice trailed away, her confidence withering up in the blaze of Mel's furious glare. Why was the truth so unconvincing? 'Ask Emily,' she said. 'She'll tell you.'

'Emily! Right – the woman who gets her knockers out to illustrate your brilliant prose. Very reliable witness. What goes on in her mind is beyond me.'

Netta was silent.

'I'm just completely gobsmacked,' said Mel. 'I should have known, that day you turned up at that DeeDee Chapinsky lecture, all tarted up. You'll have a great career, writing for the *Sun*. You wrote it as if . . . as if you hated us.'

'Mel – honestly – how many times? It wasn't me! Pilar and you are the best people I've ever met . . .'

'How can you say that? How can you expect anyone to believe it? It's all here – the facts – in black and white . . .'

But Pilar's voice cut across them. 'You really are something,' she said. 'You really are something very special, aren't you, Ms Royce?'

'What do you mean?'

'It's getting to be a bit of a habit, isn't it, this betrayal lark? Perhaps you're getting a taste for it?'

'What . . . how can you . . . ?'

'How can I what? Don't look so bloody wounded! And don't lie like this! Again!'

'Again?' asked Mel. 'Is there something I should know?'

'Pilar – for God's sake . . .' The tears were rising in Netta's throat. She thought of the recurring nightmare she had, when she was unable to move, desperate to escape, paralysed by some invisible dream-force. But the real nightmare of her waking life was the opposite of paralysis. Rushing foolishly in was her vice. She knew it, but her mouth was still opening and shutting, anxious to make further uncalculated remarks.

'It's you . . . it's bloody you!' Pilar threw the newspaper on to the floor. 'How could it be anyone but you? Your voice is in every line. You've completely and utterly screwed it up. With everyone. Big time,' she said. 'I can't believe that I've spent so much time with you, and not realized how . . . how damaged you are.'

'And dangerous,' said Mel.

'Dangerous?' Emily was standing at the top of the stairs, puffing on a cigarette. It was slightly disconcerting to see her fully dressed. 'What's this . . . tales of unsafe sex? Personally, I find "safe sex" a contradiction in terms.'

Netta had never been more pleased to see her. 'Emily – tell them! Tell them Bryan wrote that piece! They think it's me . . . tell them!'

Emily seemed not to hear her. She picked the paper up off the floor. 'They've come out incredibly well, don't you think?' she said. 'Just ever-so-slightly Rubenesque, but it works for that audience. I'd have to lose some weight for the catwalk. For an acting role, they can be any size at all as long as they're smooth and blemish-free . . . although for certain vulnerable, off-centre character parts, I suppose even ageing ones would do.'

'What are you on about?' asked Netta, trying to keep her voice calm.

'My boobs. Provocative but not perky. Mammaries with intellect. I do think I have a certain presence. It's an inner light – they can't teach you that. Dear old Roman Polanski will be on the phone soon, I expect. Behold – the new Nastassia Kinski!'

'Aren't you ashamed?' asked Mel. 'Don't you feel really cheap and trashy and used . . . ?'

'Emily, everything isn't about you,' said Pilar. 'Take your mind off your tits for one second, please. Now look, tell me honestly. Did Netta write that thing, or Bryan?'

Emily kept her gaze firmly locked on to her own mammary glands. 'Netta did.'

'*What?*' Netta grasped her by the shoulders. 'Emily! Look at me! How can you say that?'

'That's what Bryan told me,' said Emily, fixing Netta with a dogged stare.

'But you were there . . .'

'You told him to write about Greenham. And he said you helped him to write it.'

'*What?*'

'Of course,' said Emily, shaking herself free. 'Why would your name be on it otherwise? Personally, I don't see what all the fuss is about. This is a showcase for both of us. We'll have our names in lights.'

'Jesus.' Netta's arms fell to her sides. 'This is mad.' She realized for the first time that Emily didn't just admire men, she had a psychotic addiction to being on their side. Flora certainly had a lot to answer for.

'You've lied to us, Netta,' said Mel implacably. 'I'm sorry to say that, but it's true.'

'Why don't you ask him yourself?' said Emily, doing a sudden hair-toss, presumably in honour of the absent male. 'He's doing an open mike slot at the Tunnel Club tonight. He's going in for stand-up comedy now. He's brilliant. Pop star, writer, comedian, megastar . . . I don't think there's anything that Bryan can't do.'

The Tunnel Club was famous for two things – its drunken clientele and the appalling aspiring comedians who were screamed off the stage on 'try-out' nights. And these two facets of its personality complemented each other perfectly: the more ferociously inebriated the crowd, the more harrowing and visceral the death of each performer. It wasn't just careers that were terminated at the Tunnel; the crowd could crush personalities, too. This was the closest thing that 1980s London could offer to the Coliseum in ancient Rome. But it didn't look much like the Coliseum. It was a dingy little place, tucked away at the back of the Mitre, which was a dingy little pub in the middle of a dingy area of south-east London which nobody could be bothered to build on. There were no colonnades, no tiers of shouting slaves, no lion-infested vistas of sand and blood. It was a long, low, dark room, with a bar along one side. The area nearest to the stage was a no-go area for middle-class women, being exclusively the preserve of pink-necked lager louts and their formidable squaws. These were people who knew what was what: the comedy police. They could spot tedium or toff tendencies from a hundred paces. They could smell fear, and they rather liked it. But above all, they knew what was funny, and what wasn't.

Netta pushed her way through the crowd, elbowing through the crush of bodies, the sudden onset of gratuitous after-shave, or a shirt that hadn't been changed for a few days, half-heard conversations held between sips and gulps. 'See that Joan Collins Fan Club bloke? He's a poof, but he's nasty with it, so it's . . .' 'Look, if you chuck him again, it's a relationship. If you do anything that many times, it's a relationship . . .' 'What d'you think – 2000 turbo or turbo 2000? Nought to ninety in . . .' She was not bothered about being polite. She wanted to find Bryan. Behind her, she knew Mel and Pilar were fighting their way to the bar, but she didn't want to drink. She wanted to keep a clear head, and anyway, she had an odd, metallic taste in her mouth. But it was hard to see anyone, all around her were backs, plastic glasses passed above her head, shouted repartee and catch-phrases she didn't understand. The first act was on stage: two women were doing a magic show. They were undergoing one version of the Tunnel put-down – being totally ignored. One was thin, with spindly, unconfident legs. The other had droopy, low-flying breasts. Eventually, the crowd noticed this, and started shouting obscenities at her. After a short while, she started crying and wandered off, and the skinny one gathered up their toy rabbits and collapsible wands, face set with hatred.

'She wants to work those into her act,' said a voice behind her. 'The fat girl, I mean. Fantastic material – knee-level tits. It's a fucking gift. And she should ditch the bunnies.'

Netta turned. Bryan was smiling at her in an agreeable manner. 'You have a bloody nerve,' she said. 'What's going on? Why the fuck is my name on that article?'

Bryan looked hurt. 'I thought you'd be pleased. Aspiring young journalist like yourself. This could be your big break, you know . . .'

'What?'

'They wouldn't put my name on it, the arseholes. Said it had to be a girl. So I thought it was only just and fair, in an unjust, unfair world, for your name to go on it.'

'You are beyond belief . . .'

'World domination, darling, go for it. It's all there, waiting. Whereas I have to go on stage here, and get torn limb from limb.'

'Why?'

'Just to get a stab at posterity. Earn my fifteen minutes. There's no time to waste, you know. Emily's got her tits, I've got–'

'I don't mean why go on stage? I don't bloody care. I mean why did you think I would want to be associated with something like that? Didn't you realize what my friends would think? Mel lives at Greenham! Not to mention my landlady—'

'Half of it is you in any case,' said Bryan, looking at his watch.

'Half of what?'

'The words. And they were good, as well. You should be proud.'

'Oh, right, the missing essay. The essay you nicked. The essay I hadn't even —'

But Bryan was edging past her. 'I'm on after this act,' he said, as a man appeared on stage to a rage of cat calls. ('Hello, I'm a schizophrenic,' he said. 'You can both fuck off, then,' shouted a heckler from the back. The crowd was getting into its stride now.)

'Brace yourself,' Bryan said.

Netta scowled up at him. 'What do you mean, brace yourself?' she yelled, trying to make herself heard above the baying and hooting. 'How could things possibly get any worse?'

19

There was a short interlude between the last act going off – at a slow run, under a rain of beer glasses – and Bryan going on. Interest in what was happening onstage had risen now, and the crowd began to shout, 'Who's next?' and chant, 'Why are we waiting?' Finally, a dishevelled man with a mess of black hair and heavy spectacles shambled on stage with a fag in his mouth. 'That was shit,' he said impassively. 'This next act's probably a bit shit as well ... or it could be average.' If Netta hadn't been so angry with Bryan she might have felt a little concerned on his behalf. As it was, she felt she would rejoice in his complete annihilation. Stealing essays? Putting her name into tabloid newspapers? She still couldn't understand why he'd done it. No wonder Mel and Pilar thought she was making it all up. Scowling with anger and anxiety, she wriggled her way to the front, so that she had to crane her head to look up at the stage.

For a moment, the lights went down, and all she could see was blackness. Then, seconds later, they flashed up again, to reveal a figure, head bent, standing with its back to the audience. She knew it must be Bryan, but at first it appeared to be a person of indeterminate sex: too tall to be a woman, but wearing a long, flowery overall, and with black, bouffant, bouncy hair. Without turning round, the creature began to sing: 'We are women, We are women,/We are strong, We are strong,/We say No, We say No,/To the Bomb, To the Bomb.' The voice was a man's falsetto. The crowd waited, the cries had died down to a few shouts of 'This is crap!' and a one-man chant, 'Bor-ing! Bor-ing!' Then Bryan spun round. He was wearing violent red lipstick, and had a flowery hat perched on top of his head. In his right hand he held a potty. In his left he held what looked like a man's head, with fake blood dripping on to the stage. The crowd was silent for a second. He raised his left hand, and more blood – or perhaps ketchup – plopped on to the stage.

'I'm a peace woman,' he said in his normal tones. 'That is, I'm in favour of peace for women.' He lowered the head. 'You can't beat it. Singing around the campfire. Sharing a slightly used Tampax. (We're all environmental, you know.) Touch of tongue Olympics while you wait for the lentils to brew.' Mild and expectant laughter followed this.

'People say to me – Greta, they say (that's my name – Greenham Greta) – Greta, they say, the spark's gone out of my sex life. You're a woman of a certain age – but I don't see you going short. Why are your cheeks so rosy? How come you have a spring in your step?' He paused. ('Go on,' yelled a frontline yob. 'Tell us your secret!') Bryan gave a tremendous, full-lipped smile. He really did look as if he had achieved some ultimate sexual goal. 'I'll tell you my secret, young man. I'll tell you my bloody secret – I've unleashed the power of my anatomical jewel.' ('Come again?' said Frontline Yob.)

Now Bryan looked magnificently around the room. 'I'll come again with pleasure,' he said. 'I'll come all over your ugly bloke's face.' He paused again. 'What shall we call it, girls? Vagina? Pussy? Fanny? Pudenda? Or prat, maybe? Anyone know that prat means fanny? And they both mean – oh, the *naughty* word! The word you can't say because it's abusive to women! Excusez moi! It's abusive to women to say our anatomical jewel is the ultimate obscenity! It's offensive to our sex to ban us from calling a cunt a cunt.' A mixture of clapping and shouting now, and Bryan began to shout to make himself heard. Then, he began to sing again, bastardizing the tune of Tammy Wynette's 'D.I.V.O.R.C.E'.: 'My C.U.N.T. is fine with me/My sweet V.A.G./I love to make it sing along,/With my V.I.B./Your C.O.C.K. faces redundancy,/Poking out so T.E.D.iously,/ So why don't you just f . . . fade away/And let me find true ecstasy?' The audience were soon singing along to this. A couple of Frontline Yobs got up and waltzed about on the stage. Then Bryan held up the man's head again. 'Women and violent-men, I give you – cunt-rap: "'Allo blokes, it's Greta 'ere,/Got bad news for your sexist fear,/Cunts are tops, cunts are sublime,/ Don't need your willies any time/The cunt is nature's best invention,/Takes us to a new dimension,/You just squirt your sperm away,/Our orgs are Christmas every day."'

After this, he began to declaim: 'Our cunts are the symbolic and physical zenith of our existence. Famous cunts in history have caused empires to rise and fall. Yes, though they often play supporting roles to cocks, cunts deserve star billing in the marquee of every woman's life . . .' Netta had no idea whether the clapping and whooping that drowned this out was genuine or ironic, or aggressive, or really quite okay. 'Positively Cunts!' shouted

Bryan. He lifted both arms – and seemed to notice for the first time that he was holding a decapitated male head. 'Positively Cunts – and Death to Men!' he said, to more cheers. 'Join us – or collude in the oppression of your own clitoris!' The stage went dark again, the air was full of hoots and wails. Netta felt a hard tap on her shoulder.

'I take it that's another of your little projects with Bryan,' said Mel. In the temporary darkness, Netta could only see her outline and the angry spikes of her hair.

'God! Why am I suddenly supposed to be in cahoots with Bryan the whole time? It's nothing to do with me! I'm fucking furious with him . . .'

'You gave him that leaflet,' said Emily, who had appeared from nowhere.

'What leaflet?'

'The Positively Cunts leaflet. That's where he got all his jokes from. It's all real, that's the beauty of it. As Bryan would say, you couldn't make it up.'

'You are the bloody limit, Netta,' said Mel. 'I should never have agreed to you moving in. Big, big mistake. But you looked so sweet and innocent, the day you got into the bath with us.'

'You didn't actually live there, at the time,' said Netta, furiously. 'You still don't, officially.'

'No,' said Pilar, as the lights came up again and a man with a guitar appeared on stage. Her face was pale and lumpy: Netta saw that she had been crying. 'Mel doesn't live there, officially. And neither do you, officially, from now on. You've got a month to find somewhere else.'

'Oh, fuck off,' said Netta. 'Just fuck completely off, all

of you, for ever! I'm sick of the whole thing – stupid right-on Newspeak! Brain-washed, brain-dead, half-baked – most of that stuff Bryan was amusing them with wasn't even exaggerated! I've heard Jude come out with most of it!'

'Crap!' said Mel.

'It's not crap! She said anatomical jewel! That leaflet – that fucking leaflet – it really did say "collude with the oppression of your own clitoris". No wonder you're a laughing stock.'

'Who's a laughing stock?' asked Pilar very quietly.

'Greenham. Lesbians. *Feminists*.'

'Just why the hell are you being so foul and vitriolic?' cried Pilar.

'And offensive?' asked Mel.

'Because you're talking such rubbish! And you've fallen for the whole Jude-line. Can't you see how stupid she sounds? Now Greenham Greta is probably going to get booked all over London – and serves you right. All men are rapists indeed! It's pathetic – just pathetic! Of course they aren't! Why do you even talk such bullshit? What's the point – it's just mob rule, fashion, group hysteria. You should listen to yourselves–'

'There's no need to be confrontational,' said Pilar. 'You know I think it's lovely to be a girl. But you're behaving as if you hate us . . .'

'And arguing like a man,' said Mel. 'Feminism is impor-tant. It's not about group hysteria, it's about trying to make a point of view heard that the rest of society is drowning out! Can't you see that? Look at the mess men are making of the world! We can't just leave them to it.'

'Oh yeah, right – and it's so dangerous and they're such animals that we can't even walk the streets at night. And you insist on using that stupid women-only cab firm. Real life's just not like that. You're living in a Cowboys-and-Indians world. Thatcher versus Scargill. Reagan versus the Ruskies. Women versus Men. Ra ra ra.'

'Are you saying you don't believe women are oppressed?'

'Yes, I fucking am. We're middle-class, privileged, lucky. Simple as that. Of course women should have more power. But you take things too far.'

'What do you mean, too far?' asked Mel quietly.

'Reclaim the night and all that crap. Everyone knows that if I walked out of that door tonight and went home, all alone, nothing would happen to me! It's perfectly safe. We aren't living in a war zone.'

'Oh, Nettie,' wailed Pilar. 'You should listen to yourself! Lashing out like that! I thought we were friends! I thought we understood each other!' She burst into tears and disappeared into the crowd.

'I hope you're satisfied,' said Mel. 'Is this what you call free speech? The opportunity to slag people off if they don't agree with you? Aping male aggression?'

Waving her hands in a gesture of dismissal, Netta said, 'I'm sick of this. I'm off to Reclaim the Night.' She grabbed her coat and pushed her way out of the bar. Once outside, she gasped with the sudden cold. But she could soon warm herself up. She began to walk as fast as she could, and it was only after some time had passed that she stood for a while, and began to gaze around her, frowning. She had hardly looked out of the taxi window on the way over, and the landscape had been nothing more than a dark screed of emptiness beyond the harsh, sporadic street lights. She turned a full circle, attempting to get her bearings, her painful gulps of breath clouding the air. In the winter darkness, it was a lonely and forbidding sight. This was a part of London which tourists would never see: the Blackwall Peninsula, a great scar of derelict land. An old gasworks had been built here once. Now it was closed, and all around it was poisoned, a vista of rubble and broken concrete. Post-nuclear, thought Netta. Post-nuclear and post-people. Car headlights flashed to and fro on the tarmac road which crossed the wasteland like some eerie causeway. But there were no pedestrians. And nowhere to hire a cab, women-only or otherwise. She looked both up and down the road – which was the way home? She wasn't even sure about that. Was the Blackwall Tunnel to her left – or to her right? All she could see was moving points of light and surrounding darkness. Finally, she decided that the Tunnel was to her left, turned right and began to walk along the road. Almost straight away, an old Ford Escort winked its indicator and pulled over. She thought of the abuse she and Pilar had been subjected to on the way to Greenham – suddenly, that seemed rather cosy. Now, there was just her, and the car, which lay in wait ahead of her by the lonely road. She thought of running out and waving down another car – but what would be the point? She had no more reason to trust another motorist than this one. Slowly, she walked to the passenger window. The driver leaned across and wound it down.

'Want a lift anywhere?' said the man inside.

Netta almost laughed with relief. 'Oh, for goodness' sake!' she said. 'Tom Birtwistle! Are you following me?'

She had never seen Tom's flat before. For some reason, she had never believed that he would be able to have a proper life, away from his sister and his mother and the bright chaos of Dartmouth Villa. She had no trouble picturing him at Greenham, lurking in the bushes, as she had seen him on her visit. But in London, she could only imagine him eating cold soup out of a tin, or perched uncomfortably in a frugal bedsit. (Although she had never seen such a thing: 'bedsits' were where people lived in 1960s novels.) She thought he was the least domestic person she had ever met. But here they were now, in an attic room high above Mornington Crescent, and Tom was frying garlic and telling her a funny story about impersonating a policeman at Greenham – she wasn't really following it, leaning out of the window and watching the people far below, little birds of paradise flitting in and out of the Camden Palace.

'I thought this was a squat,' she said, taking the glass of red wine he had poured out for her. She looked around at the walls. Tom must be the last person in Britain to have a pin-up of Che Guevara. A less surprising choice was the ubiquitous anti-nuclear poster of Ronald Reagan, looking like Clark Gable, and Thatcher in Scarlett O'Hara mode. Netta read out the caption in a Southern Belle accent: 'She promised to follow him to the end of the earth. He promised to organize it.'

Tom laughed. 'Why is this not a squat? What did you expect?'

'I dunno. It's so . . . civilized. I thought you'd be lying on a pile of filthy tarpaulins with a bunch of junkies.'

He laughed again. 'What planet have you been living on?'

'I'm new to the metropolis,' she said, suddenly feeling weirdly coy. 'Relatively speaking. Things aren't much like this in Crewe.'

'What *are* things like in Crewe? I've often wondered.'

'Not like anything much, to tell you the truth. It's very tempting to rush down to the station and jump on the first train that comes in. Plenty of choice, you see. Heart to heart, city to city.'

'And did you ever?'

'Did I ever what?'

'Jump on the first train.'

'Yeah, once, when I was about twelve. My mum had just died. It was the fast train to Middlesbrough.'

'God almighty,' said Tom, turning back to the frying pan and tipping a tin of tomatoes on top of the sizzling onions. He didn't seem to be very interested in hearing about her return journey. 'I wouldn't worry about it. You don't need a fascinating home town. If you're beautiful, you don't need to come from anywhere.'

She found she couldn't reply. Unhelpful headlines flashed into her mind. Be witty! Show nuclear insight! Look enigmatic! Then she remembered the article. 'I didn't write that thing in the paper,' she said, suddenly serious. 'The *Chronicle*, I mean. It was Bryan.'

'Don't worry, I know,' he said. 'He came and interviewed me in a tree. Quite surreal. He was really fired up about it all. Then they refused to use his name, apparently. Serves him right, making me sound like some kind of sexual misfit. He doesn't care who he screws up.'

She drained her glass. The wine was rough and vinegary. 'It's such a relief to hear you say that. None of my friends believe a word I say. I'm just a walking feminist Thought Crime.'

Tom looked at her empty glass. 'That's all the wine I had, unfortunately,' he said. 'We'll have to switch to vodka.'

''S fine,' said Netta, already seeing the walls rippling slightly. 'I adore vodka.'

The truth was that Netta had only ever drunk vodka once before, and the evening had not been an unqualified success. After a small glass she found the room doing even stranger things, even though she ate as much of the meal as she possibly could. (Her appetite was small, however, reduced by life with Pilar to the occasional rumbling which could be satisfied with a piece of warmed pitta bread and half a tomato.) But she was pleased to discover that there was no longer any problem thinking of the right thing to say. Once they had finished, they pushed the plates to one side and sat side by side, smoking a joint, giggling at each other. He put some music on – Pink Floyd, Animals, he told her.

'Not very fashionable, are you?' she laughed.

He sounded nettled. 'In what way?'

'You know . . . Pink Floyd . . . Che . . .'

'Fashion is all very well for women.'

'Ooh, Tom. Sexist!'

'Don't you start! I'm sick of women telling me what I'm allowed to think. Bryan got it about right, I think.'

'When?'

'Tonight. Greenham Greta. The peace women are splitting down the middle because of all that stuff. They'll end up a laughing stock.'

'So you agree with your mother?'

'Fuck, no! It'll never come to that.'

Laughing again, she pulled on the joint and felt the familiar, slightly veggie vagueness wafting into her brain. Getting stoned had always seemed to her to be of mainly masculine value, as it involved saying very little and retreating into a brooding, private world. Drunkenness, on the other hand, was more usefully girly, as it made conversation easier, faster and sillier. But she liked the idea of retreating into a brooding, private world with this particular man. She liked it very much indeed. 'I didn't see you at the Tunnel,' she said, processing the words she had just heard. 'Were you with Emily?'

'No, nobody,' he said.

'Just on your own?'

'Yeah, why not?'

'But you didn't say anything to us. You could've said hello.'

'I was quite happy where I was.'

'Watching the acts?'

'Watching you.'

He leaned forward and kissed her. Her arms went around his neck, her glass of vodka toppled over. After a while, Tom pulled back, almost nervously. 'There's something I need to say to you.'

'What?' Her head was resting across his chest and she was looking up at him. She felt completely happy, the bad

271

things all pushed away to the corners of her mind.

He hesitated.

'What do you want to talk about?' she asked, kissing him gently on the lips again.

'I want to tell you my life story.'

'You already have. At Greenham. Remember?'

'I missed out the most important thing.'

'What was that?'

'About why I'm the way I am.'

'And what way are you?'

Tom pulled away, stood up, and poured himself a drink of water. He seemed heightened, manic, Netta thought. Then he sat down again, and began to talk. Impossible to believe that usually he was so taciturn. It was as if he thought he would never see her again, and this was his one chance to say everything. And so, nodding but not comprehending, she drank it all in. She saw a mushroom cloud go up: the mushroom cloud that haunted his imagination when he was a child. Other children had Daleks; Tom had radiation sickness to keep him awake at night. She saw Tom, sweeping floors in an old farmhouse, his childhood home in Wales before his family moved to London. Tom as a little boy, then a teenage Tom. Still sweeping. ('That was my area, you see, floors. Each one of us had a job to do. My hands still twitch when I see a mop.') The fields around his Welsh farmhouse seemed real to her, she could hear the sheep baa-ing, that peculiar note of comatose complaint, feel the fields spinning around her. Hang on, what was this? Dizzy. Really dizzy. She struggled out of his memories, suddenly herself again, needed water. But the liquid was something else; she knocked it back anyway. Would dancing help? Confusedly, she thought they were at a party, but where had all the people gone? 'I never dance,' said Tom, or perhaps he said nothing. His eyes, dark and gazing into her. Had anyone ever looked at her like that before? He was kissing her. Soft and searching. A lover's kiss. Now he was telling her something else, she could see Flora looming over them, a giantess, could hear sobbing. Saw girls turning away from him, contemptuous. Saw him walking alone, further and further away from everyone else. But not from her. No. She felt herself swooning into his world, felt as if she could turn into him, if she really tried.

Then – was he crying? He was naked, she was next to him, stroking his hair. Oh, it was that one. Erection stuff. His bad, bad, mother. Feminist Flora with her frizzy hair. Emasculating, said Tom. You're beautiful, said Netta. She touched his face, touched his body. It was like being born again, or the imaginary conversations she had with her mother. For a moment, she saw the attic room quite clearly, clothes tossed all over the floor. Two people on the bed. One of them was her. Her jeans, jumper, her old DMs – where were they? But there was something wrong. By touching him so gently, and with such tenderness, she had pressed some magic button. And he was not the same. No. He was not the same. He was kissing her again, but this time as though kisses were a means to an end, he was getting them over with so he could project himself into another state. She knew he could no longer see her as she was: she had disappeared from his gaze. She knew what she was now. A Girl. Interchangeable, something to wank off impersonal desire. The words were

273

different too, like an incantation. 'Let's feel that little cunt, wants me, your little cunt . . .' Even in her drunken state, it jolted her, that he of all people would use that word of all words. 'Tom!' She was trying to call him. 'Tom!' But she knew he was using it as a spell, a spell to break away from who he really was. It was all wrong. Something was trying to get inside her, something which hurt, there was rawness, dryness. Somebody was shouting. 'No! No! Stop it – I said No! I said No! No! No! No!' She kicked again, and pushed again, but she was slippery and naked and not strong enough. Girls are Powerful – oh yes. But not where it really counts. There was more screaming – him or her? And why did nobody come? Or did she?

20

In the morning, he reached out his arms to her. As if nothing had happened. As if they could be lovers, everything was perfect. The look in his eyes was proud, as if he had transcended his demons. She rolled over, away from him. The word 'RAPE' appeared before her eyes, tiny and far away. She couldn't claim that distant word and apply it to her own situation, this desired man who'd cried in her arms. Could she? But she knew she'd said 'No'. And that he carried on. So that was the thing they called 'Rape'. On the placards. In the support groups. At the police station. And now it had happened to her.

After a while, he got out of bed. She heard him sigh and the sound of his belt clinking as he pulled up his jeans. 'Look, I . . .' He came across to the bed and turned her over, gently this time, reminding her of last night, him yelling: 'I'll FUCK you and I'll FUCK you and I'll FUCK you,' with each thrust. 'That was the first time it's . . . worked for me,' he said. 'For years. Perhaps ever. You . . . blew my mind.'

'I said "No",' she said, not touching him, not looking at his face.

'You kind of said "No" at the beginning, but you seemed to really . . .'

'I said "No" because it was hurting, and it carried on hurting.'

'We were both lying there, naked, discussing my sexual hang-ups. I kind of took that as a green light.'

'I said "No", and that's what I meant.'

He laughed, a hard, painful laugh. 'So, what are you saying?'

'I can't say it.'

'You mean, you think I – forced you? Like some nutter in an alleyway?'

'What difference would it have made? How was this any better? At least then I would have been able to think it was some basket-case, some bogeyman. But it was you! You!' She felt as if she should weep, but her eyes were bitterly dry.

He stood with his head bent, staring at his hands. She waited for him to speak, still half-believing that he might have the words to make it all right, to explain himself away. But he said nothing.

'Does this mean *anything* to you?' she asked.

He nodded very slowly.

'Say something, then.'

'It means . . . everything.'

She stared at him, then wrapped the sheet more tightly around her body. She wanted to get dressed, but not till he had left the room.

He walked to the window, made as if to draw the curtains back, and then stopped. Without turning round he said, 'You were drunk. I was drunk. We had sex. The best sex I've ever had – life-changing sex. Don't make it like this. I just wanted you, and I thought you wanted me.' He turned to look at her. But she couldn't think of anything to say. The silence extended until it became a destructive force in the room.

'I suppose it was just . . . a misunderstanding, then?' he said, limply. 'Communication breakdown. I mean, I honestly and truly had no idea you wanted me to stop.'

'Of course you knew. Don't lie, as well as everything else.'

'I . . . thought you must have changed your mind.'

Not sorry for you, she thought. I am not fucking sorry for you, Tom Birtwistle. 'In the big, grown-up world, you stop when the woman tells you to stop. It's a fundamental fact of sexual relations.'

'I can't believe that you want to destroy everything there could be between us, just like that. All because of one reckless moment . . .'

'Get out.'

'What?'

'Get out of here so I can find my clothes, get dressed and get the fuck out of here.'

'When can I see you?'

'You can't ever see me. Not *ever*. Don't you understand?'

'I can't believe you're doing this. I thought we'd found something . . . done something . . . really special.'

'If I was a proper feminist, I would be calling the police.'

'Netta! For Christ's sake!'

'Just leave me alone.'

He went, but only after scrawling a telephone number on the back of a bus ticket and leaving it on her pillow. 'I love you,' he said.

'Oh, please,' she said. 'Spare me that one.'

At last, she heard his feet pounding down the stairs. She collected her clothes together in a bundle, then for a moment she couldn't think what to do with them. Only after she looked out of the window again did she work it out – she saw the little scurrying people, grey in the daylight now. That was it. She must put them on. Trembling, she replaced her body in the clothes it had been hidden in the day before. She wanted a bath, but not there. She picked up her bag and stumbled out, feeling as if she had left something behind, she must have forgotten something. But on the Tube to London Bridge she found her mind was strangely blank. She fell asleep with her head pressed against the cold window, dreaming that she was trapped behind a high barbed-wire fence. Tom, who was also mysteriously Toby at the same time, lay injured on the other side. Women were pinning girly tokens to his body: diamanté earrings, frilly knickers and photos of Tammy Wynette. She was searching for the jagged hole so that she could crawl through it again. But it had disappeared.

When she got back to the house, she saw that a notice had been stuck to the front door. 'Dartmouth Villa is a man-free zone,' it read. 'The male gender will be admitted by prior invitation, in special circumstances, or due to sexual orientation. Dartmouth Villa is in the vanguard of the new matriarchy. There are no circumstances in which Bryan Sullivan will be allowed to cross the threshold.' It was in Mel's handwriting.

'I'll smuggle him in through the French windows,' said Emily, who had appeared behind Netta, carrying a lot of shopping. 'Like Romeo. It's very tragic – we're divided against each other now. But love will conquer all, of course. I'm looking forward to the sort of feminism which celebrates women's bodies, instead of covering them up with enormous malodorous jumpers.' She was in mufti, and appeared to be wearing an enormous malodorous jumper herself.

'Sexual apartheid sounds like a good idea to me,' said Netta. 'Send the men off to the homelands.' She was surprised to hear her voice. It sounded quite normal, in spite of the shock of speaking to Emily. Netta hadn't noticed how similar she and Tom looked until now, but she saw that Emily had the same shadowed eyes, the same long, thin limbs, the same long, Elizabethan face. Perhaps she hadn't really looked at Tom till last night. Perhaps she hadn't really looked at anything till last night. And how would life be with Emily downstairs, the rapist's sister? How should that be addressed, during the next long afternoon when they lay around smoking and laughing about men? Was there an anecdote funny enough to wrap that one up? As she climbed the stone steps to the front door, she felt nauseous and weak.

'What really gets me is they've both swanned off without a je ne sais quoi,' said Emily. 'Mel's gone back to Greenham, and Pilar's staying with Gay Jeremy.' She pushed the door open. 'So it's actually human-free, for the time being.'

Netta had an overwhelming sense of gratitude and relief. To what? To God? She climbed the stairs to the empty flat. She went into the bathroom and began running hot water into the bath. Wash it away, she thought, wash him away. 'I'm going to wash that man right out of my hair' – the jaunty, pretty *South Pacific* girl, ever-so-slightly slighted in love. Smells, salts, potions, she thought, and poured various concoctions belonging to Pilar into the water till it was brimming with iridescent foam. Of course, she should not do this. She should leave the semen untouched, go down to the police station, have swabs taken, fill in forms. She sank into the water, eyes closed, wishing her mind could be closed down too. But that wasn't possible. The events of the previous night were part of her, and would never leave her. He had raped her. A man she liked – a man she had fancied, fantasized about – had raped her. The loop started playing again. She saw his face. Smelled his skin. Felt his weight. Heard her voice: 'No! No! Stop! Stop!' Had he said anything? Apart from shouting obscenities to will himself on? She couldn't remember. It didn't matter. She had lost him, and she could never have him again.

Still her mind raced giddily around, unable to reach a conclusion that satisfied it. His sperm was inside her, his kisses had covered her body. Lover or rapist? She knew which. Yes. She knew that much. The police. Even though she was cleaning herself up, she could still report him. 'So you say this man was known to you? Has he ever displayed violent tendencies before?' But what had happened between them was private and terrible. The law had nothing to do with it. He wasn't a danger to society. He wasn't evil. He was someone who had got everything wrong, so wrong that he would never be able to put it right. She thought of the policemen she had seen at Greenham: the nervous constable and his grumpy superior. The thought of men like that – even their female colleagues – tramping into this affair was sickening. The relationship she had had with Tom was as fragile and temporary as cloud – let it go, she thought. Let it go.

I can survive, as long as I never have to see him again.

'Hello?' There was a tap on the bathroom door. 'Mind if I come in?'

'Yes, I do really, I . . .'

But the door swung open anyway, and Emily entered the room. She had skewered her hair on top of her head, so you could see her large, goblin ears, and was carrying a pile of photographs.

Netta's body tensed under the hot water. 'I don't mean to be rude, Emily, but I'm really not in the mood for looking at holiday snaps.'

'I just thought I'd come up for a chat,' said Emily. 'We're sort of soi disant partners in crime, if you know what I mean.'

Netta sank lower into the bath, so that the bubbles came up to her shoulders. 'I don't know what you're on about. And I would really like to have some time to—'

'To what?' Emily was leafing through her pile.

'To think,' said Netta, though she realized that this wasn't true. She didn't want time to think; she wanted time to not-think, to fill her mind with a blank space so that no disturbing ideas or memories could fit inside it.

'I suppose you're really pissed off with Tom,' said Emily.

Netta sank even deeper into the water, not sure what to say.

'It's not his fault, you know.'

'What's . . . not his fault?'

'This stupid obsession with Greenham. And Mum. He told Bryan all that terrible stuff because he thought it was the right thing to do. And to get his own back, bien sûr, but he has good reason to be angry with Flora. She's been a bitch to us both. Always has been. When we were children, we were just an accessory.'

'What do you mean...accessory?' asked Netta unwillingly.

'Not fashion, like certain women – matching shoes and handbag, toning child. Ego. Different sort of narcissism. She had to be a mother. It was an absolute requirement. Then, apparently, Dad was no use whatsoever, so out he went. After that it was *égoisme à trois*. Three corners of the perfect feminist family, battling against the odds. When I visited schoolfriends with real mothers who cooked dinner and made the beds, I thought they were indecently spoilt.'

'But Flora wrote about motherhood and housework! Wasn't that her subject?'

'Too busy writing about it to indulge in the real thing. Are your hands dry?'

'No, of course not, I'm having a bath.'

Emily handed her a towel. 'You think I'm pretty vacant and Tom's a shit, don't you?' she said. 'Go on, dry them.'

Netta obediently dried her hands. 'I don't think anything.'

'Really?'

Netta shook her head.

'Oh, come on. You look down your nose at me. So do Mel and Pilar. You think I'm a moronic tart. But I don't suppose it's ever occurred to you that I'm like that because I find men more reliable than girls? I hear you, giggling and back-chatting away up here, while I'm down there, sorting out my Françoise Hardy collection, and it seems a lot easier to get shagged by a succession of men than it does to get anywhere with you. You know where you are with l'amour. At least, *I* do.'

'Really?' said Netta. 'What about the time you were slumped in gloom because Bryan didn't stay over? Men are just as unpredictable as women. And more dangerous.'

'Dangerous? Nonsense! With men, you know there are certain rules, and when they cross them, you can no longer do business.'

Netta nodded mutely.

'But with girls, frankly, fuck knows what's going on half the time.'

Netta nodded again. She had no idea about either friendship or l'amour.

'This is a good one,' said Emily. She passed Netta a photograph. It was shot in tasteful black and white, and showed her naked, apart from a pair of black stockings and suspenders, and a tiny pillbox hat with a veil. She was pouting over one shoulder, like a cheeky chorus girl.

'Emily . . .' Netta looked at it more closely, wondering if she was missing something. 'Emily, we don't know each other all that well. I mean . . . maybe there's more to this than meets the eye. But I just do not understand why you are showing me this picture. I thought you wanted to be an actress, not a . . . porn star.'

Emily smiled mysteriously and handed her another one. 'Is this more your kind of thing?' It was a colour photo this time, showing two children. The boy, with his black fringe hanging into his dark eyes, was unmistakably Tom. The girl was plump and pudding-faced, and the camera flash was reflected in her NHS glasses.

'That's you, is it?' Netta looked closer. 'You've certainly blossomed since then.'

'You could say that,' said Emily. 'When I was fourteen

I read Colette and decided I wasn't going to be ugly any more.'

'But you weren't ugly,' said Netta. 'You were just a child wearing spectacles.'

'I was hideous,' said Emily. 'Fooling people into thinking I'm not is still a kind of confidence trick. But I'm collecting proof now – proof that I'm not invisible. Proof that I'm beautiful – or beautiful enough.'

'For God's sake!' Netta handed both photographs back. 'This is 1985, Emily! Why are you talking such crap? You could do anything!'

'It's not that simple. You don't know what it was like, growing up with someone who sucked up all the available attention. Here's another one.' This showed Flora sitting at a table in the sun. She was beaming widely, surrounded by a crowd of kaftan-sporting chums, young men with beards and headbands, skinny brown girls with waist-length plaits. While she smiled at the camera in a rictus of peculiar triumph, their eyes were all fixed on her. Netta could see why – she gave off an odd radiance, as if she was intoxicated by her own confidence. But it took her a moment to find Tom and Emily in the photograph. They were hiding under the table, looking out blankly, each hugging their neatly bent knees, sitting close together but not touching. 'All the energy belonged to her,' said Emily. 'And now, I think both of us are trying to make up for that.' Another photo now, of Emily's breasts. They were displayed beneath the triumphant smile she had inherited from her mother.

'So, topless modelling is the way forward,' said Netta. 'It might make sense to you, but it seems bloody weird to me. I'm sorry, Emily, but the water's getting cold.'

'Don't you understand?'

'No, I don't.'

'Tom and I want the same thing.'

'Which is . . . what?'

'To be noticed.'

'Noticed?'

Emily nodded. 'It's not complicated.' She made the photos into a neat pile and squared off the edges. 'Flora made us feel as if we would always be on the outside of her big, important life. Invisible little nonentities, looking in. I reacted by . . . well. Pursuing my own glittering career.'

Netta looked at the shrivelling bits of foam that were still floating in the water. 'And how has Tom reacted?'

'Not by chasing after a brilliant career, absolument pas. He's the least ambitious person I know, in that way.'

'Some people might say that wanting to save the world was pretty ambitious.'

Emily stood up. 'That's what he wants officially. But I don't think that's what he's really looking for. He's a lost soul.'

'Lost?'

'You know what I mean. He's doesn't know how to be a man. He doesn't know what it means. All his role models are negative – blowing people up, or being irrelevant and useless like Dad. All these causes – shooting statues or hiding in the undergrowth at Greenham – they're just a distraction. It's not world peace he wants. It's something much closer to home.'

'What?'

'Unconditional love.'

21

'Now, just tread water, Netta. Okay? We're going to do this once more!' Jane, busty and commanding in her all-in-one swimsuit, was standing on the edge of the Marshall Street pool. Charlotte was in her arms, screaming and twisting with rage.

'Are you sure this is a good idea?' called Netta. 'Won't it just make everything worse? She really is in a dreadful state.'

'Ahhhh!' screeched Charlotte, writhing in her mother's grasp. 'Hate Mummy! Bad Mummy! Going to kill you . . . ahhhhh!' Her costume was pink and frilly: she looked like little Shirley Temple.

'It's just attitude,' said Jane serenely. 'She's not really scared of the water at all.'

'You're the expert. She seems pretty scared to me.'

Charlotte's limbs flailed furiously. 'Want my wings! Want my wings!'

Jane grappled with her daughter for a moment to get a better grip. 'Right, here we go . . . ready?'

'Yup.' Netta trod water obediently. Jane, face set, advanced to the edge of the pool and lobbed Charlotte into the water. Charlotte's screams rose in volume during her brief trajectory through the air, to be replaced by pathetic coughing and spluttering when she hit the surface. 'Waaahhhhhhhh!' she yelled through the coughs. 'Splub ub. Waaahhhh!' Netta swam over and grabbed her before she went under again. Charlotte's face was puce, her eyes round with fear. She hit Netta hard in the face with her fist before they reached the side. Netta grasped the bar around the pool, feeling the child heaving and shuddering with panic.

'All right, darling, it's all right now. That was the last time. It's just to get you used to the water.' But she was not sure that Charlotte could hear a word she was saying; sobs still racked her body, and a little trail of green snot slid from one nostril. 'I'll buy you an ice cream later,' said Netta, and the child's sobs died down slightly, but her body still trembled in Netta's arms.

'Want my wings! Hate Mummy! I might drown and then she would be happy.'

The lifeguard, overweight and with his feet splaying over the sides of his flip-flops, viewed the scene with an air of detached enjoyment. He seemed grateful for the break in his monotonous routine, and not in the least inclined to remonstrate with Jane or Netta for reasons of cruelty to children.

Jane dived in smugly, feet together, smooth as a seal. She had always been good in the water, streamlined and compact as she was. Netta, with her ganglier frame, found swimming an arduous business. Today, two weeks after the terrible scene with Tom, the swimming pool was the last place she would have chosen to be. She didn't like the fact that so much of her body was exposed, and wished that the Victorian fashion for long, baggy bloomers was still an option. In the changing-room mirror she felt almost comically provocative, with her breasts bulging over the top of her swimsuit, and her long, white thighs on view for anyone to see. She had only agreed to come so she could talk to Jane in private – or rather, away from Richard – and this seemed to be the sole option. Jane claimed to be too busy and tired to meet for a drink ever, and was even more consumed by her children than usual. Their accomplishments were not apparently coming up to scratch, and the incident in the river had concentrated her attention on Charlotte's apparent hydrophobia. Richard had taken the two boys to the National History Museum to be improved – Little Richard doubtless being exposed to the flora and fauna of the world at precisely the right moment in the development of his synapses – and Charlotte was here, undergoing ritual torture because she refused to give up her water-wings.

As Netta passed Charlotte's protesting little form to Jane, she felt grateful to be useful, and have a role to perform, however questionable. She had spent most of the last two weeks alone: Pilar, obviously too enraged to live under the same roof, was still staying with Jeremy. Netta had told no one about the rape. Instead, she had closed in on herself, spending her days in the library and her evenings writing essays and reading. In between times, she cleaned and tidied obsessively, imposing order on both the flat and her own body. She had also shaved her head even more closely, in case she was starting to look attractive again. But in spite of her best efforts to keep her head empty, she couldn't help thinking, and her thoughts kept coming back to the same subject. Not the rape, but Jane. Her secret loomed between them, impossible to ignore. And yet – how could she ever tell Jane what she had done? Would she ever forgive Netta? Or Richard? Whatever Netta chose to do, she knew she would feel bad. As Richard had pointed out, there was no longer an ethical option. But since Tom had done this terrible thing to her, she felt damaged and disconnected. At the same time, she felt more determined to try to sort out her life. Perhaps Jane had a right to hear about their sordid betrayal. If their situations were reversed, Netta thought she would rather know the truth.

'You're very quiet,' said Jane, sipping her coffee in the café next door. 'And a funny colour. Are you sure you're all right?'

Netta hesitated, looking down at her own drink. They hadn't spoken to each other properly till now, due to Charlotte's relentless whingeing – she had built up gradually to the full-on hysterics which had so diverted the lifeguard. Now she was busily gorging ice cream, letting out a sound that was half-way between a sigh and a sob every few seconds. Netta envied her ability to wear her heartbreak on her sleeve. She had a sense of almost consciously holding herself together, as if she would otherwise disintegrate and fly all over the room.

'I'm fine,' she said. 'Fine. How about you? You look a bit on the wan side yourself.'

This was true. Jane's face had a worn-out intensity. If only she could take parenting a bit less seriously, thought Netta.

Jane looked around at the stripped pine tables and higher forms of salad. 'Oh, completely and utterly fine. So much more on top of things at the moment. Everything's just . . .' A strange spasm crossed her face. 'Look, Charlotte, darling, wait here while Netta and I get some more cake.'

'I don't want any more cake, it's okay . . .' Netta began, but saw Jane's frozen stare, and followed her to the counter. Jane grabbed a tray and looked mournfully at the assortment of date flapjacks and wholemeal muffins.

'What is it?' asked Netta, glancing over at Charlotte, who was tearing up sachets of cane sugar and emptying the golden grains on to her plate.

'It's nothing, it's just a passing mood.' Jane closed her eyes now. Netta had a strange sensation in her stomach she could not put a name to. It intensified when she looked at the chocolate fudge cake.

'Jane . . . ?'

Now Jane's eyes snapped open as if she had been stung. She took a piece of flapjack and began to talk rapidly. 'I don't know what to say. I don't know where to start. I specifically told myself not to tell you. You of all people. But then I realized there was no one else.'

Netta swallowed and avoided looking at the cake. She braced herself. 'Tell me what?'

Jane hesitated again.

'I think it'll be better for all of us if you tell me what's the matter,' said Netta.

'Marital indiscretion is your speciality, is it?'

Oh God. 'Please tell me what's wrong.'

'I've done a terrible thing.'

'*You* have? But – what kind of terrible thing?'

'I've been having lunch with Fenton Brasier.'

In spite of everything, Netta struggled not to laugh. She coughed instead. 'You told me you bumped into him, and he recommended you for a job. It's not a crime, is it, having lunch?'

'There are different ways of having lunch, Netta. These weren't the sort of lunches during which one ate much. I drank champagne and allowed my head to be turned.'

'He's still got a crush on you, has he?' If lunch was a betrayal, where would kitchen-floor copulation register on the sliding scale of sin?

Now Jane was talking even more rapidly. 'More than a crush. He's in love with me. He's been in love with me for years, or so he said. He's got a wife and four children in an Elizabethan manor house near Ipswich. The children are Ivo, Elfrida, Christobel and Max. He's shown me all the photographs. He has gun dogs and everything. The grounds are by Capability Brown. There's even a moat . . .' Her description ended in a muted wail.

'God,' said Netta. She tried to digest this. 'But . . . you're not having an affair?'

Jane gulped. 'No. I said no. How can I? How could I even think about it? Richard's devoted to me, the perfect husband. Of course, the sex isn't always . . . but what would you expect? That day I told you I had a job interview, I was really meeting Fenton. For the last time.'

'So there was no job?'

'No job at all. I just made that up. It sounded pretty good, didn't it? Quite fancy myself at Demeter Books. I wouldn't stand a chance, of course. Just a little fantasy.'

'What . . . happened?'

'I told him I couldn't see him again, not for lunch, not for anything. And he . . .' Jane's voice cracked, and she took a glass of English apple juice from the cold counter.

'He . . . what?' asked Netta gently.

'He said I had a suburban soul.' She sniffed. 'I could

feel his attention wandering as soon as he knew he wasn't going to get his own way. He said his wife – who is terribly understanding and the daughter of a high court judge – knew all about us, that I was getting the whole thing out of proportion. Love isn't exclusive, he said. Love doesn't demand loyalty. That's just a recipe for claustrophobia, stasis and boredom. I slunk away feeling compromised by my own dull, conventional limitations. A lumpenly, monogamous fool.' She looked at her hands, clenched around the glass. 'Do you know, we never even kissed? It was more of a brief encounter than *Brief Encounter*, and yet it meant so much to me.'

'Oh, Jane.' Not knowing what else to do, Netta scooped the last slice of walnut cake on to a plate. But when its faint smell reached her nostrils, she felt something rising in her throat. She couldn't speak – and even her thoughts made no sense. She had limited experience of married men – well, just Richard, actually. She swallowed hard. 'I'm sure you did the right thing,' she said. 'But it must have been horrible. You should be proud of yourself, rather than feeling guilty.'

Jane gave a short laugh. 'Proud! That's a good one!' She paid for their food, and said quietly, 'I sometimes think . . . well . . . I know a million women have fallen into the same trap before me. But Fenton seemed to notice what I was like. Which was very flattering. But then – I know Richard has always been faithful . . .'

The room lurched. 'How do you know that?' said Netta. She tried to push the nausea down. 'I mean – maybe he hasn't. Maybe you aren't the only person who has been . . . tempted.'

Jane turned to look at her. 'Whatever do you mean? Of course he's faithful! Why would I think otherwise?'

'Well, I suppose if you've no reason to doubt him . . .' The room lurched again, and Netta's stomach rolled with it.

'I don't understand what you're saying.' Jane was glaring now. 'What do you mean? Is there something I don't know?'

'Going to be sick,' said Netta, running for the loo, but she got only half-way there, and vomited copiously all over the floor next to the cutlery area. She didn't wait to apologize, or gauge the reaction of the austerely snooty staff, but ran into the Ladies, where she threw up again, even more violently, strands of mucus and half-digested food streaming from each nostril. When the nausea subsided, she flushed the toilet several times, then sat down on it, sweating and shivering. She knew she was upset about Jane and Richard, but the violence of this bout of sickness was overwhelming. Could it be caused entirely by emotion? She hadn't eaten anything strange. In fact, she had hardly eaten anything at all. She went out to the sinks and washed her face and hands slowly, still trembling.

'Netta?' Jane came bustling in with Charlotte. 'Are you okay?'

'Yes, I . . . think it's all over now. Just a bit shaky.'

'You okay, Nettie? That was the most sick I've ever seen.' Charlotte sounded impressed.

'We'll beat a hasty retreat when you've cleaned yourself up,' said Jane. 'Staff out there aren't too happy. I had to reassure them that you aren't a drug addict.'

'Yeah . . . I'm so sorry. Must've been really disgusting.' Netta looked up and saw her reflection. A spectral figure gazed back at her, hairless, white-faced, hollow-cheeked. 'Christ. Why didn't you tell me how terrible I look?'

'I did say you were a funny colour.'

'I look totally – appalling. Like somebody from Belsen!'

'No, Nettie, you're pretty,' said Charlotte. 'But prettier before, with hair.'

'You do look rather under the weather,' pronounced Jane. 'There's nothing really wrong, is there? I mean, you're not . . . ?' She glanced down at Charlotte, then at Netta's reflected face. 'In an interesting condition?'

'Not what?'

'Bun in the oven? Expectant? Avec child?'

'Of course not.'

'Good. Because that would . . . add to life's complications, wouldn't it?'

'It certainly would.' The idea twisted slowly in Netta's head. She had been half-aware of this possibility for several days, but had pushed it to the edge of her mind. Pregnancy. Periods. Pill. She was not good at remembering to take it. Sometimes she took two at once. Sometimes, as she did not really have a sex life, she wondered why she was on the pill at all. Now she tried to focus on the salient facts, such as when she was due to finish her current packet. But all she could see was a pink haze, and tiny foil compartments identified by the days of the week.

They left the café after apologizing repeatedly. Jane gave the waitress a five-pound tip. 'You were telling me something about Richard,' she said, when they were walking along Argyll Street. 'Or aren't you up to talking about it now?'

Netta's thoughts had raced ahead by now. The image of the pill packet had been replaced first by Richard's face, and then by Tom's. She had made one stupid mistake. Two stupid mistakes. A confession to Jane would make it three. Honesty was no longer any kind of policy at all. 'I was speaking theoretically,' she said. Her voice sounded thick and strange. 'What I meant was – no one knows everything about any other human being,' she said, trying to speak more clearly. 'Not even the ones they think they know best. The people they trust.'

'Oh, quite, quite . . .' Jane gave a relieved laugh, like an exhalation of air. 'Awful, really, the smugness of monogamy. Bundled up in your domestic straitjacket, suspicious of the outside world, full of screwed-up single people . . .'

'Quite,' echoed Netta.

'Even Dad's a mystery,' said Jane. 'He's suddenly got religion. Can you believe it? He used to have a personal vendetta with God – it used to be a close-run thing between the Holy Trinity and Anna Raeburn. Now he's gone all High Church, and decided to surrender to the eternal verities. I think the main attraction is that Father House likes claret. That's his new poison – red wine. The blood of Christ, as he likes to remind me on his umpteenth glass. I've no idea what's going on in his mind, but he's talking about going back to resume his duties at the pub now . . . patched up with some vague idea about meeting up with Mum in the great hereafter.'

Netta couldn't summon up the power of speech. Once, she had wanted to escape from her father. Now, she wanted to escape from Jane. Neither goal was achievable. Her habit of diving into disaster seemed to have strength-ened the bonds between herself and her family, rather than weakening them. If she was going to avoid hurting everyone, she would have to do something drastic.

They had reached the Tube station. Jane and Charlotte were off to Oxford Street to shop. 'I didn't actually mean that you are screwed up,' said Jane. 'When I talked about screwed-up single people, I mean.' She seemed happier, now she had made her confession about her secret meetings with Fenton. First she kissed Netta, then, unexpectedly, gave her a hug. 'I do realize I've been an awful cow,' she said. 'But – I think you're wonderful. Really. We both do – Richard and I.'

'Love you, love you, love you, Nettie!' said Charlotte.

Several hours later, Netta stood at the edge of the Thames. The river was lapping quietly at her feet, shimmering as far as the wastelands of the Isle of Dogs on the opposite shore. Greenwich, she thought, trying to order her mind. I am in Greenwich. She looked up at the starless black sky. She looked down at her damp feet, and at the grubby shingle. It was a mess of washed-up flotsam and discarded litter: empty beer cans, dirty feathers and used condoms. Used condoms! Ah! Sensible people, indulging in safe sex on the river bank. Feeling around inside her shoulder bag, she found the pregnancy testing kit she had bought on the way, which she had meant to use as soon as she got home. But when she got off the Charing Cross train the thought of the empty house had been unbearable. So she had walked and walked, and ended up here, staring across the filthy river at the emptiness that lay on the other side.

She looked at her watch and saw that it was after nine. How long had she been standing there? 'Oh well,' she said aloud, and began to walk along the river, trying to clear her thoughts. After a few minutes, she thought she heard other footsteps, scrunching along behind her on the shingle. She turned, but all she could see was the empty shore. She walked on, and once more heard a strange echo of her own steps. But again she saw nothing when she looked behind her. Nervously, she hurried back to the road, and found she was in the deserted area of the old dockyards, an eerie zone full of empty warehouses and high walls, blackened with smoke. She began to walk briskly along a silent street, which she thought led towards the main road. Unmistakably, she heard footsteps behind her. This time, when she turned, she saw someone standing under one of the street lights. Who was it? Tom? Or some other rapist? Automatically, she broke into a run, and the footsteps behind her were running too. Fear gripped her, and she began to race flat out, sprinting headlong down the centre of the street, faster and faster. But she stumbled, her body felt weak and heavy, and the someone was coming nearer and nearer, a voice was calling her: 'Netta! Netta!' It must be Tom, it had to be Tom, and now she was sobbing and gasping as she blundered along, tripping over loose cobbles, fearing any moment she would fall. She was slowing down, she was too slow. She felt a hand grab hold of her arm. 'Let go of me! Let go of me! I never want to see you again! Let go!' she screamed.

'Netta?' It wasn't Tom's voice. She stopped. It sounded like a woman. 'Netta? What the bloody hell is going on?' Netta turned around to face her assailant. Pilar was staring at her, wide-eyed. 'Gawd! I thought you looked a bit funny when I saw you leave the station. Thought I'd just catch up with you, straighten a few things out. And now . . . what's wrong with you? What's *happened*?'

Netta opened her mouth, but no words came out. 'Can't . . .' She cleared her throat. 'It's not something I can really go into, just at the moment.' She sounded unnecessarily official, as if she was taking a business call on the phone. What she wanted to do was tell Pilar everything, and be friends again, and always do the right thing in a big, warm, tactile future. But she couldn't work out what it was safe to mention and what wasn't. The little boy in Emily's photograph haunted her, staring out blankly at the world. Was he a rapist? Was that his destiny, his identity? If she told Pilar or Mel about how he had forced her to have sex, this would be the result. If she told anyone what had happened, he would be damned for ever.

'Don't be stupid,' said Pilar. 'Something's up with you. Why are you running away? What are you scared of?'

'I . . . I'm scared of the dark. You know I am.'

'Come on, there's more to it than that! And if you can't tell me about what's wrong, who the hell *are* you going to unburden yourself to?'

'I'm okay,' said Netta. 'I don't need anyone.' But she felt her legs buckling underneath her, and Pilar put one arm around her, propping her up.

'Look, Nettie, you can tough it out as much as you like once you've told me what's wrong. Okay? But first, we are going to stagger to the Frog and Toilet, and we are going to have a bloody good drink, and you are going to lay it on the line. Tell me the whole story. However bad it is. All right?'

22

The Frog and Toilet was really called the Frog and Doublet, but earned its affectionate nickname due to its characteristic smell of urine. It was small, with just one room and an old-fashioned brass-topped bar. The brass – rarely cleaned – was matt with accumulated dirt. It did not do to examine the glasses closely, either. Most of the clientele were elderly West Indian men, who supped Red Stripe in their accustomed seats. The Frog was also a mild Goth pub, and the undead denizens of the local council block would wander in and drink snake-bite and get less and less animated as the evening wore on. Netta was sipping a gin and tonic, and feeling almost normal. 'Mother's ruin,' she thought. Her hand still shook slightly, and she felt a strange sense of unreality, but otherwise this might have been an ordinary night, and this a casual drink with a friend. But she had no friends. There was no one she could really trust.

Pilar swigged her own drink and watched Netta carefully. 'So – are you going to tell me what's happened to you?'

'I can't,' said Netta. 'I just really, really can't.'

There was silence for a moment. Pilar shook her head. 'I've never seen you like this,' she said. 'Is this some massive self-destruct mission? You look like a bleeding junkie, for a start. I just don't understand. Why did you write that article? Why did you back Bryan up when he did that terrible act at the Tunnel? What *is* it with you and men? I mean, no one expects any better from Emily, being a self-made moron is her life's work. But you! I thought we were really close . . .'

'I didn't write the article. And I know the act was awful – but you were all being so po-faced about it. He was only trying to wind people up, and you fell for it . . .' Netta faded away. She wondered if she was going to be sick again.

'Ever since you shagged Richard, your life's gone from bad to worse,' said Pilar.

'You could say that.'

'Does anyone else know about it?'

'About what?' Netta clutched her cold, ice-filled glass with sweaty hands.

'Richard and you being vile adulterers.'

'No.'

'Have you thought about telling Jane? Getting it all out in the open?'

'Yes.'

'And . . . ?'

'I thought it would make a bad situation worse.'

'Why? Surely living with a lie isn't what you want! Come on, Netta. Maybe I could help you, if you told me what's going on. As it is . . . I just don't understand.'

Netta felt a tear gather itself and slide down her cheek. Another followed, and then another. Still not sure what to say, and what not to say, she pulled the pregnancy testing kit out of her bag and put it on the table between their two bottles of tonic.

*

'Well? *Are* you?' Pilar was hissing through the closed door of the toilet cubicle. Netta was looking at the line in the little plastic wand. It had changed colour and made its prediction. She stared at the narrow strip. Her mind was refusing to process the information in front of it. She was staring at a symbol which had no meaning.

'It's blue,' she said, trying to focus on the lettering on the side of the box.

'What does that mean? Pregnant, or not pregnant?'

'I dunno.'

'Read what it says on the side.'

'I *am* reading what it says on the side.' She bent down suddenly and posted the box under the space beneath the toilet door. 'You look at it.'

Pilar was quiet for a moment, and Netta rested her head against the closed door.

'Well,' said Pilar. Netta could almost feel her hesitation. 'Do you want me to come right out and say it, or do you want to have another drink first?'

'Just bloody well tell me,' said Netta.

'Right,' said Pilar. She hesitated. 'You're pregnant, Net. I'm really, really sorry.'

'Pregnant?' She lifted her head and looked down at herself. Pregnant? The word itself was swollen with responsibility.

'Netta? Darling? Are you coming out? You've gone all quiet.'

'I dunno,' said Netta again. 'Maybe I'll just stay here.'

'You can't stay there for ever,' said Pilar. 'That won't solve anything. We have to sort you out.'

'I know.' Although it was completely irrelevant, she

was trying to decide which man she least wanted to be the expectant father, Richard or Tom. Oddly, she found she was trying to remember a missing Third Man, someone normal and anonymous who might be the real dad. Someone she had slept with accidentally, without noticing.

'Netta, for God's sake open the door! You need to get out, get a drink down you and make a plan of attack.'

'How can I make a plan of attack? I'm With Child. I just need to knit bootees.'

Pilar banged on the door. 'Get a grip on yourself! Are you going insane? You need to think. Come out of there and talk to me properly! Please, Net!'

Netta pulled back the latch. 'I was only joking. Imagine me with a baby! I wouldn't last ten minutes.' She thought of Toby, Charlotte and Little Richard. And then of Toby floating in the river. She wasn't even fit to be an auntie.

'I need to destroy the evidence,' she said, washing her hands.

'That's one way of putting it,' said Pilar.

An Abortion Hotline sticker leered garishly from the hand-dryer – Netta wrote the number down, using a red biro she had found at the bottom of her bag.

'Sleep's what you need, more than anything,' said Pilar, as they made their way from the riverside towards Blackheath. 'God knows how you've coped, keeping your fling with Richard a secret! You of all people, one of the UK's premier blabbermouths.' She linked Netta's arm affectionately. 'Normally, you never shut up.'

'I suppose I must have changed,' said Netta. 'I certainly feel as if I have.' Her second secret held her in a clammy grip, separating her from Pilar.

'How I've avoided the up-the-duff horror is a total mystery,' said Pilar. 'The risks I've taken! Gawd! Must be barren, non-Earth Mother type. Of course, it's all fine now. Yet another advantage of sleeping with girls.'

'Shagging men is definitely a loser's game,' said Netta. 'I'm living proof of that – or hanging-by-a-thread proof, anyway.'

'That's the spirit,' said Pilar.

They turned into their road, and could see Dartmouth Villa at the far end. Overgrown hedges lined each side of the street, hiding the other houses, and the pavement was punctuated with rectangles of unkempt grass. Rampant old sycamore trees formed a woven mesh of intertwining branches far above, sealing off the sky. In the winter darkness, Netta felt as if she was in hidden woodland, not a London suburb. The naked trees shuddered together in the gathering wind.

'Freezing,' said Pilar as she pushed open the squeaking iron gate. 'Can't wait to get inside and . . .' Then she hesitated on the edge of the dark, chaotic garden. 'Shit,' she said. 'We've run out of wine.'

'Do we need any?'

'For God's sake!' said Pilar. '*You* may be pregnant, but I'm not! And anyway, if you're not keeping the cluster of cells, there's no need to stop drinking, is there?'

Netta gazed at the gloomy house. 'There are no lights,' she said. 'Complete darkness. No one there.'

'No idea where Emily is – I think she's up to something,'

said Pilar. 'And Mel's still at Greenham, of course. It's fine. Let yourself in, and I'll dash to the off-licence.'

'Oh – no – I'll come with you!' The windows of the house had filled with shifting shadows; the rustling rhododendrons concealed ghouls and spectres.

'Netta! Don't be silly! You're exhausted. Just go inside, put the fire on, and get warm.' Pilar turned and walked briskly away.

Netta thought of following her, but felt tiredness overwhelm her. Instead, she turned and walked through the gateway. The cold cut through her clothes: she huddled her coat around her more tightly and scrunched over the gravel towards the front door, feeling for the keys in her pocket. As she climbed the decaying stone steps, she realized that her right pocket was empty, and hastily felt for them in her left. That was empty too, so she searched her bag. But the keys weren't there either. They weren't anywhere. She glanced over her shoulder – the night-filled garden seemed watchful, malevolent. The trees moaned and creaked above her head. She saw a figure – did she see a figure? Standing by the garden gate, blocking her way out. Her exit point. It was a man. A cold certainty gripped her. It wasn't the supernatural that scared her. She was frightened of something else – someone else. And with good reason. Suddenly, without knowing why, she pelted down the steps and ran around the side of the house. The wind shrieked in her ears, she charged towards the long grass of the disused tennis courts, she felt herself slipping. She staggered forward, trying to regain her balance, but she tripped again and fell to the ground. She wanted to sob, or scream, or shout. But she couldn't.

'Netta,' said a man's voice.

Her face was hidden in the freezing grass.

'Netta.'

She raised her head. 'Go away,' she said. 'Please . . . go away.' She turned and looked up into a pale cadaverous face, dark hair falling into darker eyes. The face of Christ. Tom's face.

'Where to?' he asked thickly. 'There is nowhere.' She realized he was drunk.

The fear tightened around her, but she struggled to her feet. 'Anywhere,' she said. 'Anywhere but here. You must know that. You must know I could have you arrested for what you did.'

His bloodshot eyes were fixed on hers. 'Falling in love with you is a crime, is it?'

'Oh, Tom! Don't start trying to romanticize it. You know what happened.'

'No, I don't.'

'How can you not know?'

'Please, please. Believe me. I have no idea.'

She stared at him. Could this be true? 'Even if you think I've made all this up . . . you have to leave. I'm asking you to leave.' This was all that she could say. She glanced around her – where could she go? The house was locked, Pilar was too far away to hear her call.

'Why? I need to talk to you. I need to–'

'No you don't. There is nothing to talk about.' Her teeth began to chatter.

'About – why I might have lost it for a moment – about . . . how come someone like me, non-violent, non-sexist, totally aware and sensitive and . . . Christ – fucked up by the women's movement – might end up doing the thing that you mentioned . . .' He lurched forward and grabbed hold of her shoulders and she began to shudder violently.

'Doing what thing that I mentioned? And please . . . don't. Don't touch me.'

'You know what I mean.' His hands squeezed her shoulders gently, as if he was an expert masseur.

She thought: I have to go through all this, and he doesn't even have to say the word. 'No, you tell me. *You* tell *me* what you think I mean.'

'Forcing you to . . .'

'Forcing me to . . . what?'

'Not listening when you . . .'

He paused. She waited for him to continue. She couldn't feel his hands on her shoulders any more. All she could see was his hooded, haunted eyes.

'When you weren't very . . .' He paused again, and she watched. 'Very into . . . that kind of thing . . .'

There was a long silence. 'What kind of thing?'

'When you – apparently – didn't want me to carry on . . .'

'With – what?'

'With . . . sex.'

'When I said?'

'When you said . . . "No".'

'When I said "No". And what's that called? What's the word for that?'

'I can't say it.'

'What is it called? When you stick your penis inside a woman, using force, and she screams for you to stop? Something a bit kinky? Bit of rough stuff? Or is there another word for it? A specific term?'

306

He took a deep breath. 'Rape. It's called "rape". But that's not what happened when I–'

'Rape. Thank you. That's what I needed to hear.'

'Why? What difference does it make?'

'I can't escape from this, and I don't see why you should . . .' She stopped herself. 'In terms of responsibility. You fucked up, Tom. Really and truly fucked up. There is no way back.'

He turned away, groaning. 'Jesus . . . why are you torturing me like this? Just – can't believe the way you're being . . .' He pulled a packet of cigarettes out of his pocket, found it was empty, and flung it away.

'Why am I torturing you? What about what *you* have done to *me*?'

'Yeah . . . yeah – it's all one-way, isn't it? Women are the only people who really suffer – because we are the violent oppressors. Right? In your unbiased opinion? I didn't think you subscribed to the sisterhood. I didn't think you'd see it like that.'

'It's not about politics,' she said.

'What's it about, then?'

'It's personal.'

'You know you're making me suffer as much as possible, for as long as possible! But to prove what? I mean, you've made your point. I did a bad thing, a very bad thing, and you're right to be pissed off with me. I understand, I really do understand. Now, for Christ's sake, will you please go out with me, be with me, spend a fucking evening with me, so I can show you that I'm not a complete animal? So we can start again?'

Netta felt herself swaying. Beads of sweat began to

trickle down her shivering back. 'We can't start again,' she said weakly. 'This is the end.'

'No! No! Don't you see . . . ?' He seized her arms again. She smelt the alcohol on his breath and pulled away, nausea rising in her throat. 'Don't you see – you need me? I can look after you. I'm the one you're meant to be with. It's all there, just waiting. You're everything I ever wanted – and I'm everything you ever wanted. I knew it as soon as I saw you, and you knew it as soon as you saw me.'

She tried to take a step backwards. But he held her arms tightly and stared into her face. 'Tom. Tom . . .' She tried to collect herself. 'When I first saw you, I thought you were wonderful. Okay. That much is true. But we're not in that world any more. You forced me to have sex against my will. You raped me. When that happened, everything changed. Permanently. I should have reported you to the police – that's what the "sisterhood" would do, and that's what you deserve. And that's where the lovely, romantic scenario breaks down.'

'You can't mean that! How can one moment of weakness be the end of everything?'

'It is. It just is.' Aching tears rolled slowly down her cheeks.

'Netta – darling – Netta – please . . .' He put his arms around her, trapping her, and began to kiss her neck. Each tender kiss felt sickening, invading. She gave a groan of fury and pushed him hard. 'Don't touch me! Get your hands off me! Get off . . .'

He kept his arms tight around her, and pushed her against a tree. Her face scraped against the rough bark and she felt warm liquid trickle into her eye. It's going to happen again, she thought, he's going to do it again, and yes, his hands were inside her coat, inside her shirt, he was pulling it away, and sobbing, 'I love you! I love you!'

She screamed as loudly as she could: 'Leave me alone! For God's sake, leave me alone!' At first the cry was feeble, she couldn't make her voice obey her, his lips were seeking hers, he was pushing her mouth with his own. But she wrenched her face to one side and let out a sound that raged into the night. 'Help me! Someone please, please help me!'

The front gate shrieked on its hinges, there was the sound of running footsteps, and a loud cry: 'What the fuck is going on here? Who . . . Netta? Is that you . . . ?' The horrified voice froze both of them. Tom, still and silent now, buried his head in her neck. Trapped between his body and the trunk of the tree, Netta was stiff with fear.

'Shit – what *is* this? Get away! Get off her . . .' Someone was pulling at Tom, and she felt the heaviness lifted. She realized that this voice was familiar. It was odious, contemptible Bryan.

Tom staggered towards him. 'Look, Bryan, it's not what you think. It's just a private thing between the two of us–'

'He attacked me,' said Netta. She tried the word again – it didn't sound right. 'Attacked,' she said.

'Piss off!' shouted Bryan, jerking his thumb over his shoulder. 'I don't know what the fuck you think you're doing, but get the hell out of here, and leave her alone!' He half-led, half-carried Netta to the front door. Without thinking, she put her hand in her pocket and this time she found the keys straight away. Bryan opened the door and led Netta to an old sofa at the bottom of the stairs. Tom followed them.

'Listen, listen – Netta and I need to have a serious conversation,' said Tom. 'It's between . . . friends. You don't understand.'

Bryan grabbed hold of Tom's arm. 'I went through my entire school career without beating anyone up, but if I have to start now, I will do. Okay? Now get the fuck out of here . . .' He gave Tom a hard shove towards the open door. Tom tried to speak, but Bryan, with surprising professionalism, twisted his arm behind his back and pushed him out of the house, slammed the door behind him and shot both bolts. They could see Tom's silhouette through the opaque glass, illuminated by the outside light.

'Netta,' he called. 'Let me in! You can't do this!'

She closed her eyes, and he beat his hands against the glass, over and over again in a rhythm of despair.

'Stop that!' shouted Bryan. 'You'll smash the window! Fuck off and leave her alone! Go home!'

'Let me in!' wailed Tom. 'Why should I care about anything? I want Netta! All I want is Netta!'

Unable to bear this, Netta pulled herself to her feet and clawed hold of the banister at the bottom of the staircase. She needed to get away from the terrible noise. She needed to hide. But before she could reach the first step, she lost her footing and fell to the ground. For a moment she saw nothing but a dark mist, and heard nothing but Tom's voice crying her name. Then, the sound stopped, and blackness filled everything.

23

Hot fluid was being forced into her mouth. She began to cough and splutter. Someone propped up her shoulders. 'Drink it slowly,' said Bryan's voice. 'It's warm milk and sugar.' She drank the milk and wiped her mouth with the back of her hand, then regretted it as she felt her nausea return. She blinked and looked around her. She was in the living room of the upstairs flat, lying wrapped in a blanket on the sofa. Bryan was sitting next to her, smiling in a worried way. 'What the hell was all that about?' he asked.

Netta set the cup down on the floor. 'Can't tell you.'

'Why can't you? What did that cunt do to you?'

'Just can't. And Bryan – can we forget the c-word for now? I can't cope with any more controversy.'

'Okay, okay. You're the boss.' He frowned at her. 'Have you told anyone about – whatever it was?'

She shook her head. 'Classified information.'

'When you said . . . attacked . . . ?'

She shook her head again. 'Why would I tell you? You'll just put it in the *Daily Chronicle*. You're the last person I would . . .' She stopped. 'Going to throw up now,' she said, and rushed to the bathroom. This time, being sick was easier. My expectations are lower, she thought, as she splashed her face with cold water. Her mind was uncannily cool and detached. I have to do something, she thought. I have to get away. She went back into the living room.

'Thanks . . . for helping me,' she said, folding up the blanket. 'Can you go now, please? I mean, thanks for seeing Tom off. But I don't need you. I feel much better now, Pilar will be back in a minute.'

'Right.' He looked at her without moving.

'Bryan? Did you hear me? I am totally not in the mood for spending any time with dodgy men. So off you go.'

'I don't blame you for hating me.'

'Very big of you.'

'I'd hate me, if I was you.'

'Good. Now go.'

'I'm not all bad, you know.'

'Let's just say you're bad enough.'

'Can I tell you something?'

'As long as it's something short.'

'Right. What does your father do for a living?'

'He used to be a teacher, and now he runs a pub. Why?'

'Mine was a hospital porter.'

'Oh. Sorry, Bryan, but someone just – jumped on top of me – and I'm really not in the mood to hear your family history.' Netta went into her bedroom and hauled a suitcase on to the bed. Bryan hesitated on the threshold, as if anxious not to invade her privacy. She didn't invite him in, but started opening drawers, randomly removing clothes, and packing as quickly as she could.

'My point is that it's about the most crap job you can have. Wheeling people around, full of tubes and shit. Heavy, hard work. And you're invisible – unless you're a cheeky chappie type. My dad was never like that.'

'Was?' She looked up from a pile of faded M & S underwear.

'He died five years ago, when he was pushing a corpse into the morgue. A really fat corpse. My dad was small and skinny.'

'Oh dear.' She opened the wardrobe, took out her only suit, and folded it across the mounds of jeans and T-shirts. 'I'm really sorry.'

'Yeah.' He paused. 'It was handy really. All they had to do was stick him into a drawer. He hated causing trouble so it's what he would have wanted, as they like to say when someone croaks. Thing is, it wasn't just the job that killed him.'

'No?'

'It was me.'

'You . . . killed him in the morgue?'

'I had a sort of scuffle with him that morning. The nearest I ever came to having a fight. Until today.'

'Why did that kill him?' Now she was crawling under the bed in search of shoes that made a pair.

'Rage. Frustration and rage. His eyeballs were pulsing out of his head. I pushed him up against the kitchen door and ran out of the house. He was yelling abuse at me as I legged it off to school. He had the heart attack about two hours later.'

Netta thought for a second. 'Why do you want me to know this?'

'Because what happened to my dad has made me the way I am. I'm ambitious, Netta. I want to make something out of my life. No one helped him, and no one's going to help me. I *have* to be ruthless. I *have* to be impatient. And if people don't like it — that doesn't usually bother me.'

'I'm sure you'll go far.'

'No, that's not what I mean. I've treated you really badly. That's why I came round — to try and make up for it.'

'I thought you'd come to see Emily.'

'Ah, young Emily. A bit too similar to me in some respects. No shame. She's moved on, apparently. Some film director johnnie saw that photo, and off she went.'

'Not Polanski?' Netta wedged the shoes at the edge of the suitcase and looked around, wondering how much more she could carry.

'Not Polanski, no. I think he comes from Thames Ditton.'

'Are you very upset?'

'Christ, no. Who cares? She's a bloody nightmare. It's you I'm worried about. The point is — I wanted to be a top journalist to justify my dad — on his behalf, if you know what I mean. Then I got my big break, and I asked you to help me, and you were so fucking lah-di-dah about it, as if I was the lowest form of life. By the way . . .'

'What?'

'Why are you packing?'

'I have to leave.'

'But you're ill.'

'I'm okay now.'

'Where are you going?'

'I haven't decided yet.' She found some money in the top drawer of the dressing table. 'I still don't understand why you stole my essay and put the article in my name.'

'The gits at the *Chronicle* said it had to be written by a woman. I did all that work – chased all over Greenham, sat up a tree with crazy Tom, listening to him ranting on about his psychological issues, dug up all kinds of stuff they never used – and then they decided it wasn't even going to have my byline. I was still pissed off with you, and yours was the first name that came into my head. I thought there was a kind of poetic justice to it, given that I'd used your essay . . . and why did I use your essay? I didn't need to steal it, darling. You left it in the fucking refectory that day we were at DeeDee Chapinsky's lecture. I was going to give it back to you, but when I saw what it was about, I decided to hang on to it. Oh, I know it sounds really shit. It *is* really shit. I was totally hacked off myself. That's when I decided to broaden out to stand-up comedy, which now looks like it might work out. I haven't got time to wait around. Life's too short, and who the fuck is going to notice you if you don't push yourself forward? But I'm sorry. Very, very sorry. I was a cun . . . I was a total wanker.'

She shrugged, and glanced at him dismissively. 'Why bother to apologize? I'm surprised you're here at all.'

'I like you quite a lot,' he said. 'Surprising as it may seem.'

'You've got a funny way of showing it.'

'Well, I . . .' Bryan seemed as if he was about to say something, then changed his mind. 'What's up with you, baldie Netta Royce, escapee from marauding nutters, throwing up one minute, on the run the next? Is there anything you'd like to tell me?'

'I'd be a fool to tell you anything,' she said. 'You must

be the least trustworthy person I've ever met. Even if it didn't end up in the bloody tabloids, you'd use it for one of your hilarious routines.'

'Well, who are you going to tell, then?' he asked. 'Or will you take the secret of your weird behaviour to the grave?'

'Probably.' Her voice was hard, but tears began to trickle down her face, and she found that she was shaking with sobs. Bryan stuffed his cigarette into an empty beer can and took her in his arms. She wept freely and with relief. After a while, she straightened up, smiling apologetically, and dabbed herself dry with various tissues. 'Sorry. Stupid . . .'

'Not stupid at all.' His voice was tender now. 'I suppose now isn't a good time to tell you that you're still ultra-shaggable? Even without any hair?'

She stopped smiling. 'Bryan, it's a crap time. It's the crappiest of all crap times.'

'Yeah,' he said, stroking her cheek with an ironic grin. 'Sort of knew it was.'

'Well, that is perceptive of you.'

'Just call it masculine intuition. And . . . just to prove I do really have the gift – you're pregnant, aren't you?'

She nodded.

'If you won't shag me, at least tell me what's going on. What happened with Tom? Why were you crying like that?'

'Why should I tell you?'

'Because I might be able to help. And I won't tell a soul. Really and truly. I'm on your side, Net. You've got to believe that.'

She took a deep breath, and she told him the whole story: Jane, Richard, the kitchen table, the Greenham fall-out, Tom – everything. Afterwards, she was surprised to find that her mind felt light and clear.

Bryan lit another cigarette and thoughtfully flicked ash into the beer can. 'Yeah,' he said. 'What you might call a comprehensively bollocks situation.'

'Yes.'

'You're sure an abortion is out of the question?'

'I think so. I have to go through with this. I can't face screwing up again.'

'It's kind of the modern way, you know, Net. A baby will cut down all your options. And no one is asking you to be a martyr.'

'I just couldn't go through with it. Don't ask me to go into all the whys and wherefores. I don't want to argue like a man.'

'So you can't tell anyone. Can't let your sister know it could be Richard's baby, and can't tell Tom it might be his. And can't tell anyone Tom raped you, because he'll be kicked out of normal society, and you still feel sorry for him for reasons of gratuitous humanitarianism.'

'That's right.'

'What are you, sodding Joan of Arc?'

'Quite the opposite, as you know.'

He leaned forward with sudden intensity. 'So – you want to get away?'

'Yes.'

'Right away?'

'As far away as possible.'

'How does New York sound?'

'New York?'

'I'm not joking.'

'You're not – not asking me to elope, are you?'

'Sadly, no. I'll be staying right here. You'd be doing this on your own. Hold on . . .' He rooted around in the pocket of his jacket and pulled out a folded piece of paper, which he handed to her. 'Read that,' he said.

She unfolded the paper. It was a letter, typewritten on thick, cream paper. At the top, there was a picture of a reclining poodle, wearing shades. Next to it appeared the wording '*The New Bitch*: the magazine for women who know it all'. Below was the address in New York. She stared at these words, and at the name scrawled at the bottom. 'I don't understand it,' she said. 'What's going on? I don't know anybody in New York. I've never even been there.'

'Read the bloody thing, for Christ's sake,' said Bryan. 'It's only a sodding job offer! From our dear friend DeeDee Chapinsky.'

'But . . . I didn't apply.'

'This *New Bitch* magazine is hot stuff. Chapinsky wants to replace *Ms* and *Spare Rib* – it's ironic, iconoclastic – attacking the feminist old guard. Right up your street.'

'I don't want to attack the feminist old guard! I want everyone to love me! And why the hell would she offer *me* a job? I'm a first-year communications student. There must be loads of people who are better qualified than I am.'

'Look – for God's sake – you need to think about this. It's the chance of a lifetime.'

She tried to compose her mind, and began to read:

Dear Netta Royce,

I read your article in the Daily Chronicle *with great interest, as I am launching a new magazine which aims to turn the women's movement around. Women are underestimating themselves in seeking equality with men. Women aren't celebrating what they have, because they don't even recognize that it exists. Eve was Adam's downfall, not the Serpent. The Serpent was part of Eve's psyche, and with that she cast us all out of the Garden of Eden. Sugar and spice? The female of the species? I don't think so.*

The New Bitch *is here to celebrate all that is mean and nasty and beautiful in the essence of femininity. It's here to call a girl a girl, smear lipstick on collars, drape itself decoratively over dreary, desk-bound corporate America. What I want to avoid is all those tired old clichés about oppression and our alleged victim status as a gender. Also, the masochistic assumption that wearing make-up or using our boobs to get ahead is a bad thing in itself. Women have always been smarter than men; it's the biological determinism of childbirth that holds us back. If we want to storm the citadel, then hard work, not whining and kvetching, will win the day. Young women like yourself – inspired by the example of your very own Margaret Thatcher – hold the future in your hands. I don't want writers who sit piously on the moral high ground, claiming mistresshood of all that is pure and clean and lovely in human nature. I want writers who show what women are really like: dark, cruel, sadistic, powerful, demonic, perverse, murky, decadent and pagan.*

If you can produce more material of the quality that you put into your article – not to mention your quite fascinating essay, for which I thank you – then I would like to hire you to work

*with me on this exciting new launch. Call me to arrange an
interview date — I need to get my team in place by the end of
the month.*

*Sincere regards
DeeDee Chapinsky*

Bryan looked at Netta expectantly. 'Well? What do you reckon?'

She shook her head. 'She sounds barking mad. Even worse than in that lecture. Does this magazine really exist?'

'Launch issue is out in three months,' he said. 'And you could be working on it.'

'God, I dunno.' She started to read it through again, still shaking her head. 'And you sent her my crap, unfinished essay! Whatever for?'

'She called the *Chronic* wanting to speak to you — thinking you must be a staffer. Told me how great she thought your piece was, and I happened to have your essay in front of me. So I got her address and sent it. Some of the stuff you wrote in there is brilliant, you know, Netta. You have to take this chance. I'd kill to do something like that . . .'

'Yes, nice turn of phrase. I'd have to kill to do this. And I can't do anything like that. I'm pregnant, and I'm staying pregnant.'

'Why? No one would expect you to go through with having a baby.'

'I'm not going to do any more bad things, that's all. I have to pay for what I've done.'

'Pay? That reminds me.' He scrabbled in his pocket and

pulled out a wad of ten-pound notes. 'Look, this is what they gave me for writing that piece. My twenty pieces of silver. It's yours. Buy a ticket to New York and go for it.'

Before Pilar returned, Netta had hidden both the letter and her suitcase. She needed time to think. Apologizing profusely for being so long, Pilar opened a bottle of champagne and they drank it in bed, wearing thick pyjamas and woolly socks.

'Have you still got your bra on under there?' asked Pilar.

'Yes, why?'

'I dunno. Don't you trust me?'

'Don't be silly! My tits feel like barrage balloons. I have to keep them caged up.'

But there was a strange tension between them. Sharing a bed was a habit of Mel and Pilar, and they used to picnic contentedly and paint each other's toenails. Netta had never been involved in any of this. Now she felt awkward, and the friendship she had craved seemed remote and theoretical. Even so, it was lovely to be cocooned with Pilar, locked safe inside the house.

'This is delish,' said Pilar. She put her glass down and regarded Netta seriously. 'Friendship,' she said. 'There aren't many rules for it, are there?'

'Not really.'

'When I first saw you, I thought you were such a nice, sweet thing.'

'I thought you were much too glamorous and scary.'

'And we were both wrong. There's a moral in there somewhere.'

'You only think that because you're an English student. There's actually no moral in there at all.'

'I don't care either way, quite frankly. As long as we can be honest with each other. That's what really matters.'

Netta took a sip of champagne. It tasted sickly and metallic at the same time. 'I might not have an abortion,' she said. 'I might go ahead and have the baby.'

'Oh, do leave off!' said Pilar. 'Where would we put it?' She looked around at the plentiful belongings which almost filled her large room. 'And imagine it, screaming all night.'

'I suppose I'd have to move out,' said Netta.

'What, into a Peckham tower block and live on the eleventh floor? I'd do anything for you, Net, but for God's sake. You've plunged into enough disasters now – just draw a line and try to be more realistic. You're a talented, brilliant woman. You can't have a baby while you're doing a degree.'

'No,' said Netta. 'Would you mind if we turned the light off and went to sleep now?'

They kissed each other chastely, and the room was plunged into darkness.

In the morning, Netta woke early. The sky beyond Pilar's closed curtains was palest grey. In the street below, she could hear the soothing whir of a milk float, and the clinking of bottles. She turned and studied Pilar's face: she looked so still and beautiful. Each eyelash was visible against her white face. Her red hair spread around her in auburn spirals. Silently, holding her breath, Netta slid out from underneath the heavy warmth of the duvet and crept out of the room. She dressed hastily, and sat down and wrote a note:

Dear Pilar,
I am going away. I might have a job, or I might not. Whatever happens, you are right. I can't carry on being a student, or living here. One day, I hope I will be able to be honest with you, and tell you the whole story. At the moment, I can only let you know part of it. But I will always think of you as my friend. You are right — there are rules for falling in and out of love. Friendship is something you make up as you go along.

Don't forget me.

Love, always,

Netta

24

'Which street did ya say again?'

Netta looked at DeeDee Chapinsky's letter, which was now coming apart in her hands. 'West Forty-sixth,' she said. 'Don't you know where that is?'

'Sure I know where that is,' said the taxi driver. 'I fuckin' live here, don't I?' He was a mean little man, small with a sharp, uneasy face and slicked-down hair. She knew that he was overcharging her, as the cab jerked slowly forward in the crawling traffic. She also knew that she was going to be sick.

This had happened so often in the last few days that having an abortion was surely unnecessary: nothing could possibly be alive inside her. In fact, it was hard to believe there was anything left inside her at all. She could see herself in the rear-view mirror, a wraithlike transparent ghost of the person she had once been, eerily projected into this hectic, hectoring city. Everything she could see was perpendicular, heaving skywards; everything she could hear was deafening and indecipherable.

'Is it near here?' she asked. 'Only I'm not well, and I–'

'It's where it is – where it's always been.' He slammed on the brakes. 'You gonna throw up in my cab?'

'No . . . I . . .' But her hand was on the door handle. 'Yes . . .'

'Forty bucks . . . and you're outta here.' She gave him fifty and he sped away, much faster now she was no longer a passenger. Relief was her first emotion as she bent double, vomiting in the gutter. A nervous couple man-oeuvred past her, the woman politely clutching the man's arm. To them, she was part of the lurid scene, which must be coped with. She straightened up and looked down at her black suit. It didn't fit her very well, and it wasn't keeping her warm in the freezing New York weather. She shuddered. What might have been an Audrey Hepburn look on someone with a smaller frame was stretched over her body, condom-tight. The high neckline cut into her throat (not a good feeling when the bile began to rise) and the skirt rode up unprofessionally when she sat down. So here she was in the middle of New York City, in her micro skirt and tiny jacket, smeared with her own vomit. She didn't even know which street she was in, and glancing at her watch, she saw there was seven minutes to go before the interview was due to begin. There was no time to get there. They would never give her a job anyway. She was only here to salve Bryan's guilty conscience.

'Do you know where Forty-sixth West is?' she asked a passer-by, but they pushed past her, expression fixed. Worse than London. She rushed to the end of the street, feeling as if she was being garrotted by her collar, pulling her skirt down at the front and the back. She saw the street sign: '46th East'. Was that good or bad? She turned on her heel and rushed in the opposite direction, hobbling in her cheap plastic heels. The plate-glass windows caught her as she passed – the crop-haired anorexic in her stupid suit. She watched her heels clacking along the icy pavements. Movie picturesque. If only she could will herself to be a girl in a film script it would all come right. But it was real. The long stretch of sidewalk, spliced by churning streets of sweating traffic. Walk/Don't Walk. The fast-paced citizens who would not look at her. The homeless drunks, stalling at each garbage can. The sky above. She twisted her neck to look at it, storey above storey above storey zooming stratospherically upwards. She had the giddy sensation of looking down, not upwards, as if she might tumble away from gravity and towards heaven. A sort of ground-based vertigo. The glass structures glittered in the morning sun, complacent in their permanence. This, then, was the epicentre of the West, not London, squat and dreary, a muddle of Dickensian grey, split by a filthy river.

As she peered up, she found she had barged into another passer-by. 'Oh, sorry – sorry . . .' she began, but then stopped.

'Hello, young stranger,' said the passer-by.

She gulped. The passer-by was Richard. 'Hello,' she said. 'I thought you were . . . in London . . .'

He didn't smile. 'I'm at a conference. Nothing to do with you. Or, at least, our meeting is coincidental.'

'Phew, that's a relief,' said Netta, very brightly. 'Hate to think I was . . .'

'What?'

'Oh, you know. Having an impact of any kind.'

He laughed softly.

'I'm afraid you've made a profound impact. An impact I have been trying to ignore, and failing miserably.'

She opened her mouth to speak, then realized that she

did not want him to know why she was there, and folded her arms over her chest in a vain attempt to conceal her suit. He stared at her for a moment. 'I saw you at the airport and followed you.'

'Followed me?' With a lurch of panic, she thought of Tom at the Tunnel, the way she had stepped into his car, relieved and happy to see him.

'Yes.'

'Why?'

'Because everything seems – boring and pointless and grey and empty – when you aren't there. Because you plunge in, and say stupid things, and wear your heart on your sleeve, and mess things up, and because you jumped into the river and pulled Toby out, and because you used to look like an angel and now you look like a funny little punk, and because I want to gather you up, and look after you, and be with you, and because . . . because I want you . . .'

'Want.'

'Love. I love you.'

'No you don't.'

'Yes I do.'

'No you don't. You're being completely illogical. You're arguing like a woman.'

'What on earth do you mean? That *your* cognitive processes are superior to *mine*?'

'What you want is someone new. A holiday from everyday life. And you could have that.'

'With you?'

'No! But you could have it with umpteen women in this city, while you are at this jolly old conference of yours.

Isn't that the usual way? Like Hollywood – if it happens on set, it doesn't count. But an affair with your sister-in-law . . . that would be a bit more destructive.' She thought of Pilar. 'This is *family*, Richard. Don't fuck with family.'

He stared, completely still. The knuckle of his right hand was white as he clenched the handle of his leather briefcase.

'You must have noticed how I've been with you.'

'Rude and aggressive, mainly.'

'I was at war with myself. I've been in hell. When I saw you at Kennedy Airport, I thought – it's kismet. It's meant to be.'

'Now you really *are* arguing like a woman. Kismet? What's that got to do with anything?'

'I can't help it. I can't stop thinking about you.'

'Oh, but you can.'

He closed his eyes. 'I can't, Netta, I can't.'

'Jane did.'

Richard opened his eyes and frowned. 'Jane did what?'

'Stopped thinking about a man who thought he was in love with her. Who tried to seduce her.'

'Who was it? Who the hell had the nerve . . . ?'

'It doesn't matter who it was, the point is . . .'

'It's someone I know, isn't it? It's one of those creeps who used to lounge around in her room at Oxford, bloody old Etonian bastards, looking down their –'

'Richard, I –'

'How dare he? How bloody *dare* he?'

'The point is, she turned him down . . .'

Richard looked behind him, as if the would-be seducer might be waiting to pounce. 'I think I'm going mad,' he said, swooping round to face her again. 'What's happening to me?'

Netta realized she could see the street sign she had been looking for, directly opposite. But she was later than ever now. 'Why don't you go to your conference, and then call her?'

He looked at her strangely. 'Call her?'

'Just to say hello.'

'I suppose I could,' he said, uncertainly. 'Just say, "Hello", and see how she is?'

'At home with the children. Holding it all together.'

'She could have done so much more, you know.'

Netta reached up and kissed his cheek. 'Maybe she still will.'

He caught her to him and held her tightly. Then, before she knew it, he had hailed a cab and was stepping inside. She watched him go, thankful that he had been too agitated to ask what she was doing in New York herself. Perhaps he really was in love with her, after all. She gave a thin little shrug, then realized that his coat was draped around her shoulders. His parting gift. She wanted to cry, but pulled a hideous face instead. Then she crossed the street and walked until she came to a tall art deco building. She looked for the floor number in the letterhead, but couldn't see one. So she pushed through the doors, crossed the wood-panelled entrance hall and got into the lift, hoping to see the magazine listed there. But there was no mention of it. Looking at her watch, she saw that she was now thirty minutes late. Might as well go home. Except, she didn't have one, just the cheap hotel room where she had left her suitcase.

Just as she was standing there uncertainly, she caught sight of a woman about her own age opening a door on the other side of the hallway, and apparently going down a flight of stairs. She followed quickly, having no other plan of action. The stairs were narrow and uncarpeted and smelled musty. At the bottom was a dark wooden door with a window set into it, too high to see through. Below the window was a small brass plaque which read 'The New Bitch'. She took off Richard's coat, which was trailing on the ground, and tried once more to pull her skirt down.

On the other side of the door was a small dingy room with no windows. Each wall was covered from floor to ceiling with bookshelves, filled with books, magazines and papers, not ordered in any way, as those in a library or schoolroom might be, but haphazardly, with heaps of newspapers wedged precariously here, phone directories bulging out there, and elsewhere loose manuscript pages stuffed in chaotically. In front of this jumble of paper and general detritus was a row of chairs. At the end of the row of chairs a door leading to an inner room. On the door another brass plaque, this time announcing 'DeeDee Chapinsky, Editor'. On the row of chairs sat a group of terrifying-looking girls. All of them were as thin as Netta, but thin as if they meant it, with narrow waists and trimly coordinating outfits. Each one had a perfectly correct chin-length bob: one blonde, one red and one brunette. The brunette bob was the one Netta followed down the stairs. When she walked through the doors all three swivelled to look towards her at precisely the same moment and all three gave her a look of perfectly judged indifference. Netta nodded, affecting a similar disinterest, and sat down in the last remaining seat.

After a few moments a fourth girl came out of the inner office. She too had bobbed hair, of deepest midnight black, and white skin. In fact, she was immaculate, apart from the fact that she was sobbing into a large handkerchief. She didn't stop to speak to the other interviewees, but ran out of the other door, her sobs rising in volume as she ascended to street level. Then the blonde girl disappeared into the office, only to emerge in a similar state of distress. She didn't cry, clearly being a stoic sort of person, but trembled from head to toe. There was a loud crash seconds after her departure, as if she had collapsed at the top of the stairs outside. No one acknowledged this or went to help her, and Netta decided to stay where she was. Concentrating on not being sick was her mission for the day. She thought of the afternoon with Jane's children on Hampstead Heath to try to distract herself, and her comment to Toby: 'It's a dog-eat-frog world out there.' He hadn't thought it was very funny, and perhaps it wasn't. But she smiled at the thought. Which was very useful, because the girl with the red bob had now reappeared, and stalked out of the office, eyes tight shut, face set with misery. The brunette went in and this time Netta edged closer to the inner door, trying to work out what on earth DeeDee Chapinsky could be saying. But all she could hear was the rise and fall of her distinctive voice, and then suddenly a piercing yell, 'Wasting my valuable time!' and then what sounded like 'Mediocrity SUCKS!' The brunette appeared and ran out before Netta could attempt to read her expression. The inner door stood open.

'Yes?' The question was peremptory. 'Is that it for today, or do we have other time-wasters who are too timid to even cross the threshold?' Netta got up and made her way unsteadily into the inner office. It was tiny, just about big enough for a large old-fashioned desk, which dominated the room like a vast teak altarpiece. On the far side, head only just peering out above the piles of books and magazines which covered its surface, sat DeeDee Chapinsky. Even at close quarters she was of indeterminate age, and could have been an eight-year-old dressing up as her grandmother, or an eighty-year-old who had raided an unsuitable boutique. She was wearing a purple dress and a bright red jacket, and the largest glasses Netta had ever seen. This gave her a comical, froglike air, and looked incongruous with her perfectly symmetrical bob. Which, of course, entirely explained the sleek uniformity of the other girls.

'I'm sorry,' said Netta. 'I'm slightly unwell.'

'Slightly unwell? Jesus.' DeeDee Chapinsky rolled her eyes behind her glasses. 'You must be the Brit. What's your name again?'

'Netta Royce.'

'Royce, of course. The Greenham girl. Great piece.' She looked up with a glint which may have been a smile. 'Take a seat, take a seat, I'm seeing Susan Sontag in twenty minutes,' she said. 'I met you, didn't I? In London, England? You were dressed as some kind of hooker.'

'I'd been clubbing.'

'Whatever. What do you think of Sontag?'

'I . . . is she the one with the white streak?'

'Yep. Good image. Navaho feel. I've always liked that look. But what about her body of work?'

'Well, I . . .'

'Greer?'

'Germaine, or Garson?'

'Germaine.'

'She wrote . . . *The Female Eunuch* . . . and she's Australian. Isn't she?'

'What about Steinem?'

Netta writhed. 'Edits *Ms*? Quite pretty?'

'Good, as far as it goes. Friedan? French? Dworkin?'

'Dworkin is fat with frizzy hair . . . and she's into men and the power of pornography,' said Netta. 'Or is it women? Anyway she's against it. Pornography, I mean. She's a woman-only person . . .' Desperation and nausea threatened to overwhelm her. She stared around the room for inspiration. 'Do you know what it all reminds me of?' she said.

'Jesus.' DeeDee Chapinsky was staring at her, her eyes almost as big as her glasses. 'No, tell me. What does the history of the women's liberation movement remind you of?'

'Maths homework,' said Netta. 'Can I go now, because . . .'

But DeeDee Chapinsky had risen to her feet and marched round the side of her desk. Her red high-heeled shoes carried her at a crippling angle. She came between Netta and her desk and stood leaning against it, arms folded. 'So that's what the women's movement means to a modern young woman like you? Maths homework?'

'Well, I'm not as well informed as I should be and I'm sure a magazine like *The New Bitch* will be looking for someone more . . . political, and I really have to go now, because I need to–'

'Got any ideas?'

'What?'

'Ideas. Ideas for my magazine? You dragged yourself all the way from London feeling slightly unwell so I just wondered if you might have, you know, in that charming, languid, ironic, British way of yours, bothered to come up with anything you wanted to say.'

Netta had in fact scrawled some thoughts down on the plane. 'Friendship is finite.'

'Crap.'

'A woman's guide to the new pornography.'

'Boring.'

'When beauty is the beast.'

'Trite.'

'Deadlier than the male – why women make better enemies.'

'Bullshit.'

'Barefaced cheek – nudity for the over-forties.'

'Sick.'

'The dark side – celebrating evil women.'

'Obvious.'

'Oh, for God's sake!' Netta got up, crossed to the wastepaper basket and vomited with professional aplomb. Practice made perfect with everything. 'There,' she said, wiping her mouth. 'You've reduced four women to hysterical breakdown, and now I've thrown up in your hallowed portals. Why have I thrown up? Because I'm pregnant.

Why am I pregnant? Because I'm a fucking fool, that's why. Why am I a fucking fool? Because I'm a woman. Because I'm nice, nice, nice from morning to bloody night. Because I value myself as the sum of other people's opinions, not for anything I achieve for myself. Because I want to be attractive and sought after and acceptable to everyone – men, women, children and bloody dogs. Betty Friedan? Gloria Steinem? Marilyn French? Maybe if I'd read them all, they'd show me the way. But I haven't. And I'm in the dark. And I'm up the duff. And I don't give a shit about the old guard. All I want to do is sort myself out without taking any crap from people like you. So you can take your job, and stuff it up your . . .'

'It's yours.'

'It's what?'

'It's yours.'

'What's mine?' She looked involuntarily at the vomit which formed a layer over the screwed-up bits of paper and discarded polystyrene cups in the bin.

'The job,' said DeeDee Chapinsky. 'Assuming you'll do the decent thing and get a termination. This is the twentieth century, you know. Not the nineteenth. You need to live your life.'

'Isn't that my decision?' asked Netta. 'As in – a woman's right to choose?'

DeeDee looked at her. Netta realized that she really was smiling this time. 'Let's call it your probation,' she said. 'The day you walk into this office and announce you've brought a brat into this mad world is the day I find an eager replacement.'

'OK,' said Netta. 'It's a deal.'

'Aren't you gonna thank me?' asked DeeDee Chapinsky. 'I've got English majors from Sarah Lawrence who would die to be in your shoes.'

'I think that would be a tiny bit dishonest,' said Netta Royce. 'Don't you?'

DeeDee went to her desk and pulled on a huge leopard-skin coat. 'Ms Sontag awaits,' she announced. 'Now. Issue number one. I want ideas on my desk, tomorrow morning seven-thirty – OK?'

'What's the theme?'

'Oh – anything you like from your perfectly adorable list. Friendship is finite: I like that one. Trash the idea that girlfriends are there to mop your brow for eternity. Junk the whole damn thing. Female friendship is a royal pain in the ass.'

She marched out of the office without another word. Netta, feeling New York swoon around her, followed a few minutes later, carrying her own vomit in a neat plastic carrier bag.

Epilogue

Someone had planted a nuclear bomb inside her. It had been ticking away for nine months. Now, they had come to take it away. A gaggle of peace women, dressed as cute little ducklings. They were against violence, so why were they hacking at her stomach with pick-axes? It must be a dream. Opening her eyes, she saw the blackness of her apartment. A deep, familiar blackness – she could almost touch the walls from where she lay in bed. She was conscious, in control, in her right mind. No bombs. No ticking. No peace women. The green numerals on her clock said 3.42. She closed her eyes again, and curled into another part of the bed. But they were still there, the peace women, still digging. She was shouting at them.

'Once they've been invented, what can we do? You can't uninvent the wheel, and you can't ban the bomb. Adam bit the apple. Mankind split the atom.'

The peace women whooped, 'You can't say Mankind. You have to say Humanity.' They lobbed hand grenades at her stomach and she gave a shout of pain, and when she woke up the bed was swimming with liquid.

'Your waters have broken', said a little voice inside, her internal midwife. She had no idea she even knew that much. Her hands clawed the air. What was this pain? She felt her belly and found a great, hard lump. Oh yes. This was the thing. She should have read those childbirth manuals. She shouldn't have pretended that the only part of her body that existed was her head. Too late now. Biology was taking over. The nuclear countdown had started.

'Jesus Christ!' She tried to straighten up. Must do something. Must – what did pregnant women do? A proper pregnant woman would not do anything. She would be driven to the hospital by her husband. If there was no husband? The digging started again, and this time she rolled out of her wet bed and on to the floor. The blackness wasn't caused by the absence of light. The blackness was made of pain, her head was encased in agony. All she could see were flashing points of light. She might die here. Where was the phone? Feeling around on the floor, she found it under the bed. Couldn't see the dial, couldn't get rid of the stars in her head. Dialled randomly.

'Who is this?' An American voice, blurred with sleep. She crashed the phone down. American? Then she remembered – I live in New York City. I am a grown-up and I have no diapers and I am having a baby. A telephone number appeared in her mind, in green numerals like those on the clock. And now she could see the numbers on the phone dial, as if they were at the bottom of the ocean. Punching at them rapidly, she held the receiver so tight to her head that she felt a new pain as it dug into her skull.

'Hello, this is DeeDee Chapinsky,' said another American voice. Please God, not the answerphone. But this was the way DeeDee always took her calls, even at four o'clock in the morning.

'DeeDee?' she screamed. 'It's coming! And it's terrible! And I don't know what to do . . . You have to help me . . . I know what you think, but you're my only friend here . . .'

'You know what? I told you to have a termination, and you never listened. Now you call me and want me to join in with the whole sick crazy baby mess. Like you want me to be your birthing partner, some gross lesbian fantasy girlfriend? Are you out of your mind?'

'DeeDee – I'm asking you as a friend. Please. No matter what you think of me. You don't have to keep me on the magazine. You don't even have to . . . aaahhh!' She dropped the phone and fell to her hands and knees, head bowed, feeling the pain enclose her as if it was she who was being squeezed through the birth canal, and not this unseen, unwanted child.

'Netta? Netta? You still there . . . ?' DeeDee's voice was shouting at her from the floor.

'I don't . . . I don't know . . .'

'Don't move. Don't die. I'll be right over. Don't . . . just do deep breathing . . . like in *Moonlighting*, right? You see that episode?'

'Bruce Willis falls in love with a woman . . . aaahhhh! . . . at the antenatal class.'

'You got it. She does this breathing thing. I don't know much about babies, but you have to do that breathing thing . . .'

'Okay.' Netta tried to breathe, though it hardly seemed feasible when the pain pressed the sight out of her eyes.

'And – before I get over there – great issue. I don't think I mentioned that. The nude interview with Madonna and Doris Lessing – perfect! Just . . . in case you don't make it . . .'

'But I'm still sacked, now that the baby is . . . nearly . . . nnnnhhhhhhh . . . nearly here?'

'Sweetie, diapers and dazzling careers just don't mix. In any case . . .'

'NNNNNGGGGGGHHHHH. Sorry?'

'It's just phoney baloney if you're gonna die anyway.' And she was gone.

After that, the haze of pain released Netta from reality. There was no bravery involved in enduring the agony of childbirth, she realized, because when it reached a certain level, nature took pity and made sure that you were out of your mind. First the room changed, so that, while remaining dark, the walls disappeared into a black, distant fog, against which scenes from her past were played. She saw Margaret — because she was about to follow her to the other side of the grave? — standing at the school gates with her bright, insatiable smile, waving ironically. Saw Mel and Pilar, climbing the steps to Dartmouth Villa, wearing silly costumes, feather boas and long satin gloves, propping each other up and laughing hysterically. Saw Bryan, pounding away at the typewriter in the *Metropolitan Student* office. Tom, smoking his endless cigarette, brows lowering, eyes staring at her intensely. Jane, weeping at the kitchen table. Richard, removing his glasses. Charlotte, flying through the air into the pool. Little Richard's snot, Toby and the ducks. She was trying to speak to them, but what was she trying to say?

'OK, lady, now see if you can get on to this stretcher.'

'Ngghhhhh. Nggghhhh.' The paramedics were trying to rescue some kind of warthog. Some grunting, inchoate thing. It was uncooperative. 'NGGGHHHHHH! NGGGHHHHHH!'

'OK, OK, we're trying to help you. Don't panic . . .'

'Going to die!' screamed the warthog. Then, with a terrible new fear which came through to her in a shard of absolute clarity, so that the warthog vanished, she could see two men bending over her, the walls had returned, the pain was real. 'My baby! Is my baby all right?'

'Your baby is fine. Everything is fine,' said a voice. 'Now get on to the fucking stretcher!'

'DeeDee?'

'Yes, it's your lousy guardian angel. I'll be godmother before I'm through.'

She clutched on to a hand, which she hoped was DeeDee's. The pain was blinding again, a box seemed to be clamped to her head, all she could see was the floor of the apartment, giving way to the floor outside, then the lift.

Struggling to focus her mind, she said, 'You have to send a letter to my father. I've been writing to him every week, but he doesn't know where I am . . . If I die, you have to send him the letter in my bag. And there's a post-card to my sister. I only send her postcards.'

'I'll do a deal with you,' said DeeDee. 'If you *don't* die, will you tell me some of these Gothic, European secrets of yours? Like, just who got you in this mess in the first place?'

'Maybe . . . nnnnnngggggghhhhhh! But I wouldn't . . . nnnnnnnngggggggghhhhhh . . . wouldn't count on it, if I were you.'

'Any time now,' said a man's voice. 'Head's engaged.'

'Sheesh, not in the lift,' said a second. 'Let's get her to the ambulance, for Pete's sake . . .'

'I don't want anything on my coat,' said DeeDee's voice.

'Blood, gore, puke or afterbirth. This is not a fake. This is real corpse skin I'm wearing. Dumb animals were massacred in droves so I could look this good. I don't want one human birth to ruin the damn thing.'

'Lady, then stand well back,' said the first voice. 'D'you think this is our Sunday best?'

Now New York shrieked by. Netta shrieked with it. 'Is it okay? Is it okay?' she yelled between the rocking, harrowing periods of insanity. The fervid activity, the silence of the two men – she thought not. 'DeeDee? DeeDee?' Someone held her hand tight.

'I'm with you, honey,' said DeeDee. Christ, it must be bad.

Then there was something else. Something else. A new sensation. 'Right – push!' She pushed. 'Again!' She pushed again. 'Keep going!' She kept going. And going. The warthog was back. 'Nnnnggghhhhh. Nnnngggghhhhh.' She thought of Mutant and Mel in the throes of sexual congress. 'Nnnnggghhhhhh! Nnnnggghhhh!' Now the past was shrinking, vanishing. One reality remained. The baby. All she wanted was the baby. The rest of the world must take on a new shape around it. All she wanted was . . . 'Waahhhhhhhhh'. A tiny figure, tangled and bluish, sailed through the air and landed in DeeDee's lap. Netta could see again. She propped herself on her elbows.

The paramedics cleaned her up. 'It's a boy,' said the first paramedic. But, of course, Netta knew it would be.

'Is he all right?'

'He's beautiful.' He passed the child to Netta.

'Ruined that coat,' said the second paramedic. 'Shame. Sure it cost a few bucks.'

'Forget about it,' said DeeDee. 'It kind of adds to the overall effect. Completes the circle. Life, death, life. Could be the next big thing.'

'He gotta name yet?' the first paramedic asked Netta. The baby was lying in her arms, already rooting for a nipple.

'David Chapinsky Royce.'

'Oh, smart girl,' said DeeDee. 'Now we're family, I *have* to give you your fucking job back.'

Acknowledgements

Thanks to Veronique Baxter for her advice and patience; to Claire Bord; and to everyone at Penguin, especially Mari Evans and Louise Moore. I am also grateful to Di McDonald of the Nuclear Information Society, and to Hazel Rennie and the women at Aldermaston Women's Camp. Special thanks also for helping me with my one-woman tent. I have tried to be true to the spirit and determination of the Greenham women but have changed some of the details about the camp for the purposes of fiction – Rainbow Gate did not exist, and Netta's day trip does not take place on an actual Embrace the Base day. The phrase 'anatomical jewel' comes from Inga Muscio's book *Cunt: A Declaration of Independence*, which is also the inspiration for some of Jude Blackman's thoughts on the subject of cunt positivism. And though DeeDee Chapinsky is, like all the characters in this story, a fictitious creation, she shares her admiration for Amelia Earhart and disdain for conventional feminist ideology with Camille Paglia.